THE AMARANTH CHRONICLES:
DEVIANT RISING

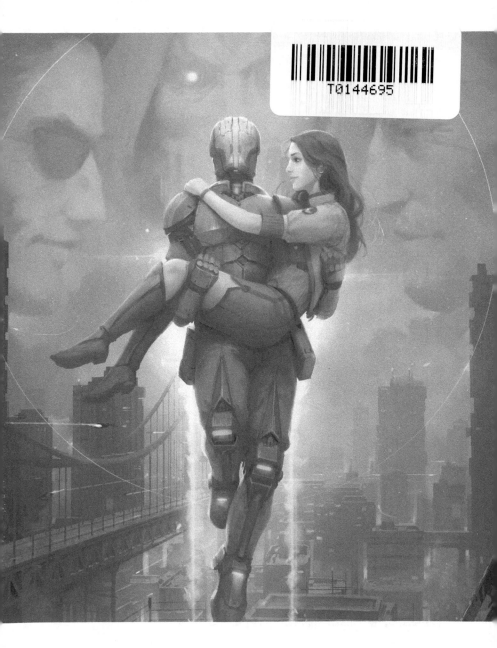

ALEXANDER BARNES & CHRISTOPHER PREIMAN

T0144695

This is a work of fiction. Names, characters, organizations, places, events, and incidents are either products of the author's imagination or are used fictitiously.

Copyright © 2017 Alexander Barnes & Christopher Preiman
All rights reserved.

No part of this book may be reproduced, or stored in a retrieval system, or transmitted in any form or by any means, electronic, mechanical, photocopying, recording, or otherwise, without express written permission of the publisher.

Published by Inkshares, Inc., San Francisco, California
www.inkshares.com

Edited by Ryan Quinn and Tyler Sparrow (Sparrowsfeather.com)
Cover Designed by Alexey Yakovlev kypcaht.artstation.com
Interior Designed by Kevin G. Summers (literaryoutlaw.com)

ISBN: 9781947848016
e-ISBN: 9781947848023
LCCN: 2017956955

First edition

Printed in the United States of America

This novel is dedicated to all those who believed in our crazy dream, even in the face of overwhelming reality.

PROLOGUE

LITHIA KNEW WHAT was in the crates in front of her. She had ordered this particular batch herself. Having both dreaded and waited for this moment, she took a few steps forward. Her boots echoed on the deck plate of her ship as she leaned down to open one of the smaller crates.

She keyed in a sequence on the crate's safety lock. A split second later, the lid yawned open, exhaling a soft mist from its lips. Inside was a single plant. It seemed to be reaching up to greet her with its burgundy brushlike bristles. The aroma of damp soil washed over her. Lithia scooped up a handful of dirt from the inside of the crate. She moved it to her face and smelled it before letting the soil fall through her fingers. It smelled so alive. It's amazing how a smell can bring back a vivid memory. A simple, familiar scent can trigger a moving recollection, like a key opening a door you forgot was locked. For Lithia, the aroma of wet soil was home. It transported her back to her childhood, when the world was new and vibrant. It was the smell of the first chilled breeze on a cool summer evening. It was the moment the sun dipped below the trees and began to wink away beyond the edge of the world. It was the perfume of satisfaction after a long day of helping her mother tend to the arboretum. Even after all this time, she could still remember the sound of the little dolphin wind chimes that hung from the porch.

The family arboretum was always an adventure waiting to happen. Every plant and every flower was a character in a story. Her mother had told her countless tales about each of them. About why each flower was important and why it was unique.

Lithia had been only seven Earth years old the day her mother told her the legend of the amaranth. Lithia had found her in the back of the family arboretum working on a patch of flowers. Lithia thought she had smelled, sneezed at, and picked the petals off every flower the universe had to offer, but she had never seen one like this before.

"What kind of flowers are those, Mommy?" the young Lithia had asked, furrowing her brows at the crimson, brushlike appearance of the plant. Lithia's mother looked up from her work; she raised her eyebrows and smiled. Her mother's smile was beautiful, and the swell of her pregnant stomach lent to the nurturing warmth of it. It radiated all the goodness and happiness in the world. When her mother smiled like that, Lithia almost didn't mind that her father was rarely there.

"If you come over here and help me, I will tell you a story about it." Her mother beckoned to her with a small trowel.

She loved her mother's stories. They were nothing like her father's, which were all about swashbucklers and cowboys. Her mother's stories were legends and fairy tales. To this day, Lithia didn't know whose stories she liked better.

Lithia had run over and hugged her mother, who let out a chuckle. She'd gotten so big, it was all Lithia could do to get her arms around the bulge in her stomach.

"Tell me the story, Mommy!" Lithia had exclaimed.

"Not so fast," her mother had said. She'd held her at arm's length for a moment and examined her face before letting her go. "You know . . . you're beginning to look more like me every day. I wonder if your brother will look more like me or Daddy."

Lithia wasted no time and knelt in the dirt to help. She had been helping her mother since she'd gotten too big to garden comfortably on her own. She'd flung dirt to the side, making a hole for the flower sitting in a large pot.

"These flowers look strange, Mommy. I've never seen anything like them before. What are they?"

Lithia had little interest in gardening, but as long as she could hear a story, she'd keep working. At least until the story was over.

"These . . . these are very special flowers."

"They don't look so special," Lithia had said.

"Looks can be deceiving. If I tell you a story, do you promise never to forget it?"

"Yes, Mommy."

"Once upon a time, an amaranth and a rose grew side by side in a garden just like ours . . ."

"This is just a story about growing flowers? I thought it was going to be about magic!" Lithia had exclaimed, jabbing the trowel into the dirt and standing up.

Lithia had been an obstinate child, but luckily this was matched by her mother's patience. She remembered her mother smiling and silencing her by pressing the flowerpot into her hand. "Remember what I said. These are special flowers."

"They're just flowers! They don't look special," Lithia had whined.

Her mother had struggled to her feet and smiled down at Lithia. "Would I tell you a story just about flowers?"

Lithia had looked up and cocked one of her eyebrows. Her mother had the upper hand. Lithia poked at the ground faster, making up for lost time.

"Once upon a time, an amaranth and a rose blossomed side by side. The rose was beautiful, lush, and red. It was the color of love and passion. The amaranth felt plain in comparison. It was so jealous of the rose that one day the amaranth said in frustration, 'You're so beautiful and you smell so nice, no wonder you're everyone's favorite!'

"The rose was shocked. She looked at the amaranth and replied, 'But my beauty is fleeting. My petals will fall, and my beauty will die. Your blossom will never fade. You are everlasting.'"

"You mean, amaranths never die . . . not even if you don't water them?" Lithia had asked as she finished planting the mysterious flower.

"No. You still have to water them, but they are a symbol of everlasting life. That which never fades, even after being cut."

"I don't get it . . . they live forever?"

"You'll understand someday, Lithia. Just promise me you'll never forget the story," her mother had said, pulling her daughter into an embrace.

Lithia then pulled away, giggling. She buried her face in the freshly planted flower and inhaled. The cool, crisp aroma filled her lungs.

Lithia pulled herself from her childhood memory and back to the real world. The memory of that warm summer afternoon so many years ago got fuzzy, blending into all the other magenta-colored afternoons from her childhood. She slid back to the present, away from the family orchard and the habitation dome she'd grown up in. Snapping back to a cold metallic room, bathed in a soft amber glow, she felt a sudden longing for those warm, fresh, fragrant days back on Venus.

The cargo control room she was standing in began to blur as a few soft tears beaded in her eyes. She'd known this trip would bring back memories like this, and she reassured herself she could handle it. That those warm, naive childhood memories were far behind her and in a place that could no longer get to her. She knew things were different now as she stood in the cargo area of her vessel, surrounded by industrial loading equipment, and staring at a large stack of shipping crates marked: Flora.

Lithia leaned her face toward the flower in the middle of the crate and inhaled again. The cool, crisp aroma filled her lungs like it always had, but this time there was something different. Those warm, innocent memories seemed more real for only a few fleeting seconds as sensations from simpler times washed over her before fading into smaller disjointed recollections. She remembered how tall the roof of the dome they'd lived in had seemed, and how the glass shimmered at night. She remembered leaning back on a hill behind her house, wondering if the sky over other planets, like Earth, was just as beautiful. She remembered that, at the time, she'd had no idea Terrans didn't live in domes like her family did on Venus.

She took a few steps back from the crate and away from her flashbacks. Her world had changed so much since those days.

If only time machines were real, maybe she could go back and tell herself to truly treasure those afternoons with her family. They would all be gone one day.

She needed to draw the line and stop herself. When the impending dark cloud of her teenage memories began to collect on the horizon of her mind. When the smell of freshly cut grass and curried chicken began to dissolve into the smell of ash and embers and the terrible things that took those wonderful, blissfully innocent days away.

Lithia found herself pushing those dark clouds away with the resolve of the present. She needed to seal up the crate and get back to the bridge to take control of her ship.

She dug around in her jacket pocket and pulled out a large, shiny metal earring. She cocked her head to the side, never losing eyesight of the amaranth in the crate. She snapped her earring in place and ran her finger along the outside edge as it covered the length of her ear, finally coming to a loop at the base of her earlobe.

There was a split-second tingle, like ice-cold water running down her spine, as little twinkling lights in her field of view assembled into strings of numbers before arranging into a little computerized helix symbol. The word "Connected" blinked below before both images faded away.

Lithia knelt to close the crate and then left the cargo room. She considered washing her hands before returning to the cockpit but decided not to. She wanted to keep the richness of those memories with her as long as possible. Sometimes her memories brought her so much peace and comfort. The smell of dirt triggered it every time. Now it was hers to take back in the delivery ship she affectionately named the *Amaranth*, to a place far away from where she grew up. A placed called San Francisco.

CHAPTER 1

Virtuoso

LITHIA CHECKED HERSELF in the mirror once more. She couldn't afford for a single red hair to be out of place or a single eyelash to be goopy. She made sure she concealed the soft patch of freckles on her nose and plucked every stray hair from between her eyebrows. This was her routine before every show. The butterflies would come, and her mouth would go dry. It wasn't so much from the fear of messing up. Lithia could play, she knew she could play, and even if she missed a note, it wasn't like anyone in the audience would notice anyway. The nerves weren't from anything so simple as that. They were from being watched. Those people out there might not know a damn thing about music, but they did know fashion, style, and all the little things that most people only understood in passing. They had turned it into an art form, and they would pick her apart for missing even a little bit. The picking apart was something else they had turned into an art form, one that took just as much practice as Lithia's piano and one they spent far more time working on.

Lithia tried to calm herself, tried to remind herself that she didn't care what all those puffed-up snobs thought, but it wasn't quite true. She cared what they thought because her aunt cared, and if they weren't pleased, Aunt Petra would make Lithia pay for it.

"It couldn't get more perfect if you spent all day on it, sweetie," said a female voice from behind her.

Lithia turned to confront whichever spoiled little princess had come to poke at her, but then she smiled when she saw who it was. There wasn't a lot Lithia liked about these shows, but she liked Myra, the stage manager. She wasn't a performer herself, but she was blessed with a drive to do nothing more than help bring music to the people. Myra managed to both charm and disarm all but the haughtiest of social players.

"Thanks, Myra, you know how I get," Lithia said. She wanted to hug the woman standing there, smiling motherly, with a bundle of red roses clutched in her hands.

"I do, sweetheart, and I get it. You couldn't drag me out in front of those people, even if you paid me," Myra said, pinning one of the roses to Lithia's dress. It clashed slightly with the soft pink Aunt Petra had insisted on, but Myra's flowers were something of a tradition, one even Aunt Petra couldn't do away with, even though she had tried several times.

"If I had known who these were for, I might have tried to sell you a different color. Something white maybe," Lithia said, smiling and adjusting the rose.

"No, you wouldn't have. You might not be able to poke at your aunt and the rest of them, but I can," Myra said, moving down the row of vanities, handing flowers to the other musicians and singers who were firmly planted in front of their own mirrors. Lithia noticed that Myra didn't actually pin flowers on any of them herself.

Lithia turned back to the mirror to give herself one last check. Regardless of what Myra said, she was sure there was some imperfection that her aunt would claim completely destroyed her performance. When she got a good look in the mirror, she saw two faces looking back at her: her own slightly pale expression, slightly powdery from the makeup that would keep her from shining under the hot stage lights, and over her shoulder a sneering, dark-skinned face, one Lithia knew well.

"Hello, Lithia. Where did you get that lovely dress? I'd love to get one just like it for our housekeeper for her birthday; she has your pale complexion."

"Hi, Abha. So you have a new housekeeper? Aunt Petra said you had to let the last one go. Something about her and your father, right?

You know I have a terrible memory for all that gossip," Lithia said sweetly, a smile on her face that never quite reached her eyes.

"What did you just say?" Abha said, all pretense of friendliness gone from her voice.

"Oh, nothing. Nothing at all. Just something I heard. I'm sure it's not even the slightest bit true, you know how these rumors get started." Lithia turned away from the raging girl. She knew she had struck a good blow. Honestly, she'd probably gone a bit across the line, but while she despised the social games her aunt forced her to learn, it didn't mean she didn't know how to play them. If Lithia was forced to play the game, why not try to win?

"Don't you turn your back on me, you Venusian trash," Abha said.

Lithia could feel her blood rising. Even through her makeup she could see the color fill her face, but whatever it was Lithia was going to say, she wasn't given a chance.

"Lithia, it's time," Myra said, rushing over and inserting herself between the seething Abha and the equally furious Lithia.

Lithia forced herself to calm down. She couldn't let Abha do this to her, not before she went onstage. If Lithia missed a note, Abha would take credit for it, and Lithia could not abide such a petty woman.

"Okay, Myra, I'm ready."

The crowd was silent as Lithia stepped out under the hot lights. She paused for a moment, just looking out at the sea of faces. Lithia wondered if even one of them understood anything about what she was about to do, if any of them knew even the first thing about music. She doubted it, but she could hope.

Lithia found her seat at the large, old-fashioned grand piano at the center of the stage. She took a moment to adjust her Helix settings, focusing on the piece of music in her mind so that the notes would swim into her field of view. She declined the option to see how closely her playing was to the recording in its system, and she told her device to hold all incoming communications until she was offstage. The modern distractions dealt with, Lithia considered the large antique instrument in front of her. Its lines, its shape, its form. Unlike most things, this thing looked exactly like what it was, a thing of beauty that served no other purpose than to create even more beauty.

She started to play and the notes became something she felt. The audience ceased to exist for her, and any anxiety she'd had faded away. It was like everything besides her music receded as Lithia's fingers hovered over the keys. The music seemed to pour out of her, riding waves of emotion. Lithia put everything into that piano, her anger, her nerves, her frustration that the audience would pick her apart. Everything in her, both good and bad, fueled the notes that came raining out of her fingertips.

There wasn't much of the performance Lithia could recall. It flew by in a blur, the combination of emotion and music making everything flow together. Her aunt was waiting for her backstage after the show. She was talking to someone Lithia didn't recognize, but it was one of the very few people Lithia had ever seen more finely dressed than her aunt. The way Petra talked to her, she was someone very high in the social order.

"Your niece plays beautifully," Lithia heard the woman say.

"Why, thank you. She did come very close, didn't she? Ninety-two is better than most. You know, she didn't want to play at first. She fought us tooth and nail when we got her first piano. She didn't want to learn. She thought playing in the dirt and things like that were better pursuits for a girl her age," Aunt Petra said, a practiced smile crossing her face for a moment.

Lithia didn't know which statement bothered her more: the quoting of her score, as if music were some sort of competition with winners and losers, or that Aunt Petra was trying to take credit for Lithia's piano. *Tooth and nail?* Lithia had to fight for the piano, and it was only when Lithia had pointed out it would be something Aunt Petra could show off to her friends that she finally gave in. Lithia took a few deep breaths and forced a smile onto her face.

"And here she is now," Aunt Petra said, beckoning Lithia over sharply.

She walked over to where the woman and her aunt were talking.

"Lithia, this is Rebeca Luen, head of the city's counsel of the arts," Aunt Petra said.

Lithia shook the woman's hand. She had to keep her excitement contained for fear of embarrassing herself—or Aunt Petra.

"It's a pleasure to meet you, Lithia," Ms. Luen said, smiling. "I'd have to say you were the standout of the night. Looking at you up there so composed, so beautiful, and so talented."

"Thank you," Lithia said. She was honestly a little dazed. It was rare that she had ever actually been complimented on her playing. On how she *looked* while she played, all the time, but never on her actual talents.

"I think we'll be calling you very soon, Lithia. There is a real future for you in music. If you want it, that is," Ms. Luen said.

"She might not be ready for that yet," Aunt Petra said, turning away from Lithia and speaking to Ms. Luen. "I'm sure your patrons wouldn't accept anything less than scores of a hundred."

Her aunt's statement was true as far as it went, but Lithia was sure it wasn't the real issue her aunt had with it. As her Aunt Petra had told her time and time again, "Music is fine for a hobby, when you're young . . . but it's not a future. Not for our sort, anyway." That was one of their longer-running fights; the only other one that could rival it in duration or fury was the fight about Lithia's future. She honestly wasn't sure what her aunt expected. She didn't want her to fly and she didn't want her to play, but those were the only things Lithia ever showed even a little interest in. Actually, that wasn't quite true, Lithia knew exactly what her aunt expected. Lithia was to marry someone Petra picked and neither of them would have to work. Instead, they would host parties and have children to be a "credit" to her and the rest of the family.

"Some, perhaps, but for the true connoisseur, the score doesn't matter. For them that's not a true measure of skill. Lithia feels the music. She breathes it and it flows through and out of her," Ms. Luen said.

"We'll see," Petra said, bidding their good-byes to Ms. Luen and steering Lithia back into the crowd.

"Where is Uncle Amir?" Lithia asked once they were out of Ms. Luen's earshot. It wasn't what she wanted to say, but what she wanted to say wouldn't have gotten her anywhere, and at least finding her uncle would get her home.

"I sent him to get the car. He should be waiting for us out front already," Aunt Petra said.

True to Aunt Petra's word, their car was waiting for them just out front, Uncle Amir sitting in the driver's seat smiling quietly to himself as other cars zipped past him overhead.

"Lithia, you were magnificent," Uncle Amir said as they got into the car and flew up into traffic.

"Thank you, Uncle," Lithia said. He had little-to-no interest in music, and even less understanding, but he meant it when he said it. Anything Lithia did was wonderful in his eyes. Whatever else Amir was, he was always sweet and supportive of Lithia, and she loved him for that.

"She was sloppy," Aunt Petra said. "I don't know who did your makeup, but I'm going to make sure you don't have them again."

"But the music was—" Amir started.

"No one could pay attention to the music. How could they? The person playing it looked like she was covered in baking powder, which was good. Ninety-two? Lithia, I expect at least a ninety-five from you if I'm going to keep humoring your little hobby," Petra said. Lithia thought Amir might respond in her defense, but a quick glance at his wife made him stifle whatever it was.

Lithia wanted to take a deep breath and sigh, but that would be enough to set Aunt Petra off again. Instead, she simply leaned her head up against the window next to her seat and watched the Lower Terraces shrink behind them. Uncle Amir continued to fly the car back up to the level where he and Petra made their lives. It was odd how something as large as the concert hall could so quickly become small. Right now it was little more than a pinprick in the distance, and in a moment, it wouldn't even be that. The old-fashioned structures with Roman-style pillars and Victorian trim on the first Terrace were slowly being replaced with the larger homes and upscale businesses that made up the Upper Terraces. Soon even they would be visible only with effort from the highest levels.

Still, while everyone was trying to go higher, Lithia wasn't. If Earth had to be her home, and for the moment it did, she preferred to be lower. Even the first Terrace was a bit too high for her, but the higher she went the worse it got. The Upper Terraces looked like someone had taken a jumble of different design aesthetics and put them into a blender. Everything was an orderly jumble of disparate elements in oddly repeating arrangements. As she looked at one building surrounded by giant Greek columns supporting a multilayered pagoda-style roof, she wondered if the owner had considered how the building might look before they decided to copy their neighbor's newest edition.

The highest Terrace was different, though, and far worse. Below, the people were pretending to have some level of design and charm. Up top, where residents had all the space they needed, there was no need for fancy design and exotic materials. Not that there wasn't a bit of that still to be seen, but mostly there were big blocky mansions and skyscraping towers. The people at the highest level of society tried to top each other in how much space they could take up and how far down they had to look to see their neighbors.

As the car rose higher and higher, Lithia started singing a little tune, "All the little angels ascend up to Heaven. All the little angels ascend up high. Which end up? Ass-end-up. All the little angels ascend up high."

The rest of the ride home was spent in silence except for Lithia's quiet humming. Considering some of the post-show conversations they'd had, Lithia was content. Still, she was relieved as the car drifted to a stop on the small pad in front of her aunt and uncle's home.

"Go upstairs and get that makeup off. You look like you never see the sun. You don't live in the Undercity; it's bad enough you dyed your hair that horrible shade of red. I'll not have you looking like those Right to Light punks," Aunt Petra said.

It wasn't worth arguing, not tonight. Tonight she had plans, and nothing Aunt Petra could say would be enough to make her risk having to break them.

CHAPTER 2

A Different Kind of Broken

LITHIA DIDN'T WASTE any time making her way through the front door and upstairs. She was ready to tear her dress off and wipe off her makeup, but she needed to see her brother first. As rough as her day had been, she knew of at least one person in the house whose day had almost certainly been worse.

Lithia went to the door she knew from long experience to be locked. There was no music coming from the other side. That was a bad sign. No music meant things were worse than usual.

"Bobby?" Lithia called as she knocked first gently and then more forcefully. "Bobby, you back yet?"

No response came from the other side of the door. It remained as silent as ever, but a moment later it did slowly creak open.

Lithia didn't go into her brother's room often, partially because her brother's room, as Aunt Petra put it, smelled like something that crawled out of the bay and died, even despite everything several house-keepers had tried. The big reason, though, was that her brother valued his privacy. Lithia didn't want to intrude on that if she didn't have to. She usually let him come to her when he needed, but therapy days were often different.

"Hey, Bobby," Lithia said as she cautiously pushed the door the rest of the way open and stepped through.

At first, Lithia thought that the door must have opened on its own. While there looked to be several living things in the explosion of a room, her brother Bobby didn't seem to be among them. It took a moment for Lithia to see her brother under the old clothing, sheets, and food wrappers piled high on the bed.

"Hey! There you are!" Lithia smiled as she walked over to her brother, concealed in the trash. "For a moment I thought raccoons had gotten you again."

She paused for a moment, waiting for a response, but when one didn't come from the sunken, sullen teenager, she continued the one-sided conversation. "Did you get them to lower your dose? I know you were going to talk to them about that." This did get a response from Bobby. He grunted something she couldn't understand and rolled over to face away from her.

Lithia sat down in the space his movement had created in the pile of blankets, clothes, and trash and put a hand on his arm. Bobby sharply pulled his arm away and too late did she realize that it was the arm his medical cuff was clasped on. He hated anything that drew attention to it. Most of the time, that included touching the arm they had strapped it to. The cuff gleamed in the soft sunset through the window as Bobby pulled his arm away, and what Lithia saw she didn't like.

"The rash around the bracelet's injection sites isn't getting any better. Bobby, you're not using that cream they gave you, are you?" This wasn't really a question, Lithia knew her brother too well, but she had hoped he'd use it.

"Why should I?" This time Lithia could understand the grunts her brother made in response.

"Because that has to hurt . . ." Lithia said kindly.

"Doesn't. Nothing does anymore. Whatever crap they are pumping into my veins makes sure of that. I think it makes me forget what pain is." Bobby rolled over as he said this, and the look on his pale, clammy face broke Lithia's heart. Bobby didn't look like he had been raging or crying, or any of the other emotional extremes he usually experienced. Those Lithia was more than used to, but the blank, tired, and numb expression on her brother's face almost killed her.

"What did they give you?" Lithia asked.

"I don't know. They don't even tell me anymore. They just put a canister in the cuff and tell me to get it refilled in a month." Bobby's eyes looked like they wanted to start dropping tears, his mouth looked as if he wanted to snarl, and even his voice had the tone of a shout that had long since lost its way.

"Does it help?" Lithia asked, not really knowing what to say as she watched her brother again slip into blankness.

"I feel dead. I guess that's a start," Bobby said coldly.

"Don't say that, Bobby. Soon we'll get out of here. Soon you'll be of age and I'll help you rip that cuff off and blast it into a star," Lithia said.

"It won't help, Lith. With the cuff I'm broken, without it I'm still broken, just a different kind of broken," he said, staring up at the ceiling fan.

"Stop that! You're not broken!" Lithia didn't mean to raise her voice. It wasn't what her brother needed, but she couldn't give him what he really needed, and that was killing her inside.

"I *am* broken," he said as Lithia watched his eyes track briefly to his bracelet before darting away. The cuff was a long-term chemical dispenser, but its resemblance to an old-fashioned handcuff had long ago prompted them to just start calling it the cuff. At first it was an attempt to make a joke of Bobby's situation, but as time went on and Bobby felt more and more trapped by it and life in general, it stopped being funny. The cuff had become a symbol of his captivity in his own body.

Lithia grabbed her brother's wrist, her hand wrapping around the cold, tight, and slightly damp metal. "This is not you, Bobby. And the only thing it's a sign of is that Petra's a bitch!"

She took the cuff and examined it for a moment. The device looked simple enough. It didn't look that much more complicated than the wrist monitors in the *Amaranth*'s hypersleep chambers.

"What do you think you're doing?"

"Nothing, Bobby. I'm sorry," Lithia said, looking at her brother.

"Then get out," he said, a bit of color coming into his cheeks. "Just leave me alone."

"Don't you want to hear about the concert?" Lithia asked.

"Let me guess. You dazzled them all and Aunt Petra gave you a new car because of how proud she was, and then three men asked you to marry them," Bobby said.

"Well, I did get a ninety-two . . . for whatever that's worth," Lithia said.

"Only a ninety-two? Aunt Petra must have been so disappointed."

"Oh, depends who she is talking to. You know her. Brag when I'm not there, but make sure I never actually hear anything good about myself. Otherwise I might start believing she's actually proud of me or even loves me or something," Lithia said, moving a little closer to her brother again.

"Oh, she couldn't let you think that," Bobby said slowly getting into their favorite activity: Petra bashing. "Would kill all the sympathy she gets for taking in us poor orphans out of the goodness of her heart."

"I know. She's soooo good to us," Lithia said. "That's why the judge had to issue an order requiring her to let us come to Terra."

"You were at the hearing when that happened. Please tell me how red she turned when the judge told her she'd have to take us in," Bobby said as the ghost of a smile crept onto his lips.

"Let's just say my hair is a tribute," Lithia said, matching his ghost with a live one.

Bobby grinned openly at that thought and it thrilled Lithia. I am going out tonight. You can come with me if you can keep it quiet. I can think of a couple of girls who might be very happy to meet you," Lithia said, leaning over and giving her brother a playful shove.

"I don't think so," he said. "Just not feeling like dealing with people right now."

"Hey! I'm people," Lithia said, acting hurt.

"You're not people. You're just Lithia."

"Not sure how to take that . . ." she replied.

"Oh, it's a good thing. I hate people. I only sort of hate you," he said confidently.

"Thanks. You sure?"

"Yeah, I'm sure," he said.

"What if it were a few boys who might be happy to meet you instead?" Lithia inquired.

"Well, that's a bit better," Bobby said. "Yeah . . . no . . . I just want the world to fuck off right now."

"That's fair. Well, I'll be heading out in about twenty if you change your mind," Lithia said quickly, wrapping her brother in a tight hug before he could put up his arms to stop her.

"We'll see if I let you in here again," Bobby said, pushing her off him.

"No problem. Though if you don't let me in here, that opossum is going to come back eventually."

"I liked him," Bobby said, looking over at the hole in the screen of his window. "I named him Whiskers."

Lithia laughed as she made her way out of her brother's disaster and to her own room. Now, he would be . . . well, not exactly okay, but close enough for the time being. She couldn't wait to strip off the horrible pink dress and wipe away the powder and goop that had been layered on her face before the show.

Unlike Bobby's room, Lithia's was pristine. There were no piles of clothes on the floor, nor did she keep stacks of dirty dishes on her chest of drawers. Instead of the air being musty, stale, and with a hint of dirty socks, the air in her room was sweet and teased with the scent of jasmine from a candle she had accidently left burning. Lithia snuffed out the flame and wiped away the melted wax from the polished dresser top as quickly as she could. She shuddered to think what her aunt would do if she found out that Lithia had left the candle lit. The candle notwithstanding, nothing else about Lithia's room was out of place.

Lithia hung her dress up on a hook at the back of her closet alongside half a dozen others that made up her concert wardrobe. She didn't know why she bothered to keep them, though. Inevitably, her Aunt Petra would discard all of them and provide new ones next fall. Lithia considered tossing a few of them in her bag and taking them with her the next time she left the house. Surely she knew someone who might want them, and anyways, her closet was getting too packed to find anything, even despite Lithia's almost compulsive attempts at organization. She went back over to the dresser and opened a small jar. The smell of alcohol and other astringents was almost overpowering as she dipped a small brush in and started dissolving the thick layer of artificiality that had been plastered over her face. After using a cloth to wipe away the cleaner and the last dregs of makeup, she looked at herself in the mirror before applying just the slightest bit of eyeliner and a dab of color on her lips. Lithia was getting ready to head out into the Undercity, the part of San Francisco far below the Terraces. It was a place where you didn't want to draw attention, because attention would often mean attention from the desperate or the untreated mentally ill who called the place home. Still, it was a place she loved. Yeah, it had its problems, but despite them, Lithia had made more and better friends there than she had at any other time since coming to Earth. She knew that the little makeup she did put back on was unwise, but for her, the slight danger was also part of what made that place attractive.

Lithia kept a few tattered and torn sets of clothes from her teenage years in a special drawer under her bed. She had piles of comfortable, ripped, stained denim jeans and hooded sweatshirts made from some thick, soft material that you just couldn't find in the Upper Terraces. The smell of many campfires and the cold, damp aroma of rainwater saturated every stitch of clothing in the drawer. She quickly found her favorite set of jeans, the ones with the tattered, faded, and frayed ankles. She could almost still pick out a faint yellow mustard stain near one of the pockets, but she didn't care. These were perfect Undercity fatigues and she put them on like armor. Dressed in them, no one would guess she spent most of her time living the life of a rich resident of the highest part of the city. No, she looked like everyone else in the lower sections. Perhaps a little better fed and groomed than most, but that alone wasn't enough to set her apart.

She could have probably used the front door; there wasn't a lot her Aunt Petra could do to stop her from going anywhere, but she didn't want the fight. There were still many ways Petra could make Lithia regret it. Only some of them would be targeted at Lithia directly, and she was not prepared to drag her brother into this long-running battle with her aunt. Instead, Lithia climbed out the window, careful to pull it closed behind her. She went down the thick latticework of vines that clung to the side of the house.

Lithia turned back for a moment, looking up into her brother's window. The lights were off, but the fact that it was open and there was a bowl of food sitting on the ledge made her smile. If Bobby was already trying to attract a new roommate, he really must be feeling more himself. How scavenging animals managed to get this far up into the Terraces, she couldn't fathom, but she hoped any new pet would be a better houseguest than the previous one.

The walk to the tram into the Undercity was a long one, and Lithia had to take the pedestrian elevators down several levels before she got to a public train station. Everyone she passed along the way gave her the kind of looks that seemed to say louder than words that they knew she was up to something.

The train Lithia caught was almost empty, as usual. Very few people in the Terraces ever used the public trains. It would fill quickly, though. As the train went farther down into the older and lower parts of the city, there would be standing room only.

Lithia smiled as she watched the people filter on and off, the real population of the city making their way to work, home, or to the few diversions they could afford. Lithia wondered what their lives were like, what their stories were. When she was younger, she would make up stories about them, little dramas about people and lives she would never know.

When the train doors opened on the very lowest stop, Lithia pushed her way through, along with the crowd of people trying as quickly as they could to get off the train and vanish into the places they claimed as home. For the people above, it was a quick and cheap way to keep the poorest of the poor out of sight and out of mind.

Lithia stood on the old platform as people around her either made their way up the cracked stone steps to the streets above, or filtered onto one of the other trains on this level. When Lithia had first started coming down here, the only trains were the up and down lines, but a few years ago, some engineer trying to make life down here a little better had started restoring ancient electrical trains and getting the tracks back into good repair. One of these trains pulled out of the platform beside her, its metal wheels screeching deafeningly. She thought about catching one of them to get her closer to her destination but in the end decided not to. It wasn't far and she felt like a little walk to help her sink into this place before she actually met anyone.

Lithia made her way up the broken steps, popping off her Helix earring and slipping it into her pocket. Very few people who lived down here had access to the earrings, and a few people even feared them. Lithia didn't want to draw the focus of one of the anti-Helix gangs, or worse, the Right to Light movement.

The street was cold as Lithia emerged from the old rundown station. Upper levels of the city had long since blocked out most, if not all, of the warm sunlight and turned this level into a place of perpetual night. Here and there, old sunlamps had been put in as San Francisco developed. They still shone dimly, but mostly if there was light, it was coming from an old streetlamp, or even more often from a trashcan fire. That was life in the lowest level—cold, dark, damp, and often slimy.

She walked down the torn and cracked street. What must this place have looked like when it was new? When the sun could still reach it? When the old beautiful buildings weren't crumbling and covered with the thin layer of mossy slime that was the only thing that seemed to grow down here?

It must have been the greatest city in the world. Lithia pictured the ruined facades gleaming and clean, sun shining through spotless clear glass in their windows. She stopped to look at the remains of a massive dome. It, and the columns that had once held it up, had crashed down into an old dried-up pond. Scattered around it were the remains of carved women, their broken forms highlighting the loss of what must have been some great palace. It must have looked breathtaking centuries ago, when it was first built. Maybe it had been a grand music hall or maybe some sort of palace of fine arts. Either way, there was something almost sad and funereal about the way the ruins just laid there in the twilight under the massive city above it.

Lithia turned onto a large old stone road that the locals called "One oh one" for some reason. It was as ruined as everything else in this part of the city, but the worst of the rubble had been cleared off to the sides so that the people who called this place home could use it as a makeshift walkway. She walked along the cracked asphalt road, occasionally passing people who were headed out to the bay. The bay may have been long devoid of anything close to life, but for the people down here, it *was* life. The bay was one of the few places where the concrete jungle of the Terraces couldn't block out the sunlight for the city below. Standing on the beaches and cliffs, people could watch the waves roll lazily in and feel warm sun on their skin. From up on the walkway, Lithia watched them as they stood on the shores below, a few of the braver ones risking going out to the Golden Gate Market.

What had once been a massive grand bridge at the mouth of the San Francisco Bay had long ago given up all pretense of utility and had slowly transitioned into a sort of combination market and carnival, a place where tourists came to pretend to learn about the old city while eating overpriced food from carts and buying souvenirs from places they didn't realize they hadn't seen. Her destination wasn't the bridge, though, and after a walk down a steep trail, she came to a small stretch of cool, clean beach. Lithia smiled, stepping out onto the soft sand as the sun was just finishing its descent down into the sea, casting the sky in dark pinks and brilliant blues.

"Lithia!" came a chorus of voices as she made her way to the water.

A small group of somewhat ragged people broke away from a weak pit fire farther down the beach and ran toward her. A young man pulled ahead of the others as they came, reaching Lithia first and wrapping her in a hug that might have been rib crushing if the man had ever had enough food to put on real muscle.

"Was starting to think you'd never get here," the man said, finally releasing Lithia as the rest of the group caught up.

"I've been looking forward to this all day," Lithia said, smiling. She let them lead her to the beacon of their small fire.

CHAPTER 3

Bonfires of Baker Beach

LITHIA DRANK DEEPLY from the flask in her hand. The harsh homemade alcohol burned as it went down, and its warmth spread through her body. She coughed a bit as she passed the flask on to the blond woman sitting next to her on the log. She looked around her. There were maybe ten other people clustered around the fire, but Lithia only knew four or five of them by name. The woman took a deep draft from the flask in her hand. Lithia smiled as she saw a sick look come over Siri's heart-shaped face before she spat out the alcohol over the fire. Everyone joined Lithia as they turned to see the fire sputter blue before returning to its crackling orange and yellow.

"Easy, Siri," Lithia said. "I think that stuff may have been made from hopper fuel."

Lithia handed Siri another flask, this one filled with cool water.

"Thanks for the warning, Lithia," Siri said, grabbing the flask and taking a gentle drink before handing it back.

"You insult me," came a hurt voice from Lithia's other side. A young man was standing there, several more flasks and bottles clutched in his arms, the light of the fire reflecting in his dark hair and eyes. "I would never use hopper fuel in my drinks."

"What is it, then?" Lithia asked.

"No idea. Something I found in an old funeral home. Tastes like crap, but it kills flies and goes down smooth," the man said.

"You're so full of shit, Vijay," Siri said, patting a seat next to her, hopefully. But Vijay ignored her, squeezing his slight frame in between Lithia and another man.

"Here, try this instead. It's a little less harsh," Vijay said, passing over a thick brown bottle.

"What is it?" Lithia asked, narrowing her eyes.

"Why do you always ask those questions?" Vijay replied, putting his arm around Lithia and passing her the bottle.

"Because I know you," Lithia said.

"Then you know I would never give you anything unsafe. I test all my stuff before serving it to anyone," Vijay said.

"Getting drunk in the back of a truck while you're brewing does not count as testing," Siri said, grabbing the bottle from Lithia and uncorking it.

"How did you know?" Vijay asked.

"Because we know you," both Lithia and Siri said as one.

"But seriously, what is it?" Lithia asked, leaning over to sniff the bottle in Siri's hands.

"No idea, actually. Some fruit I snatched last time I was on the upper levels. Soft little yellow things, all covered with fluff. Might have been from off-world."

Siri looked like she might spit out this last gulp too at hearing that, but she managed to force it down as she ran her fingers through her dirty-blond hair.

"I'm drinking something made from fruit covered in fluff? I may not know much about growing things, but generally, fuzzy fruits are the ones even we throw away," Siri said.

"Nah, think they were supposed to be that way. They didn't seem rotten or anything, and a bunch of rich people were buying them," Vijay said.

Lithia smiled and finally took a long drink from the bottle Siri handed back to her. The taste was sweet, spicy, and a little bitter, like apricots and cinnamon.

"See? If our own baby can get it down, it has to be safe," Vijay said, pulling Lithia in just a little tighter.

"That doesn't mean anything. She drank your embalming fluid too. She might just be looking for something that will finally kill her," Siri said, but she took the bottle as she did.

"I know what they are. They're face squid eggs. You know you guys are going to have to get inoculated soon or . . ." Lithia let a small smile come to her face as she took the bottle back again and drank another big gulp.

"But-but what about you?" Vijay said, turning a little pale.

"I already was. Everyone who goes into hypersleep has to be inoculated to make sure there isn't an outbreak," Lithia said, offering the bottle to Vijay.

"But I let them sit for a week in yeast and other stuff. They can't still be dangerous," Vijay said, staring at the ground.

"You'd think that, but actually egg is a bit of a misnomer. They really aren't eggs as much as a cluster of spores covered with a protective skin. They can survive in space and any environmental conditions we've yet found," Lithia said, her eyes boring into Vijay.

"So I've just given everyone . . ." Vijay turned to face the fire and started spitting up everything he'd had to drink.

Lithia couldn't contain herself anymore and started laughing so hard she fell off the log they were using as a bench.

"They're apricots. There's no such thing as face squids, and even if there were, why would they be selling them in an upper-level shop?" Lithia said through peals of laughter.

"I don't know," Vijay said. "Rich people keep some weird things as pets. Saw this one woman once with this tiny hairy guy on a leash who was eating a banana. Actually kind of liked him. This old man slammed into the little guy and he just went off, screeching and throwing shit," Vijay said.

"The old guy?" Siri asked.

"No, the little hairy guy. Just remember thinking I've been there, man," Vijay said, wiping his mouth and turning to help Lithia up.

Lithia took Vijay's hand and found her seat again between Vijay and Siri.

"Look what you've done," Vijay said, looking Lithia dead in the eye. "Everyone's spitting out my good upper-city stuff."

"Serves you right. Brewing with stuff you don't recognize. That could have been anything," Lithia said. "What were you doing in the upper city, anyway?" Lithia went on, a note of curiosity in her voice.

Lithia knew Vijay sometimes made his way to the upper city. She also knew that oftentimes these little trips ended with Vijay in serious trouble.

"It was nothing major. Just a little walk around the back of a few stores. It's not like anyone ever realized I was there."

"You're sure?" Lithia asked.

"Completely. Anyway, even if someone did see me on some sort of door-mounted security sensor . . . well, it's not like I'm in the system anyway."

"Eventually they'll start some program to get the Helix down here, and then they'll know," Lithia said.

"That's a joke. I mean, maybe if we had something they wanted, but they don't want people like us hooked into their system," Vijay said, anger and frustration coming out in his words.

"It's true. They keep saying they have—" Lithia started, but she was cut off by Siri.

"Lithia, we love you, but trust us. No one cares about us as long as we stay down here. There won't be any program to get us hooked into the Helix."

"Yeah, maybe if we lived out in the Colonies or somewhere like that. They're giving those guys free Helix earrings, but down here it's like we don't exist," Vijay said.

"You don't understand. You can't. You don't live here. You come down here and you hang with us, you bring food and clean water and you're cool. But when the night's over, you get back on that train and you leave. We don't get to do that. This place is our home all the time," Siri said, putting a hand on Lithia's arm.

Lithia didn't know what to say. What Siri said was true, she didn't live down there. But she did understand. She knew it was hard. That was why she brought the things she did when she came, not because they expected them; they didn't. Lithia brought the food, the water, and even sometimes clothing, because she wanted her friends' lives to be a little easier. She'd have done more if she thought they'd let her, but they wouldn't. Vijay and Siri were proud. They stole to live, but that was different than just being given something. In many ways, pride was the only thing they really had, and Lithia would not be the person to take that from them. If they lost that, they'd be like almost everyone else down there. The Undercity was where people came when they had nowhere else to go and no hope, and to see her friends give in to that would be too much to watch.

"Lithia, it's not your fault. You didn't choose to come from up there any more than we chose to come from down here. It's just the way it is," Vijay said, standing up and leading a somewhat unsteady Siri away.

Lithia sat at the fire, considering everything the two of them had said. Vijay sat Siri with a couple of other girls and started walking back over to where Lithia sat. Was she an outsider there? Was she just some slumming rich girl who didn't understand the world she lived in? Vijay sat back down, taking one of her hands in his and wrapping his other arm around her, pulling her in tight.

"Don't let it bother you, Lithia. Siri knows you get it, we all do. She's just had a rough day and a little too much to drink," Vijay said, speaking into the top of Lithia's head.

"She's not wrong, though. I don't know what it's like, not really. I don't know what it is to be hungry and not know where my next meal is coming from, or any of the other things you guys deal with every day," Lithia said, her voice muffled by Vijay's somewhat threadbare sweatshirt.

"It doesn't matter. None of it does," Vijay said, a hand gently patting Lithia's back.

Maybe it was the cold, or the drink, but Lithia was happy to let Vijay comfort her. His arms felt firm, and his chest was soft as she closed her eyes.

"That's it, Lithia. In the morning everything will feel better," Vijay said. But his voice sounded like it was so far away.

"I just want . . ." Lithia mumbled.

"I know, I know," Vijay said softly, and Lithia felt the soft pressure of his lips on the top of her head as the world slowly drifted away.

CHAPTER 4

Deviant Rising

FIRST OFFICER SARA Rin sat in the captain's chair on the bridge of the Strife Merchant Marine Corps vessel *Deviant Rising*. Captain Pacius had locked himself away in his office just off the bridge for some time. She hadn't been keeping her eye on the clock, but she estimated that he'd been in there at least an hour and a half . . . maybe longer. She was by no means unaccustomed to the long, silent deliberations he held with himself when he was alone in his office, but she didn't think he was in there alone. She quickly checked the command display on the side of her chair and saw she was right. The governor of Strife had been trying to reach the *Deviant Rising*, and Captain Pacius specifically, ever since they had left their world three weeks ago. Pacius had done his best to put off the governor, but now, as their destination grew closer, he had no choice but to finally sit down and talk to the man. It was anyone's guess how the conversation was going, but beyond a shadow of a doubt, the context of that conversation was negative.

First Officer Rin readied herself for her next entry in her log. She took a deep breath and hit "Record."

"First Officer's log, nineteenth of Augustum, standard year twenty-six forty-two. We are nearing Occasio Ultima, more commonly referred to as simply 'the Gate.' The ship's crew has, to this point, performed ably, but tensions are running high. It is difficult to blame them. They know we're heading to the Gate. Some believe our final destination might actually be Earth itself, and I've heard more than one crewman speaking of what they'd like to do with Earth when they thought I wasn't listening.

"I must confess some sympathies with their feelings, if not with their expression. I'm not immune from the belief that Earth has far overstepped all reasonable bounds with its attempts to force the Helix on the colony of Strife. Some have suggested that the Helix and its interface accessories, commonly just called 'earrings,' are a way to make sure Strife continues to supply Earth with the wheat, corn, rice, and other crops that it depends on. This seems farfetched to me. No matter how strained things become between Strife and Earth, I can't see us ever allowing so many to starve. Though I can concede that many in the UPE government on Earth would do exactly that if the roles were reversed. Perhaps that is it. Perhaps they are simply judging us by the standards they set for themselves . . ." Rin paused for a moment, tapping her fingers on the armrest of the captain's chair before continuing. "Intentions aside, I hope the captain fills them in soon or we're going to have a breakdown in discipline among the crew, one that could spell disaster for us all."

Rin hit the control to stop recording and turned back toward the bridge. At this time of night, there were only three other members of the bridge crew on duty: Lewis Carry at navigation, Charlotte Wessels at tactical, and Daniel Stevens at communications. All were good mates, but young. Rin doubted Carry had ever even been on a ship's bridge before she had suggested him to the captain for the job, and the others weren't much better.

"Navigation, what is our ETA?" Rin asked the young man at the station.

"We're going to reach Occasio Ultima in about seven hours," Carry said, not turning his head from the station.

"Excuse me? Did I ask you *about* how long it was going to take? Mate, take a look at those controls again and give me a proper ETA."

"Sorry, ma'am. At current speed, we'll be arriving in seven hours and twenty-three minutes."

"That's better, Carry. You can leave the word *about* out of your vocabulary while you are on this bridge," Rin said.

"Yes, ma'am."

"Communications, is the captain still on his call?" Rin asked, turning her attention to Stevens.

"The captain terminated the connection twelve minutes ago, ma'am," Stevens finished, and Rin couldn't help but smile. These new crew members were going to come along just fine.

"Very well. Navigations, the bridge is yours. Contact me if anything changes between now and when we drop back into normal space," Rin said, standing from her seat and walking the short distance to the captain's office. She touched a control outside the door, and a moment later, she heard the deep, slightly raspy voice of the captain tell her to enter.

The captain's office was small, with little room for more than a tiny desk, three chairs, and a potted plant that had died some time ago. The only other decoration in the office was an old-fashioned revolver set in a glass case behind the captain's desk, and it looked almost as battered as he usually did. The firearm was illegal in UPE space. If it were found out that he possessed the antique, the captain's ship would be confiscated and his license revoked. It would mean imprisonment if the UPE found out it was in firing condition. It was, in fact, in firing condition. She had seen him have to use it on several occasions during their time together. Lieutenant Rin preferred the firearms the Strife Merchant Marine Corps offered, not only far more modern and reliable but also, thanks to their status in the SMMC, completely legal anywhere, outside of a planet in the Sol system. Only the UPE's own troops were allowed weapons there.

Captain Pacius sat behind his desk. He looked exhausted but still had the determination painted across his face that had carried him this far. Rin knew before she even asked that the conversation with the governor had not gone well. It was printed on the captain's face. But still, she found herself compelled to ask, "How did everything go with Governor Maher?"

"The governor thinks we're playing with fire," Pacius said, sipping a glass of tea and never looking up from the computer on his desk.

"And you?" Rin asked.

"Obviously I think we're doing what we have to," Pacius answered and paused for a moment. "We are playing with fire, though," he said.

"We're not the ones who are going to get burned, though, sir," Rin said.

"Oh, we'll get burned. I have no doubt of that. There is no way we walk away from this clean. There will be a price. I'm ready to pay that price when the time comes, however," Pacius said.

"Perhaps I should rephrase: we're not the only ones who are going to get burned," Rin said, though she didn't quite know why. She knew what the captain was up to, she had known for weeks, since before they set out on this mission, but she was the only other person on the crew who knew the whole story. And beyond knowing the whole story, knowing all of Pacius's plan, she agreed with it. What they were doing was for the best. But right now she needed a little reassurance; reassurance that the captain understood everything that could come from their actions tomorrow, and that he still believed it was right.

"I know. I've thought about it for a long time. I've thought about it every time they load us up with more Helix earrings and send us home. Every time we haul enough grain to cover a city all the way to Earth, and then we are treated like we should be grateful that they are willing to take it from us. Sara, the people aren't happy with the UPE right now; they're not happy with Earth. The governor thinks he can still smooth things over through official channels, through words and fake smiles, and maybe he could have forty years ago, back before they stopped paying for the grain, back when we didn't need their permission to fly our own ships, but not today. Today words aren't enough. Today it's gone too far for that, and tomorrow they'll understand how serious we really are. Tomorrow the people's voices are going to be heard. Sara, this is our last chance to keep the Helix from being forced on us, our last chance to keep some shred of our independence from the UPE and Earth, and yes, it's going to have a price. But there is always a price, and maybe it's one we're going to have to pay," Pacius said, a bit of his energy returning.

Rin felt inspired by his words and his passion. She had known Xander Pacius for years, both as a member of his crew and as a friend, and there were few people she believed in more, and no one she trusted more. If Captain Xander Pacius of the *Deviant Rising* believed he was on the right course, then Sara Rin would always be right behind him.

"My shift's about to end, but you look like you need the sleep more. Why don't I stay on the bridge for a few more hours while you go get a little sack time," Rin said, looking over the captain. After his mini speech, what little energy he seemed to have regained had left him.

"No, if you think you can sleep, go. I'm up and I doubt that's going to change anytime soon," he said.

"You know most of the other SMMC captains think you're a madman?" Rin asked.

"So people keep telling me. I really have no idea why."

CHAPTER 5

If History Should Recall Our Names

SARA FOUND HERSELF slowly sliding back into the waking world as she stared at the ceiling above her bunk with only a vague idea of what time it was. Was her alarm moments away from ringing or had she only been out for a couple of hours? She groaned and leaned over to the end table on her right, fumbling around for her DIT. She nearly knocked it off the table but caught it by its chain just before it hit the deck plate. Why had the SMMC made such tiny little plastic cards standard issue? Digital Identification Token? More like "Drop It every Time." To her amazement, her DIT read 0500 hours. She wasn't due on the bridge until 0700 hours. Instead of trying to fill the next two hours with a little more sleep, she tossed off the covers and slipped back into her uniform. As far as she was concerned, she was now awake, and she was sure the captain needed her. Leaving her sleeping quarters, she walked down the corridors of the *Deviant Rising* with a hurried speed that few young cadets would have on their first tour in deep space.

The morning shift was just about to start and the hallways were beginning to bustle with the early business that would normally accompany a vessel with nearly fifteen hundred people on board. The shifts were designed to overlap by an hour, so while some were heading to bed, others were hopping in the shower before their daily duties.

Sara contemplated heading to the cafeteria and grabbing a cup of coffee, but even she had to admit she was a lot more alert than she would have normally been at this time. Deciding to skip the detour, she made her way to a lift that would take her to the bridge. The lift that came to greet her was empty of personnel, and so she knew exactly what she would find when she stepped onto the bridge: Captain Pacius standing over somebody's station, checking and double-checking everything some poor third mate was doing and insisting that he was as alert as ever, despite looking like hot death. The worst part was he would probably be telling the truth. Rin looked forward to the day she became a captain so someone could tell her the secret of staying up for days on end and not missing a beat. Even when she was in her twenties, the best she could ever do was forty-eight hours, and even then she suffered.

As the lift carried Rin to the bridge, her mind drifted to what would happen when the *Deviant Rising* reached the Occasio Ultima star system later that day. The captain was sure that what they were doing was right, so sure in fact that to him it was the only real option. After listening to him speak, Rin was sure too. The problem was that Rin kept thinking about the consequences that their actions could bring. The captain believed this would open a few eyes, force the UPE to step back and listen to what Strife and the other colonies were saying, but Rin wasn't so sure. It was possible things would play out like the captain thought, and for Strife's sake she hoped that's how it would go, but she couldn't shake the image of warships in orbit around Strife, UPE soldiers standing beside lines of Strifers as technicians clamped Helix earrings onto them. Maybe the captain had these thoughts too; maybe they haunted him like they haunted her. Or maybe he was so convinced of his rightness that he couldn't conceive of things not working out.

When the lift opened onto the bridge, Lieutenant Sara Rin scanned the room. It was busier than she might have expected for such an early hour, but other than that it was exactly as she thought it would be, right down to Captain Pacius leaning over the navigation station, a cup of coffee clenched in a hand that trembled only slightly. She stepped out of the lift and onto the bridge and took up her post next to the captain's chair.

"So if we drop the cargo there, it will take how long to drift into the star?" Rin heard Captain Pacius ask the officer at navigation.

"Abo—er, the same, sir," came the reply.

"I don't love the idea of it taking months to drift into the star. The cloud of debris could disrupt transit to and from Archer's Agony station," Pacius said.

"Isn't that kind of what we're aiming for, sir?" the navigations mate asked.

"Not if it's going to damage anyone's vessel. No, we better drop out of sprint closer to the star. Maybe at point oh-oh-seven astronomical units. We'll need to arm a nav beacon to drop as well to warn any nearby vessels of the debris cloud."

"That might bring us a little close. Transit around the Gate gets pretty congested at that distance."

"What if we fired our cargo into the star?" Rin proposed. All the heads on the bridge turned her way.

"First Mate, you're not supposed to be on duty for a couple more hours," Pacius said.

"Just following your example, sir."

Maybe it was her imagination, but she could have sworn Captain Xander Pacius paused just long enough to shoot her a proud smirk.

"If we don't decompress the cargo bays before releasing their contents, we can turn them into crude cannons, firing everything inside. I doubt it would shorten the trip by all that much, but it would do something, and it's a solution the other ships will be able to implement as well." The mate at navigation pondered her suggestion and quickly ran a few calculations.

"It would shorten the time, Captain," the mate said.

"By how much?" Pacius asked.

"Several weeks," he replied.

"Is that really the best we can do?" Pacius asked.

"Without irradiating everyone on the cargo decks, I think so."

"Very well, work out the details with engineering and cargo control. Once you have everything, prepare some instructions we can send to everyone else once they arrive at the party," Pacius said, turning away from the navigation station and taking his seat.

"That wasn't bad thinking," he whispered to Rin as he sat down.

"Thank you, sir. So, does this mean you've made an announcement to the crew?" Rin asked.

"Not yet. But I have started informing those few who need to know before we get there," Pacius answered.

"So, the entire crew will know in about twenty minutes," Rin asserted with a very slight smile.

"If it takes them that long, I'll be disappointed," Pacius said with another one of his trademark smirks.

Rin was just about to sit down at operations and look over the morning duty roster when the captain spoke again, "Have you ever looked at one of these?"

He was pinching a small chrome hemisphere between his right pointing finger and thumb, studying it intently through one eye. On one side of the little chrome half sphere it had a short needlelike spike and a short and stiff but flexible wire running from it.

"It's a Helix earring," Rin answered. Where was the captain going with this?

"I mean, have you ever really looked at one of them? They're so small, so deceptively simple. But they're so powerful. One of these has more computing power than all the computers built before the turn of the last century. With one of these things, you can access almost any information you could ever want, perform almost any task, communicate with people on the other side of the galaxy instantaneously, and store the complete memories of a lifetime. And you'd only be scratching the surface, because its real trick is far more impressive. It does all this by reading your mind, all you have to do is think . . . and it reacts . . ."

"It is remarkable," she said into the pause.

"And yet it's something we're about to take a stand against," he continued.

"Sounds like you're ready to address the crew," Rin said, perking up.

"Not really, but I should. Better to get it over with before the rumor mill turns this adventure into something even more ridiculous."

"Sir, there is nothing that the rumor mill can do to make this more ridiculous than reality already has. Firing Helix earrings into a star that is also a gateway to another galaxy as part of a political protest is sufficiently ludicrous."

"There could be chicken suits involved," Captain Pacius joked, a bit of tension leaving his face.

"It might be worth asking the stewards department about that. I wouldn't want to disappoint anyone," Rin replied as professionally as she possibly could.

"Maybe next time," Pacius said, and from the smile on his face, Rin knew he was already envisioning the two of them commanding the bridge, covered in yellow feathers, beaks gleaming. Rin suppressed a smile at the thought herself.

"Communications, give me a channel to the entire ship," Pacius ordered, turning away from Rin and rising to his feet.

"Sir, you're live in three," the mate at communications said, silently counting down his fingers for the captain.

All around the bridge, heads turned from their stations to watch and listen. Most of them had picked up something of what was going on, either from conversations with the captain or from the ever-present rumors that a ship like this more or less ran on, but not one of them wanted to miss hearing the whole story from the captain's lips directly.

"Attention, crew of the *Deviant Rising*. This is Captain Pacius speaking. For too long, the United Planets of Earth have held Strife by the throat. I don't have to give anyone a list of reasons to hate them. They've already given us the only one that matters . . ."

Captain Pacius paused and pulled from his pocket the Helix earring he had been considering earlier. He held it out in front of him and let it catch the light from the main view screen.

"They've assaulted our very freedom by hoping to shackle us with their technology. Today we say, 'No more.' When we arrive at our destination, we will be joined by a fleet of civilian ships from all over the Frontier. In full view of one of the Frontier's busiest space stations, we will throw overboard these chains they've tried to tether us with . . . I've never been much for speeches, but today I hope to send a clear message. If history should recall our names, then I have no doubt someone more eloquent than I will put words in my mouth that are worth remembering, but until then, my speech will have to do. Thank you all for the exemplary service."

Even on the bridge there was a cheer, one that had to be echoing all across the *Deviant Rising* and her crew. For so long, the United Planets of Earth had regarded most of the Frontier as nothing more than an indentured labor force, Strife Colony in particular. The crew had reason to be elated.

"You all should be aware that the actions we're about to take are illegal and will likely bring action down on myself and possibly the rest of you. At this time, any crew member who wishes to lodge an official objection to our actions may do so with their superior officer. But when the time comes, I expect everyone to do their job. That is all."

The captain gave the signal for communications to cut the channel and sat back in his seat.

"You know, Captain, the chicken suit might have actually helped that speech," Rin said, as straight-faced as ever.

"I'll keep that in mind for the holo version."

CHAPTER 6

Showy Acts of Rebellion

"IF YOU'RE THIS unsure, Trevor, you can go, but the rest of us are staying here. We've come too far to stop now." Rin sat in the captain's office as Captain Pacius spoke into the holo receiver on his desk. The other ships that were to be involved in the protest had been arriving more or less constantly for the last couple hours, and Pacius had spent most of that time in conference with their captains, each of whom seemed to have their own ideas about how they should proceed with the protest.

On Captain Pacius's desk were the miniature projected images of three people. Though after the last few hours, Rin could honestly no longer keep track of who was captain of what. Pacius didn't seem to have the same problem, though, addressing every one of them by name, and knowing details of their situations that only a crew member would know or care about.

"It's not that I'm unsure—" one of the miniature captains started, but Pacius cut him off.

"Trevor, if you're not completely with us, it is probably better you take the *Heisenberg* and head back. I know where we are right now, but I don't pretend to know where we're going from here. What I do know is I need everyone here to be with me on this," Pacius said.

"No, I'm here."

"Good. Then if that's everything, Captain, I need to get back to my bridge. The show will be starting shortly, and I want to make sure everyone out there has time to get good seats."

The miniature captains winked out of existence one by one.

"Well, that went well," Captain Pacius said once his office was free of holograms.

"But everyone just argued with you and each other, and three ships left. Is that what we call going well?" Rin asked.

"Three ships left, but twelve stayed, and while they may have spent the last two hours arguing with me, and even now probably are still arguing with each other, they are still here, and when the time comes, they'll follow, even if it's grudgingly," Pacius said.

"You're probably right."

"It's been known to happen. Now, let's get back to the bridge. Who knows what's come of it with only second and third mates in charge," Captain Pacius joked.

"I shudder to think, sir."

The two stepped out of the small office and surveyed the bridge of the *Deviant Rising*. To Rin's relief, everyone was at their stations, nothing seemed to be on fire, and everything was still working.

"Navigation, is everyone in position?" Captain Pacius asked.

"Most are, sir. Though a few are still on their way." Rin looked over at the mate at navigation and saw Carry doing his best to hide his excitement and nervousness. Rin wished there was time to have a quiet word with him before everything got started, but unfortunately there wasn't. The *Deviant Rising* would just have to make due with a navigator who looked as if he was torn between doing a little happy dance and bolting from the bridge in abject terror.

"Very good, let me know when they are," Captain Pacius ordered.

Suddenly the mate at communications spoke up. "Captain, we're receiving a message from Archer's Agony. They're warning us that our course has us colliding with Ocassio Ultima and wish to know if we need assistance."

"Inform them that everything is all right and that we do not require any assistance at this time," Pacius ordered before continuing under his breath for himself and Rin, "That should make damn sure they're looking our way when everything gets started."

Rin smiled and looked up at the large view screen that dominated one wall of the bridge. An image of Archer's Agony Space took up almost a third of it. The large space station that served as the first port on this side of Ocassio Ultima resembled nothing more than a junkyard slowly revolving in space with the aid of several almost circular rings. The most impressive feature of the station was that it had not yet broken into a thousand individual hunks of scrap a century ago. Somehow, against all odds, Archer's Agony held together and was now the permanent home for several thousand people and the temporary home for tens of thousands more.

The only other prominent thing on the display was the bright red mass of Ocassio Ultima, the gateway star. Ocassio Ultima was by all appearances a typical red dwarf star, much like its twin Epsilon Eridani. It was the sort of star that would normally draw little if any attention, but neither star was what anyone considered normal. Due to a process that no one even came close to understanding, the twin stars were linked, linked over countless light years, and provided a bridge from one to the other for those who knew how to navigate it. Rin always thought that the stars should look different somehow, show some sign of their unique properties, but they didn't. It was by simple chance that Captain Archer discovered the Gate so long ago, and nothing short of a miracle that he was able to return to tell others of it, even if that return trip ultimately cost him his life.

"Sir, the last ships are in position," Carry said from navigation.

"Very good. Communications, inform the ships that dumping should start in one minute."

Rin sat in silence with the rest of the bridge as the minute passed, and then one by one the *Deviant Rising* and the other twelve ships blasted their cargo free, using the air in their cargo bays to give their loads that little bit of extra acceleration as they went.

It was almost a magical moment for Rin. They had done what they came to do and nothing had happened. Rin had not realized how tense she had been in the lead-up to this, not until that tension was suddenly gone.

"That's the last of it," a mate at one of the engineering stations said.

"Sir, we've got something coming in fast, just out of the Occasio Ultima gate." The words came from Wessels at tactical.

"What is it?" Captain Pacius inquired.

"Can't tell. The star is making it hard to see."

"Put it up on the screen," Captain Pacius ordered.

At first all they saw was a small point of light, a blip where the sensors told them something was, but rapidly it grew, becoming more and more massive. Something enormous was coming their way and icy fear seized Rin when she realized what it might be.

Suddenly the *Deviant Rising's* entire front viewport was blocked by an enormous shadow that seemed to emerge from the star itself. The shape was sharp and angular at first, but as the vessel took up a position in front of them, the full outline of this ship became visible against the backdrop of the star behind it.

The sharp angles, flat profile, and thruster shape of the ship before them was clearly designed for speed as much as it was firepower. The ship bore a striking resemblance to a giant squid. That is, if a giant squid was made of knives and was eleven thousand meters long. It loomed above the *Deviant Rising* like a massive ocean predator sizing up its prey. A swift sensation of terror washed over Rin's body, causing the hairs on the back of her neck to stand on end.

"My god . . ." Captain Pacius whispered, "It's the *Enigma* . . ."

"Captain, we're being hailed. Audio only."

"Attention, Frontier vessels. This is Captain Shard of the UPE *Enigma*. You are in violation of UPE code 1773–1216. You're ordered to stand down and surrender immediately."

Rin's stomach sank. She knew the *Enigma* by reputation. Everyone did. And now that she could see it on the screen, it became all too real. Like every UPE capital ship, it had enough firepower to turn a moon into glass and enough troops to make sure even the cockroaches were gone. But the *Enigma's* reputation went beyond that. The *Enigma* was a hell bringer, and its captain took delight in flexing the muscles of his ship and people. The *Enigma* had been involved in more violent incidents than any other ship in the UPE Navy. Now, it was ordering them to stand down.

"Open a channel to the fleet!" Pacius ordered. "This is Captain Pacius on the *Deviant Rising*. Continue to dump your cargoes. We've come too far to let the UPE intimidate us now."

"Sir, are you sure?" Rin called out when he had finished addressing the other ships.

"The *Enigma*'s not going to push the issue, not this close to the station and with all those witnesses, not for a protest that's already over," Captain Pacius said. Rin hoped he was right.

"Sir." This time it was Wessels at tactical. "They're targeting and firing on the other ships."

Rin watched in horror as one by one the ships that had joined them in the protest started taking damage. At first she hoped they were only firing to disable. But then the screen was overwhelmed by a pulse of light that could only be the drive core of one of the ships going critical.

"This wasn't supposed to happen," she heard Captain Pacius say beside her. "Most of those ships aren't even armed. This wasn't supposed to happen. No one was supposed to die."

"Sir! That was the *Heisenberg*."

"Are you sure?" Captain Pacius barked.

"Yes, sir!"

"Okay . . . navigation, move us between the *Enigma* and the other ships. Tactical, target any incoming ordinance you can and destroy it before it can reach us or the other ships, but prioritize the other ships over us. We can take a larger beating than they can. Communications, put me through to the fleet." Pacius didn't pause to check if his orders were being followed, and he didn't need to; his crew might lack the discipline of a proper naval vessel, but when it counted, the *Deviant Rising*'s crew was just as skilled. "Attention, fleet! Get out of here as fast as you can. We will do our best here to cover you."

The view screen started showing little dots where the *Deviant*'s fire was destroying the incoming ordinance, but it was clear it wasn't enough. Too much was still getting through to the other ships.

"Tactical! We need to get their attention. Divert some to the *Enigma* itself. We'll not be able to hurt them, but we might piss them off enough to look our way."

"Attention, all crew, proceed to your nearest emergency escape locations. I am ordering a complete abandon ship," Captain Pacius said before turning to Rin. "That means you too, Sara. Get to an escape pod now." As if to punctuate the captain's statement, the ship started rocking and shuddering from impact after impact. Rin saw a ball of fire engulf tactical and heard a short piercing scream before Second Mate Wessels was simply not there anymore.

"Captain, with all due respect, fuck no. You need me here," Rin yelled, shoving Carry out of his seat at navigation and ordering him into an escape pod.

"Okay, Sara, guess it's you and me, then. I'm diverting weapons control to another station. You try and keep us in one place as long as you can."

"Yes, sir!" Rin barked, turning to the controls and realizing that simply keeping them in one place while under this kind of fire was going to be all she could do.

"Xander!" but Rin was cut off, as all the air was sucked from her lungs, and she felt an intense heat unlike anything she had ever experienced. There was a quick blinding pain, and then nothing, merciful nothing.

CHAPTER 7

Deviant Lost

CADEN PATH WAS not a man normally given to excessive sympathy. This was not to say he was a cruel man; words like "sympathetic" or "cruel" simply didn't fit who and what he was, or at least who he allowed himself to be. They implied a degree of feeling that Cade couldn't afford himself in his life with the UPE. Still, as he stood outside the doors to the hanger where the survivors of the *Deviant Rising* protest were being held, observing them through a personal uplink to the *Enigma*, he felt a hint of something that might be called sympathy. They had brought this upon themselves, it was true, but as they were being lined up, stripped, disinfected, and fitted with Helix earrings, they seemed so pitiful, so broken.

Cade stepped away from the doors as they slid open for a medical technician in a white version of the UPE naval uniform. He was pushing a gurney that carried a badly burned woman. He nearly lost it when he saw Cade standing there, his long dark coat and magnetic sunglasses serving to reinforce the fear of Cade that this man, and most of the crew, held for the ship's Lambda observer. Cade looked down at the badly burned and unconscious woman on the gurney while the medic tried to compose himself. He tried to guess the woman's age, but the mass of burns and blisters covering her face made that a fruitless effort.

Once the medic had hurried past, Cade blinked away his own personal view of the hanger and stepped through so that he might see the scene in person. In person, the collected misery was no better. Cade could now hear the prisoners' soft whimpers and smell their blood and fear. The guards had lined up the terrified men and women against a wall. Cade had seen worse, been the cause of worse even, but it was still hard to see so many people broken. Not only in body, but also in mind and soul. If it had been up to Cade, he may have handled the protest reprecussions differently. But still, there was no arguing that Captain Shard's methods had been effective. Less than a handful of these people would ever be able to muster the courage to speak out against the UPE ever again.

As Cade traversed the massive hangar, he followed a thin trail of blood that had been left by one of the *Deviant Rising*'s crew. The blood trail grew thicker as it led to the outside of one of the escape pods the *Enigma* had reeled in. The pod had been cracked open like an egg and was covered in thick, semi-dried blood. The spatter patterns on the outside of the escape pod were likely from the butt of a rifle or a baton that had sprayed the blood in such a way as to make it look as if the broken pod itself were bleeding.

Cade continued through the hall of machinery, passing docked fighters and *Deviant Rising* escape pods, his long, dark trench coat sweeping back and forth against his legs until he found a position next to the *Enigma*'s captain and his squad of soldiers.

"We believe their captain survived," Captain Shard informed Cade as he approached.

Captain Shard was clearly waiting for Cade to say something, to indicate that Shard's luck in possibly not killing the man they had been sent to collect was somehow an accomplishment, but Cade remained silent, simply looking the shorter man up and down.

"We think he's in there." Shard gestured at a pod they were currently standing in front of." They've already removed a woman who was in the pod with him, but when they realized who the other occupant was they called for me," Shard continued, noting that Cade showed no signs of concern.

"I understand," Cade said flatly.

"Yes . . . so, I called for you. So you could confirm his identity before we took any further action. If he is Xander Pacius, then we can't allow him to rejoin his crew, and if he's not, then there is little point in spending any more time on him."

Cade accepted the simple truth in Shard's words, but also knew it for a half-truth. The real reason Shard had called for Cade was because he desperately needed to show Cade that his rash actions had not doomed their mission. Shard had lost his temper when the *Deviant Rising* had altered course and started firing back, and he knew, because of that, his life was in very real danger. At this point, Cade would be completely within his authority as the ship's observer to execute his captain and appoint a new one. Being a member of the United Planets of Earth Navy, Shard had seen other observers do this before.

"Then let us see if Xander Pacius is among the survivors. That will change a great many things," Cade said, noting the way Shard's face paled slightly at his words.

The pod smelled of sweat and burned flesh as Cade leaned inside to get a look at the remaining occupant. The man, still tangled in the pod's crash webbing, didn't have the same defeated look of most of the survivors. This man had a hardness in his eyes, despite the profound weariness that was also clear on his features. Cade looked the man over, impressed despite himself. There was clearly a core to this man who would not break easily.

Cade scanned his files on the *Deviant Rising's* crew. While they did not have information on the crew in its entirety, the UPE required all officers of the SMMC to be registered and licensed. So he did have information on everyone rated as third mate or above. Cade compared the man in front of him to the image of Xander Pacius that was now hovering in his field of vision. His systems told him that there was a 99.5 percent chance that the man was Xander Pacius, but for Cade there wasn't even that little fraction of doubt. It seemed Captain Shard's life was indeed safe for the moment.

"Captain Xander Pacius?" It wasn't really a question, but more of a way to give Pacius an avenue to start cooperating with them. Cade doubted if Shard and his people gave a damn whether or not Pacius was cooperative, nor would the UPE Naval Command or Lambda HQ, for that matter. So long as Pacius gave them what they wanted in the end. But Cade was not inclined to make things more difficult for this man if he didn't have to.

"Where is Sara Rin?" Pacius asked.

"Your first mate?" Cade asked in response.

"The woman your people yanked out of the pod. The one who was covered in burns!" Pacius spat.

"I don't know," Cade lied. The moment Pacius had mentioned her name, he had scanned the information the *Enigma*'s crew was collecting on the new prisoners. "But I can try and find out. If you work with us."

That had triggered something in Pacius. He didn't want to talk to Cade or anyone else on this ship. His profile coupled with his demeanor made that clear, but he did care about his crew. Sara Rin maybe most of all. Cade could use that, although he would have to do it carefully.

"We don't have time for this," Shard said from behind him. The continued life of Xander Pacius clearly returned a measure of confidence in Shard's own continued existence. A confidence Cade was not sure he shared. "Get him out of the pod and take him to Interrogation Room 4."

"Captain Pacius, please excuse me a moment," Cade said. He leaned out of the pod and turned to look Shard in the eye. Behind him, Cade heard a pair of soldiers approach Xander Pacius to cut him off the escape pod. "Captain Shard, this situation needs to be handled with some delicacy. Let us not resort to torture right off," Cade said, more for Xander Pacius who he was sure was listening to every word. Maybe yet another of Shard's impulsive and shortsighted actions could be turned to his advantage.

"The man is a pirate and a threat to the entire UPE. We don't have time to play nice," Shard said, trying and failing to meet Cade's obscured eyes.

"Understand me, Captain, this is a matter that we can't afford to rush. We'll not likely have another opportunity like this one, and I will not allow you to jeopardize it. You will first try speaking to the man. We may get lucky, and he may see reason. If that fails, I, not you and not your trained dogs, will be the one to extract what we need from him. Am I completely understood?" Cade said calmly, looking down at his captain. Shard was fuming, but he was also scared. Cade's look, as well as his words, had reminded him that he still hung from a very thin thread.

Shard turned back to his soldiers, who were dragging a struggling Xander Pacius across the deck to the station where he would have his Helix earring installed.

"Take him to guest quarters and stay there with him. The observer and I will be there shortly," Shard said, not bothering to turn back to Cade before hurrying off.

Cade watched as Xander Pacius was stripped and doused in disinfectant before a medical technician extended a hand and clamped the earring into place on Pacius's right ear. Again, Cade was impressed despite himself as Xander Pacius barely flinched when the needles pierced his flesh and began running the almost invisible wires from the piercing site to his brain. Cade had seen people cry out during the procedure before. It was far from painless. Most civilians opted to have their pain receptors temporarily blocked before installation. The *Enigma*'s prisoners were not given that option, though.

Cade absentmindedly rubbed a spot just next to his orbital bone. Captain Pacius might be in pain now, but there were far more painful things in this universe, many of which he might know before long.

CHAPTER 8

Reasonable Observations

CADE STOOD WITH Captain Shard outside the doors to the guest quarters where Xander Pacius was being held. He could tell by the look on Shard's face that he was working himself up to saying something. What that something was, Cade had a reasonable guess. But he was content to allow Shard to speak it in his own time, if at all. Shard attempted to meet his eye several times, anger, fear, impatience, and, most of all, uncertainty warring on his face. In general, Cade approved of his captain's attitude. It meant that Shard might finally be learning the importance of thinking through irreversible actions. It was a lesson Shard had, to this point, managed to avoid learning in his service in the UPE Navy, trusting to a general ruthlessness and natural ability to climb the promotion ladder.

"When we get in there, you're going to let me speak," Shard eventually said, making each word sound like he were chewing glass. It wasn't what he wanted to say. That was clear.

"Of course, Captain. It would be beyond the scope of my duties to interfere. I am an observer, my duty is to observe," Cade said, managing to convey in his normal flat tone the idea that what Shard had said was beyond obvious.

"Good, because despite everything that has happened over the last few hours, this is still my ship and this mission is mine." That was closer. Shard was trying to figure out where he stood with Cade as well as reassert some authority.

"I understand your concerns. I have only ever attempted to advise to make sure that your actions are completely in the best service of that mission. After all, neither of us want me to resort to the other aspect of my duties as an observer. In a time like this, stability is generally favorable over that kind of shake-up," Cade said, watching as Shard's face went just a little paler.

"Of course," Shard said, shrinking a little bit.

"So we're going to go in there and I am going to observe while you attempt to reason with the man," Cade added into the silence that followed Shard's brief answer.

Shard nodded grudgingly. Cade's threat was clear and, for the moment, anyway, that threat would keep Shard in line. The truth was that however much Cade disapproved of Shard, the UPE Navy had very different feelings. As such, Cade was reluctant to take any permanent measures against him unless he was sure those actions would have Lambda's full support. So Cade would push Shard, either into being a better captain, or into doing something Cade would be able to act on with security . . .

"Good evening, Captain," Shard began as they entered the room. The chamber they entered was sparsely furnished, but spacious, with a large viewport that took up most of one wall. This was the navy's idea of comfortable. Shard extended his hand to Xander Pacius, who was sitting stiffly in a high-backed chair near the viewport. Pacius ignored the extended hand, opting to continue looking out into the depths of space.

Cade angled himself so that he might have a similar view to Pacius's and saw that he had a clear view of the field of debris that used to be his ship . . . along with several others.

It was difficult to see, even with Cade's eyes, but he thought he could make out several very large sections of hull that would have belonged to a ship matching the design of the *Deviant Rising*.

Shard glanced at Cade before he withdrew his hand.

"Captain, have you had time to consider your situation?"

Pacius turned away from the viewport to finally look Shard in the eye. "You destroyed my ship, along with several others, without provocation. There isn't really much to consider."

Shard didn't respond at first. Instead, he made his way over to a small cabinet near the chair in which Pacius was sitting. He opened the cabinet, revealing several bottles of various size, shape, and color. "Captain, we both know it's more complicated than that. Even if it weren't, you still have your crew to consider. Neither of us want anything . . . uncomfortable to happen to them," Shard said.

Shard selected a short bottle containing a thick red liquor and made his way to a seat near Pacius.

"Captain, we don't need to be adversaries. If you work with me in this incredibly difficult situation, things can go much easier for you," Shard said, pouring a measure from the bottle into three glasses and setting them on a small table. Both Cade and Pacius ignored their glasses, but Shard sipped at his contentedly.

"I would rather work on a drive core naked," Pacius hissed through gritted teeth.

"You and your crew are in serious trouble, Captain. You fired at a UPE vessel and led a protest that destroyed UPE property. I urge you to reconsider. If you cooperate with me and give me all the information I need, then for the rest of this trip you will be treated as a guest. When we return to Earth, I will inform my superiors of how helpful you've been, and I will advocate for leniency for you and your crew."

Pacius stood up. "Your ship's log will prove you fired first. We only retaliated in defense. We've damaged no property of yours. But today you've killed thousands of innocent people."

Shard stood up to join him, but the difference in the two men's heights caused Shard to meet Pacius's chest rather than his eyes. "I am oh so very sorry you feel that way," Shard said. He walked over and looked out the viewport at the debris field.

"Our ship's logs will show that we had little choice. We had to stop a mounting threat."

"What is it you want?"

"I want to know how many SMMC vessels were involved. Who sanctioned this protest, and how many other terrorist acts are being planned?"

"Terrorist? How can you call our protest a terrorist action?"

"Your protest destroyed millions of credits worth of property and cost the lives of, at last count, one thousand three hundred and fifteen people. It is clear that your real intentions were to shake the people's confidence in the UPE and its ability to govern and protect its citizens. I am honestly hard-pressed to categorize it any other way," Shard said, turning away from the viewport to look at Pacius once more.

"You're the one who did that!" Pacius said. Cade privately agreed.

"I guess it comes down to perspective. Either way, Captain, I need to know who else organized this. We can track down the other ships and their captains, but I doubt they'll know much. It would be a shame to have them interrogated for no reason. I would much rather have you just tell me who's giving you your orders and have done with it."

"No one gave me any orders. I organized this. It was me. I contacted the other captains, and they all followed me. There was no plot, no conspiracy, just me," Pacius insisted, though Cade was reasonably sure he was not telling the entire truth. It seemed Shard agreed.

"You're lying! You really expect me to believe one man, one captain, was able to muster a fleet of that size without assistance? You may have fooled your crew, but I am not so naive! I urge you one last time, Captain. Tell me who your other comrades are. Tell me what your future plans are and this can be much easier for you."

Pacius looked directly at Shard. "I already did."

"Very well. To be honest, I didn't expect this to work. But I was asked to try before I moved to more direct forms of extraction." At this Shard looked over at Cade, who was standing unconcerned in the corner.

Shard walked back over to the door and knocked on it sharply. It opened, revealing a pair of guards who had been waiting outside.

"Bring Mr. Pacius to Interrogation Room 4. I think he'll find it a bit more conducive to conversation."

This time Cade didn't argue.

CHAPTER 9

Aurelium Ignition

STRIFE WAS BEAUTIFUL this time of year. The sky was warm and gold. The sun peeked through the clouds and reached down with its long fingers to the tall grass that covered the mountains below. The smell of tall golden meadows wafted through the air. It was the aroma of life at the beginning of a gentle summer. You could hear the buzz of grass crickets playing their symphonies between every blade.

The air was warm and sweet with the smell of summer. A light breeze blew through Maintenance Hangar 13. It was too beautiful of a day to be working with the hangar doors closed. Aurelius had opened them at the beginning of his shift. This hangar was up on a range of hills. Out the back doors, there were rolling golden mountains with little dark emerald patches of trees. Out the front, the massive doorway framed a view of the city of Blades. It was the only metropolis on Strife, and Aurelius found himself staring out at the city. Maybe in another fifty years these hills would be covered in overpriced condominiums, but for now it was a hell of a place to spend post–boot camp days in the SMMC.

Like most mornings, Aurelius was on his back under a vehicle. His hands were covered in grease and his overalls were dotted with oil, and he loved it. He was trying to tune out the sounds of rushing water coming from a hose. Someone was washing down a craft or trying to get the oil stains off the floor. Aurelius was just tuning out the noise when an ice-cold puddle caught up with him and shocked him out of his happy place.

"Ow!" he yelled, creeping out from under the craft. "Dude! What the hell? I'm working here!"

His buddy Benny laughed. "Sorry, Strifer. My bad."

"Can you do that later? I'd like to get through the day without being electrocuted."

Benny shut off his hose. "We know how hard that is for some people."

Aurelius shot him a look.

"Sorry, just trying to polish up the place."

"Here . . . I could use your help."

Aurelius pulled off a panel and began tweaking something inside.

"What's up?" Benny asked.

"Flow regulator says both turbines should be getting power . . ."

The craft was dead silent.

"Doesn't sound like anything's getting power," Benny said.

"I know. That's the problem. I need you to hop in and run a diag."

"You can't do that?"

"Not while I'm down here, genius."

Benny hopped into the cockpit and flicked through the controls. The craft began to hum and vibrate.

Aurelius pulled a coin out of his pocket and held it over one of the engine housings. He gently let it go. It hung, floating in the air a few inches off the craft. He flicked it with one finger, and it began to spin.

"Okay. That's all I needed. You can get back to beautifying the place," Aurelius said.

Benny hopped out of the craft and looked up at Aurelius. "What are you doing? What is that?"

"My own diagnostics."

"Oh god." Benny shook his head. "Not that again. Strifer, why don't you learn how to do it the right way?"

"Takes too long. Plus, I'm no good at the math."

Aurelius wasn't kidding; he was "math dead." The complexities of tuning a faster-than-light engine were overwhelming and laborious. This wasn't the way he worked on them back home. He had learned everything from his father, who didn't have the money for the latest and greatest tools; he had to resort to other means. Aurelius had learned every one of his father's diagnostic techniques; balancing a coin over the antigravity generator was one of his favorites.

Benny picked up a socket wrench and began checking the screws around the craft. "Yikes. Remind me never to fly in one of your hoppers."

Aurelius rolled his eyes.

"What, do you need a tutor or something?" Benny asked.

"Tried that. I just don't have the patience for it. I guess it's the technobabble I don't get."

"Technobabble?"

"Yeah, the tests look like Terranese to me."

"Rough, Strifer, rough. What's the biggest engine you've ever worked on?"

Aurelius pointed to the hopper.

"You're kidding me!"

"Wish I could say I was. My pa used to service hoppers about this size. That's where I learned to do this kinda stuff. Like he always used to say, 'If you can't fix it with duct tape, then you're not using enough duct tape.'"

Benny frowned. "I seriously hope you're joking, otherwise, I'm not flying in anything you service. How long you been in the hangars?"

"Nine months," Aurelius answered.

Benny stopped mid-ratchet. "Nine months? Holy shit, Strifer! Maybe I should double-check the whole damn craft! I never heard of anyone taking more than four to test out!"

"I know!" Aurelius laughed. "I know, I know."

"Shit. Sorry, dude."

The honest truth was Aurelius was a damn good mechanic. Good enough that he had a reputation for it.

"That's bad. Like, real bad. How do you expect to get drafted to a ship?"

"Well, if my good looks don't help me, I guess I'll just have to get real lucky when they need someone to replace the lightbulbs," Aurelius joked.

Benny didn't laugh; his attention was elsewhere.

"Hey . . . hey!" Aurelius said, snapping his fingers to bring Benny back.

"Huh?"

"Quit the daydreaming and help me with this."

"I wasn't daydreaming," Benny said. "I was checking out that cruiser coming in over the capital."

Aurelius pulled his head out of the engine. Sure enough, a large SMMC cruiser was coming in and docking at the Spire in the center of the city. This wasn't uncommon, but it was still a sight to see as it darkened several city blocks beneath it.

"Never seen the *Freedom's Reach* before?" Aurelius asked.

"Nope. It's a lot bigger than the other ships I've seen dock."

"Yeah. It's the governor's ship."

"That guy gets his own ship? I wanna go into politics. Think of all the skirts you'd get with a ship that size." Benny laughed.

"It's not the size of the ship that matters—it's the size of the mass core that counts." Aurelius couldn't help himself.

"And you wonder why people think you're a dork?"

The coin Aurelius had placed was beginning to wobble. That wasn't good; it told him something was wrong in the antigrav assembly. He hopped down and powered off the craft.

Aurelius went around back and removed a panel under the engine. "Hey, help me here right quick."

The two of them removed each screw and dismounted the antigrav generator. It was heavy, and setting it down on the ground was a two-man job, ironically.

"You're gonna be here a long time if you don't figure something out," Benny said.

Aurelius smiled. "I've made my peace with it."

"Maybe you just gotta focus a little. You know, grow up a bit."

A cocky smile creeped its way across Aurelius's face. "I don't wanna grow up. I reckon it's a trap."

"You can't stay here forever, Blaze!" Sergeant William Barber barked as he entered the hanger, causing Aurelius and Benny to drop their tools and salute.

"At ease," the sergeant ordered.

Sarge was intimidating as hell the first few weeks of boot camp, but after that, he grew on Aurelius, so long as he wasn't crossed.

Sarge had a touch screen in one hand and his signature cigar in the other as he walked up to Aurelius. "What the hell is wrong with you, Blaze?"

"You're gonna have to be a little more specific than that, sir!" Aurelius said with a shit-eating grin still on his face.

Benny snorted, attempting to swallow his laughter.

"All right, chuckles," Sarge said, blowing a mouthful of smoke at them. "Benny, your three and a half months are up. And I'm pleased to see that your tests are good . . ."

Sarge flicked through the pages of a document on his pad before continuing. "Congrats, you're getting moved to a ship. Looks like you're being sent to the *Ember Cascade*. They need good engineers. You'll have to kiss Aurelius good-bye and hope he learns from your example."

Sarge shook his hand. Benny looked elated; he had been looking to get this post for a while.

"You're dismissed," Sarge ordered, saluting Benny.

Benny headed for the hallway off to one side of the hanger. He walked slowly, probably so he could eavesdrop.

The look in Sarge's eye made Aurelius nervous. He knew he was gonna get barked at for something; it happened all the time. Sarge pulled up his last test scores. "Aurelius Blaze. You know, your scores on your retake really shouldn't be lower than the original."

Aurelius stood silent. What could he say?

"What the hell is wrong with you, Aurelius?"

"Sir, did you read my essay answers?"

"Yeah, I did. In fact, I read them a few times . . . but I still don't understand them. That's why I'm here."

The test mostly focused on mixing the right fuel-to-mass-field ratios and checking the plasma flow in boson fields. It was all hieroglyphics. Aurelius was relieved Sarge came down to talk about it. If he had a chance to demonstrate the idea from his answer, maybe Sarge would go easier on him.

"I want you to explain, in plain English, what this 'alternative method' is."

"Sir, I understand the need for the test. You gotta know these things when you build a ship, or when you work on one midflight. I get it. But in a real hot situation, all that stuff in the books won't help you, and you're not gonna have time to double-check your long division. You need to be able to think on your feet, think on the fly."

"This is the way it's done. This is the way it's always been done, and this is what gets things done safely."

"Sir, if I could demonstrate?"

Aurelius connected a cable from the craft to the antigrav generator now sitting on the ground. He leaned in the cockpit and turned it on.

"You have a coin, sir?" Aurelius asked.

"Where the hell are you going with this?"

"All I need is a half Strife or something."

Sarge dug through his pockets and handed one to Aurelius.

"That'll do."

Like before, Aurelius held it about six inches over the antigrav generator and slowly let it go. It sat there floating in midair, as if on the end of a string.

"The coin's being suspended by the antigrav field," Aurelius said.

He flicked the edge of the coin with his finger, and it began to spin. "Now, if any of your calculations are off, even a little, you'll be able to see it in the spin of the coin."

Aurelius flicked some controls. The coin began to rotate slower, then fast again. "If there's a problem, you'll know right away."

He flicked a switch that caused the coin to wobble irregularly and the generator sputtered out.

Sarge was silent. Aurelius couldn't tell if he liked the idea, or if he even understood it. After a moment, Sarge spoke up. "What if you don't have a coin?"

Aurelius spent the next ten minutes showing Sarge different everyday items he could use instead. A pair of sunglasses, a screwdriver, or a shiny bubblegum wrapper. If there had been more time, he would have shown him all the other techniques he had learned to diagnose and fix other very complicated problems.

"Seriously, sir. No one's ever done it this way before?" Aurelius asked.

Sarge let out a low whistle and ran his fingers through his hair. "Nope. Fifteen years in the corps, and I've never seen it done this way. Where'd you learn to do something like this?"

"My dad. He taught me everything I know. Said I had a real keen understanding of engines."

"All right, Mr. Blaze. This is neat, but not what I got from your test."

"Yeah, I know. It's too bad there's no show-and-tell section."

Sarge scratched his head. "That's damn inventive, but tricks like that ain't gonna get you further than this hangar, and you've already been here too long."

"I know, I know . . . I'm trying. What can I do, sir?"

Sarge took a long, hard drag on his cigar. "Think I'm gonna have to move you somewhere."

Sarge's tone scared Aurelius.

"I told you not to get too attached to this place," Sarge said with a wink. "Well, I'll leave you to it, then," he said before walking out of the hangar.

After a moment, Benny came running back in. "Did you just get booted or something?"

"God, I hope not."

"Damn, dude. Sorry. That's a pretty cool little trick, though."

"Yeah. Fat lot of good it did me."

"Well, I really should get out of here and pack up. Hey, let's go out and get a beer tonight. I know you could use one right about now."

"Gina's Bar?" Aurelius raised a brow.

"Yeah."

"Sure. Congrats on your new post, by the way," Aurelius said.

Benny's mouth worked silently for a moment. "Uh . . . thanks. Well . . . I'll see ya later, Strifer," Benny said, walking out.

"Yeah . . . Sure," Aurelius said as his friend left the hanger. "I guess a drink will do me good." Aurelius turned from the door his friend had just left through and returned to his tinkering on the hopper. Tomorrow this hanger might not be his home anymore, but today it still was, and today there was a grav assembly that needed figuring out. Aurelius could spend days doing work like this; he liked fixing things but his destiny was in space, traveling the stars and seeing the sights, saving people in danger and all that space-adventurer shit.

The thought that it might not happen didn't bother him as much as it should. Yeah, he was bummed, but mostly because the corps was the best place to learn how to do the repairs he wanted. It wasn't the adventure he'd be sad to give up, it was the tools, the grease, the stuffy and overheated hangers filled with junk and noise and activity. That was what was pulling at his heart. That, and the strange thought that his older brother would be disappointed with him somehow.

CHAPTER 10

Three Sheets to the Wind

AURELIUS HAD ALREADY hit several bars that night, Benny somewhat wobbly, following in his wake. But even when they showed their leave notice to the duty officer and started out, they knew what their final destination would be.

Even on weekends, Gina's Bar was busy. It was the closest place to unwind near the hangars, which meant it was popular with recruits and enlisted men. The drinks were weak, the place was loud, and if you didn't get there early, there wasn't a place to sit. People came for the atmosphere—it was fun, and everyone knew the staff. For Aurelius, it was the only place he'd want to have a last drink before the SMMC kicked him out.

"Hey, everyone!" Aurelius called as he finally managed to kick the door open. It'd taken him three attempts, but he was fairly sure no one inside noticed those. "Your favorite grease tech is here and the party can finally start!" No one turned Aurelius's way at this declaration, but surely it was only to avoid being blinded by his awesomeness.

"You go get the drinks. I think I need to stay here a moment. Otherwise, I might fall off the floor," Benny said, trying to keep his gaze steady on the boards that threatened to betray him.

"Got it. But if I come back and you're floating or something, I'm keeping your drink," Aurelius said before making his way to the bar, past a few tables that kept jumping in front of him.

Gina, the owner, smiled as Aurelius finally reached her. "Didn't think I'd see you in here tonight. Mostly it's the folks getting ready to ship out throwing one back one last time," she said.

"And that . . . and that I am, Gina. Shipping out tomorrow. *No* idea where I'll be going, but I'm going. Not being held back in the hangers anymore," he said. Then he leaned in closer to Gina and whispered, "Benny, though . . . poor guy. They said he was too stupid to leave the dirt. Trying not to make him feel bad, though. We've been telling everyone all night I'm the one staying back and he's the one jettin' off into the stars."

"Is that really how it is?" Gina asked knowingly.

Aurelius hesitated a moment, trying to figure out if his game was up already. He didn't remember Gina being all that sharp, and he wondered how she saw through his cunning story. "You got me, Gina. They're never letting a kid like me into space, so I came here to see if you could get me there instead."

"Are you asking for directions?" Gina looked him up and down.

"That depends," Aurelius replied. "You coming with me?"

Gina hesitated. "I think the drinks have gotten to your head."

"Oh, yeah? Well, I heard alcohol kills brain cells slowly, but that never bothered me because I'm not in a hurry."

Gina laughed as she poured him a shot of something light blue and fuming. "You stay here and have your drink. Gunna go get Benny before he purges all over that big guy."

Aurelius turned to see Benny looking green and trying to lean against one of the largest guys Aurelius had ever seen. The big man was staring down at Benny with a look of irritation that was slowly turning into horror as what was about to happen dawned on everyone.

"No, I got this. Benny's my ground-poundin' buddy after all. Gotta look out for 'im."

Aurelius pulled himself to his feet and ran over to where his friend was about to lose his lunch and life in quick succession. He was aiming for Benny with his tackling lurch, but that damned treacherous floor decided that Benny wasn't the only one it didn't like that night. Aurelius hurled into the large man, who shoved Benny away just in time to catch the soon-to-be washout before impact.

The order of events that followed was a bit jumbled, but as best Aurelius could figure, the beer in the giant's hand went flying. Most of it went splashing down to the floor, but enough went down Aurelius's back so as to briefly make him consider if he'd need to do the rest of the night's drinking in his underpants. At the same time, he heard a crashing sound as Benny attempted to catch himself but instead took a table, several drinks, and at least one woman with him to the ground.

The giant pushed Aurelius off of him and towered over him. "This yours?" he said, turning to Benny with a disgusted look on his face.

"He might be," Aurelius said, standing himself and checking to see how much beer was really dripping onto his pants.

"Well, keep a better eye on him. Little guy comes up to me like he's gonna puke, and when I pushed him the fuse away, he started getting all cuddly like I was his sweetheart or something."

"I think that means he likes you," Aurelius said.

"Fuse that. Guy was going to vent all over me and no one's ever gotten laid with recruit chunks down their shirt," the giant said.

"They say it's not what's on the outside that counts," Aurelius replied.

"Are you a complete idiot?" the man asked.

"Not a complete idiot. Lost some parts a while back," Aurelius answered.

"'Bout to lose a few more, I'm thinkin'," the man said, advancing.

"Hold on, no need for all that. There was no real harm done." The man was getting ready to hit him, and Aurelius became suddenly stone sober.

"I think there is. First, you two come bothering me, getting ready to sick up. Then you start coming up all smartass. I'm thinking you need a little lesson in manners," the giant said with a sickening grin that showed far too many bright white teeth.

"Not being a smartass, I'm a dumb ass, trust me. A smartass wouldn't be in this situation, would he?" Aurelius said.

The giant paused at that, a war going on behind his eyes. He looked to be torn between using Aurelius to clean the bathroom or something worse. After what seemed like a short eternity, the man cracked a smile. Not the evil 'I'm going to kill you' one he had been sporting earlier. This smile seemed to carry genuine amusement.

"Either you're the dumbest man I've ever met, or you've got a set larger than moons," the giant said.

"Well, they do have a few craters," Aurelius said with a grin that matched the giant's, though his was as much relief as anything else.

"Yeah. It's dumb. Still, get me another drink and we'll call it balanced."

"A drink?" Aurelius asked.

"Beer. I was drinking it. You and your friend spilled it," he said, taking a small step forward.

"I don't—" Aurelius started but then realized that he was still holding a miraculously un-spilled shot. "Actually, here, have this." Aurelius handed over the slightly damp shot glass.

"What is it?" the man said, taking it from Aurelius's hand.

"It's—it's—it's blue," Aurelius said.

The man looked at the shot in his hand, then down at Aurelius who was grinning up at him. Eventually he seemed to come to some decision. He smiled at Aurelius and threw back the blue liquid.

"Damn. Like antimatter," the man said, closing his eyes and nodding.

"All for you, buddy," Aurelius said, sensing that the danger might have finally passed.

"You're not bad, Strifer. Let's get pukey here some water," the giant said, helping Aurelius bring Benny back to vertical.

Together, the two of them were able to get Benny into a seat at the bar where he seemed to start recovering.

"Did I miss something? Who's the big guy?" Benny groggily asked as he drank his water.

"Jerula," the man said, turning to take in Benny.

"Guess his name's Jerula. He's the guy who almost caught your lunch a few minutes ago," Aurelius added.

"He mad?" Benny asked.

"He was for a little bit, but I sorted everything out," Aurelius answered.

"Oh, good. Drink?" Benny asked.

"Not for you, pukey," Jerula said.

"But it is your turn to buy the next round," Aurelius finished with a grin.

"Oh . . . okay . . ." Benny said.

They didn't think they'd get much out of Benny the rest of the night, but that didn't stop Aurelius and the giant Jerula from ordering another drink.

"So, what's your story?" Aurelius asked.

"I'm a soft tech. You know, a hacker," Jerula boasted.

Aurelius was struck by the irony. A guy built like a Thunderball linebacker a software technician? He knew soft techs were the sort of counterpart to his hard tech training. Jerula was the guy that made everything do what it was supposed to, once someone like Aurelius got all the parts working. Still, the image of this guy didn't line up with the career choice.

"You any good?" Aurelius asked.

"I am like a god. No machine would ever disobey my programming," Jerula answered.

"And you're so humble about it."

"Strifer, gods can't be humble. If we were, who would ever know to worship us?" Jerula said, turning to Aurelius with a look of complete sincerity plastered across his broad dark face.

"So you're a god? How'd you get a gig like that?" Aurelius asked.

"You don't get a gig like this. You have to be born with the greatness inside you, and if you don't got it, you don't got it. Sorry, man, you might have good taste in drinks, but a god you ain't," Jerula answered.

"I might be. You don't know. I might just like to keep it low key," Aurelius shot back before finishing a drink and gesturing for Gina to bring them another round.

"Hey, Gina. While we have you, take a good look at this pretty-boy Strifer, and then at my ebony glory, and tell me which of us looks like a god among men to you," Jerula said as she poured them each another couple shots.

Gina looked them both over, considering the two drunks looking up at her from their stools.

"I don't know. Jerula, you got that strong statuesque magnificence thing going for you, but Aurelius here . . . well, if anyone has the luck of a supernatural being, it's him."

"How do you figure?" both Aurelius and Jerula said together.

"Anyone else with Aurelius's attitude would have been booted out years ago, but damned if the little bastard hasn't found himself a home in those hangers," Gina said, pouring herself a drink and sitting down across from them.

"Nah, a god would have moved on from the hangers," Aurelius said, trying to sound a bit more cheerful than the thought actually made him.

"Why do you say that? Gods don't always get what they want. Gods just have a way of getting what they need," Gina said.

"So I need to be in the hangers?" Aurelius said, taking a sip of his drink, then eyeing it suspiciously as if it might leave on its own if he didn't do something about it soon.

"I think you live for those hangers. Even if you got a posting tomorrow, those hangers are yours, kid. Everyone says so," Gina said.

"What, this guy? He can hardly find his way to the can. There is no way he's that good," Jerula said, taking a swig from his own drink.

"Kid knows tricks most of the other techs haven't ever seen. Even Barber doesn't know how he does it."

"Barber? Sarge said that? Always thought the old jackass hated me," Aurelius said.

"He's just like that. He sort of hates everyone, but only while they are his responsibility. He just doesn't want you going out there and embarrassing him or worse . . . the corps." Gina patted Aurelius on the back and stood up to see to another customer who was calling for a refill.

"So Sarge actually likes us," Aurelius said, trying to take in the planet-shattering news.

"Don't go that far. She just said he didn't quite hate us. "Like" is another thing completely. There is no way Sarge likes you. I only barely like you, and that's mostly because you keep buying drinks," Jerula said.

"Oh, come on, you love me. I can see it in your eyes," Aurelius said.

"Strifer, that's the antimatter."

The night got blurrier as time went on. Aurelius woke Benny up at one point to drink a toast for getting posted to a ship. Later, Aurelius found himself with Gina in his lap doing her best to feed him her tongue, while a pretty young recruit lead Jerula away to a booth for a game of tonsil hockey.

Aurelius didn't remember much else other than trying to find his way back to his room sometime before sunrise and dropping onto his bunk, the night's beer-stained clothes still clinging to his body.

CHAPTER 11

Fizzies, Foes, and Giants

"HEY . . . HEY, STRIFER. You alive?" a voice barked.

Morning came sliding to Aurelius, accompanied by a massive headache. He cracked open his eyes, trying to keep the light at bay. The outline of a very large and dark man standing above him shifted into focus.

"Thought I was gonna have to call medical," the voice chuckled.

Aurelius sat up. Apparently he had crash-landed on someone's dorm room couch. But he'd have sworn he had made it to his bunk, so where on Strife was he now? The dark, blurry figure towering over him tossed him a small jar of pills. Aurelius studied the jar uncomprehendingly.

"They're Fizzies, take them," the figure said as it slowly coalesced into someone Aurelius was almost sure he recognized.

Aurelius recited the commercial numbly: "Fizzies, Fizzies when your stomach and head are in a tizzy."

"Oh, good. We can rule out long-term memory loss. How's your short-term? How much do you remember from last night?"

Aurelius thought about it. He laughed. The truth was at this point he was happy he remembered his own name, but the name of the giant standing in front of the couch was a mystery. "Oh, god . . . I don't know. I think I remember knocking a drink into your lap?" Aurelius said, trying to fight through the fog of the night before.

"Yeah, you're getting there," the man said.

"You're Jerula? I think I remember you almost killing me. You didn't, did you?" Aurelius asked.

"Yeah. Didn't really wanna get kicked out of Gina's, ya know? You're lucky."

"That I am. Would you have really hit me?" Aurelius asked.

"What do you think?" Jerula asked. "You remember trying to kiss me?"

"Huh?" Aurelius quickly parsed his memory. No, nothing. "Very funny. I am sure I'd be remembering that."

"I'm serious. You tried to kiss me. I told you that you weren't my type, and you followed me all the way back here, crying the whole way. I felt bad and let you crash out."

Aurelius paused. That couldn't be—he was reasonably sure he remembered kissing a brunette. He remembered how great her . . . eyebrows were, though that might have been a dream. Aurelius quickly checked Jerula's eyebrows to make sure.

"Oh, man, I totally had you there for a second."

"You're an ass," Aurelius said.

Aurelius put a hand on his head. Life was painful right now, and all he could do was wait for the Fizzies to kick in.

"So, Gina . . . she single?"

"I dunno," Aurelius answered.

"She seemed kind of single last night," Jerula laughed.

"What makes you say—" Aurelius cut himself short as a disjointed series of still images of the previous night's shenanigans blew past his mind's eye. "Oh, yeah. I knew I remembered kissing a brunette . . . I should probably call her . . ."

"I wouldn't if I were you," Jerula said.

"Why not?" Aurelius asked him.

"We may have left without paying," Jerula answered.

"Shit. I'll have to pay a visit over there this afternoon. Hopefully Gina won't be too pissed," Aurelius replied.

"Well, we may have also left a mess in the bathroom."

"What kind of mess?" Aurelius asked, searching his mind for any memory of the event.

"The kind with spillover. You're going to want to give Gina a little time to get over that kind of thing. You can send her the money. Think that will be safer for everyone," Jerula said.

"I don't remember that," Aurelius said.

"I'm betting there's a lot you don't remember this morning."

"Guess so. Hey, where's Benny?"

"Who?" Jerula asked.

"My bunkmate. I came out with him last night," Aurelius said.

"I'm sure he's fine. He was passed out the last time I saw him. How much trouble could he have gotten into?"

"Wait, did we . . . ?" Aurelius quickly pulled his dog tags out from under his shirt. He held up the business-card-sized piece of plastic attached to the end of his chain so that its reflective side was facing up. A hologram popped out of it, displaying some notifications. He checked his messages, and sure enough there was one from Benny flashing "Priority." You assholes left me at the bar last night!

Aurelius was getting ready to shoot Benny a reply when he saw he had another priority message flashing in the queue, this one from the commandant of the academy.

It said, Mr. Blaze, report to my office at 0830 hours to discuss your assignment.

"What time is it?" Aurelius asked Jerula as he sat up.

"Man, it says right there on your tag," Jerula replied.

"I'm having trouble with numbers and letters right now," Aurelius said.

"It's 0845," Jerula said, checking his own tag.

"Shit!" Aurelius said, springing to his feet, which was a mistake—as a wave of nausea and pain threatened to send him right back down to the couch.

"Yeah, that's why I tried to wake you. Your tags have been going off for the last hour," Jerula said.

"I got to be someplace!" Aurelius said, quickly making sure he was wearing everything he needed and bursting through the room to the door.

"What about Benny?" Jerula shouted after him.

Aurelius hit the path to the commandant's office at a sprint, people quickly moving out of his way as he charged passed, barely seeing them in his haste. He wasn't able to maintain the fast pace for long, though, and the jog through the cool morning air was exactly what he needed to shake off the grogginess. The hills were mild, and the tepid morning air gently blowing through the trees helped him pull himself together. He could see intermittent shots of the city of Blades all around him as the buildings peeked out from between the trees.

When Aurelius finally arrived, he stopped just outside the unassuming building at the center of a large square. Quickly checking his tag to see exactly how late he was, Aurelius decided to take a few moments to compose himself. He was already twenty-five minutes late but he figured it was better to make it an even thirty and look a little presentable than to head in looking like he had been running a marathon and smelling like he was leaking hopper fuel.

Aurelius found a small fountain to the side of the path with a few benches around it. He smiled at the people sitting there enjoying the early morning sun. Then he bent over the rim, splashed some cold water over his face, and ran his fingers through his hair. When he was satisfied that he was as good as he was going to get, he made a quick wave to the people watching him amusedly, and said, "It's been one of those mornings." He walked the final stretch to the commandant's office.

In another time and place, he'd be nervous, but right now he was too hungover.

The receptionist was on break. The door to the commandant's room was open, and the unmistakable smell of a cigar wafted out of the room. That meant Sarge was around. Shit.

"Mr. Blaze, get in here," a familiar voice said from around his cigar.

Aurelius walked in as confidently as he could and snapped to attention, trying to cloak his hangover.

"When the commandant requests your presence, he doesn't mean in thirty minutes or less. He means immediately," Sarge said, puffing on his cigar.

"Understood, sir. I was walking through the park when I got the message. Won't happen again."

There was no hiding it. Aurelius looked like hell, not like he had just taken a casual walk.

"Is the shower in your dorm malfunctioning, Hard Tech?" the commandant asked.

"No, sir. Just haven't had time to use it this morning."

"I hope she was worth it," Sarge said.

The commandant was sitting in his chair, reviewing Aurelius's profile. Sarge stood next to his desk, holding a copy of his retake test. There were two other men in the room. One was dressed in the gray and blue uniform of the SMMC. He had the rank insignia of captain just above his SMMC wings. The fourth and final man wasn't wearing any type of military or academy uniform. He looked downright out of place in his denim blue jeans and oil-stained work shirt and cap. At least Aurelius wasn't the only one in the room who didn't look like he was in the corps.

The commandant paged through Aurelius's record that had stacked up over the past two and a half years. It was mostly minor stuff, but several incidents involving instructors popped up. Aurelius knew his trade well, really well, and was never shy to inform an instructor when he knew a different, and usually more time-efficient, way of doing something. Several of them had taken hits to their egos and had written him up. This wasn't something Aurelius was new to, but he had learned to temper himself and, more importantly, justify himself more delicately.

"You say he's been in the hangars for nine months? Can't seem to test onto anything else?" the commandant said.

"Nope," Sarge said, "I've never seen a kid like this one. He's full of 'alternative' methods of diagnosing and fixing problems."

The commandant glanced through some notes. "This kid has been in the hangars too long. You've been too easy on him."

"He just can't seem to play by the rules. I don't think there is any place for him on this campus."

The fact that two of these four men were talking about him like he wasn't even in the room made him profoundly uncomfortable. Who were the other two men? If this was some sort of discussion before they moved him to another department, or even dropped his contract with the corps in general, why had they summoned him? Surely they could have made some sort of decision and sent Aurelius the paperwork. That's when he noticed the casually dressed man swiping through a copy of his record. "I'm surprised you didn't know that coin trick, Barber," he said.

"Any reason I should?" Barber asked the man, his cigar flaring slightly as he spoke.

"It's an old trick. It's not pretty, but folks doing home repairs have been using it for years. It's not as exact as some people think it is, but in a pinch it works," the man said absently, continuing to flip through the file.

"We believe in teaching our cadets the right way to do things here. Our calibration tools and techniques focus on a best practices model," the commandant added.

"I've no doubt of that, but there are times when you're not going to have those tools. It's good to have other options, even if you never use them. An old friend told me that once," the casually dressed man said.

Aurelius listened to the four men go back and forth, talking about one trick or another of his, one disciplinary issue or another. It was all he could do not to speak up, but at this point any breach of protocol might very well be the last straw. Instead, Aurelius tried to figure out who this man was. He almost looked familiar. Was he another one of the quartermasters? Was he a director that had crossed his path before? Where had he seen this guy? It was driving him nuts. He knew this man from somewhere, and it seemed that he somehow had a say in Aurelius's future, but who was he?

"What about this here? Says that while you were supposed to be confined to your dorm, you were found in the hanger waist-deep in an atmospheric loader . . . why?" the man asked, finally turning to look directly at Aurelius.

It took him a moment to find his voice. He was nervous, but he hadn't realized exactly how nervous, until now. This man may have dressed like a farmer who just finished fixing a harvester, but there was something about him, something that felt like an almost casual note of command. Something that made Aurelius not only want to answer, but also to impress.

"Sir, the lift systems on those things are tricky. I knew the other guys hadn't had much experience with them, and I worried that one falling out of the sky might cause some problems down the road," Aurelius said.

"You were so sure your fellow techs in the hanger couldn't have handled it?"

This was from the man in the captain's uniform, the first time he had spoken since Aurelius had entered the room.

"I needed to be sure, sir," Aurelius said, trying to take in all of them.

"I like it. Tha' boy shows the take-charge spirit we're looking for," the casually dressed man said, and something about the way he said rang a bell someplace in the back of Aurelius's mind.

"You can call it spirit if you like, but I see it as a cadet who shows no ability to follow the orders he's given. Time and time again, he's shown no ability to understand that those above him might know a little more than he does," the commandant said.

"Commandant, are you telling me you've never known more than a commanding officer, not in all the time you've been serving?" the casually dressed man asked.

"Well, of course not, but there is a time and a place," the commandant said.

"Of course there is. He's young and gifted and very aware of it. It's going to take a little more real world to teach him those times and places. He ain't gonna learn them here," the man responded, taking off his cap and looking at Aurelius appraisingly. He had thinning gray hair and his face showed the lines of both age and stress, but his eyes were piercing and clear. They gave Aurelius the impression he was looking right through him. It was at that moment Aurelius realized who this man was, this man who looked like he had just walked in off the street, but who had everyone in the room deferring to him.

"Kid, I like you. Moreover, my captain likes you. Barber—sorry . . . Sarge—he thinks you can be whipped into something like shape, but considering everything, they thought I should meet you first," the man said.

"So you've made up your mind, then?" the commandant asked, his tone clearly indicating he already knew the answer, and very much disliked it.

"I think so. You can veto it if you want, this is your academy, but I'd suggest you not. Give us Aurelius, and let us do for him what this place couldn't," the man said, a little smile coming to his face as a look of almost outrage boiled up onto the commandant's.

How could he have been so stupid? He had been seeing this casually dressed man's face on holograms for the last five years. He was usually in a suit and speaking to the world from his desk, appointed with the SMMC flag behind it, but now there was no mistaking it. This man was in fact Strife's own governor, Christopher Maher. This was the guy, the guy on top, the guy elected and trusted to run it all.

"You could stay here," the governor continued. "I know Sarge would be happy to have you in his hangers forever, or we could have you transferred to one of our major repair installations for the rest of your contract. But I would prefer you sign onto my ship. We have a long trip ahead of us. We're going all the way to Sol . . . to Earth, in fact. What do you say?"

Aurelius couldn't believe it. He'd been expecting to be kicked out, or at the very least shipped off to scrub floors on a mining station.

"Governor . . . sir . . . of course. I do have one question, though. When do we leave?"

"Kid, you're going to be seeing Strife from orbit tomorrow night," Maher said.

A warm elation washed over Aurelius. For the first time all morning, he hadn't felt lost in a fog. He couldn't believe it. He hid his jubilation as best he could behind a vindicated smile.

"If you screw this up, you'll be in a slush suit strapped to the side of a mining ship while you wash the space dust off its name badge, understood?" Sarge said, a smile briefly replacing his usual sneer.

"Yes, sir," Aurelius sounded.

"You're dismissed."

The five men saluted and Aurelius found himself dumbfounded. He couldn't wait to tell Benny he had been picked up by a ship, let alone the governor's ship and by the governor himself.

Sarge stopped Aurelius before he walked out of the room. "Mr. Blaze . . ."

Aurelius whipped around to face Sarge. "Sir?"

Sarge dug through his pocket and pulled out a coin. Smiling, he tossed it to Aurelius,

"Go get yourself some Fizzies, kid."

CHAPTER 12

There Were Four Lights

CADE TRIGGERED A command, turning on the high-intensity lamps in the next room. For a normal crew member, this would involve pulling up a command list on their Helix and picking the option that corresponded with the lamps. But for Cade, it was a simple mental command. His brain told the ship to do something, and it understood. What did that say about his mind? Even for other Lambdas, it wasn't usually so easy to interact with technical systems and artificial intellects, but for Cade it was the most natural thing in the world; Cade's world, at any rate. Not for the first time, Cade wondered how much of him was still human. That thought went far beyond wondering how much of him had been replaced in the name of enhancements over the years. Perhaps he had crossed that line from man to machine, and if so, had it happened before or after they started augmenting his body?

Cade shrugged off the all-too-common thoughts and stepped through the door into Interrogation Room 4. In many ways, the room wasn't that different than one in the medical bay. It was sterile and full of diagnostic equipment designed to monitor the various bodily functions of its occupant. The key difference was one of intent. While both rooms were designed to keep their occupants alive, only one was designed to keep them healthy, and it was not the one that Cade was now in.

Xander Pacius had been strapped to a metal examination table for days. At the moment, that table held him at a nearly vertical angle, forcing him to stare directly into the four high-intensity lamps that hung over the door.

Cade calmly walked over to a panel on the wall and manually turned down the lights just a little bit. This was an important step and one he took every time he came to speak with Xander Pacius. It showed the man that Cade was in fact capable of small kindness. It kept him from seeing Cade as merely a tormentor, because should the dynamic ever shift in that direction, then the only way Pacius would give Cade the information he needed would be if Cade shattered his mind completely, and Cade didn't want to do that. Not if he didn't have to.

Still, it might come to that. Over the last week, Shard's superiors were becoming increasingly impatient for Pacius to speak. This meant little to Cade, but his superiors at Lambda were much of the same mind. One way or another, Pacius didn't have a lot of time left.

"Good morning, Captain Pacius," Cade said, taking a small cup of water and walking over to place it to Pacius's lips. At first Pacius had refused the small cups of water he was given. Pacius knew the game they were playing, the matching of wills, but that minor rebellion hadn't lasted. Being thirsty didn't get either of them anywhere, and now he drank almost gratefully every time he saw Cade.

"I hope you're as well as current circumstances will allow."

Pacius cast a dagger look at Cade as he finished drinking. He hated Cade, for what he was and for what he was doing. In the end, Cade was okay with this. It didn't change anything for him, though it more than likely would end up costing Pacius quite a bit.

"How well do you expect me to be? I've been hanging from a wall in the dark for days," Pacius spat.

"Fair enough, Captain." Cade sat down in a seat across from Pacius, one he had positioned precisely so that Pacius could crane his neck to see him, but only just. "Is there anything I can do for you before we get started?"

"You can let me know how my crew is doing," Pacius said, and Cade wasn't surprised. Pacius had said some variant of this every time they had spoken over the last week and a half.

"Captain, I want to, but we've been through this before. I can't tell you anything until you start telling me about the things I need to know. Tell me . . . tell me if elements of Strife's Merchant Marine Corps are planning a coup."

"So we've started, then?" Pacius said.

"The UPE needs to know. We need to know how far your demonstration goes. It is my responsibility to obtain it. Tell me, and I can return you to your crew."

Pacius said nothing for a long time. At first he had insisted that he had been acting alone. He had hoped to convince Cade that there was no involvement by other SMMC captains or governing entities, or from STR1-FE's government. Cade had made it clear early on, though, that they knew he had spoken to Governor Maher shortly before the incident. Now he just remained silent. Still, Cade had to try. After all, any day might be the day Pacius broke down. For Pacius's sake, Cade hoped it was today.

"Captain . . . Xander, I have no illusions of your opinions about us. I'll spare you the speech about how bad this could be for Earth or the entire UPE. I doubt it will move you. Your sole incentive for telling me is a cessation of the questioning and a return to your crew."

Pacius continued his silence, not even bothering to glare at Cade.

"Very well, can you at least tell me why you dumped the Helix earrings? Surely, Captain, you can tell me this and then I can help you."

Pacius remained as silent as ever.

"Is it possible you've grown too weak from hunger to answer?" This wasn't the case. Cade knew exactly how diminished Pacius's body was. They had been monitoring his vitals from the moment he was hung from the wall, and while they had been depriving him of both food and sleep, he still had quite a bit more time before such deprivations prevented him from speech, and surely Pacius would break before then. Still, Cade didn't have that time to wait anymore.

Cade stood up and walked to the door. He opened it and stepped outside for a moment. When he returned, he was pushing a cart with several covered platters on it. Cade could tell from the look on his face that Pacius could already smell what Cade had.

"Captain, I really hope you don't mind if I take my lunch while we talk. With all the things going on, I have hardly had time to eat in three days. But look who I'm talking to. You know better than most, I imagine," Cade said, pulling the cover off one of the platters to reveal a large plate of curried chicken. The smells of the strong spiced meat were getting to Pacius. He looked at the food, slack-jawed and longing. Then he snapped out of it, shaking his head and scowling. That was good; Cade needed to twist that knife just a little bit more.

"I need to hear something. Tell me something. If you do, I can feed you." Pacius's eyes flicked to the food and hovered there, but again, he looked away and set his jaw.

"If you don't talk, I can't help you."

The conversation went on like this for some time. Cade asking for an answer or just for some cooperation, and Pacius remaining silent.

"Xander, please talk to me. If you don't, I can't protect you anymore," Cade said, hoping the insinuation that things would only get worse might do what isolation, exhaustion, and hunger had failed to.

"I've already told you everything. I told it to you from the start. There is no more to tell, nothing I have that you don't," Pacius said, sounding like a much older man.

The two sat in silence for a while after that. Pacius had clearly said all he was going to and Cade considered what might come next.

Eventually, Cade stood up and brought the other platter over to Pacius. Cade released his arms from their shackles. The severity of the days kept strung up had taken their toll. Pacius collapsed to the floor like he had no strength left in him. He slowly rocked back onto his knees, working his hands where the straps had held him immobile. Cade handed him the platter of chicken. Pacius hesitated for a moment, suspicious that this was just some new trick, some new way to break him.

"Your crew has been fed. It's okay." That was all Pacius needed to hear. He dove on the platter, no longer trying to resist.

"I thought you couldn't feed me until I talked," Pacius said around a mouthful of chicken.

"Captain, I am sorry. Things will be much harder for you now," Cade said, turning away from Pacius. For the first time in ten days, he walked from the interrogation room without bothering to turn out the lights or lock the door behind him.

Cade walked down the hall, nodding to miscellaneous crew as they passed. What could he have done differently? It didn't matter; Captain Shard himself would be taking over the interrogation. He was the man who destroyed Pacius's ship. The man responsible for all the death that had happened. Pacius would be lucky to get out in one piece at this point, and there was little Cade could do about it.

As Cade turned the corner, he spotted Shard approaching. "Don't you want to observe? Isn't it your job?" he asked.

"No, Captain. I will go over the transcripts once you've broken him," Cade replied coldly. He continued down the corridor contemplating the man, Xander Pacius. Cade respected him. Any man who could give up nothing after a week and a half strapped to a wall in a dark room with no food and almost no water was worthy of respect. Pacius was a man with convictions. Despite himself, Cade pulled up the feed from Shard's Helix earring and could see and hear everything his captain was experiencing. He owed it to Pacius to at least watch.

"I know you are a subversive working to destabilize the Frontier. I know you are trying to bring it into open revolt against the UPE! Now you will tell me the names of your coconspirators!" Shard said.

Shard barked a command at a technician, and Pacius started screaming. He looked expectantly at Pacius, waiting for an answer to his question. When Shard didn't get one, he barked, "Turn up the intensity."

Pacius's body convulsed with the feedback the technician was flooding into his nervous system through the Helix earring. At that intensity, it probably wasn't long until it completely torched every synapse in Pacius's brain.

"Who is working with you? Who's giving the orders?"

Shard gestured for the technician to stop the Helix onslaught, but only waited a moment before ordering its resumption.

"I will ask you again, Captain. How far does this go? Is the SMMC planning to revolt?"

This time, when the neural attack stopped, Pacius actually spoke.

Pacius's words came out in a rasp—which even Cade's sensitive ears, combined with the high-resolution sound pickup, couldn't make out.

"What was that, Captain?" Shard asked, moving a bit closer.

Again, Pacius spoke in a whisper that Cade couldn't catch.

"One more time," Shard said, closing the final distance between him and his prisoner. His ear was almost at Pacius's mouth, and—Shard screamed as Pacius bit down on his ear with all the might his body still had in it.

Shard pulled away, a river of blood running down his cheek, a matching one running from Pacius's mouth. The prisoner was grinning with an insane glee, and he spit something wet and fleshy onto the floor in front of him. Cade didn't need the near-perfect video feed to know what it was.

Shard stepped away from Pacius, a look of pain and rage on his face. Not saying anything, Shard used the hand that wasn't gripping the side of his head where his ear used to be and drew his side arm. Without a moment's hesitation, Shard fired. Cade's eyebrows raised as Pacius's kneecap disappeared in a red mist.

Cade sprung from his seat and dashed to the interrogation room. When he got there, Shard had his gun pressed against Pacius's forehead. "I will enjoy killing you. Don't think I won't. And no one will ever think to question me."

"That's enough, Captain." The command in Cade's voice brought Shard up short. He turned around to look at Cade standing in the doorway and quickly took in his firm expression.

Shard put his thumb on the hammer on the back of the gun. He was testing Cade, who was more than eager to accept his challenge. Cade pulled up the sleeve on his left arm. At a glance, nothing was out of the ordinary, but ever so slowly his hand started to subtly change. Cade shifted the components in his arm, shifting metal supports and cabling, retracting lines of artificial muscle, adjusting them to allow the long blade that this arm concealed to emerge. Cade could have done this quickly if he had needed to, the prosthetic was capable of reconfiguring at speeds almost too fast for the unaided eye to follow, but right now, it was better to allow Shard to see it happen and give him time to understand what it meant.

"Put it down," Cade said, the long thin blade resting against his leg.

"Your role is to observe, Cade. The mission is mine. You had your chance. For ten days you had your chance, now Pacius dies. He dies for what he did to me!" Shard almost screamed.

"Captain Julio Cesar Shard, you are in violation of your orders, both mine and those of the United Planets of Earth. Holster your side arm now or I will have no choice but to exercise my authority as the Lambda observer of the UPE *Enigma*," Cade said, without emotion or inflection.

Shard looked at Cade, and Cade could see fear in his eyes. This was the closest Cade had ever come to killing him, and he knew it. Shard feigned composure and holstered his weapon, his eyes never leaving Cade and that long blade protruding from his hand.

"Captain, order your men to take Pacius back to his crew now," Cade instructed.

Shard straightened his shirt and pushed past Cade into the hall. He was bound for the ship's infirmary, but he did give the order before he left.

CHAPTER 13

A Short Crucifixion

CADE HAD BEEN summoned to the captain's office. He thought it was to submit his report on the interrogation, but it turned out Shard didn't care. Shard was screaming. He had been for some time, and it probably wasn't going to stop anytime soon.

In the monitor behind them, they watched Xander Pacius. He was lying on a cot in a large cell with his surviving senior staff. They had placed themselves around him like some sort of honor guard for their bloodied and bandaged captain.

Even now, Shard was trying to figure out some new way to make Pacius talk or, more likely, punish Pacius for what he had done to Shard's ear. What Shard wanted was revenge, but failing that, he wanted some magic solution to their problem. The prisoners weren't any more helpful than Pacius. A few were willing to talk, so willing that Cade or Shard usually only had to ask a question before they got a litany of facts. The problem was these facts were mostly lies told to avoid further interrogation.

"We've interrogated over half the crew, and we have nothing I can use!" Shard bellowed, not for the first time.

"Captain, have you considered your tactics may be to blame?" Cade said evenly. He had been making this point to Shard now for some time, and it showed no signs of sinking in. Cade wondered if it would have been better to simply execute Shard back during the incident with Pacius, then Cade could have gotten on with the questioning without his disruptions.

"What do you mean?" Shard asked, automatically. It was evident he wasn't actually going to listen to the answer, and wouldn't understand it if he had. Still, it was in Cade's nature to try.

"They're scared. Terrified even," Cade said eventually.

"Of course they are. They should be," Shard said, confirming for Cade that he had indeed completely missed the point.

"They are so scared, they will say anything to avoid looking like Pacius. In a very real way, you've broken them."

"So?"

"In the time since their capture, they've seen you destroy civilian craft, destroy their ship, kill many of their comrades, and even cripple their captain, all for little or no reason. All of this in an attempt to extract information, an attempt that was a failure."

The session with Pacius had become a point of contention between the two of them. Cade wasted few opportunities to remind Shard that it was his rash actions that had led them to this impasse. "Most of them will now tell you whatever they think you want to hear. The rest see their captain, see that he didn't talk, and see it as an inspiration. They won't talk now no matter what you do to them."

Shard began pacing the room, absently scratching at the mass of bandage that was covering his reattached ear. He was considering something, and for a fraction of a moment, Cade thought he might have actually gotten through.

Those hopes were dashed, though, when Shard spoke again.

"Maybe if we step up the interrogations."

"I don't see how you would do that, short of crucifixion," Cade said flatly.

"Or maybe start executions. If I start killing some of them, the rest will have to start giving me things I can use."

Cade stood up and walked out in disgust. As the door closed behind him, Shard was still pacing.

Cade had given everything to the UPE. He walked the halls of the *Enigma* contemplating his meeting with Shard and, for the first time, wondered if he had made the right choice. He had volunteered for this post. Knowing tensions were high in the Frontier, he wanted to be right in the middle. Shard was a loose cannon, though. That's why the UPE had sent him out here. They admired his brutality. Cade had hoped to provide a sense of restraint to the man, or at the very least be a visible reminder of the consequences for damaging the mission.

Cade had never questioned his duty before. All his adult life he had served aboard UPE starships. He had given them his skills and his life, and in return they had made him a Lambda. They had given him power. If Cade needed to, he could eliminate any officer he felt necessary in the course of his duties. Cade had done this several times, and it was never an act he took lightly.

Shard was endangering the interests of the United Planets of Earth in the Frontier. There was no question there were terrorists in the gaps between the stars, but Cade no longer believed Pacius and his crew were among them. Shard, however, couldn't separate acts of defiance from acts of terrorism. To him, they were one and the same. Shard needed to find a connection, a link between terrorism and the SMMC for his own reasons, and those reasons had nothing to do with protecting the Frontier worlds.

The main reason Cade hesitated terminating Shard that day in the interrogation room was that their primary order was to stop the protest at Archer's Agony, and to capture Captain Xander Pacius of the SMMC. Even though Cade objected to how Shard had accomplished this, there was little doubt he had accomplished it. Their secondary orders were to restore and maintain order in the Frontier. While he doubted the efficacy of Shard's approach, he couldn't justify eliminating him to his superiors, not when by all accounts Shard had accomplished their primary objectives so decisively. Shard was following orders, and he was following them with the fervor and tenacity that had seen him promoted through the UPE ranks. Those who posted Shard to this mission knew who he was and had to expect that things would have gone something like this.

What power did Cade really have in this situation? He had little authority to directly affect the course of the mission. The only real thing he could do was remove Captain Shard, and he couldn't justify it. He was also powerless to help those held captive by Shard. This, more than anything else, was bothering him. He had dealt with prisoners before and seen worse interrogations than Shard was performing. Cade had even conducted a few himself, but those had all been for what Cade believed to be good reasons.

This one was different. All these people were guilty of was not wanting the UPE to control every aspect of their lives. That was how they saw the Helix earrings. Cade could understand and even empathize with them. He had seen all the good the UPE could bring to a planet if they chose to. The events of the last few weeks had really shaken him, though. Everything Cade had ever done was because he believed it was, in the end, for the greater good. But what about now? If people should not rule themselves, then who should? Should it be men like Shard? Men who would kill at the slightest show of defiance? What about the men who employed him? Men who knew exactly what he was and turned him loose on people? Cade couldn't do much about the few ills in the UPE, but maybe he could do something about this one. Maybe he could help Xander Pacius, who had said nothing, even when he thought it would cost him his life.

Cade would free their captives, and Shard would have to accept it because, as far as he knew, the orders would be coming from his own command structure, Lambda Command, an authority above the UPE Navy.

So, resolved, Cade set out to forge an order from Lambda. It was an order to cease all interrogations and immediately release all prisoners. The relief it brought to his conscience made him feel like it was the best thing he had ever done. His superiors wouldn't like it, but he believed he could make them understand. If asked what he was hoping to accomplish, he'd say he was trying to save lives.

Cade and Shard stood on the observation deck as members of his crew escorted the *Deviant Rising*'s survivors down the embarkation ramp and onto the space station Archer's Agony. It had only taken a couple hours for the *Enigma* to reach Archer's Agony after Cade had sent the orders. Shard had fumed the whole way. Even now, as they were watching their prisoners walk to freedom, Shard was insisting, "If I had a little more time with them, I know I could have gotten something."

"Possibly. It doesn't matter now," Cade said, watching a couple people help Xander Pacius down the ramp.

"Those damned cowards in command don't have the thrust needed anymore. They're too used to peace. They don't understand the threat these people pose to their precious security."

"You know as well as I do that Lambda Command will have what they want."

Shard gritted his teeth. "I promise . . . that man, he's a terrorist. And I will kill him personally one day," Shard said, trying to bore a hole in the back of Pacius with his eyes.

Cade took a moment to marshal himself before replying, "I am sure we will see him again."

Of that, Cade had no doubt.

CHAPTER 14

Departure

AURELIUS TOOK THE fastest shower of his life. He wasn't going to be late for destiny, which was docked at the Spire in the center of the city. Part of him still couldn't believe Sarge and the governor himself had reached out to him personally for this assignment. He couldn't imagine Sarge sticking his neck out for anyone else like he had done for him. Did he know the governor personally, or had Aurelius's record stuck out enough to warrant the attention of the most powerful man on the planet?

Aurelius smiled. He could have his dreams, right? Either way, this was a once-in-a-lifetime opportunity. He wasn't going to let Sarge or Governor Maher down.

Aurelius glanced around his room. The SMMC dorms were small, which meant it didn't look bad that he kept it so Spartan. Two single beds, a dresser, a table with chairs, a kitchen sink, and a cupboard were the only furniture in the room. Across the wall opposite the door was one big window overlooking the northwest side of the campus. Being up on the eighth floor of a fourteen-story building meant he had a great view. He often found himself just gazing out at the city looking for where he could see the ocean in between the buildings.

He might actually miss this place. He was going to miss the view, at least; his roommate Benny; and even Sarge, if he was being honest with himself. But Strife itself, maybe not. Strife had always been where he lived, but Strife was still just a place. Had he been booted out of the SMMC instead of assigned to the governor's ship, it would still have been saying good-bye. In a lot of ways, that was just how he felt. Aurelius always understood why people loved Strife. There were the large open skies and the relaxed attitude of the people. But for Aurelius, all that meant was that there would be ships. Fixing them, cleaning them, sitting in them, and considering what they might feel like in the air. Without those things, Strife wouldn't have been home, so leaving the world itself wasn't really saying good-bye to anything real, not for Aurelius.

Aurelius took a quick look back at the empty dorm room to make sure he hadn't missed anything. The room was completely clear. The only thing not part of the generic corps-assigned room was a black shoulder bag sitting on one of the narrow beds. That bag contained everything in the world Aurelius owned, everything he had taken when he left home, and everything he had managed to collect in the intervening two years. It wasn't much, but Aurelius didn't need much. He had his work, a good set of "going-out clothes," a few sets of work uniforms that weren't too stained with grease and other substances, his personal tools, and that was it. The thought gave Aurelius a pang of regret, like a momentary mental twinge that had him almost picking up the comm and calling home. Maybe to talk to his mother and hear her voice, maybe to see if she could send over some pictures or books, something to wear that wasn't either stained with food or grease, or maybe just some pictures from before . . . but no. That part of his life was over. That door was closed, and he was glad. He kept telling himself that, all the way to the monorail platform.

The monorail would take Aurelius to the Spire. He could see the immense needle of a building from where he stood, rising up into the clouds. All the buildings around it looked like blades of grass collecting around the ankles of a giant thin-stock mushroom. Strife didn't have any major orbiting stations. There were a lot of different reasons for this, but in the end, the only reason that mattered was that, with the Spire, it didn't really need them. Everything docked at the upper levels of the Spire; small cargo haulers, huge long-range exploration vessels, even military ships. If it couldn't or didn't want to land somewhere in the city, it docked at one of the enormous disks that extended out from the top of the space scraper. They would unload their cargo and people, and do whatever else they needed to, in the very outermost part of the planet's atmosphere before moving on.

The cars that moved people up and down the outside of the Spire were cramped, only room for three or four people at best, and that was without baggage, which was usually handled by the roomier and less comfortable freight cars. But Aurelius wasn't going to let his bag out of his sight. He drew several nasty looks from the car's other passengers for this, but as he looked out the window, at the lights of Strife, the expansive plains, and the calm placid oceans as he went higher and higher, he didn't care. All pangs of leaving were forgotten and every doubt ignored. Aurelius was headed into space. He was about to be a serving member of a SMMC ship. That was the dream, wasn't it? It was what his father had wanted, what his brother had wanted, and it was what Aurelius wanted.

Maybe it was the fact he could already feel himself leaving his world behind that made him reach for his dog tags as he ascended higher up the side of the Spire and away from the world. The need to share with someone what was happening was nagging at him. Not just anyone, but one of the only people in the world who would really appreciate what Aurelius was about to embark upon. His father would be so proud, probably brag to all his friends for a few weeks, maybe while opening a few drinks, and live on the stories he'd be telling about his space-faring son. Never mind that Aurelius hadn't done anything yet. Little things, like the facts, were optional in his father's stories. Aurelius smiled, just thinking how the stories would always stretch, sometimes with a seed of reality in them, other times not. But in the end, he didn't make the call. He couldn't call his father if he was unwilling to also call his mother, could he? He wasn't talking to them for the same reasons; he couldn't reopen that door any more for his father than he could for his mother.

Eventually the car stopped on Aurelius's level. He stood there for a second, letting the other passengers squeeze out, before slinging his bag over one arm and walking out into the lounge where the new crew of the *Freedom's Reach* would shortly be boarding their new home.

Aurelius had seen spaceports before, if not in person, then in thousands of holos, and he knew what they were meant to look like. This lounge did not look like one. The entire place wasn't a bustling hub, travelers rushing from one dock to another, shops trying to sell them last-minute souvenirs to bring home. It was just the same slightly battered and dirty chairs and desks that the corps used everywhere else and the same slightly tired-looking personnel that seemed to man all the groundside operations Aurelius had ever seen. Still, these surroundings couldn't dampen his excitement. This was his moment, and soon this place and Strife would be a memory, something he'd think about from time to time, maybe even revisit every now and then, but they would be in the past.

One day he might call Strife home again, when he finished his service and had the money to set up his own shop for fixing hoppers and all those little things that were so critical to keeping ships in the sky. But that was way off, years, if ever, and now he wasn't worried about that. Ahead of him was adventure, or something close to it anyway. At the very least he'd be adventure adjacent. Maybe he wouldn't be the brave space captain, but damned if he couldn't fix the hell out of the captain's squeaky chair.

"Attention: Will all new crew members please return to the docking area? The hatch doors will be opening shortly." The announcement brought Aurelius back to the present. He picked up his bag and made his way to the short line of people getting ready to step aboard their new posting.

The *Freedom's Reach*, such a grand name. As Aurelius looked out the windows, he thought that the massive ship might have once been worthy of the title. But the hulking ship he was looking at now was on its last legs. That wasn't unusual for the corps. Everything was used until it couldn't be repaired and sometimes well beyond that point. Aurelius suspected the only original parts left were in the hull, and only because the thick metal skin of the ship, with its pockmarks and extrusions, looked to be at least sixty years old. The mile-long rectangular hull of the ship was cracked in places, the patchworked repairs evident in the mismatching of the paint. Even the large cylindrical power core that ran down the length of the ship had the impact marks indicative of having been in service for a while. The only things that looked new were the doors on the large front docking bay and the rear winglike rudders that held clusters of thrusters. Both showed signs of recent work, and Aurelius saw several areas where the external plating hadn't even been installed yet.

Aurelius pulled his attention away from the view of the ship. He'd have all the time in the world to explore it both inside and out. Instead, he focused on the line of people boarding with him. Most of them were junior-level techs. It made him wonder if this ship had been pulled out of mothballs for the governor. That would explain its age and all the techs coming aboard. Most of the senior crew would have been here for weeks already. Clearly Sarge knew that it would take his special kind of brilliance to keep this ship running, either that or he was seizing his last chance to get Aurelius as far away from him as possible. Aurelius figured it could go either way.

He moved forward in the line as each new crew member stepped through the hatch and had their tags updated with posting and ship information. It wasn't long before it was Aurelius's turn. As he stepped onto the ship and placed his tags in the reader, he was struck with how stale the air was. It was a sign of the atmosphere having been recycled again and again by filters that were just barely up to the job.

As the line dispersed into the busy corridors of the ship, he could hear a low thrum. It was something he felt more than heard. The engines, the conduits, the generators, all of their activity combined gave him the impression that his back teeth were vibrating ever so slightly.

As he walked down the long industrial corridor, looking for his assigned bunk, there was one thought in his head. It wasn't his parents, or anything else from the world so very far below. No, all Aurelius could think about was what they were going to let him get his hands on first. He couldn't remember the last time he was so excited.

CHAPTER 15

Freedom's Reach

THE AIR QUALITY on board had a processed feeling to it. It was musty and stale, almost like a hospital or a large dense office building. There was a noticeable "well-used" quality to the ship. He saw evidence of its age; back when voyages took longer, ships had to feel like a second home. Most people would have been turned off by it; Aurelius was in heaven.

A computer-generated voice from his tags directed him to main engineering, the section that housed the vessel's massive Star Drive. He was to report to the chief engineer to receive his briefing.

The double doors ahead of him unlocked and slid open. The room inside was bathed in light from transparent metal that lined the main reactor like windows. They formed caustic light patterns on the walls like an indoor pool, waving and shimmering. This was the ship's beating heart, where its power and soul emanated from. He stopped to take in the sight. Personnel scurried around the room double- and triple-checking systems. A test of one of the systems changed the azure light pouring out of the engine core to an emerald green before slowly fading back. Aurelius cracked a giddy smile. He imagined he looked like a kid opening a birthday present.

"Where's the chief?" he asked a crewman.

The crewman pointed to a little office overlooking the room. Aurelius could have taken a lift up to the second deck but thought it would be more fun to shoot up one of the ladders. Aurelius knocked on the chief's door. The plaque outside read CHIEF JEREMY MARCUS. After a moment, a voice told him to enter. The office was minimalistic. No toolboxes or equipment racks like he would have expected. It was more like something out of an office building. The chief engineer sat behind the desk in the center of the room. Aurelius approached and stood at attention. "Hard Tech Aurelius Blaze reporting for duty, sir."

"At ease," Chief Marcus ordered, pointing to the empty chair across from his desk. He pulled Aurelius's profile up on his screen. "Another level-two hard tech. Welcome aboard, Mr. Blaze."

Hard tech level two? This was awesome news. It meant he'd be working on important stuff. Maybe even the Star Drive itself.

"You'll have to forgive the lack of communication on your orders. Being Governor Maher's ship, we have to do things a little differently."

"Understood. Just glad to be a part of it," Aurelius said.

"Save the ass-kissing for promotion, hard tech." The chief smirked. He logged Aurelius into the ship's systems and issued him a bunk number. His tags blinked.

"By the way, are you afraid of spiders?" the chief asked, his eyes never leaving his screen.

"No?" Aurelius replied.

"What about enclosed spaces?"

"Not really . . ."

"Suddenly open spaces?

"I don't think so . . ."

"Falling from forty meters or higher?"

"Hadn't thought about it . . ."

"Spontaneous midair vaporization?"

"Is that a possibility, sir?"

"No . . . no . . . you should be fine," the chief said, punching away at his controls. "After you've taken time to familiarize yourself with our mission, you'll be added to the duty roster and you'll start getting work. We usually don't let the newbies touch anything fancy for a while, but you'll be able to get your hands on that engine core in due time."

"Oh, was I staring, sir?"

"We've all been there. I think that'll do it for now. You're dismissed."

As Aurelius was leaving, he caught a glimpse of a sign just outside the office:

Proudly accident-free
2 days

Aurelius went hunting for his bunk, wondering why the chief had asked him so many strange questions. Around the corridors and through a couple of bulkheads, he found it: a good-sized room with a single round table and short booth seats in the middle. There were four bunk beds embedded into the wall to the right and all the lockers and storage cabinets in the room were painted to look like wood, which only accented the hardwood floor stretched across the majority of the deck. This room was designed to accommodate four people, and considering it was sitting on an old heap of metal, it was strangely comfortable. There were two crew members already in the room. One was a tall, wire-thin man with his dark hair pulled back into a tight, short ponytail, and the other was a shorter woman with chocolate-colored skin covered in the dark lines of intricate tattoos. As they both turned to look at him, he noticed a lock of her hair had been dyed a bright metallic blue.

The tall man was the first to speak, reaching out to grasp Aurelius's hand in a surprisingly firm grip. "Hey! Dead man's boots! I mean . . . Hi, I'm Paul. You must be the guy who's here to replace old Jenkins."

"Hey, I'm Aurelius. What do you mean, replace? Who's Jenkins?"

"You mean, you haven't heard?" Paul asked.

"Why would he have? It only happened a couple days ago," the woman said, standing up from the bottom bunk at the far end of the room and joining them. "My name's Nyreen. Don't let Paul here scare you. That accident was a once-in-a-lifetime type of thing."

"It'd have to be—" Paul said.

"Wait . . ." Aurelius said, starting to feel a little nervous. "What? What accident?"

"Nothing to worry about. Word to the wise, though, never tape your arc welder to the head."

"Why would I . . ." Aurelius began to say before shaking his head. "What happened to this Jenkins guy?"

"Don't worry about it," Nyreen said. "You're here to replace him."

"I mean, it's not how I'd have wanted to get this posting," Paul added, "but you gotta take 'em where you can get 'em."

"There's supposed to be one more guy coming, but he hasn't arrived yet."

"He replacing someone too?" Aurelius asked.

Both Paul and Nyreen gave him a look normally reserved for especially slow toddlers. "No. They just needed another tech."

"Oh . . . kay . . ." Aurelius said.

"He should be here anytime," Nyreen continued. "So that means you get first dibs on bunk."

"Cool," Aurelius said, moving to throw his bag up onto the vacant top bunk.

"That one was Jenkins's," Nyreen said, almost in mourning.

"Nyreen, that's not fair," Paul said. "At the end, he was leaking down onto the bottom one too."

Aurelius still had no idea if this was a hazing ritual or if they had really lost this Jenkins guy to some sort of horrible accident. "Did they at least change the sheet?"

"Yeah. But I don't know about the mattress," Paul said, scratching his chin.

He took a few steps back and turned to face the room. "Maybe I'll just take one of these benches."

He threw his bag onto the round table in the middle of the room and sat down.

"We'll let you read your mission briefing and get settled in," Nyreen said, taking a step toward the door and motioning for Paul to follow her.

"Thanks," he said, watching the two disappear down the corridor.

Aurelius read the mission briefing on his dog tags. Apparently Governor Maher had business to attend to on Terra Luna, Earth. What it actually was could be anyone's guess, but it meant he was in for a journey. It would take two and a half weeks to get to Earth, with a three-day shore leave in San Francisco, then two and a half weeks back. This was a hell of an opportunity. He made a note to thank the hell out of Sarge when he got home. And to think he always thought Sarge hated him. There was no mention of Aurelius being there to replace anyone in the briefing. It made sense, but he wondered if his new bunkmates had been messing with him.

"Aww, shit. You gotta be kiddin' me," a familiar voice said from the doorway.

Aurelius looked up from his handheld screen. Who he saw standing in the doorway felt like just one more joke in a day that had already had so many. Jerula stood there with his bag slung over his shoulder. "It's pukey's buddy! He isn't here too, is he?" Jerula said, looking around as if Aurelius had been hiding Benny in a locker.

Aurelius laughed. "Well, I'll say it's a small freakin' 'verse. Now I'm really glad you didn't hit me last night. Woulda made this awkward."

"I still might if you don't give me top bunk," Jerula laughed.

"Yeah, no problem," Aurelius said. With a month in deep space ahead of him, at least Aurelius wasn't going to be bored.

The giant clasps holding the *Freedom's Reach* in place began to snap open one by one. All docking tubes and refueling cables detached from the hull and retracted into the massive dock that stretched out of Center Spire. Once everything was clear, the ship began to back out of its gangway. The ship took several minutes to turn around, orienting itself toward its destination as it rose up from Center Spire and higher into the stratosphere. Booster systems that were powering its flight up through the clouds began to sputter out and detach, falling into the ocean just off the coast of Blades. They made splashes that were several stories tall before the waiting watercraft retrieved them for the next SMMC vessel launch.

The engine room was buzzing with activity. Aurelius hadn't been assigned any real duties yet, but the chief had instructed all tech crew to report for disembarking. Aurelius watched in awe as the dormant power plants came to life. Spinning and humming, he felt that dull vibration that had been with him since he boarded the ship shift into a true shaking of the decks. The *Freedom's Reach* was coming to life all around him, its old hull groaning under the new stresses.

"Hey, Jenk—I mean Aurelius. Come over here!" the chief called.

"Sir!" Aurelius replied, having to shout over the thrum of engines cycling through their warm-ups.

"You wanna push the button?" the chief asked.

"The button, sir?"

"Yeah, the button that takes everything out of power-up and gives control to the nav geeks on the bridge," the chief said, pulling Aurelius over and showing him a long metal lever that was sticking out of the enormous power plant connected to the central turbine.

"When I say so, pull that thing and hold on, because down here things can get a little rough."

Aurelius was barely able to contain his excitement. He looked at the simple dented, tarnished, greasy lever as if it were made of pure platinum.

The chief was listening intently to the whirring, grinding, and buzzing all around him, seeming to take note of every change in speed and pitch.

"Not just yet . . . just a little bit more . . . almost . . . now, kid!" And Aurelius pulled.

The ship rocked and bucked. Aurelius was almost thrown from his feet as the *Freedom's Reach* lurched forward.

"That's some kick, isn't it, kid?" the chief said, helping Aurelius keep his footing.

"It was something, all right," Aurelius said. "You ever get used to it?"

"Hell, no, kid, but you do learn to enjoy the ride. Now don't stick around here, run to one of the ports. You're not going to want to miss the view as we leave," the chief said, steadying Aurelius and pushing him toward the door.

Aurelius staggered slightly as he made his way down the corridors to one of the lounges that butted up against the outer hull. When he finally reached one, it was crowded with off-duty personnel. Aurelius had to squeeze himself into the nearest spot to the viewports that he could.

The Spire was glittering in the late-evening sun, the clouds below giving it a carpet of soft peach, transitioning to bright orange. Above, there was a field of bright stars, swirling nebulae, and—somewhere off in the distance out of view, but never out of anyone's mind—the Eridani Gateway. Even now, up on the bridge, a helmsman was undoubtedly setting a course for that mystery that gave the Frontier human life.

CHAPTER 16

A Three-Man Job

THE FIRST WEEK passed by uneventfully; in fact, it was downright boring. Other than his duty shifts, Aurelius wasn't prepared for just how slow life on a starship could be. What was worse, without the rising and setting of the sun, it felt like one long, unrelenting night.

But this was the way it was at the bottom of the barrel. He was the lowest rank on the ship. He wouldn't always be the guy fixing the chicken soup machines. By the end of the trip, he'd have his hands elbow deep in the Star Drive. The chief engineer wasn't kidding about not letting him touch anything fancy. So far, Aurelius had been assigned all the low-man repair gigs. Everything from changing the lightbulbs in sick bay to fixing the alarms on the baked potato machines. You know, the more important aspects of starship maintenance. His responsibilities hadn't brought him back to main engineering at all. He had spent most of the time trying to stay out of trouble; it was easy. There was even less recreation on the *Freedom's Reach* than there was work for someone of his rank.

The first bit of excitement was coming up, though. They were nearing the Epsilon Gateway and would be passing through it soon.

Shipboard time was late afternoon. The morning shift had begun to clock off, making their way to their bunks. The evening crew had just awoken to their duties. Aurelius made his way down the corridor of Deck 6, Section C. He was in a hurry, walking with an upbeat tempo, which only made it harder to unwrap his soy-based protein bar. He hated them, but he didn't have time for anything else. The tool bag slung over his shoulder didn't make things any easier. He had to fight with it to keep it from knocking the protein bar out of his hands as it swung with each hurried step. The wrapper made an unmistakable obnoxious crinkling noise, echoing down the corridors.

Once he got enough of the wrapper out of the way, he sunk his teeth into it. Terrible. It tasted like cardboard and bug spray. How it could pass for food was anyone's guess.

His boots echoed with the wrapper as they smacked against the floor. The ship's decks and corridors were like most others in the SMMC fleet. The paint was chipped, the air was stale, and the deck plates were covered in boot prints. Most of the ship was always three-quarters lit. If something was important, it got fixed, or, in most cases, was not allowed to break down in the first place. Like the chicken soup and baked potato machines. But if it broke and they could make do without it, it stayed broken.

Aurelius had finally gotten a shift in main engineering. He was excited and in a hurry. There were no vending machines in the engineering sections of the ship, which meant he might actually get some decent work.

The section wasn't as chaotic as the last time Aurelius had seen it. There were only about half as many people, and the room didn't feel like it was going to wrench itself off the ship, but it was still a hive of activity.

Aurelius quickly spotted the rest of his work detail. Paul, Nyreen, and Jerula were standing in a cluster by one of the caffeine dispensers and talking, waiting for their shifts to start.

Aurelius walked over to them, taking an offered cup and leaning up against the wall.

"So, this your first time down here?" Paul asked.

"Nah, Chief had all the new techs down here when we undocked from the Spire," Aurelius said.

"You could have fooled me," Jerula said.

"He does have that kid-in-a-candy-store look in his eyes," Nyreen added.

"Can you blame me?" Aurelius said, looking around him at the power plants, the engines, and the huge spinning cylinder, viewable through the rear viewports. "This place *is* a candy store. I can't wait to start taking things apart and putting them back together."

"Hold on there, zippy," Jerula said.

"Yeah. Today you're going to be fetching coffee for people and holding my tools," Paul said.

"I've had a bunk bed next to yours for a week. I know what you do with your tool and I'm not touching it."

"Well, someone has to help him with it. He tends to let rust collect when it's just him looking after things," Nyreen added.

Aurelius was a little let down. He was just so close to it all. He could reach out and touch all the things he'd been dreaming about since he set foot on the ship, but he wasn't allowed to yet.

"Relax, Aurelius. It won't be forever. We all start out at the bottom. We gotta see what you don't suck at before we trust you with anything serious," Nyreen said, seeing the look on his face.

"I've got to go calibrate one of the power regulators. Why don't you come along? I might let you see if you can figure out where the problem is," Paul said, putting his cup down and gesturing for Aurelius to follow him.

The next three hours of their shift passed with Aurelius listening to Paul explain what he was doing while half buried in the guts of something Aurelius would have given an arm to be working on.

"See, sometimes you get buildup down here in the vent conduits. Mostly junk the filters can't quite deal with, and it causes the malfunction warnings. All you gotta do is get in there and blast the worst of it off the collectors. The whole thing takes about five minutes," Paul said, his voice slightly echoey from the vent his head was stuck in.

"So it's a lot like the soup dispenser," Aurelius said, trying not to let the boredom show in his voice.

"Well, yeah, but you get to use a plasma torch," Paul said weakly.

"The thing to remember, is you'll mostly be doing stuff like this. Well, until you become the chief and can make other people do it for you. The big stuff matters too much to be tinkered with too often. Mostly it's just the soft techs playing with numbers and flows. When something cool does need tinkering with, that's usually a bad day for everyone, and if the stress doesn't take all the joy out of it, the chief will by looking over everything you do and shouting. It might be hard to accept, but learn to appreciate the crap jobs. They are basically the best times you're going to have," Paul finished, pulling his head out of the vent and looking down at Aurelius.

"If you say so," Aurelius said, frowning. The crap jobs may have been fine for Paul, but Aurelius doubted he could ever be content with lightbulbs and air vents.

"Seriously. I can tell you don't believe me, but you'll learn to love the boring stuff," Paul said, brushing off the front of his clothes. "Usually if something big messes up, lives are on the line, and nobody wants that. Anyway, what's next on—"

Aurelius was nearly thrown from his feet as the ship lurched and rocked. He grasped for a handhold but only managed to catch the front of Paul's shirt.

"What the hell?" Paul shouted, steadying himself and looking around. Aurelius looked around too. Everywhere, emergency lights were flashing, klaxons were blaring, and people were scrambling, but that wasn't what worried Aurelius. What caught his eye, and evidently the eyes of a few other members of the engineering staff, was the big energy collector that took in power from the huge rotating cylinders and fed it back out to different areas on the ship. The collector was silent, a single red light flashing on it, and its access consoles were running through some sort of emergency shutdown.

"What the hell was that?" Chief Marcus barked as he burst from his office.

Aurelius shook his head as the chief pushed past him toward the main monitoring station.

"Attention, crew. The *Freedom's Reach* is in emergency mode. After stepping down from FTL for our final approach to the Gate, we were struck by a large piece of debris. We're assessing damage reports now. Please log any damage or injuries in your area to your section chief. More in a moment."

Chief Marcus pulled up a holographic diagram of the ship on his console. The image displayed the impact location and the damage left by the debris. To everyone's amazement, there was a large piece of another ship embedded in the port steering strut. The look of fear on the chief's face was palpable as he buried his mouth in his hand.

"Damage reports are starting to filter in," a crewman off to his right said as he pulled up a scrolling list linked to a diagram of the ship.

Aurelius saw Jerula and Nyreen enter the room. Jerula wasted no time approaching the command console and the chief. His eyes darted back and forth as he assessed the list of compromised systems. Aurelius didn't need to read the entire list to figure out the ship had automatically triggered the core's standby mode. He was no soft tech, but even he knew it was to prevent the reactors from becoming unstable in an event like this.

"How did the bridge not see something that big?" the chief asked.

"Didn't the captain say we were approaching the Gate? If we're within an AU or less, the solar winds could be obstructing our view of anything."

"But a piece of debris that big? It's the size of a three-story building," Paul added. "Where does a piece of debris that size even come from? It looks like a piece of a ship! What happened here?"

Just then a chime came over the chief's dog tags. He was getting an incoming call from the bridge. "Chief, this is Maher. What's your assessment of the situation?"

"Not good," the chief said. "Very not good. We've got all sorts of scrapes and bruises from minor debris, but we've got a giant piece of another ship caught up under our skirt."

"I see that," Governor Maher said. "Can we safely pass through the Gate, though?"

"No way. Our maneuvering options have been cut in half. The tidal forces of one of the transmission vortexes would toss us around too much. I'm not even sure we could resist the gravitational field of the star right now. We've gotta get that thing cut loose from the hull before we can assess the damage to the maneuvering engines."

"Can we launch a utility craft?" the governor asked.

"Maybe to cut away the bulk of the object, but I'd recommend an EVA to get it free of the hull. We're going to need a scalpel to remove it, not a butcher knife."

"The captain says it's too dangerous to send out a standard EVA team," Governor Maher continued. "Archer's Agony station tells us they've been cleaning up a debris cloud in our transit trajectory for the last few weeks. Anyone we send out there is going to be in a shooting gallery."

"That shouldn't be a problem," Chief Marcus said. "We've got three prototype slush suits on board that should handle things just fine. Problem is, this is a three-man job and we've only got two people on staff rated to use them."

"I don't like it, but if you have to send someone out untrained, then do it. It won't help to keep someone back if we all end up dead."

"Aye-aye, sir. Marcus out."

The chief took a moment after his tags went silent. He surveyed engineering once, twice, three times, and finally closed his eyes and massaged his temples with one hand. After several painfully long seconds he called for Paul and Nyreen to join him. The three spoke together for a few moments, Nyreen and the chief exchanging heated words. Aurelius couldn't hear the whole conversation, but he did catch a few words. "Jenkins was the only other one rated for a slush suit," and, "It's dangerous . . . qualified."

Not knowing what possessed him to do it, Aurelius strode over to where the three were talking. "Sorry to interrupt, but it sounds like this Jenkins guy was the only other person qualified to do this thing, and people keep reminding me I am replacing him. So if you need a third body for the suit, I'm in," Aurelius said, meeting the chief's eyes with his own.

"No. No way am I putting you in a slush suit. If I wanted to kill you, there are more fun and less expensive ways to do it."

"He has a point, Chief," Paul said, interjecting himself into the conversation for the first time.

"I don't care if he's replacing the captain. These are my suits, and this is my department, and I don't really feel like writing a letter to anyone's family this afternoon."

"Chief, Paul and I can look after him. We're both rated for the suits and we'll have Jerula running support if anything really goes wrong," Nyreen said.

"Did someone say my name? Please tell me you're not volunteering me for an EVA," Jerula said, stepping up beside them.

"Nah, you get to stay here," Nyreen said.

"Good."

"You're going to help us babysit dead man's boots here while *he* does it," she finished.

"Why does that not seem much better?" Jerula said.

"Because it's not," the chief said. "At least if I was cramming Jerula into a suit, I'd know for a fact that the body in it had a brain," the chief said.

"Is that really fair to say . . ." Paul started before turning to Aurelius. "I mean, he's not been here long, but he picks things up quickly."

"I have a brain, sir. And as much as I'd like to joke about where I bought it, right now it's telling me that we don't have the time to be sitting around discussing this. We all heard what the governor said," Aurelius said.

"Paul and I were going to get him certified eventually, and we don't really have a choice. We *could* cram Jerula in the thing—"

"The hell you could!" Jerula interrupted.

"—but I feel it's probably safer if we just start the kid's training now," Nyreen continued.

"I don't like it," the chief said.

Aurelius looked the chief directly in the eyes. "Got another hard tech in mind, sir?"

CHAPTER 17

Start Jetpack in Oxygen-Rich Environment

THE SUIT WAS a little tight after Aurelius finished fastening. Despite the tightness, it seemed he and Jenkins must have had a somewhat similar build.

"Generally speaking, these slush suits are designed to keep the person in and the harshness of space out," Chief Marcus said, monitoring the team of three as they suited up. "But these here, on this ship, are far stronger, more versatile, and easier to move in than standard suits. These suits can be pummeled by debris like a cosmic punching bag and rarely rip or tear. The suits are so strong, that the person inside usually dies from untreated impact trauma before anything else. They're just as good at keeping the void of space out as they are at keeping all of your bits in. Hence the name 'slush suit.' Nowhere are they more important to have than on the governor's ship. These are the new top-of-the-line prototypes with extra impact reduction. A pirate boarding party could ram through one of our airlocks at full thrust with one of these babies and probably live to tell the tale. The entire SMMC only has a half dozen of them in total. They're worth orders of magnitude more money than the three of you are, so I want them all returned in one piece."

"Is that his way of telling us to be careful?" Aurelius asked Paul under his breath.

"Mostly you, I think," Paul said. "We're a bit far out to be replacing you at this point."

"Good. I wouldn't want to be someone else's Jenkins," Aurelius said.

Aurelius stepped into an airlock with Paul and Nyreen. Between the three of them, they carried a toolbox and laser cutter. The laser cutter looked like a cross between a rifle and jackhammer. A simple voice command caused their helmets to seal up tight.

"The utility craft has just finished cutting away the bulk of the debris. Your job is to dislodge the rest. I want this done clean and by the numbers," the chief said over the comm. "Depressurizing now."

There was a rushing noise as the air evacuated from the airlock. A moment later, the outer door unlocked and slipped open silently. Paul raised a little metal shutter over a button on his forearm. "Magnetizing . . ." His boots became fixed to the floor. Aurelius and Nyreen followed. Now they could step out of the airlock and onto the hull. Aurelius's steps had to be slow and deliberate. If one foot wasn't on the hull at all times, they ran the risk of breaking contact and flying away. In place of tethers, the suits had safety measures to ensure at least one foot would always be firmly magnetized to the hull, but safety tech wasn't a full replacement for being careful.

Paul led the team, one foot in front of the other. Aurelius couldn't help but gaze out at the expanse of emptiness around him. There was a strange loneliness to it. He couldn't tell if the tiny twinkling lights were all stars or if some were far-off ships.

Jerula's voice came over the comm. "All right, boys and girls. Looks like this is going to be nice and simple. We've still got a good chunk of another ship lodged in us, but if the three of you can get that dealt with, actually fixing the steering strut should be child's play. The captain has positioned the ship to hopefully protect you guys from the worst of the Gate's effects, but be careful. Get the new guy killed and I'll have no one to drink with."

"I've got better things to do tonight than die," Aurelius replied.

"Not if you don't get moving. We've got a job to do, and right now I don't see anyone doing it," came the chief's voice, cutting over everyone else. "So if you've got a moment, maybe you could attend to it, please."

Aurelius pointed his hand at Paul, making a little gesture that resembled a squawking bird. Both Nyreen and Paul cracked smiles.

"Okay, guys, be careful going forward," Paul said. "Your mag boots are going to hold you to the hull, but we're going to have to make at least one short jump to get where we're going. Only disengage magnets when you're sure you're ready to jump. Also, your suits have a jetpack for these sorts of situations, but you only have a little bit of fuel and you're going to need the pack to both go up and come down, so let's not waste any of it. Jerula, can you give me and Nyreen readouts on Aurelius's fuel gage, I'd like to keep an eye on it while he's learning."

"No problem," Jerula confirmed.

Paul led the way out across the hull. He advanced them around antennae and over vent panels and protrusions Aurelius couldn't put a name to.

"We can see the damage, sir," Paul said.

There, down the length of the ship, was the massive fin-like stanchion that held the steering thrusters out from the hull. It had a sizable impact scar with a car-sized piece of sharp, serrated steel poking out from the wound.

"The utility craft got as much as it could," Chief Marcus said. "We're going to need you guys to dig out the rest before we can assess the damage."

Eventually Paul, Nyreen, and Aurelius came to a break in the hull. They wouldn't be able to continue without the use of their suit's jump-pack systems.

"End of the road, guys," Nyreen said, dangling a foot over the gap before letting the magnets in her boots snap her footing back to the hull.

"All right, Aurelius. The jetpack engages when your suit does. The systems on board scans the local area and can tell when you're adrift."

Paul stepped forward to the very edge of the gap in the hull. He pressed the button on his forearm and his boot unsnapped from the metal beneath him. He used his feet to push off from the contour in the ship in the same way a swimmer pushes off the side of a pool. The jets on his backpack fired up, pushing out a little jet of hot plasma before dying back down.

"See! It's just like swimming! If you want to go faster you stretch out like this," Paul said before stretching his body out a little into a pose a comic book super hero might recognize. The jets on his backpack fired up and carried him forward faster and faster as he began to stretch out into a planking position.

"If you want to stop, pull your legs forward, then spin around and direct your jet in the other direction," he said, swinging his legs back underneath him.

"Those are the basics," Nyreen continued. "Oh, and you lean your body in the direction you want to go. It's a lot more intuitive than it looks."

At this point, Paul was a good hundred or so meters downrange. Nyreen stepped to the edge of the hull and followed him, demagnetizing her boots, pushing off from the ship, and letting her momentum carry her a few meters before engaging her jets.

"Just like swimming . . ." Aurelius said under his breath as he stepped to the edge of the gap in the hull. Nyreen and Paul had clearly done this before. They seemed oddly at ease with the idea of floating around the outside of this behemoth of a ship with not so much as a tether. Aurelius had been waiting for an opportunity like this, but it was remarkable how small he felt right now. It brought an unease to his stomach that was made of both nerves and excitement. Not wasting another moment, he stepped to the edge of the hull and followed Nyreen and Paul. He felt a vibration in his boots as they demagnetized. A second later, he pushed off from the hull as gracefully as he could. After just a short drift, he realized that he might have pushed a little too hard with his right leg. His drift was becoming increasingly off target.

"Just stretch out a little bit. Keep your eyes focused on the strut at the back of the ship. You have to look where you want to go," Paul said, pointing to the massive series of crossbars sticking out of the back of the ship. From their point of view, the scaffolding that held the steering fin seemed more like a massive tower sticking up out of the ground.

Aurelius tried to follow Paul's example and began to lean forward. His jetpack fired more abruptly than he had anticipated, throwing him forward. He panicked a little, flailing his arms and trying to stabilize himself as he wobbled, which didn't help at all in the lack of air and gravity. He was drifting downward toward the ship.

"Keep your eyes on the end of the strut and stretch out," Paul said, sensing his panic. Aurelius couldn't help but look directly at the hull beneath him. That was his first mistake. His second mistake was stretching out like superman. His suit reacted and blasted his jets, sending him flying toward the hull.

"Shit!" the chief barked over comms.

"Don't stretch out that much!" Nyreen called out.

"Look at that strut!" Paul yelled.

Aurelius had to fight his natural instinct to keep his eyes on the hull as he flew closer and closer to it. He kept his head up and locked his eyes on the steering fin on the end of the scaffolding sticking out of the ship. His pack continued to fire and pulled him away from the vessel. It rocketed him toward their destination.

"See! You're getting it!" Nyreen said, watching his flight stabilize.

"Strifer," Jerula's voice came over their radios. "You're going a little fast."

"How do I slow down?" Aurelius asked, fighting the anxious tremble of his vocal cords.

"Pull your feet back under you, then turn around and lean forward," Paul said.

Fighting to keep sight of where he was heading, he followed Paul's advice. He pivoted around and faced his two companions and leaned forward slightly. As his suit was designed to do, his pack fired and began slowing him down. That's when he noticed the little speedometer in his HUD. He had been going over sixty-five kilometers an hour, relative to the ship, but was now slowing. He watched the holographic needle in his field of view drop to under ten kph.

"You're going slow enough that you should be able to catch the hull under your feet and remagnetize now," the chief said.

"Don't forget to turn around!" Paul reminded him.

Aurelius pivoted around. Rather than hoping to catch the hull with his boots, he was close enough to the base of the scaffolding to grab it with his arms and pull himself in. Once he had a firm grip, he activated his boots and, for the second time that day, he was standing on the outside of the ship. He let out a long sigh as Nyreen and Paul landed next to him.

"See. Not so bad," Nyreen said, patting him on the backpack.

"Don't. You might send me off into space again," he said, mostly joking.

"Okaaaay . . . not exactly how I planned to get us here, but here we are. You two ready to get to work?" Paul asked, starting to unpack the laser cutter and gesturing for Nyreen to help him.

"After that, I feel like I'm ready for anything," Aurelius said.

"Good. Nyreen, you've got better aim than I do; come guide this thing as I direct you. Aurelius, I'm going to need you to start pulling away the chunks as she cuts them free," Paul said, stepping away from the controls so Nyreen could take her place.

"Got it," Aurelius and Nyreen said almost at the same time.

Aurelius hadn't expected to see the beam of the laser, so it surprised him the first time the metal Paul was pointing at turned phosphorescent white before a seam became visible.

"Grab it!" Paul yelled, snapping Aurelius back to the reality of his task. With a quick lunge, he grabbed a chunk of metal about the length and width of his forearm.

"We keeping this for something?" Aurelius asked, holding up the chunk.

"No, just throw it away from the ship. Eventually the star will get it. I just don't want it floating around us while we're trying to work," Paul answered.

"Got it."

The next half an hour went by more or less smoothly, Paul pointing out chunks to cut free, Nyreen lasering them with almost surgical precision, and Aurelius pulling debris free as gently as possible so as not to damage anything more than it already was.

"So, I've got good news," Paul said, looking into the hole. "The damage doesn't look so bad. It looks mostly structural. Now that the debris is cleared, the thruster should be able to move freely again. With a little spot welding, we should be able to get underway and fix this thing up proper once we're not approaching the corona of a star."

"That's good, get the plate on quickly, then, and get back to the ship. I've just been informed that a large cloud of debris is heading our way," the chief's voice responded.

"Big enough that you're worried about us being out here?" Paul asked.

"Big enough that the ship needs to move to avoid getting hit with larger chunks than the one you guys just cut loose."

"All right, guys, you heard the man. We're working under a time limit here. Jerula, can you give us a countdown display and prep the airlock for us?"

"Already there. The door will be open for you, and you should be seeing the countdown . . . now."

The countdown appeared in Aurelius's HUD showing the time remaining before the ship could move fast enough to avoid impact. The timer had just over ten minutes on the clock.

"Okay, guys, getting the panel down should take no time at all, so let's get to work. Nyreen, head up toward the bow end and work your way back. Aurelius, head stern and work your way back here, I'll secure everything while you two weld."

Aurelius walked along the edge of the hull plate as fast as he could. He wasn't aiming to do a good job. Right now, fast was more important than good. Good could come later when good wouldn't mean painting the interior of the slush suit with their insides. Right now, it just had to hold long enough for more standard repairs.

As Aurelius's path finally intersected with Nyreen's, he checked his countdown timer.

"All right, we've got three minutes until it starts raining sharp, heavy metal things. We need to get to the airlock," Aurelius said.

"Nyreen, if I lead the way, can you guide Aurelius and take him tandem on that jump?"

"Sure, but I think he's got it," Nyreen replied.

"I'm sure he does, but with everything going on, let's not chance—" A large object slammed up against Aurelius and broke his boots' grip on the hull, carrying him away in a tumbling spin.

Suddenly the tape in Aurelius's mind felt like it had been cut. Somehow there was a gap between moments. He had just been staring at the *Freedom's Reach* hull beneath his feet and now, suddenly, the ship was hundreds of meters away and retreating into the light at an alarming pace.

"Aurelius!" Paul yelled as pieces of debris began to rain down and smack against the ship like a hail of bullets.

"I can get him!" Nyreen said.

"No! You two get back to the ship! Jerula, is that lock ready for them?" The chief came through louder than anyone else.

"But, Chief . . ."

"Nyreen, listen to me. We're already taking small impacts all over the ship. I don't like the idea of leaving him out there either, but recovery is not an option at this point."

"I am still here," Aurelius said, the horror of his situation not quite sinking in. He knew he was heading away from the *Freedom's Reach* at an astounding velocity, and he could hear them talking about his recovery not being an option, but something about it just didn't or maybe couldn't hit home. He should have been terrified, or furious, but he really wasn't. Mostly he was wondering if this would count against the plaque by the chief's office and if people would start telling Aurelius stories. More than anything else, he wondered how he was still alive and conscious after being hit so hard.

"He's still alive!" Jerula exclaimed.

"Sit rep, Blaze!" the chief ordered.

"Well . . . I'm alive but in pain. Clinging to a chunk of metal . . . and rapidly flying away from the ship," Aurelius said, checking his ribs for any breaks. "I've had better vacations."

"Roger that. Are you injured?"

"Not terribly."

Aurelius felt a thud as the back of his suit hit something. Turning his head, he saw that it was a colossal part of a ship's hull. It looked like a section near the center of a ship like the *Freedom's Reach*. There were huge letters stenciled on the hull, but Aurelius was too close to read them. At first he thought it was a section of the *Freedom's Reach* and that somehow he had come full circle, but he knew that couldn't be the case. Out in the distance, Aurelius could just make out the *Freedom's Reach*.

"All right, we're in," Paul said, his voice sounding flat and numb.

"Got it. How's Nyreen?" the chief asked.

"She took a minor hit, nothing the suit couldn't handle. I think she's shaken up more than anything else. Any chance of recovering Aurelius?"

"We can't send anything out. We have to leave in two minutes. It's going to be up to him to get back."

The moment was surreal. They thought he was really gone, and they were writing him off. The blinking dots on his suit's radar indicating Paul's and Nyreen's position seemed ridiculously far away.

"But he has to be alive," came Nyreen's voice. "We heard him transmit!"

"He did, but our trackers have him making hard impact with a large piece of a ship, and then nothing. He's not moved or transmitted for over a minute," the chief said.

What? It couldn't have been that long. He tried to look down at his countdown, and found the numbers too blurry to read.

"Okay. Either I've done some serious damage to this thing, or I was hit harder than I thought." Aurelius's voice almost didn't sound like his own coming over the static.

"Aurelius?" came Jerula's voice.

"Yeah, I'm still here. You guys can still see me, right?"

"Yeah, we can see you, but you're a ways out there," Jerula said.

"I figured. I was thinking I could try and fire myself back to the ship. Any chance a full burn from the suit can get me there in time?" Aurelius asked.

"It could if you had a full tank, but you don't, you used a lot learning to fly earlier," Jerula said.

"What are my options, then?" Aurelius asked. "I don't . . . hang on a moment, I need to do some calculations. You know, it's funny. I always told Sarge that you can't rely on all those fancy tools and calculations in a pinch, but look at me now."

"Aurelius . . ." Jerula's voice was shaky.

"I'm listening. Right now you sound like you're underwater, but I'm listening."

"There's just no way you can possibly make it back in time . . ." Jerula said.

"What do you mean?" Aurelius asked.

"I'm sorry," Jerula said. "Even if you had enough fuel, you were never trained to use the slush suit's tracking system to direct you toward the ship's airlock. You have enough oxygen to last you for a couple of hours once the ship leaves. I'm sorry, Aurelius. I'm so sorry."

The blurry numbers in Aurelius's HUD flicked away piece by piece, as if it were a timer counting down to the end of his life. His mouth worked wordlessly for a response as his brain struggled to put words to the reality of his impending death. This was it. He finally got an assignment to a ship, and this was how it ended. He guessed there were worse ways to go than suffocation, though. At least Paul and Nyreen had made it back safely. Would they jokingly call his replacement recruit Aurelius? He clenched his fists and set his jaw, closing his eyes.

Then they snapped open.

"Yeah," Aurelius said, fixing his boots to the hull that had so rudely come up and hit him in the back. "You can tell me all about how sorry you are when I make it back to the ship."

"Aurelius . . ." Jerula said.

"Can you give me a view of the airlock? I want to see Paul and Nyreen. Patch them into my helmet too, if you can. I want them to have a good look at my face so they don't mistake the memory of me for Jenkins in case this doesn't work."

"In case what doesn't work?" Jerula said. "Aurelius, what are you—"

"Just do it!"

A small screen winked into view on Aurelius's HUD. On it, in the open airlock, Paul and Nyreen were standing at stiff attention, saluting out toward open space. Toward him. He could swear that he could make out a wetness in Nyreen's eyes beneath the gradually fading tint of her slush suit's UV filter.

"That's so sweet, guys. I'm flattered. Can you do me one last favor, though?" Aurelius asked.

"Whatever you want," came Nyreen's trembling voice.

"Could you stand a little bit farther apart?"

Paul and Nyreen gave each other puzzled glances, but moved to opposite ends of the airlock. The two blinking dots on Aurelius's HUD radar separated the barest amount, but he'd have to work with it.

"Oh, and Jerula?" Aurelius said.

"Yeah?"

"Have a few drinks ready for when I get back. I'm going to need them after this."

Aurelius kicked off from the hunk of hull and launched himself as best he could toward the exact middle of Paul and Nyreen's blinking dots. Aiming was difficult, though. For Aurelius, the ship was a black outline against the almost impossibly bright mass of the star that outlined it. If not for the dimmers and other filters in his faceplate, Aurelius doubted he'd be able to see anything. Luckily his HUD accounted for his teammate's elevation as well as direction. These really were top-of-the-line slush suits. It was too bad that all of its fancy airlock-tracking tools and computations were going to waste at the moment.

As he got closer, he used the last of his fuel to make final adjustments to his flight path using Paul's and Nyreen's locations as a guide. Aurelius waited numbly as he felt his jetpack sputter and finally stop. Once he was sure it had kicked, he used a voice command to vent his suit's last couple of hours of oxygen, shooting him forward with a kick.

"What the hell are you doing?" the chief yelled. "That oxygen was the only thing keeping you alive out there!"

The ship loomed in Aurelius's view, getting larger and larger. When he was sure he was as on target as he was going to get, he turned to get a better look at the object he had impacted with.

Aurelius could just see it, hurtling away from him, a massive chunk of a ship. The lettering that was too big to read before, he could now see clearly. "Rising," Aurelius mouthed as he read. Presumably it was part of the ill-fated ship's name, and somehow it made Aurelius feel better as his lack of oxygen made the edges of his vision grow black.

"I can't believe I'm getting the chance to say this, but you're going to want to brace yourself . . ." Jerula said.

Aurelius turned back to the *Freedom's Reach*, which seemed to have grown alarmingly in the brief moment his attention was diverted.

". . . because this is going to hurt."

Aurelius had felt more painful things in his life. One time, as a kid, he had gotten his arm stuck in the hatch of an orbital surveyor his father had been working on, and it had shattered several bones and crushed some muscle. This wasn't quite that bad, but a jet-propelled impact with the back of the *Freedom's Reach* wasn't that far off either.

"He's hit the airlock directly," Jerula said with awe.

"We've got him, closing the airlock now," Paul said in response.

The floor of the airlock was cold as they peeled him out of the slush suit, and Aurelius winced as his sore body made contact with it.

"Damn, dead man, you gave us a scare," Paul said, his eyes beaming with elation.

"He going to be okay?" Nyreen asked.

"His suit says he has a good number of bruised bones, and a minor concussion. He's going to be fine," Jerula said over the radio.

"Hey, Jerula," Aurelius said from his resting spot.

"Yeah, Strifer?"

Aurelius grinned from ear to ear. "Where are my drinks?"

CHAPTER 18

The Epsilon Gateway

THE MEDICAL STAFF was wrapping up a series of tests on Aurelius. He had a CAT scan, X-rays, and blood work done to make sure his rocket ride hadn't knocked anything loose.

"Everything looks good," the nurse said, a smile creeping across her face as she tried to keep from making direct eye contact with him. "Your cholesterol is just a tad high, though."

"Weird. Didn't think jetpacks could do that," he teased.

"Oh, definitely." The nurse laughed, patting Aurelius on the arm and smiling coyly. "Anyway, I see nothing that will keep you here. If ya hurry, you should be in time to watch the ship go through the Gate."

"Thanks," he said, hopping off the exam table. His feet had barely hit the floor when the door to the exam room slid open. Jerula, Paul, and Nyreen came stomping in.

"All right. All right. No pictures, please. I know I'm great, the hero of the hour and all that, but really I'm just a guy," Jerula announced, waving around his mobile access pad like a flag. He leaned over to smile at the nurse. "I'm free this evening, if your shift ends soon."

"And you did what exactly?" Aurelius asked.

"So, is he a goner?" Paul asked the woman.

"He'll be fine. Your other friend, though, had better keep his hands to himself if he doesn't want to lose something," the nurse threw back with a wink.

"Depending on what it is, it might be worth it." Jerula smiled.

"I love how you guys just barge in. If you were trying to catch me naked, you're fifteen minutes too late," Aurelius said, buttoning up his corps-issued crew jacket.

"It's nothing your bunkmates haven't seen before," Nyreen said, throwing her arms around Aurelius.

"I guess we're stuck with him," Paul said sarcasticly. "Thanks a lot, Jerula."

"When you're a hero, you just do it. Even the new guy is worth saving."

"Well, I guess so. Bad enough replacing Jenkins. Don't want to have to start over from scratch again," Paul said, mocking him grudgingly.

"Sorry, but only the good die young," Aurelius bragged. "The devil's got a restraining order out on me."

"He really should give me the name of his lawyer," Paul said. The five of them, including the nurse, broke out in laughter. All bullshitting aside, Aurelius could tell his friends were glad he was still alive and in one piece.

"Hey, I heard we're passing through the Gate here momentarily. I wanna see it," Aurelius said, shifting the moment back to the present.

"One step ahead of you," Jerula said. "Got a nice space for us camped out in the forward hangar bay, but we better get back to it soon before someone else takes it."

The *Freedom's Reach* was about to pass through the Epsilon Gate, and Aurelius wasn't gonna miss it. Jerula had made a "kickback" out of a stack of boxes that overlooked a massive window embedded in the external hangar bay door. The ship was headed right for the red dwarf star that was the Epsilon Gate, the wormhole that would bring them closer to Terra Luna, Earth. The transparisteel "glass" filtered out the blinding shine, rendering the star visible to human eyes without searing them.

A row of ships of all different shapes and sizes stretched out for hundreds of miles ahead of the *Freedom's Reach*. They slowly began to disappear, one by one, into the space inside a long swinging arm of prominence as the star reached out a burning grasp into the cold void of space.

This was the point in space, the mechanism, that humanity had found the Frontier with. Singularities opened and closed along the star's magnetic field. Some blinked in and out of existence for fleeting, nearly undetectable amounts of time, while others held their structure for minutes, hours, and even days. It allowed ships to pass from one side of the phenomena to the other. The wormholes in the fabric of space-time all led to the star on the Earth side.

The hangar was quickly filling up with crewmen and personnel both on and off duty. They all had their attention transfixed on the star outside the ship as it grew larger and larger.

"Now, if only I had snuck some beer out of the lounge. Never seen something so beautiful in my whole life," Aurelius said.

Jerula was more engaged in whatever was on the screen of his mobile access pad than at the once-in-a-lifetime view.

"Are you kidding me?" Nyreen asked.

Jerula looked around. "What?"

"We've got front-row seats to God's majesty, and you're here with your gizmo!" Paul exclaimed.

"I see it. It's out there!" Jerula said. "Just wanted to catch up on a few things."

Aurelius took a seat next to his friend. "I think the CO would be fine if you didn't clock in any overtime on the grounds that you were watching yourself pass through a theoretically possible but totally improbable space phenomenon."

"Huh? What did ya say?"

Aurelius shook his head and handed each of his friends a protein bar from his pack. "Not a fine Merlot, but if ya wanna toast . . ."

Jerula picked through the handful of breakfast bars Aurelius set out on their makeshift table. "I hate those things. They taste like alcohol and feet."

"Not quite the way I'd so keenly put it, but yeah, pretty much . . . feet. Mmm, dem's good eatin'."

The four of them laughed.

The cargo bay slowly began to fill with other crewmen wanting to sneak a peek at the Epsilon Gate.

"You know, I've never been this far away from home before. Was stuck in the hangars for nine months after basic. Then all this happened so fast. Can't help but wonder if this is my one big shot at something. You know, that moment where you know you've 'made it.'"

"I've always wanted to see the Epsilon Gate," Jerula replied. "But you shouldn't see this as your one and only shot at something. You never really 'make it.' There's no such thing as just one shot. You can always 'make it' again."

Aurelius nodded. "Good advice."

"Besides, things happen when they are ready to happen. This was just your time."

Aurelius's friend was wise, far wiser than he let on.

The group watched intently as the crimson light from the star enveloped the ship and bleached the massive hangar in a shimmer like that of sunlight reflecting off a giant pool of water. Aurelius could easily imagine the early pilgrims being totally confused the first time they passed through the Gate.

"Have you seen anything like this before?" Nyreen asked, extending her arm out and letting the light play against her dark caramel skin.

"Not in real life," Paul said.

"What about you, Aurelius?" Nyreen asked

"It sort of reminds me of a dream I sometimes have," Aurelius said.

"What was that about a dream?" Paul asked.

"I meant it's like something out of a dream." Aurelius's attention never challenged the spectacle just outside the vessel. His brother and he had once sat and listened to an old spacer try and describe it to them, but even the imagination of a child wasn't quite up to the task of characterizing exactly what the inside of the Gate looked like. Still, it was that old spacer that had sparked something inside his brother, something that would eventually lead Magnus to leave home, and for Aurelius to follow. He didn't know what to expect from the space beyond the Gate or from Earth herself.

CHAPTER 19

The Right to Light

VIJAY'S HEART WAS pounding in his ears. The crowd around him was reaching fever pitch and he was right there with them.

"We deserve better!" yelled a man. He was standing atop a piece of old playground equipment that made up the center of the old Sergeant John Macaulay Park.

The crowd echoed him as he finished, and Vijay was no exception. The group had been there since early that morning, and the man had been working them up for the past hour. By now everyone was hungry, cold, and, above all else, invigorated with anger and hatred.

"What a perfect system they've created with the Helix! We have to have those earrings if we want a job, or if we want to rent a space to sleep. We even need them if we want to buy something to eat, but we can't get them! Oh no, if we want one we need to pay! But what am I supposed to pay with? What are any of us down here supposed to pay for one with? Did someone strike oil? Did the folks at that old church suddenly decide to do something more useful than sell flowers and read moldy old books? There is nothing in the Undercity, and with the damned Helix now being required for every damn thing, there's going to be even less!"

Vijay could tell what the man was building up to; everyone in the crowd could. They all knew what he was going to say, and they all knew they were more than happy to go along with it. The people in the Undercity were angry, and this was the only thing left to them, the only way they could remind the people above that they were still there.

"They'd like to forget about us, sweep us under the rug and pretend we're not here, but we are! We're not on their network! We're on no one's friends list! We're not checking in, or linking up, or logging on, but we're still here!"

The cheer that followed was deafening, and Vijay's throat was raw when it ended.

"It's time to remind them, it's time to remind them of the people left behind, the people left in the dark! We're going to remind them! Today we come out of the dark because we have as much right to the light as any of them!"

"Right to light" became the slogan of their movement a long time ago, but as the crowd boiled out of the park and onto the streets, it sounded new to him. To Vijay it sounded like a realization, the sort that after you have, you're never quite the same again.

Vijay made his way up one of the alleys that connected the Undercity to the streets above. He had a hoodie pulled over his head, and his face was masked with a brown bandana. Rounding the corner, he met up with three other hooded young men. One of them opened his backpack and pulled out three crowbars and a brick.

"Is that all you could find? That's it?" a teen in a red bandana asked.

"Yeah, that's all I could find. But that's all we're gonna need."

The teenager with the pack passed out the crowbars. Vijay was stuck with the brick.

"Better make it good. You've got one shot," said the adolescent in the red bandana.

Vijay hid the brick in the front pouch of his hoodie. In the distance, there was a loud explosion. A roar of angry people followed. "Right! To! Light!" they chanted as the riot began.

Vijay and the hooded pack ran down another alley and out into a large open area. It was packed with people from the Undercity. They were screaming, holding signs, and throwing various objects. They were angry and yelling loud enough for the sky to hear them.

The "police" had come out in droves; they must have been expecting the riot. Not just city officers in full riot gear, but rather civil defense units, specially trained officers with fully armored tanks.

With weapons anchored to their backs, they lined the streets in lockstep, slowly advancing on the Undercity civilians. The police were more than willing to match the rioters' violence tenfold. They wanted to make the consequences of their actions unbearable. Nothing was open for debate. The Right to Lighters knew this.

These demonstrations had started off peaceful enough years ago, but every time they assembled, they were met with increasing violence from the police, and at this point neither side tried to pretend the demonstrations were going to be tranquil acts of civil unrest. No one remembered which side had escalated it to this point. These days, all demonstrations ended violently.

The police fired their usual blast of tear gas directly at people. The idea being to deal out a little damage, break a few bones, even take a life or two. The police would have opened fire with truly lethal munitions if they could get away with it, but they needed to cling to the pretense that they were just trying to keep order.

The police tracked people through the smoke on their infrared scanners. Anyone who they caught was beaten till they couldn't fight anymore and then dragged away, sometimes never to be heard from again. It was a witch-hunt for "domestic terrorists," with the same fatal results.

The rioters started to smash shop windows on the Terraces. They saw the owners as sellouts; after all, the Right to Lighters weren't trying to stop the Helix, they were fighting for it. They were fighting for what they couldn't afford, what they couldn't access. It had been taxed and regulated out of their grasp. The people on top didn't want anyone from the Undercity crawling out and into a better life. They feared it would compromise their own.

Vijay ran with the group down the street, smashing every car and shop window they could. There was a sign outside a corner shop that read No Earring? No sale. Vijay picked up the sign and threw it through the store's frontage. The noise it made was deafening as a wall of glass came shattering down.

Vijay and his group continued down the street, breaking any image of the Helix, any reminder of it they could. Ads showing the latest ear-ring upgrades: more memory, more RAM, bigger Wi-Fi range, greater entanglement ratio—they smashed them all.

They came to the end of the block. Up on a wall was a Helix-Node. He and three of his friends climbed up a fence and onto a fire escape and began beating on it, smashing it with their bricks and crowbars. The node began to hiss and pop with sparks. With this node down, everyone in the vicinity would lose Helix access. The Helix had these axons spiderwebbed across the city. Destroying one was a minor victory, but it was one of the only victories they had.

The group jumped down quickly. They could hear the soldiers' shooting getting closer. The four of them went tearing down another street. At the end, there was a large building; a reflection of a walker fell against it. They could hear its heavy hydraulic footsteps heading their way.

"Shit! We're cut off!" The kid in the red bandana panicked.

They spun around and ran the other way. Officers in full combat gear came around the corner, chasing people with their weapons. The block was crowded with people, only some of whom were actually causing trouble. The police were out to show force. They didn't care who was involved.

Again, tear gas canisters came flying in and exploded on the ground. They filled the entire block with a haze of lung-scarring smoke. People screamed, scrambling for buildings and climbing up fire escapes.

Vijay and his friends began coughing. Their bandanas weren't protecting them from anything. They ran through the smoke, almost completely blinded, down an alleyway, and out onto another street. Every corner of every alley, street, and basement was filled with the terrible smoke. At the end of the block was a department store with floor-to-ceiling windows. It was a popular luxury furniture store. The patrons who locked themselves inside were well dressed in expensive, imported clothes and the newest Helix earrings. They had a front-row seat to the melee outside, and all they did was watch. They all stood there, uploading video and sarcastic remarks to the Helix Network. These people thought they were elevated above the struggle. This was the opportunity Vijay had been waiting for, the opportunity to use his weapon. He reached into his pouch and pulled out the brick. He heaved it through the air and into the department store window. It shattered, shaking the entire store with a deafening crash as if the bonds of the Helix itself had been smashed. The terrible white smoke poured in. Everyone inside began coughing, wheezing, and sneezing.

Vijay wasn't out to hurt anyone. He, like the other Lighters, were out to get a message across, a message these people in the store now felt loud and clear in their lungs.

He whipped around to make his exit. What was done was done, and if that was all he could contribute for today, he would be content. The big heavy booming steps of one of the four-legged autonomous machines came pounding up to him. It reached out an ice-cold metallic hand and grasped Vijay by the throat. It had him lifted off the ground in a manner of seconds, and with its forward scanner it seemed to be looking him directly in the eye, as if trying to stare into his soul. The machine stood motionless while Vijay gasped for air. His heart tried to beat right out of his chest as everything around him seemed to slow down. Was this thing going to kill him? His whole body shivered with the thought. Or was this thing going to drag him off to wherever the civil defense team made people disappear? Little red dots began to fill his view.

Suddenly, the stinging white smoke all around them lit up a bright orange as if the fires from hell had come to meet them. A fraction of a second later, a burning bottle came flying out of the thick fog and exploded against the face of the machine. The flames erupted, hitting the surface of the machine with a thousand burning fingers that licked at its thighs. The AED responded by dropping Vijay from its grasp.

He fell from the grip of the machine with enough force to drive what little breath he had left from his lungs. Vijay struggled to catch his breath as the drone looked for whoever had thrown the homemade bomb. Vijay pulled himself to his feet with some effort and, not really bothering to check where he was going, started running. The smoke was so thick he couldn't see anything in front of him anyway. He never bothered to look over his shoulder to see if he was being followed. Right now his only thought was getting as far away from the AED as fast as he possibly could.

The adrenaline coursing through his veins carried his feet several hundred yards as he did his best to feel his way down a series of short alleyways. It was then that he realized he was all alone.

Vijay looked around. "Shit! Where did everyone go?" he muttered. He had lost his gang. He could hear the popping of the civil defense unit's guns getting closer and closer. Through the smoke, he could hear the walkers. *Boom! Boom! Boom!* Their heavy mechanical feet shook the ground under him. He started coughing and wheezing. He lost his balance and fell up against a car, sliding onto the ground. He started to see spots again, little twinkling lights.

"Vijay!" a girl's voice shouted. Through the smoke and fog, he saw an outline. The outline came closer, resolving itself into a person. He knew this girl. Her bright red hair gave her away even in the haze.

"Lithia!" he coughed.

CHAPTER 20

Redhead in Shining Armor

THE NEXT THING Vijay knew, he was being thrown over the redhead's shoulders and carried down an alleyway. A light breeze held back the smoke as they struggled down the corridor to the next street. The blasting wind of the city washed away the terrible smoke, filling their lungs with clean San Francisco air.

Once they'd made it out of harm's way, Lithia put him down. "What the hell do you think you're doing? What the hell, Vijay? What the hell?" Lithia screamed, slapping him.

"How'd you know it was me?" He coughed, leaning against a building and pushing his palms into his thighs.

"Because I bought you that hoodie and bandana! I didn't know you were gonna use them for this!" she yelled as she tore the cloth mask from his face.

If it hadn't been for her bright crimson hair, Vijay might not have recognized Lithia. She was wearing the same tattered, grungy clothes people from the Undercity wore.

"Vijay, what the hell were you doing back there?"

"Trying to make a statement. I think they heard me loud and clear."

"You're lucky I was nearby. Like, really lucky. I had no idea I was gonna be dragging your ass out of the fire today."

"Well . . . thanks," he said, coughing out the last of the gas. "I owe you one."

"You owe me one? Really? You know how you can pay me back? Don't ever do something like that again! Don't follow those Right to Lighters. Don't go to rallies, don't go to riots! I know you guys think you're some noble renegades, but the only thing it's gonna do is get you killed. Don't do it!"

"Lithia . . . I don't have much of a choice. I don't think you could understand."

Lithia looked him in the eye. "No one can hear you if you're dead. You keep up with those guys, and that's exactly what's gonna happen. I'll be sneaking out of the house to go to your funeral."

Vijay started coughing again. This time, though, it had nothing to do with the tear gas. She wrapped her arm around him tightly and began to lead him away again. "C'mon. Let's get you out of here, Vijay."

Lithia's arm never relinquished its grasp around him as the two descended a series of walkways onto the old streets of San Francisco's Undercity. Pro-Lighter propaganda was carved and etched into every flat surface imaginable as they descended back into the all-but-forgotten darkest areas.

"I hope your friends made it out," Lithia said.

"I know they did. They're faster than me," he said, choking a little bit, which summoned Lithia's hand to his back. I'm good," he said as he shrugged her off. He straightened up and swallowed against his emotions. He couldn't look weak in front of her. "They must have upped the chemicals in this gas," he said, wiping his eyes and clearing his vision. Hey . . . this is near where we first met," Vijay said. "Yeah. Right at the end of California street. You remember?" He glanced sideways at Lithia. Was that surprise on her face? Surprise that he had cared enough to remember? Or surprise because she had forgotten and he hadn't?

"Was it?" she asked.

"Yeah. There's an old rooftop patio where you were playing music with a bunch of people."

"Yeah, I remember that. Siri and I found a lounge where they had that old piano."

"I had passed by that place like a thousand times. That was the first time I had ever heard the piano playing. That's why I went in."

"Was it really?" she asked, grinning proudly.

"Yup. I'll never forget it. Was the first time I ever met you."

"You came up to me and offered to buy me a drink after the song," she said. "I asked you a drink of what."

"It was your sarcasm I liked so much," he said. "You were playful."

"Was I?" She smiled.

"Yeah. And you were dressed totally inappropriately."

Lithia jerked her head away from Vijay. "What? What do you mean?"

"I mean I could tell you were from somewhere . . . somewhere in the Upper Terraces. You weren't a lost soul like the rest of us in there that night."

"And you remember what I was wearing?"

They circled one of the massive pylons that held a section of the Terraces above them. They continued to walk down the bitter cold alleys of the Undercity.

"Of course I do. A beautiful girl in something she bought at Frontier Outfitter's trying to blend in with Undercity rats makes an impression."

"This place is nothing like the Upper Terraces. It feels like the sun has never shone down here," Lithia said.

"Well, of course not. It's literally locked away in nearly perpetual darkness," Vijay said, gesturing at the amber lights overhead hanging from the scaffolding. The lights were the Undercity's only illumination.

There was a chill to the air. As they walked, they saw their breath reach out from their lips and into the softly amber-illuminated spaces under the grand city above. On the coldest days, the rain from above would return to this place as freezing ice. The Undercity was a bitter-cold wasteland left in ruin. Most of the old brick buildings were crumbling. The districts away from the coastlines and up on hills fared best, but still, this place was Vijay's home, and when Lithia stepped into it, it felt like the warmest, brightest place in the universe.

The two of them began climbing one of the large hills that separated districts of the Undercity. The neighborhood got less sketchy as they ascended. Up here, people were bartering and trading goods at little makeshift shops.

Lithia and Vijay continued up the hill. This was one of the few hills tall enough to poke through the trestles of the Upper Terraces. The top was bathed in sunlight that washed over them in a golden glow that was warming in a way Vijay seldom felt. He noted the street signs, CALIFORNIA and TAYLOR, they read, welcoming them to the top of the hill. All around them were people stretched out across a lawn, enjoying the open sky. He couldn't help but notice that some of them wore robes while others were in the same roughed-up clothes that were common lower down.

There, across the top of the hill, stood one of the last intact vestiges of history from a time before the Upper Terraces. A monumental gothic cathedral sat as washed in sunlight as the day it had been built. The front facade was a massive monolithic structure with two colossal towers reaching up into the sky. Between them was a pitched roof that had a large round stained-glass window carved into it. Clearly this building was inspired by the post-Roman era, but something about the craftsmanship of the building told Vijay it had been constructed centuries later.

A plaque outside the cathedral read, WELCOME TO GRACE CATHEDRAL. Underneath it, a quote read, FOR THERE IS NOTHING HIDDEN THAT WILL NOT BE REVEALED, AND THERE IS NOTHING COVERED UP THAT WILL NOT BE UNCOVERED. – GOSPEL OF THOMAS.

"Pretty epic," Vijay said. "I can see why someone from down here would want to work here. Can't imagine why you would, though."

"My parents were Magdalenes. We're down here to help people. I can't imagine working anywhere else."

The two of them walked through a park just outside the church. It led to a large staircase and up to a quad where a class was being taught outside to a bunch of young children. A woman in a robe stood in the middle of a gathering. She was saying something about self-motivation and determination that sounded good on the surface, but the fact that the woman was reading from a book set off Vijay's religion alarms.

"Never really pegged you for a religious nut," Vijay said.

"What?"

"I'm just saying, I've never seen you get up on your soapbox before."

"Um . . . despite what you may see here, it's not a religion. It's more of a philosophy. Sorta," Lithia said, folding her hair behind her ear.

"Coulda fooled me," he said, gesturing to a cross in the quad.

"It's too difficult to explain. But if you're interested, maybe you should come to a service or two . . . hear what they have to say."

"Maybe. But it looks like a religion. It has a church and people walking around in robes quoting and interpreting from a book," he said.

Lithia and Vijay walked up the steps and around the right side of the building. Rather than stepping into the church itself, they made their way to a structure attached to the stately building. They passed through an old wooden door outlined in heavy rod iron and into the building before descending down an old brick-and-mortar stairway. The walls were old and made of stone and brick just like a dungeon out of a fantasy video game. For a second, Vijay expected to see a burning torch or two, but instead there were little multicolored holiday lights strung up along the ceiling, lighting their path in alternating patches of deep crimson, bright emerald green, and fluorescent blues. Where were they getting the power to run the lights? All of a sudden, he could smell the overwhelming aroma of flowers and wet dirt. The final step brought them into a corridor with archways overlooking a massive garden of flowers. He peered over the edge of the railing and down into a large plot of dirt that had bushes, flowers, and short trees. A single dirt path ran through the rainbow of plants that filled the space beneath him. He tried to follow the winding trail with his eyes, but had to stop as the twists and turns started to dizzy him.

The garden was open to the sky above. The light came rushing down onto the flower beds, highlighting their bright colors and making the shadowy gaps between trees and hedges seem even larger and darker.

"Come on," Lithia said, drawing his attention back from the winding turns and riot of growing things below.

Lithia took Vijay by the hand and all but pulled him down a narrow flight of wooden stairs to the garden below. If the path and colors were overwhelming to Vijay from above, the smells down here were almost more so. The entire area had a dusty, earthy scent that was punctuated by the perfume smells of flowers. Vijay had no names for the plants of all kinds that surrounded him. There were sky-blue flowers growing in thick patches next to vines of the deepest green he had ever seen. At first, Vijay thought they must be growing over the face of an enormous wall, but when he got closer, he could see pinpricks of light peeking through little gaps. Beyond the walls of vines were boxes filled with fragrant yellow and red flowers in precise little rows. Their vivid color struck a contrast against the dreary, dark neighborhood. Down here had to be the most peaceful place anyone could imagine, and it was breathtaking.

Lithia led Vijay over to a metal stand poking out of the ground. It was an old-fashioned drinking fountain. Next to it was another, child-sized, one. A modern-looking unit was hooked to the taller of the two.

"Here," Lithia said. "You can drink from that one."

The metal around the edges was dented, rusted, and showing signs of weather. The fountain looked ancient, and he had no idea how to turn it on. Lithia pointed to a button on the back of the spout. "Press the button with your thumb."

A stream of clean, ice-cold water came arching out. Vijay quenched his thirst and rubbed some of the water on his face, trying to wash off residue of the gas.

"So, what do you do down here?" he asked.

Lithia picked up a watering can and began to fill it with water. "I take care of this place. I planted everything here. Had to go to some pretty disparate places to get some of these things."

"How'd you get wrapped up into all this?"

"Well, I'm from Venus. I grew up doing this stuff. My family owned an arboretum in the biodomes. My mother was a green thumb and my dad was a tradesman."

"Really? Why?"

"You have no idea how important flora and fauna can be for air processing. It's cheap and reliable. Keeps the air fresh and has an effect on people. Keeps up people's morale when they've been in space for a long time."

"What would the Magdalenes want with a flower garden, though?"

Lithia walked over to a patch of flowers and began watering them.

"Well, flowers, if you hadn't noticed, are pretty hard to come by down here. They're a symbol of life. There's not too much life down here, but I don't have to tell you that."

"Yeah, no kidding."

Lithia walked over to a stack of little round planters. She picked them up and handed one to Vijay. "Here. Help me." She handed him a trowel. "When they're ready, I dig them up and sell them to people. You wouldn't believe how a flower can brighten someone's day."

"Yeah . . . I guess down here we need all the brightening we can get. Pretty thoughtful," he said, "but I guess they have to seem thoughtful if they're gonna indoctrinate people."

Upper city or lower, everyone had heard the stories of how the old religions nearly brought humanity to an end several times in the past. Now, anything with even the appearance of religion was met with caution at best.

Lithia scowled. "I told you. It's not like that at all. We don't go around preaching. We don't go around knocking on people's doors, bothering them at home. We don't go around telling people we can save them from a divine retribution. We live in a more civilized time now. Nobody believes in that crap."

"I dunno," he said, helping her remove a round purple flower from the ground.

"I could never get into all the mysticism."

"It's not about magic and talking snakes. The church is focused on recording history as objectively as possible, so that no one can corrupt it or use it for power. So that no one can use it to sway people into believing something that isn't true. We just use the church and the historic character of Mary Magdalene as symbols. That's it."

"So then why do the Magdalenes do all this? Why put in a flower garden? Why care about what happens to people down here?"

"Because it's the right thing to do," she said. "We—"

The voice that interrupted them was warm and drifted through the garden almost like music. "We aren't here to tell people what to believe or how to live their lives. Churches, mosques, and synagogues did that for centuries. We're simply here to safeguard history and knowledge. To make sure the powers of evil never use history to manipulate people. What we have to offer is corroborated by cold hard facts and not fairy tales."

Vijay looked up from his flowers and scanned the area around them for the source of the voice.

Lithia didn't bother looking, she simply finished potting the little white flowers she was working on and stood up.

"Good morning, Mother Priestess."

"Good morning, Lithia. I'm glad to see you made it in one piece. I tried calling you earlier to tell you that you didn't need to come in today. Too much rioting going on," the warm voice said. It sounded like it was getting closer, but all the tightly packed plants made it difficult to be sure.

Lithia almost unconsciously brought her hand up to the place her earring would have normally been before quickly pulling it away.

"Guess I forgot it," she said, and it sounded to Vijay like she was feeling a little embarrassed, which was odd, as Vijay hadn't heard anything like that in Lithia before. Honestly, it felt wrong to him. That wasn't his Lithia. His Lithia was shameless, fearless, and proud. She didn't feel embarrassment because she left an earring behind, even a Helix one.

"Far be it for me to turn into your aunt," the voice said, "but do you have any idea how dangerous it is to be out on the streets without it?"

Vijay chimed in, "Yeah, you wouldn't want to be caught without their precious earring or you might be considered less than human."

Vijay knew Lithia well enough to know that leaving it at home was her own act of rebellion, and he wasn't going to let anyone say anything to her about it.

"Your friend is absolutely right, Lithia. I understand the penalties are heavy if you're caught without it," the voice said, either missing Vijay's sarcasm or not caring.

Lithia shot a look at Vijay, the sort of look that said there would be a conversation about this later. "I won't forget it next time."

"I'm serious, Lithia. You don't need to come in while the violence is going on topside."

"What about the garden? I can't let these flowers die. I've put too much work into them."

"If the flowers die, then they die. We'll find another way to bring in money, though I doubt it will get that far. You aren't the only one of us who likes to get their hands a little dirty for the people," the voice said, which Vijay was sure was coming from just around the corner now.

"Even if you have to turn into Christians and beg for it?" Vijay jeered.

"If it came to that," the woman said. "The funny thing about pride is that sometimes it makes you overlook options that are right in front of you. But I doubt it will get that bad." The voice seemed to have a touch of amusement in it, and that touch made the already musical tones seem to ring. A moment later, a woman came into view, stepping around a bend in the maze of flowers.

The woman had long reddish-blond hair and was wearing a robe that might have been white were it not almost completely covered with dirt and a yellowish sort of powder. If Vijay had to guess, he'd have put her age at mid forties, but there was something about her that made her look both much older and at the same time much younger.

"Keep an eye on this one, Lithia. I like him. He's got a fire that most down here lose far too young. Keep him from doing something that will make someone put him out," the woman said, walking over to where Vijay and Lithia stood. "I'm Priestess Tarja. Lithia insists on calling me Mother Priestess, but honestly, Tarja will do. Titles make my skin feel a little tight." She reached a hand out and grasped Vijay's in a grip that was much firmer than he expected.

"He's Vijay, and that's really why I brought him here," Lithia said, making Vijay turn his head to look at her in puzzlement.

"Oh, really? Is this the sort of thing I shouldn't ask too many questions about?" Tarja asked, dropping Vijay's hand and giving Lithia a light, loving hug.

"Hey, I don't need—" Vijay started, but Lithia cut him off.

"I found you gasping and in the arms of an AED. You need anything they can give you."

"Oh, sounds like you two had an interesting morning. I'll not ask too many questions. It's your story, and anyway, I can't tell anyone what I don't know," Tarja said, giving Vijay a look that seemed to say that there was little she didn't know.

"So, can he stay here, just until things quiet down a little bit?" Lithia asked.

"As long as he chips in, he can stay here as long as he'd like, but we'll not keep him. Vijay, if you want to leave, no one here will stop you, but I trust Lithia, and I'd bet you do too. If she thought you needed to be here, I'd give that a little thought before you run back out into the cold," Tarja said.

"I really will be fine," Vijay said to Lithia and Tarja both.

"Just consider it. I'll be inside getting cleaned up before lunch. Come find me if you decide to stay," Tarja said, turning and making her way back into the church.

"Vijay, I really do think you should stay here. The police . . . they'll be looking for you. I'm sure they've got a good image of you, and if any cop sees you . . . that's it. Down here you'll be safe. No one looks too closely at the Magdalenes," Lithia said, turning to look directly at Vijay. There was worry in her eyes, real worry for him and what could happen to him.

Lithia took his hands in hers and Vijay could tell that she was trying to say something.

"Lithia," Vijay started, looking back at her. "I'll do anything you want. I always have." Vijay looked into Lithia's eyes a moment longer before leaning in.

Lithia's breath was warm as his lips met hers, and Vijay knew that this was right. Everything that had come before could have only led here.

"What are you—" Lithia said, pulling away sharply.

"I was . . ." Vijay started, but the look on Lithia's face stopped him. He had expected something like the same wide smile he could feel on his face, but Lithia's face was blank.

"I thought we were . . ." Vijay started again. "Lithia, it's always been you and me, at the fires, just walking around, it's always been you and me."

"Vijay, we're friends. You may be the best friend I've ever had, but that's it," Lithia said, gently touching him on the shoulder.

"Of course," Vijay said. It felt like something inside him weighed a thousand pounds, and he hoped whatever it was would drag him down into the ground.

"Vijay, stay with the Magdalenes, please. I need to go deliver these flowers," Lithia said, turning away and gathering up an armful of small pots. "I'll come check on you again in a few days," she said, stepping away.

Lithia almost ran up the stairs back to the church. When she was finally out of sight, Vijay sat down hard in the dirt. He didn't know where he had gone wrong with Lithia, but he had for sure changed things in a way that could never be put right again.

CHAPTER 21

This One Was Filled with Vampires

LITHIA SAT ON the tram unable to get what had just happened out of her head. Vijay had kissed her. How could he have kissed her? They were good friends, but Lithia had never given him any hint that there might have been more. At least she didn't think she had. But still, something had made Vijay think it could happen. Lithia didn't think about Vijay that way, though, not really. He was good-looking enough, and fun, even if most of his fun came out of one of those bottles that always turned up with him, but, well, he was just Vijay.

The kiss wasn't bad, though. No. She shook her head. She couldn't think that way. If she thought that way, then things would get complicated, and she didn't want that. Things were complicated enough as they were. But when she saw him again, would he want to talk about what happened? Would she? Would he try it again? Did she want him to try it again?

No, dammit. Thinking of Vijay as more than a friend would only hurt him. The most agonizing part was that she did actually love Vijay. He was the only person who saw who she was, saw it and honestly and accepted her. He knew she was rich, but never asked for anything. He knew she was musically talented, but never expected her to play for them. But she didn't feel a romantic love for him. She couldn't feel that for Vijay. She had thought about it a few times, mostly when she was younger and feeling lonely, but it couldn't work. Vijay was from the

Undercity, and whether they liked it or not, he was going to stay there. It wasn't his fault. No one got out of that place once they went down, but it was still true. Lithia had plans. It was only a matter of time before she left Earth forever and never looked back, and she couldn't take Vijay with her. Even if Lithia did take Vijay with her when she left the planet, he'd be lost. He wouldn't understand anything about living and working on a ship. She honestly wasn't even sure if Vijay knew how to read, though that at least the Magdalenes would help him with if he stayed.

He might not stay, though. That was another thing about Vijay, he wouldn't accept help from anyone. That wasn't his fault either. It was the world he lived in. The Undercity was full of more good people than bad, but enough bad was down there. There were too many people more than happy to take what little you had. Too often, a smiling face was just a cover for something predatory. That was life. Lithia had seen Vijay tempted; good and bad had little meaning when the real question was whether you'd have enough food to make it through the next cold snap. And if her friend was better than that, it was only because Lithia helped.

As the tram came to a stop, Lithia stood up and moved out through the doors into the sunlight. This really was a different world, and it felt like she was leaving her troubles with Vijay below, though she was only exchanging them for a new set.

There was a park in front of Lithia. Green grass stretched across a wide field in front of single-family homes. These homes were huge for the Terraces, a place where living space was at a premium. Number 705—Lithia's home.

Lithia entered the house and set her things down on the bottom step of the staircase. Her uncle wasn't home yet. The house was quiet, other than a rustling in the kitchen.

"Hey," Lithia said, entering the kitchen.

"Eww . . . what are you doing here?" her brother Bobby said, pulling his head out of the refrigerator, lunch meat in hand.

"Nice to see you too. Enjoying your afternoon graze?"

"That supposed to be a joke?" he asked.

"You're shoving meat in your mouth."

"Jealous?" he asked, poking his head out of the refrigerator again.

Lithia smirked. Her little brother had such a strange and morbid sense of humor.

"Can't you eat at the kitchen table like a civilized person? I swear you're like a farm animal with its head in a trough," Lithia mocked.

"But then I'd have to walk all the way back to the fridge to get more . . ."

Lithia poked Bobby in the gut. "The exercise could do you some good."

Bobby frowned. He was pudgy around the gut, and Lithia's sisterly jab only served as a reminder.

"I'm serious, Bobby," Lithia said, shuffling her brother away from the fridge so she could dig through it.

"Pass me a soda," Bobby said, clanging his fork against the table to get her attention.

"What kind do you want?"

"Surprise me," he said.

"You're adopted."

Bobby froze mid-chew. "Oh, you're so funny."

"Thank you. I'm here all week, folks."

Lithia rummaged through the fully stocked refrigerator. It never failed to surprise her how even with a full fridge, there was nothing she ever wanted to eat. "You ate all the lunch meat?"

"Uhhhhmmm . . . ummfh humffmer fhoo."

Lithia couldn't understand him with the last of the sandwich fixings buried in his mouth. She shook her head, returning to her scan of the refrigerator.

"Oh, hey. I just remembered the tyrannical queen of bitchcraft wants to speak to you," Bobby said indignantly.

"Any idea what she wants?"

"It could be anything. The ship, your school. But if I had to guess, I would say it was the dirt on your clothes. Oh, and the six unanswered calls. That probably didn't help."

A rush of panic washed over her. Aunt Petra wasn't someone she wanted to cross, more like someone to live around.

"So, how'd your last therapy session go?" Lithia interjected, trying to hastily change the subject.

"Nice try, but if you don't go see her immediately, my ass will be the one in the fire."

Lithia tried to keep her cool, digging around in her pocket for her earring. Finding it, she snapped it on. A holographic image appeared in her field of view, the earring projecting an image directly into her optic nerve. A little pop-up showing six missed calls from her aunt bounced up and down. Aunt Petra was going to be pissed. Really pissed.

"She's probably got her ugly face in a book somewhere out back," Bobby said.

Lithia noted the open bottle of wine on the kitchen counter and knew exactly what that meant.

The entire backyard was domed by glass. Aunt Petra laid on a chaise lounge. Her wineglass was like a fishbowl filled with crimson medicine that got her through the day. Her eyes were buried in a book.

Books were rare and a staple of the rich. They were considered the perfect expression of technology—no batteries or updates required, and they were usually the closest to the author's original vision. A book was a thing of beauty and the voice of freedom and the very essence of civilization. Unfortunately, this book was probably filled with teenage vampires.

"Sit down," Aunt Petra said, never taking her eyes off her book.

Lithia dreaded whatever was about to come next. Her aunt was a controlling and unreasonable person when sober. When drinking, she was something else entirely. Lithia sat for several minutes while her aunt finished the chapter she was reading. Putting the book down, Aunt Petra looked up at Lithia. "You have some explaining to do."

The statement chilled Lithia to the bone. She had no idea what her aunt was talking about and definitely wasn't going to volunteer any information.

"What about?" Lithia asked.

"You know exactly *what about*." An uncomfortable moment of silence passed. "You were gallivanting in the Undercity again."

Lithia thought she had gotten the smell of campfire off her clothes. How did she know?

"You were drinking. I found a bottle cap in your jacket."

Oh, Mary Magdalene. She had been caught red-handed.

"You were with that boy again, weren't you? If I can't trust you to keep your earpiece on and not to hang around unsuitable men, then I can't trust you to go out without a chaperone!"

Lithia hated the prospect, but her aunt had been threatening it for years and never followed through. Aunt Petra pointed to Lithia's hair. "I let you dye your hair like a common whore, then you go out acting like one."

"The sun did it! It always turns this color this time of year," Lithia fought back, unable to think of a better lie. She felt incredibly indignant toward her aunt; she had no right to be treating Lithia this way. She was an adult by Earth law, which meant her aunt could no longer make decisions for her. "I'm twenty-two years old, Aunt Petra! I'm an adult. I don't understand why you have a problem with what I do."

Her aunt got really quiet. That was always a bad sign. After a pensive moment, she spoke. "I am your aunt. I've been your guardian since your parents died. I paid for your education, a far better one than you would have ever received on Venus, and you live in my home. Everything you do is a reflection on me. When you act like a whore, you tarnish our family's good name."

Lithia looked away. Her aunt always called her a whore when she was drinking. "You tarnish the family's name all by yourself when you go out and act like a drunk. You think your friends don't talk?"

"I drink to hide my shame. The shame of having a niece who hangs around that Undercity brothel! Do you realize I have to lie to people when they ask where you are?"

"You lie because it has become second nature. It has nothing to do with me."

Aunt Petra continued as if Lithia hadn't spoken. "I've tolerated it for years, but I have limits."

"You tolerate it because you have to. It was in my parents' will. You don't let me go to the Undercity out of some sort of charity. The Magdalenes are holding my parents' ship in trust, a ship they wanted me to have."

"Your parents had no business giving you a ship and no business making me responsible for it. No respectable Terran woman needs a ship."

"But I'm not Terran! I'm Venusian. That has bothered you ever since I came here, because it was something you couldn't control."

"You *are* a Terran. No one knows you're Venusian. No one who matters, anyway, and you will act like a respectable Terran woman!"

"You wouldn't have what it takes to be Venusian. Venusians have to think, they have to act. They don't sit around all day drinking and reading bad romance novels! I am a Venusian like my parents, and for Venusians, our freedom is important. We have ships, we go places, and despite what you and the rest of Terra Luna thinks, we are better for it! I am a Venusian. I will act like one."

"You are an ungrateful little bitch, and I have taken you in out of the kindness of my Terran heart." Lithia's aunt stood up. "I will not be disobeyed in this house by a red-haired Venusian whore!"

Aunt Petra slapped Lithia. She stood there for a second. The shock paralyzed her, not because of the pain, but at the utter overwhelming sensation of feeling degraded by the woman that should have been taking care of her. The sting brought back memories of the hell she had endured there. It was by no means the first time her aunt had lost control and hit her. It had been a while, though. Her silence was her loudest cry.

"Now, get out of my sight. I don't want to see you again until your hair is a respectable color."

Lithia ran up to her room, up the staircase lined with red wallpaper. The gold zigzag patterns mocked her as she ascended to the safety of her bedroom. Her eyes filled with tears. Lithia wasn't the only one her aunt had gotten physical with over the years. At one point or another, she had gotten raw with everyone in the family.

Lithia leaped onto her bed and buried her face in her pillow. She hated her aunt. The woman had tried to control every aspect of her and Bobby's life. She had to make them look like the perfect little makeshift family to all of her friends. They all had their own children and already saw Lithia's family as an eyesore. Families who weren't perfect weren't accepted or invited to social events. To their aunt, this was death.

A pressure change in the air meant someone came in. Lithia sat up. Bobby was standing in the doorway. Lithia quickly swallowed any sign of her tears. "So how much of that did you hear?"

"Everything," he answered.

Bobby looked at Lithia's face. No doubt a red mark was rising quickly to her cheek, summing up the conversation.

"I hate that woman," he said. "I hate everything about her. I wish we could just leave, you know. Just jump in Mom and Dad's ship and leave."

"Where would we go? Where would we get your meds if we did that?"

"I wouldn't need meds if it weren't for her."

Lithia was actually fairly convinced of her brother's statement. After all, he hadn't had *issues* before their parents died.

"You're underage. You can't run away. They would come after you."

"Then you could just go. I could follow later when I'm old enough. I could find you."

This was probably the most noble and caring thing Bobby had ever said to her.

"I couldn't do that. I can't just leave you here. You'd bear the brunt of her warpath."

Lithia hated to put down one of her brother's rare moments of teenage selflessness, but it was true. She put a smile in her voice that she in no way felt. "Either we both get out of here or neither of us does."

She couldn't wait for the day they could just take off in her ship and go back to Venus or wherever.

Bobby patted Lithia on the knee and grinned playfully. "Now clean up that makeup. You look like a whore."

CHAPTER 22

If Everyone Knew They Could Change the World

THE UNITED PLANETS of Earth had recalled the *Enigma* and her captain back to the skies over Earth. They needed a face-to-face with both the man who had carried out the strike against the terrorists from STR1-FE and the man who had ultimately let the survivors escape back into the Frontier.

Cade had been stationed on the *Enigma* for the last nineteen months and had seen Captain Shard command it through several situations that ended uglier than the encounter with the terrorists from STR1-FE at Archer's Agony. The only reason Cade suspected this one was different was because this event was regarded as a failure. The fact was Captain Shard should have been able to keep things from becoming as violent as they did. Now, no matter the cover-ups and propaganda that were published, something of the story would reach the people of the Frontier, and that story had the *Enigma* firing on a group of unarmed civilian ships lead by a SMMC extremist.

Still, Cade doubted Shard was in any real danger. The UPE navel structure needed, and actively rewarded, men like Shard. And after a few levels of functionaries had had their hands on the report, Cade was sure it would say exactly what they needed it to to slap Shard on the wrist and send him back out into the Frontier.

Cade was another story. He had been ordered to report to Lambda headquarters as soon as he had arrived in orbit. The only information he had about his current status was "Under Consideration." He had been ordered to stay in San Francisco and not to contact anyone in the government or the navy, but beyond that, he had been given complete freedom.

As he walked through the small hangar where his personal Dagger-Class fighter was kept, his order wore on his mind. He quickly ran through the flight pre-checks in his neural link as he walked along-side the long, angular craft. It was no wonder these small, one-manned fighters had been dubbed "Daggers." They were sleek and sharp with two wings that protruded from either side and swooped forward in a slicing motion. Every aspect of UPE ship design followed the same philosophies as their commanding ranks: fast, efficient, and lethal.

Cade looked down over San Francisco from the seat of his Dagger. Normally he would be happy to see his home again, its towering build-ings that extended far above the clouds, its sprawling land mass that reached out beyond the edge of the old bay, its monolithic seismic sta-bilizers that had made it all possible. But today Cade saw no beauty in this city that, despite not having lived in it for years, he still considered home. His return was not after a mission well done; this was no joyous homecoming. Instead, it was a forced return where the best he could hope for was a reprimand for his actions aboard the *Enigma*.

His supervisors had not been pleased. He had submitted the report of the events that had transpired during the *Deviant Rising* incident. They had felt, at best, that Cade had overstepped his authority in forg-ing the release orders. Nothing he had said could convince them that nothing more could be gained from their detention, and that Shard had lost sight of the bigger picture. They had asked why he hadn't had the prisoners executed if there was nothing more to be gained from them. Cade argued the loss of life would ultimately hurt the mission. He knew it was easier to discredit a survivor than a martyr. They had commended him on his concern for human life, a hollow commen-dation from an organization that had thought killing the *Rising*'s crew was a better option.

They ordered Cade to return to Earth for debriefing and evalua-tion. So that is what Cade did. He landed his Dagger at a small public pad about a mile away from his destination, if you didn't count vertical distance. He took an elevator to one of the lower streets; this level was the original street level of San Francisco.

As Cade walked down the streets bathed in a perpetual twilight, he thought to himself that the age of the properties was probably little comfort to the poverty-stricken people who lived here. The farther down he went, the cheaper the property became, and, as a result, the more desperate the people. Despite everything, Cade liked it down there. He felt things were more honest; if someone stabbed you in the back, they didn't smile in your face while doing it.

As Cade walked through the gloomy Undercity, it began to rain. Cold water poured from the lips of upper streets. It made everyone head indoors. Not that it was really all that much better for most of them. By the time Cade found his way to the stately church, the streets were deserted.

Cade pushed his way through the double doors of Grace Cathedral. He instantly felt the warmth that his current situation had deprived him of as the thick, earthly smell of sage washed over him. The main chapel was filled with people. Cade took a place at the back row, and his eyes were drawn up to the few remaining stained-glass windows that lined the chapel. Most had been broken over the years, but a few had survived. Cade quickly found his favorite. It depicted a man with shaggy white hair and piercingly intelligent eyes. As Cade stared, he could almost believe Albert Einstein was staring back at him from the window, his famous equation etched into the glass beneath him.

Grace Cathedral was home to the Magdalenes, not out of reverence for anything in Christianity, but to remind people of the importance of historical preservation. The sect gathered histories and preserved them for future generations. It was said that the last three hundred years of humanity's history had been recorded and stored in the giant server bank in the old Chapel of the Nativity. That had to be untrue.

He was only half-listening to the familiar middle-aged woman preaching from the pulpit as he scanned the rows of pews, watching faces and trying to see the people behind them.

"You are all singular unique beings, but those in power act to hide the truth. They create a world where your potential is suppressed. Your capacity for action hindered . . . hindered because they fear you. They fear what you could do because the alternative is a world where everyone has the ability to change that world. We look back at the past, we look up at the stars, and we look forward into the future as we've done for centuries. But it is not in these places that we find our celestial gift. The truth reveals itself when you look within yourself and find a vision and purpose for your spirit. Something that invigorates you with the spark of life, and something that you have a burning desire to become.

"The average and mediocre man has spent his life majoring in minor things. He'll never reach his purpose because he has allowed his fears to paralyze him. He has allowed the world to tell him he is powerless to change his life, let alone the world. The beauty of his dreams will slip away, back to the noise of the universe in which it came.

"Nurture what is inside you as much as, if not more than, you nuture outside pursuits. Plant the seeds you need to grow a healthy crop of self-enlightenment. Take the time to make yourself large in your own estimation, and so will you be in the estimation of the world.

"So, friends, look into yourselves and throw off the lies you've been told your entire lives and take charge. Take charge of yourselves and change the world around you. Every one of you has this power; the power to grow yourselves into something large that can reach out and make a change.

"How very bad it would be for those in power if everyone knew they were just as capable of changing the world. How very disruptive would it be for people to know that we, all of us, have absolutely amazing powers. There's no wonder *out there* that can compare to what's inside all of you. Don't let that go to waste. Don't let them cram you into the little box they've made for you."

The priestess was wrapping up her sermon and Cade tried to keep a low profile. How many of the churchgoers would be capable of understanding what she was saying? Cade glanced down at his bionic arm. He understood it all too well. He had seized the opportunities life had offered him, and there was little doubt that he had made changes in the world, but at what cost?

His attention was brought back to the priestess as she wished everyone a safe journey home. Everyone began to file out. Cade looked at her, meeting her eyes for a moment. She was in her early forties and still possessing a beauty that age hadn't diminished. When everyone was gone, she came and sat beside him. "Welcome back. How did bringing the light of civilization to those who don't want it go?"

Her tone was harsh, but something in her eyes smiled, and Cade knew she was glad to see him. Something in that smile stirred something deep in Cade. Something he could barely register, but it warmed him. Cade tried not to meet her eyes. Instead, he fixed them on the large steel cross at the front of the church. It was covered in wires, running down from it, which connected to little stations on the backs of the pews. "Not so good."

"I can't say I'm surprised," she said. "We've been hearing rumors. Nothing reliable, of course, but still, information finds its way to us sooner or later."

"Should you be telling me that?" Cade asked.

"Cade . . . if you were going to turn us in to Lambda, you would have done it a long time ago. I know I can tell you things and not fear that cybernetic soldiers will come knocking on the door."

"They wouldn't knock, Tarja."

"That's a relief. I was afraid they might come when no one was here to let them in."

Cade smiled. Tarja always had a playful way of dealing with him.

"So long as we are on the subject of the Lambdas, there is something I wanted to talk about with you."

The briefly lived smile dropped from Cade's face almost as quickly as it had appeared. It wasn't common for Tarja to want to talk about Cade's work, and when she did, things got complicated. Right now, things were more complicated than he was happy with, but whatever it was, it was bound to be important.

"Come with me. I need to show you something," she said.

She led him to a vaulted doorway in the back of the church, down a long flight of stone stairs. She led him to an ice-cold room lined with servers, with a giant holographic screen in the middle. The giant storage banks humming away along the walls did nothing to diminish the grandiosity. Painted over the entirety of the walls was a depiction of a Middle Eastern family in some sort of barn surrounded by onlookers.

"That's new. What is it?" Cade inquired.

"Oh, some of my students reproduced the mural behind that bank of servers. They felt it would bring something to the room. And I suppose it is history of a sort."

Tarja went over to the server bank and ran her hands over the painted stars depicted there. "So simple. No more than points of light.

It makes you wonder how such a thing could inspire generations of men and women to achieve so much. I wonder, if we had vivid nebulae here, like the ones over Solace or Strife, would we have reached them sooner?" It was true that space in the Frontier was more vivid and colorful than around Earth. She took a moment to shake herself from her contemplations. "But that's not what I brought you here to see."

With that, she headed for the main screen surrounded by machines. Cade knew it was at least one hundred years old. "So, you know ever since the Helix went up, we've been anonymously uploading parts of our archives to it, right?"

"Yes."

"Well, with the last batch, my students noticed something interesting. But I'm getting ahead of myself. A few weeks ago, they found some old books in what we think was a children's school not too far from the cathedral. One of the books was about the American Revolution."

"The American Revolution? I've never heard of it."

"Neither had we. We looked through everything we have and found nothing . . . nothing at all. Not a single reference. But these books must have been six or seven hundred years old. And we don't have much else going back that far."

"Okay, so you found a new piece of history. There is nothing all that unusual about that," he said. What was she getting at?

"That's not the unusual thing. We archived the books and then put them in a packet for anonymous upload to the Helix, but when we went to check how far it had saturated, we couldn't find it. Like it had been deleted from the Helix Network."

"Could it have been a mistake?" he asked.

"That's what we thought. So we tried uploading just those books, and again, nothing. They just weren't there. Something was removing them. So we checked our database against our uploads and found many things were missing. They'd been removed."

"That shouldn't be possible. Only a high-ranking Lambda agent could remove something from the Helix once it's been uploaded."

"Exactly. So we did a bit of digging around and found something disturbing. All around the Helix, things that should be aren't there. It's as if something has been systematically purging information."

"What kind of information?"

"News and history and technical information, mostly having to do with wars and revolutions."

"That can't be right. If Lambda was doing anything like this on the scale you suggest, someone would have noticed by now."

"Not if they've been doing it for centuries."

Her suggestion caught Cade dead in his tracks; the idea was haunting.

"That's not possible." Cade had to defend his organization; flawed as it was, it still served a vital purpose. "Neither Lambda nor the Helix Network have been around that long."

The priestess continued, unfazed, "Then they inherited a mission or goal from a previous group and network. Maybe this goes back to the original interwebs . . ."

She had to be wrong. Even his organization had limits. The scale she was talking about was far beyond anything Lambda would be comfortable with. The risk of discovery was too great. No, there had to be some other explanation. Lambda wasn't perfect, but it wasn't some shadowy organization sweeping things from history. "It's just not possible, and even if it were, what would Lambda have to gain from something like this? Honestly, this whole thing sounds like the plot to a bad science fiction movie."

"Cade, you're a genetically modified and artificially enhanced member of a government agency that doesn't officially exist. Your life is a bad science fiction movie." She took a deep breath and sighed. "Can you just look into it? If you're right, and it's not Lambda, then isn't it something Lambda needs to know about? Shouldn't they investigate?"

"I'll see what I can find. But I don't expect it to be anything." Tarja smiled at him as he turned to walk out. He briefly returned it, and then he was gone, fading into the shadows.

As Cade made his way back to the landing structure and climbed back into his Dagger for the trip to Lambda headquarters, the priestess's words floated around in his head. He would investigate if just to prove she was seeing a conspiracy in one of the only places Lambda didn't have one. They didn't purge information; they didn't need to. They had methods that were either subtler than that or much more direct. Either way, it didn't fit.

Cade piloted his Dagger through the space between the two cities, above and below. The trip to the Lambda HQ was quick, and as Cade maneuvered in for a landing on the roof between two other identical crafts, his mind was brought back to his initial problems. His status loomed heavily in his mind. He still had to report for his final hearing, though, and after his little trip to see Tarja, curiosity was quickly getting the better of him

CHAPTER 23

The Helix and the Pentagram

A THOUSAND DIFFERENT things were cascading across Cade's mind. He had so many things he could or should be focusing on, but for some reason, following through on Tarja's hunch was the only one that seemed tangible at the moment. Maybe that was for the better. Maybe descending into the Lambda archives was a better use of his time then idling around waiting to be debriefed by his superiors.

After numerous, tedious security checkpoints, Cade rode an elevator down into the bowels of Lambda HQ. The Lambda Helix-Node was deep underground, even deeper than the lowest parts of the Undercity. It took the elevator some time to descend into Earth, lunging toward the planet's core. When the lift finally came to a stop, Cade stepped out into an unremarkable beige hallway. It was dimly lit by thin lines of light-emitting wire running along the edge of the ceiling. The entire structure looked vacuum molded, as if a hot wax was poured into a crucible, and when it had dried, these featureless, edgeless hallways remained. He didn't pass anyone as he walked down the twisting corridors looking for a door labeled NODE. No one worked on this level, and very few people ever had need to be here. It was only his third trip down to these levels. Lambda kept all sorts of little secrets down here. Maybe that was the most ominous part. As he passed sealed door after sealed door, he began to wonder how many other Lambda—how many other people—knew what went on behind these archways.

The Helix-Node was in its own climate-controlled room at the end of the hall, and Cade felt a chill as he entered, much like the one in the Magdalenes' server room. The node itself was not very big, but it was still impressive. It was kept in a clear acrylic tube maybe twice the height of a man and just wide enough to get your arms around. Inside was a hexagonal metallic sphere about the size of a soccer ball. It was suspended in a green tinted liquid and had a single cable plugged into the bottom that ran out into a type of hub that had at least a dozen other cables running out from it. Each of these cables was plugged into a different jack along the walls of the room—all but one cable, which plugged into an old-style terminal with a keyboard and a screen just in front of the tube that housed the apparatus. This node was a top-of-the-line unit and had theoretically infinite storage and transmission capacity. Cade walked up to it and removed a cold chrome device about the size of a deck of cards from his coat. He ran a wire from the device to a jack on the node. He didn't actually need this device to interface with the machine. His own neural implants were more than capable of doing the job, but the device allowed him to make an external copy of any information he found. The keyboard and screen in front of him were really more of an obstacle than an interface for Cade. Rather than typing a string of commands, he simply connected to the node wirelessly.

A holographic interface wrapped itself around his field of view. A network of branches interconnected together with clusters and nodes stretched out into the distance in all directions. It always disoriented him at first. It was a floating sensation, like being plunged into warm water.

After the sensation passed, Cade found himself looking down at a holographic projection of the solar system. Each of the planets in the Sol system were represented by an icon with a series of statistics floating beneath it. These numbers and variables gave information about how many connections each of these worlds currently had and how the data was being sent through the Helix Network as a whole. Any one of these planetary icons was expendable, but Cade shifted his focus to Earth's. As he zoomed, the little icon for the planet slowly grew into something akin to an atomic lattice structure. It was a highly organized shape with hundreds of smaller spheres arranged as a hexagonal prism. These represented the world nodes that made up the backbone of the Helix

Network for the planet. As Cade zoomed further and further into the massive network, little wispy, light-blue lines started to appear.

The deeper he went into the structure, the more and more these wisps dominated his field of view, until they were everywhere, like billions of tiny fireflies swarming around in a massive hurricane. These were the individual users of the Helix. Every one of these tiny specks of dust was a man, woman, or child wearing a Helix earring, and their motion through the space Cade was observing represented not only where they were in the world, but also what they were accessing. Cade could expand any one of these tiny points of light and see every thought, feeling, hope, and fear of the person it represented. Each one of these ticks was, in a very real sense, a world unto its own that could be expanded just like Cade was doing with the nodes themselves. The whirlwind was almost overwhelming, so Cade focused hard on only the hubs, which now were the size of the moon in his field of view. Eventually the cyclones of users faded away, and Cade was left with a single yellow sphere that represented the node he was physically standing in front of under Lambda headquarters.

A list of commands popped out from the side of the globe he was viewing. Cade had options to do almost anything, but the one he wanted was "upload."

The Helix itself interfaced with memories, thoughts, and feelings from each user. Only a Lambda with Cade's level of clearance had control over what he was uploading. This was done for security reasons, but this also allowed Cade to be very judicious about what he put into the system.

Cade considered for a moment. He had to put out the right bait if he was going to catch Tarja's data purger in the act.

Eventually, he settled on something Tarja told him about: a text account of some old protest in the city. The overall goals of this protest were something of a mystery, but it seemed they thought by blocking streets and shutting down trains, they could achieve it. He thought about the report he read, and mentally uploaded it back into the network.

He wanted to see if anyone or anything would grab it. He saw the packet's icon move through the network to the next node. It copied itself, then sent the copies out to all of its possible connections, where it repeated the process.

It wasn't long before the packets, represented by little envelope icons, filled his entire view, having stretched out far and deep into the Helix Network.

Nothing came to find or purge these random packets. Was Priestess Tarja mistaken? If someone connected to the Helix was trying to delete or suppress information, surely they would have found the report he had released. Maybe Tarja had her facts wrong. Maybe he needed something less random. Something more specific . . .

Cade created another packet, this time a section of the history book the priestess had presented to him entitled *The American Revolution*.

He cast the packet out into the network. Immediately, the nodes lit up in response. As the packet copied and replicated itself, a symbol he had never seen before emerged deep in the distance. A Helix with an upside-down star around it began to search through the structure. What the hell was this? It started to attach itself to the nodes his packet had been copied to. It purged the data. Maybe Tarja wasn't nuts after all. Maybe there was someone or something inside the network. Clearly they were intent on purging information on this revolution.

This gave Cade the opportunity he needed. Only members of Lambda had access to Helix log files. The hope was that if something should ever take the Helix offline, Lambda would be able to recover it and piece it back together.

After the little Helix star scanned Cade's packet in the current node, it moved on to another.

Cade mentally pulled up another interface, but this time the list of commands and options that floated in his view weren't for the Helix-Node. These were his own personal lines of code. Among the commands for data creation, scanning, and movement was one, a personal addition to his software that Lambda was unaware of. The command was labeled "mask," and its intent was simple. As Cade triggered it, a slight tingling sensation ran all over his body. As far as the Helix was concerned, he was no longer there. It would still respond to any commands he gave it, but it wouldn't know it was doing so. Any command it received would be perceived as coming from some random remote location, and even then, only as long as it was performing the action. Afterward, any action it took would conveniently fail to be logged in its history.

Now that Cade was effectively invisible, he allowed himself to slowly drift down to where the pentagram-like icon was busy scanning through another node. He needed to be careful, because while the Helix itself couldn't see him, he didn't know if whatever this program was had special security measures above and beyond the usual.

Cade studied the program for a moment. It didn't appear to take any notice of him, but the real test of that was coming. He concentrated on it for a moment, willing its terminal access to manifest for him.

Again the icon seemed to take no notice of him as the list swam into view for Cade. He browsed through the options for a moment before instructing it to display its internal file structure for him. Cade's hope was that it would have records of everything it had purged from this node, but what he found was far more extensive.

There were petabytes of data imprisoned inside. Most of the purged information was indeed historical; Tarja was right. According to this program's log, there were deleted entries from virtually every time period, stretching as far back as the records for the Sumerians.

But why? Out of fear it would give people ideas? He considered for an idle moment.

The prospect shocked him like a bolt of lightning. This couldn't have been something recent. No, it would have taken decades, maybe longer, to have removed this much history from public knowledge with no one noticing. He had to grab a record of the log. He had to grab as much of it as he could before unplugging. He began downloading the files.

- c. 2380 BC (short chronology): A popular revolt in the Sumerian city of Lagash deposes King Lugalanda and puts the reformer Urukagina on the throne.
- 570 BC: A revolt breaks out among native Egyptian soldiers, giving Amasis II opportunity to seize the throne.
- 49–45 BC: Julius Caesar crossed the river Rubicon, leading part of the Roman army, and marched on Rome. After overthrowing and assuming control of the Pompeian government, he was proclaimed dictator.

- 1642–1660: The English Revolution, commencing as a civil war between Parliament and the king, and culminating in the execution of Charles I and the establishment of a republican commonwealth, which was succeeded several years later by the Protectorate of Oliver Cromwell.
- 1775–1783: The American Revolution establishes independence of the thirteen North American colonies from Great Britain, creating the republic of the United States of America.
- 1979–2046: Mid-twenty-first-century occupation of the Middle East. A series of wars by the western nations for control over the regions of central and western Asia.
- 2067–2067/2076–2081: Both lunar rebellions, led by Carol Walton, and later by her son Richard, attempted and failed to establish the lunar colonies as independent entities from the United Nations of Earth.
- 2104–2116: The War of Martian Aggression; invasion and occupation of Earth by Martian independent conglomerate, eventually leading to the United Planets of Earth.

The list went on and on. The progress bar on his download slowly crept forward, and Cade watched it intently. Each percentage represented thousands of files, pictures, video, and text associated with their historical entry, and for some reason someone wanted it hidden.

Cade was so transfixed by what he was seeing that he almost didn't notice the slight pressure building in his head. It wasn't quite like a headache. It was more like someone or something was gently but firmly trying to press something through his skull.

He had never come under attack like this in the field before, but all the same, something was trying to break through his firewalls. But that shouldn't have been possible. To attack him, something would have to know he was there.

Cade looked around, both with his eyes and with those subtle senses that being directly interfaced with the Helix gave him, but he found nothing. The only other thing there with him was the icon with the pentagram, and it was still busy scanning files . . . except hadn't it already scanned those?

Cade turned back to the progress bar. It currently read 13 percent and was starting to slow down. The files he was downloading now were from only about a hundred years ago, and contained far more data than the simple scans of books and ancient vid files from earlier eras.

As Cade considered the situation, the pressure in his head multiplied. Whoever was attacking him had clearly grown tired of subtlety and wanted to get through as soon as possible.

Cade focused on reinforcing his blocks and turned back to the progress bar. It was at 18 percent now, but where it had been moving slowly before, it now seemed to have stopped. He looked at the file it was trying to move. It wasn't all that large, just a few hundred gigs, nothing that should be slowing down like this. Whatever was attacking him was also trying to stop his download. It's what he would do. Figure out that your adversary has an objective and force them to focus on that while you attack.

The worst part was that it might work. Cade could force the download to resume and keep going, but to do that he would have to divert attention and energy away from his own defenses, and he was very reluctant to do that.

Still, maybe he had another option. Something his attacker wouldn't see coming. He looked around again, finding the icon. It was definitely moving closer to him, but that's what he expected. Cade pulled up his own command list again and selected one of the options. His virtual left hand started glowing white, and with his glowing hand stretched out in front of him, Cade drifted down to the icon.

The icon stopped what seemed like inches from him and just held there, no longer scanning, instead seeming to be at a loss for what to do next.

Cade wasn't going to give it much time to work it out, though. He reached out, grasping the icon with his glowing left hand and watched as it seemed to shudder.

The pain in Cade's head became an explosion, and he almost lost control. His walls almost came down, and he didn't even know what that would mean for him. On the other hand, his progress bar jumped to 19 percent. It had worked. Whoever was attacking him was doing so through the icon, and he had forced them to react. Cade had hurt it, probably not very much, but he didn't have to. He only had to hurt it enough that defense was as much on its mind as his. Cade continued driving his fingers into the icon. The sensation was not unlike forcing his hand through hard clay, but ever so slowly his hand sank in. It was now his will against its. The only difference between him and it was that he didn't care about winning, only lasting long enough to download as much of the data as he could.

His hand sank deeper and deeper, almost up to the wrist, and the icon's shuddering grew more violent. For a moment, Cade thought he could actually win this battle of wills against whoever was striking through the icon. The pain in his head was lessening, and his download had reached 20 percent. Then he felt it. His mind came into contact with something enormous. A will beyond his ability to measure, and somehow he knew that, until this moment, it had only been aware of him in the way you are of an itch, or an ant climbing up your arm. But now its complete attention was on him. The entire measure of that awesome will now beat down on him. The pain was worse than anything Cade had ever experienced before and he recoiled before that awareness could destroy him.

This thing, whatever it was, was tearing through his defenses like a medieval ballista through rice paper, and once it got through, it would have no problem finding him. The download bar had only made it to 21 percent. He had no choice. He yanked the cord from the node. The hologram around him collapsed and faded away, suddenly tossing him back into the real world. He was standing in front of the Helix-Node in the basement of Lambda headquarters, trying to catch his breath. That was close, too close.

He was pretty sure he hadn't been detected, so he took a couple of seconds to compose himself. He couldn't believe what he had witnessed. Tarja was absolutely right, right about all of it. Something *was* suppressing a staggeringly large historical library. Something was pushing an agenda that made this information dangerous. Something intelligent, something malevolent.

Cade picked up the little card-deck-sized chrome block he had copied the log to. Whatever was now on his device needed to be brought back to the public. But how? If it touched the Helix, it would be purged as fast as it was uploaded. He needed to get back to Tarja and the church.

He felt a sensation go off. It was like a tiny vibration just above his right ear. It was the same sensation someone wearing a Helix earring felt when they got a new message. He saw a little envelope icon pop up in the bottom right portion of his point of view. He focused on it, commanding it to open. It was an order from Lambda HQ to report to Briefing Room 1. Could they know he had jacked into the system? No. It was impossible. They had probably just reached consensus on the events of his mission. They would probably be addressing his next one. If Cade had been merely a man, he may have been afraid, but instead he felt only cold.

CHAPTER 24

Downsize with Extreme Prejudice

WHEN CADE REACHED the room, two Lambda soldiers flanked the door, both at attention with hands near their side arms. This was nothing all that unusual, but Cade decided to take note of it anyway. "Just in case" was Lambda's unofficial motto. One of the soldiers opened the door and beckoned Cade into the room. Cade was surprised to see that nobody was inside. The guard closed the door behind him. He noted the soft click of a lock being turned. Cade looked across a long conference table. At the seat that should have contained his section chief, a formless human shape flickered into existence.

"They send a hologram to do my debriefing?" Cade asked, but before he had time to wonder what that might mean, the hologram spoke.

"Please sit down, Agent Cade."

Cade complied, trying to make out some facial features on the polygonal head of the hologram. This had to be Lambda Prime, and if it was, that was a very bad thing. If Lambda Prime was involved, even by proxy, it could only mean Cade was looking at something much worse than a reprimand.

Despite not having eyes, the figure seemed to look right into Cade as it spoke. "You have served Lambda loyally for many years, but your recent actions put into question your suitability for continued operations."

Cade knew what was coming before Lambda Prime said it. "I am afraid the decision has been made to deactivate you." This meant death, and Lambda Prime said it as easily as firing a secretary.

As the hologram flickered out of existence, the door opened and the two guards reentered the room. Now their side arms were in their hands, and they were pointed right at Cade.

"You understand that there is nothing personal about this," one of the guards said, stepping forward with his gun trained on Cade's chest.

Cade stepped forward, pressing against the gun. He met the eyes of the guard that spoke. "I appreciate that. That's why I won't kill you."

The guard smirked, clearly not understanding his danger. By the time he did, Cade had slipped between the two men. The smirk dropped from the guard's face and he watched in mute terror as Cade revealed his bionic arm and it reconfigured itself, revealing a long thin blade. Cade pierced the first guard's shoulder, making the man drop his side arm to the floor with a clatter. Before the second guard had time to react, Cade's blade had extended into his stomach. The second guard's face went white as Cade removed the blade. The guard moved his hands up to clutch at the wound and dropped to the floor. Cade knelt and scooped up both guards' side arms. Both men would live, which was more than could be said for him if he didn't get out of the building quickly. He slid the guns into his coat pockets and ran for the exit.

Cade moved as quickly as he could down the halls and stairways that made up the labyrinthine Lambda building, while not attracting any unusual attention.

If he could get out of the building before more guards showed up, he could disappear into the Undercity and escape.

Cade was heading for the lobby by a circuitous route that avoided any locations where his identity would be scanned. If he walked through a scan point unaccompanied by either of the two guards he had left bleeding in the conference room, it would bring up red flags.

Things were going well as he reached the eighth floor, the lowest you could reach the lobby from directly. Cade was just about to head down the spiral staircase that lined the lobby when the alarms sounded. They must have found the guards. Cade ducked into a nearby supply closet.

Cade waited to hear the sounds of booted feet in the hall outside, but he heard nothing. He amplified his hearing to be sure. No, there was no one moving in the halls. He activated the thermal sensors in his optic implants. All the heat signatures on this floor were more or less stationary. The functionaries stationed on this floor were staying in their offices like they should, one or two huddling under their desks. Then, the pressure he'd felt in his head earlier returned. But it wasn't anything close to what he had encountered at the node. Lambda must have been trying to locate him through his Helix. Luckily, he had never deactivated his "mask" program.

Cade stepped from the closet. For the time being, at least, he was safe in the open. The building would be on lockdown now. Every internal door would be sealed. But the lobby doors would remain open. They couldn't allow the outside to see that something was wrong, which meant the lobby was still his best option for escape.

Cade walked down the hall to the glass windows that overlooked the lobby. As he looked down, he saw it wasn't deserted. Guards were running up the large spiral staircases on either side of reception, trying to get to the nearest elevator and their emergency stations. Some would be reporting to security to start forming teams that would sweep the building looking for him.

Cade's keen eyes swept the lobby for any pertinent information, anything that might play a role in his escape. The first thing he spotted was an elevator with a large "Out of Order" light above it. Cade made a note of it. The next thing he noticed was the receptionist shaking behind his desk. Good. He wasn't a combatant.

The window tint along the entryway blocked the view from the outside, showing anyone who passed a recorded image of the lobby with people going about their business.

There was a huge UPE flag hanging under him, its blood-red pyramid and hexagonal pattern standing out starkly against the night-black background. The flag hung almost all the way to the floor from a pole protruding from the wall just above the window Cade was looking through; this was his way to the ground. He would have preferred using the elevator, but in this situation, they would all be locked down. Same with the vent access. Normally Cade could have easily bypassed these lockdowns as a matter of course, but with his termination order, his access codes would have been nulled, so this was it.

He checked the ammo in the two pistols he had grabbed from the guards, and seeing they were both full, he replaced them in his coat. He punched through the window in front of him. Reaching out with his bionic arm, Cade grabbed the flag. He leaped from the window, clutching the flag and riding it down. It tore as his hand sliced it on his way down.

He was forced to drop the last ten feet. As he rose from his landing crouch, he surveyed the lobby again. This all seemed to be too much for the receptionist; his eyes had gone wide and blank in shock before he passed out. Cade ran past him and to the huge glass-paned double doors that made up the front wall of the building. Rather than stopping to see if the doors were locked, Cade whipped the pistols from his coat and shot at the windows; they cracked, and he used his running momentum to crash through. Leaping and rolling to shield himself from the shattering reinforced glass, Cade came up in a crouch, both pistols gripped in his hands, and looked up. To his astonishment, he wasn't alone.

"Stand up and drop the guns, Cade!" Shard's voice rang out in the office square. He was standing about twenty feet from where Cade crouched, and he was flanked by several soldiers bearing the *Enigma* crew patch. From behind, four AEDs had their large mounted Gatling guns aimed directly at Cade. How had they gotten there so quickly? Lambda must have figured Cade wouldn't go quietly and had set his former captain to stop him in the most visible way possible.

Cade stood slowly, allowing his guns to drop from his hands. He hadn't given up just yet, but as strong and fast as Cade was, he was no match for a volley of bullets on the scale Shard's force could bring to bear. "All right, Captain. I've dropped my weapons."

Shard drew his side arm and approached Cade with slow deliberation. "Cade, I always suspected you would be deactivated one day. You were always just a little too softhearted to be a good Lambda."

Shard stood right in front of Cade, his gun pressed against his temple. "You caused me a great deal of embarrassment. You almost cost me my command!" There was something manic in Shard's voice, something of his inner madness and savagery. "And now I'm going to deactivate you, Cade. I have dreamed of doing this for weeks now."

"You're not going to kill me, Shard," Cade said with more confidence than he actually felt, but it had the desired effect. As Shard took a very small step back, trying to figure out what ace in the hole his former Lambda officer had, Cade sprung forward.

He seized Shard's gun arm and wrenched it, pulling Shard in close. "You will never kill me, Captain. You don't have the spine. You are more than ruthless enough to make a good UPE pawn—nice and brave when you are in a position of power, but when someone with real nerve and courage doesn't blink, you flinch. And when you flinch, I win."

Cade, gripping Shard by the throat and wrist, slowly backed into Lambda HQ. "Everyone stay where you are, or I will end this piece of slime right here in the plaza!"

The statement was a formality, as none of Shard's men would dream of firing without his direct order. Sometimes the proprieties must be observed, and besides, Cade couldn't resist driving Shard's situation home just a little. The only problem was once he was back in the lobby, he still had no escape plan. It was only a matter of time before someone gave the kill order, regardless of his hostage. Right now, Cade was on top; that, after all, was what Lambda had trained him to do.

As they moved through the lobby, still staring down Shard's dumbstruck troops, Cade shifted his grip on Shard's wrist just enough to snatch the gun he was still clutching and slipped it into his coat. "You made me drop mine, after all."

"Keep it, Cade. You're still dead."

Cade wanted to say something, but then he had it—he knew how he was getting out of the building. He dragged Shard over and up the spiral staircase to the out-of-order elevator. The moment he let go of Shard, he knew the onslaught of bullets would begin. Carefully, not letting go of Shard's throat, Cade used his bionic arm blade to lever open the doors to the elevator shaft. The elevator was caught between floors several levels below him. That was good; it would make what he was planning a little easier.

Cade reached out and grabbed one of the lift cables for the elevator and pulled himself in, releasing Shard and shoving him down the stairs. As Shard fell, Cade heard him give the order to fire. And the area was drenched in bullets. Cade was already in the shaft, though, and cutting the other lift cable. As the cable gave way, Cade shot up the shaft, gripping with all the strength his real arm could muster. He needed his bionic one for the stop.

As Cade reached the top floor of the Lambda building, he was dimly aware of the elevator car crashing to the bottom. Cade was focused on the millisecond timing he would need to hook his fingers into the shaft doors and stop his ascent, or very quickly it would turn into a descent.

He almost missed his mark, his bionic fingers colliding with the almost imperceptible crack between the doors, but he got purchase and was able to pry the doors open.

The floor he was on now led to the landing pads. As he quickly moved down the hall to that door, he heard the sounds of people readying weapons and giving orders. All the guards would be rushing to the lobby right now. He approached the bend in the hall where his ambush was near. He once again extended his arm blade and drew Shard's gun.

As Cade turned the corner, he dived forward, firing Shard's pistol until the clip was empty. The answering fire was deafening, with bullets whizzing past his head and catching on his coat as he moved down the hall. When he hit the ground, he rolled, coming up in the middle of the group of waiting soldiers, his blade flashing, cutting into body armor and flesh with equal ease.

The sounds of gunfire died down. Cade had the leisure to look at what he had done. There had been ten soldiers lying in wait for him. Cade had gotten four of them with the gun in his mad dive, and the rest had fallen to his blade. Cade noticed one of the surviving soldiers, a man now missing a leg, pulling himself toward an assault rifle that had been dropped during the battle. Cade walked over and casually kicked him in the temple. The man went limp, and Cade stepped over him and out the door, thankful he didn't have to kill him.

Cade ran out onto the pad, quickly spotting his Dagger-Class fighter. He sent the command to power up.

Cade ran to the edge of the pad and looked down. The building was just at the edge of the landfill and overlooked the dark waters of the bay far below. He only had a moment to consider before sending the command for the ship to lift off and head out over the bay. Once his ship was in the air, he stepped out over the ledge and plummeted into the ocean below.

He felt the impact like a sledgehammer against his whole body. Everything was dark as he plunged down. When he finally surfaced, he saw several military craft chasing his little hopper. He ran it through every evasive maneuver he could think of remotely while he treaded the waters below. He had to make the chase convincing before allowing them to score a serious hit. Cade watched as his old hopper exploded in a bout of fire, pieces dropping into the ocean.

The military craft, evidently convinced of Cade's demise, returned to base. Cade wondered how they were going to spin this aerial shootout between the Terraces of San Francisco, with thousands of eyewitnesses, and then remembered they probably wouldn't have to. It would be removed from the Helix Network. Every report on the chase and explosion would be purged. With that grim thought, Cade turned off the implant that allowed him to control the hopper; he wouldn't need that one anymore. He began to swim back to the city.

An hour later, Cade, wet and wounded, staggered into Grace Cathedral. He was clutching an oozing wound on his abdomen that the microscopic machines in his blood were already working to seal. Fortunately, a service wasn't in progress right now, because even the most devoted congregation would have noticed a bleeding man in a wet and torn naval long coat drop into the back pew with a wet splotch and an exhausted sigh. He had left a rusty, wet trail all the way from the side entrance to one of the backmost benches. He sat there for a second, assessing the severity of his injury. It wasn't until she said something that he noticed Tarja looking over him. She wrapped him in a towel. Even he wasn't immune to hypothermia.

He could tell Tarja wanted to say something, to ask what had happened, but years of encounters with him had taught her that he would only talk when he was ready. This was just one of the many things he respected about her. So many others in his experience would have pressed him, even though they knew what his response would be. Perhaps it was because Tarja was a woman with secrets of her own and she knew what keeping them meant to people like him.

When Cade was dry, he leaned back in the pew and gave another sigh. This time it was too much for Tarja.

"You know, we don't normally do confessions, but if you have something to get off your chest, I am here to listen," she said, sitting next to him in the pew.

He rested his head in his hands. "You were right . . . right about the data. Right about everything. Someone's been purging history. I couldn't see how far back it went, but I did manage to grab some of it."

There was a look of disbelief on the priestess's face as Cade spoke, as if she was seeing something that she never expected to see, and it was only then that Cade realized he was shaking. Cade had thought that he had gotten a grip on the worst of the effects of his escape before he came in through the doors of the church, and he didn't like to think about what the shaking meant, either for his physical or mental state. Worst of all, Tarja seemed to be even more aware of his reactions than he was.

"Okay . . . so I get that," she said, a hint of terror in her voice, "But that doesn't explain why you stagger in half-dead with half the bay dripping off that ridiculous coat of yours." She tried to put as much warmth into her voice as possible.

"They were going to terminate me. I had to escape."

The priestess sat back in the pew. The two sat in silence for a few minutes.

"So, if you can't go back, then what are you going to do?" she asked.

"I have to get off Earth. Lambda will figure out I am not dead pretty quickly, and this data does nobody any good if I am captured."

"You have the data with you?" the priestess asked.

Cade reached into his inner coat pocket and pulled out the little chrome box. "One hundred fifty petabytes of it. But I can't upload it here. It would all be purged before I jacked out. I have to get it out beyond the grip of the Helix."

"The Frontier . . ." she said, staring off in thought for a few moments before turning back to him. "I think I know someone who can help. He is an SMMC captain I am in contact with. Captain Pacius. He was on Archer's Agony, last I heard."

"Xander Pacius?" Cade asked, hardly believing it could be the same man who had so changed the course of his life.

"Yes. You've heard of him?" Tarja asked.

"We're acquainted." Cade nodded.

"You never cease to amaze me."

"If he can help us, I won't be able to use the commercial liners to get out there. I'll need a ship, a private one."

"Again, I think I can help. You just leave that to me. I may have just the ship for you. And if so, it'll even come with a pilot," Tarja said, standing up. "Let me take care of the arrangements. You stay here and do a little soul searching. It looks like you could use some."

"I don't think I have a soul left in me anymore," Cade said.

"Of course you do. That is one thing Lambda never could take away from you."

The priestess walked out of the chapel and into a cloister to the side. She turned back briefly as if to say something else, but closed the doors and left Cade alone in the main chapel.

CHAPTER 25

The Dark Nature of Capitalism

GOVERNOR MAHER OF Strife had been to Earth a few times. Frankly, the place scared him. It was nothing like Strife. The people were completely different, and so was the society. It was conservative and broken, as far as he was concerned. San Francisco was a layered city where the rich lived up top and the poor lived down on the old streets. Even with his courage and determination, he'd never visit the Undercity.

It bothered him that plans to determine the future, politics, and government were always made from smoky clandestine meetings in rooms at the top of the tallest buildings. The floor-to-ceiling windows gave the impression that these men looked down on everyone else like gods, immune to the consequences of their decisions. This was not the way things worked on Strife. There, the government wasn't a giant entity or something to be feared. It was a minimal, necessary evil to get people to do what needed to be done to keep the world running, to keep the bridges up, the star lanes working, and to put electricity in people's homes. It didn't tell people who they should be or how they should live their lives. It didn't create incentives or legislate thought, and it would never ever get in the way of people being human.

This is why the Helix Network scared Maher and others like him. As far as Strife was concerned, mandating the use of a technology like this, linking everyone, unknowingly and against their will, was the loss of freedom and humanity. It didn't surprise him that Pacius and others like *him* chose to demonstrate their disgust in the way they did.

Maher had to be more diplomatic, though. He was the one who had to come to Earth, to this smoky clandestine meeting at the top of the tallest building. He was there to remind these men that they were not gods and what they were doing was beyond immoral.

He had been in conferences with the movers and shakers of the United Planets of Earth for most of the afternoon. The room was simple, simpler than he would have expected from the seat of power in the UPE, but considering the nature of that power, perhaps he shouldn't have been surprised.

Most other semi-sovereign colonies had a governing body like a republic or parliamentary democracy. In contrast, the highest seats of power on Earth were gained through capitalistic democracy. The CEOs of the ten most influential corporations on the planet made up its ruling board. It was these men who made all the decisions. It should have come as little surprise that the conference room would favor a cold efficiency over the type of grandeur that even Maher wasn't completely above.

He recognized nine out of the eleven faces sitting at the table when he walked in. They all had been on the board for the last decade or more. But two were new. The first was a dark-skinned man in his late thirties who must have been a recent addition to the assembly. The second was a man standing off to the side of the unknown councilor. Maher had taken the man for an adviser, at least at first, but now that he had stepped closer, he noticed this man looked old, way too old to be a part of this board. His posture was stiff, the cut of his old-fashioned suit too precise, and unless Maher was imagining it, everyone in the room was trying to avoid contact with the man's pale gold eyes.

Who was this guy? Who could inspire fear in these men? There was only one answer, and Maher didn't like it. This man must be a Lambda operative, an observer.

Maher had never been in the same room with a Lambda. He had no experience with these auditors, enforcers, and spies who, if some were right, were the real power behind the UPE.

He had to keep his mind off musing over fringe Lambda conspiracies and remain focused on the situation at hand, though.

Maher sat by the dark-skinned man at one end of the table. His position indicated he was the guy in charge. Maher hadn't known who this man was at the start of the meeting. It wasn't unusual for a relatively "unknown" to have a company hit it big with some new product and then just as quickly disappear as more stable companies cut him back down. Today this person was Benjamin Abel, and he led the discussion. "We were surprised at the reaction from your world. We didn't expect such a hostile response. We've been very gracious to incorporate your world into the Helix."

"Not everyone sees it that way. Most of our people feel that making this type of technology mandatory is an invasion of their privacy, an alienation of their rights. It's this type of thing that caused the protest at the Epsilon Gate earlier this month."

"That's troubling to hear. The Helix is unification. A way to gain consensus over the noise of humanity. We're aiming to bring that harmony to all united worlds. The good it brings is well worth the cost."

"Our culture, our whole way of life, is based on our freedom and self-determination. Many would rather die than relinquish that, and that's what you would be asking them to do."

"Governor, the earrings don't take away the self-determination your world seems so proud of, and certainly no one wants you to die over it."

Maher looked into Abel's eyes, searching for some sense of threat. He wondered if this man had been involved in that disaster, and decided he probably had. Depending on how long he had been the head of the counsel, he may have even been the one who authorized the *Enigma* to take such violent action.

"They see this as one more step to limit their freedom. One more step to control their lives, one more intrusion into their privacy."

"We are not unsympathetic to those concerns." Abel looked around the table. None of the board members seemed even the slightest bit sympathetic, and Maher sincerely doubted they had given a thought at all about the concerns of a planet an incalculable distance away. "But, Governor Maher, you also have to understand our position. We've spent centuries seeding worlds. We understand all too well where unregulated freedom and thought can lead. On every world where the Helix has been mandated, violent crimes have dropped dramatically, and polling the network shows the residents live happier lives overall,"

Abel said, leaning forward in his seat. "Surely, a little less privacy is worth safety, order, and happiness."

"Who the hell are you kidding? In your own city, your people are going toe-to-toe with police over who does and does not have access to the Helix," Maher fired back.

"I remind you, those people are fighting *for* the Helix, Governor. They are fighting to gain access to the device, not against it. We are uniting humanity. There are bound to be a few hitches along the way. The people down there don't yet understand how their lives are going to change because the Helix hasn't come to them yet. A few of them fear the Helix like you do, but most just want it for themselves, and in the coming months and years, we're going to do our best to make sure they get it. And when they do, they will find their lives better and more secure for it. For many, it will be the first security they've ever really known."

"No security is worth giving up the freedoms that can only exist with privacy," Maher lectured. Like every Frontiersman, the idea of giving up their privacy, and by extension their freedom, was a sore subject. The UPE had been chipping away at both for generations, and Maher felt every chip like it had been carved from his soul. "The Helix isn't the unregulated tool for expression you act like it is. It is a private network in which gentlemen, such as yourselves, can aggregate and influence the public. You generate consensus for them by weeding out anything that doesn't fit into the agenda. You reach consensus only by limiting the conversation to what you want, and you force people into arguing only those opinions you decide are acceptable.

"I cannot just stand by and allow these shackles to be forced onto my people, and shackles they are. If given the choice, then some may wear the earrings and be part of the Network. But if you force this on them, then they will resist you like Captain Pacius and his followers. You must know this."

"Captain Pacius was a man with little perspective beyond his bridge, Governor. I sincerely hope he is no longer that blinkered man. I hope the lesson he was taught sunk in, because I doubt he would like another." Maher looked over to the man who had spoken. It wasn't one of the board, but was instead the other unknown man, the one with the pale-yellow eyes, the Lambda. "You two are friends, if I am not mistaken."

When the Lambda spoke, everyone in the room looked over with a rapt attention born out of fear. Everyone except Abel, that is. He was sitting back with profound unconcern. Was it bravado, or genuine courage? If it were the latter, then this man may very well be able to keep his position among the capital cutthroats, or he would eventually just disappear like many around Lambdas had.

Abel smiled. "Now, I am sure a man such as Mr. Maher here would never have anything to do with a man like Xander Pacius. If that is what you are implying."

Maher knew his next words were probably a mistake before he said them, but he couldn't just sit back and listen to this. "Captain Pacius is a noble and honorable man whom I am proud to know. He did what he did because he felt he had to. Because he felt it was right."

"Now that is interesting, Governor," Abel said, leaning forward and appraising Maher. "I am sure you know our intelligence suspects that after Pacius left our custody, he may have joined a group of malcontents and rabble-rousers. At this moment, we believe he may be planning even more acts of civil disruption. If these things are true, then that makes Pacius and his followers very dangerous men."

"No. It is you who are dangerous. They are only victims. You turned them into that when your ship fired the first shot. They were conducting a peaceful demonstration." He was digging his own grave, and he'd be lucky to hold his office for more than a few days after returning to Strife, but it was too late to stop now.

Abel looked at him. "If that's the case, maybe you can help us find him. So all this can be sorted out before things get out of hand."

"I don't know where he is, and if I did, I wouldn't be helping you find him."

The Lambda walked over to the table, taking each step with eerie, calculated precision. "Governor, you've helped us teach him one lesson. Surely, helping us do it again is worth sparing yourself one."

The terrible truth exploded in Maher's stomach, releasing the anxiety and regret of betraying Pacius. The statement tore him open, and the Lambda continued pouring salt into the wound. "Your aid during the Archer's Agony protest was invaluable. Without the time and location, there would have been far more damage, and the consequences would have needed to be much further reaching."

Maher lost the composure he'd had earlier in the discussion. The truth was clear. These men meant to bring the Helix to Strife no matter who or what got in their way.

"I helped you because I believed their protest would do more harm than good. But I no longer believe Pacius was wrong for organizing such a demonstration."

The old man with gold eyes had an almost greenish tinge to his aged, leathery skin. His hair was ghost white and his flesh seemed to hang a little loosely from his skull. "I am very sorry to hear that, Governor, because Pacius was wrong. Those who stood with him were wrong, and those who rally to him now are wrong. Lessons are coming, lessons no one can ignore," the ancient Lambda said, stepping forward to look Maher directly in the eyes. Maher could only meet that gaze for a moment before he had to turn away. There was something about the Lambda's eyes, like an abyss with something terrible lurking at the bottom of it.

"Mr. Maher, please reconsider your opposition to the Helix. It's understandable but misguided. If you have information on the where-abouts of this deeply evil man who is actively opposing the UPE, then you must help us find him." Abel's words did something to help Maher regain some composure, and Maher turned away from the old man's menacing eyes to meet the firm but entirely human ones of Benjamin Abel.

"Let me tell you about true evil. It is to yield. To submit to tyranny and fear. It's to surrender our freedom and dignity. That is true evil."

Maher watched a note of rage come into Abel's eyes for a moment, a quick flash of emotion that he couldn't quite hide. Abel's position was a new one, and because of that, still uncertain. For a man this new to authority, to have it challenged enraged him. It forced him to react or risk showing weakness to the men of this group, who would be looking for any they could find. But let him be angry. Let him feel threatened, and let the other board members pounce on him like jackals in the coming weeks for it.

"Allow me to put it this way, Maher. I have no doubt you care about your people. In order to find Pacius, we may have to go through many of them. Would you trade his one life for a hundred or a thou-sand?" Abel gestured at the Lambda at his side. This wasn't a rhetorical question.

"I refuse to let a question like that be decided by math. I cannot say what one life is worth. Nor can I speak for the thousands, or millions, who may choose to follow that life," Maher said.

"Then, Governor, I believe we have reached an impasse. We will be passing a law mandating that all united worlds adopt the Helix by the end of the year, including STR1-FE." Abel didn't even dignify it by calling it Strife.

Abel stood up; Maher was struck by the sheer size of this man. Terrans were usually shorter than Strifers. When standing, he was easily six and a half feet tall and broadly built to go with it.

"You will be expected to enforce it, Governor, or there will be consequences for your planet and you, personally. This meeting is adjourned."

As Maher stood from his chair and turned from the table, he could feel the Lambda's cold golden stare on the back of his neck. He knew this would come back to haunt him. He just didn't know how or when.

CHAPTER 26

An Offer She Couldn't Refuse

AUNT PETRA WAS gone. She had left for a friend's home and wouldn't be back for several hours. This was almost a daily ritual. She would meet her circle of friends, and there, she would gossip over drinks. Lithia dreaded her return, but the hours she was gone were the best.

Lithia hadn't been back to the church since that day with Vijay. She didn't want anyone to see the bruise that had taken over her cheek, which by now had begun to heal and look less swollen. A little makeup, and no one would notice.

The bruise reminded her of how she needed to get out. Not just down to the church and the Magdalene Gardens but *out* out; off Earth, out and away from her aunt and everything else on this used-up rock of a planet. But she knew that was a fantasy. She couldn't leave, not without Bobby. He would never survive here by himself. Aunt Petra had already driven Bobby into a very dark place, and the medication bracelet he wore was a constant reminder to the people around him that something was wrong. If Lithia left, just took off one day, it might actually kill him.

Several months ago, she had applied to become Bobby's official guardian. The case agent had taken one look at the application and strongly suggested she withdraw it. Since then Lithia had heard nothing more about it and had resigned herself to the idea that she would stay with her aunt and uncle until he came of age and could leave with her. Until then, she would work in the church garden and try to divert as much of her aunt's ire as she could.

Lithia had just finished watering the plants on the windowsill in the kitchen when her earring began to vibrate with an incoming call, so she snapped it in her ear.

The image of High Priestess Tarja was projected into her field of view as if she had been standing right there in the kitchen with her. "Good morning, Lithia," she said. "I haven't seen you around the garden in a while. I'm hoping everything's all right."

Lithia couldn't tell her the truth. She hated to lie and felt no better than her aunt. "My aunt and uncle have had some friends from off world staying with us. I've been entertaining them. Is everything okay with the garden?"

"Yes, of course. It's fine—your friend has really taken to it. The other gardeners have sort of adopted him, in fact." Tarja smiled.

Lithia felt a twinge of pain at the mention of Vijay. She was happy Vijay was doing okay, but hearing that he was still there and doing well seemed to cement for her that things would never be the same again.

"Lithia, I've got a problem that I think you'd be able to solve."

"Oh?"

"I need you to come down to the church as soon as possible. I wish I could tell you more, but it's not something I feel comfortable talking about over the Helix. But I'm sure you'll know what to do."

This intrigued Lithia. What problem could she possibly solve?

"I'll explain as soon as you arrive," concluded Tarja, ending the call. Lithia felt a rush of excitement. She was pretty sure she could get down to the church and back before her aunt got home. Or at least that was the plan as she slipped on her Undercity gear and headed out the door.

This early in the morning, no sunlight reached the Undercity, not even where elevation could usually be counted on to earn a little illumination that wasn't generated by the residents. The amber overhead lights were the only security Lithia had as she made her way to California and Taylor Streets. At the top of the long staircase, one of the large cathedral doors was left open a crack. She looked up at the doors that depicted a reproduction of the Gates of Paradise, a two-by-five grid pattern with reliefs illustrating stories from the Old Testament, a doctrine written almost three thousand years ago and now nearly forgotten by most people. She pushed on the panel depicting Moses leading his people to the Promised Land. The huge heavy door slowly yawned open, letting out a metallic and wooden groan that echoed through the entryway of the church.

The inside of the cathedral was covered in biblical metaphor, and in a very real way, it was Lithia's paradise. The stained-glass windows were dim; the only interior light was coming from a series of candles and chandeliers lit sparsely through the main church. She used the candlelight from small standing chandeliers as beacons as she made her way across the labyrinthine pattern on the floor of the entryway and around the side of the church. There was nobody else there, and the emptiness was somehow foreboding. Lithia had never been to the cathedral so early and had no idea if services and classes were canceled or if it was always so ominous that time of day. A woman in a robe stood at a door in one of the sanctuaries.

"Morning, Priestess. I'm here to see Tarja," Lithia said.

The woman silently ushered her through a door and down a hallway. Like the ones down to the garden, it was made of stone and lit from overhead. There was something much less welcoming about these halls. The air grew colder as they descended down the old flight of stairs. A soft blue light lit the room at the bottom, and an unmistakable electrical humming noise filled the room. Could this be the way down to the server rooms? Nobody but the utmost important people within the church ever came down here. This was the archive of all of the Magdalenes' precious data. Why she was being led down here was anyone's guess.

The priestess directed Lithia to a main room as they parted ways. There was a dry, electrical quality to the air, and her breath was visible with every exhale. The final door looked just as heavy as the Ghiberti at the entrance of the church. These doors were made of a thick wood, lined with iron. There was a palm reader where the old handle used to be. She didn't know what to do but place her hand on it. It scanned her, blinking green before the door unlocked and slowly fell open under its own weight. She still had to push on the door to get through, and it was even heavier than it appeared. Inside, she saw High Priestess Tarja standing in front of a main server bank. It was incredible. Its holographic projection screen was enormous. Cables ran into the room, between bricks, and into small openings in the ceiling. These must be the same cables that plugged into the cross in the main cathedral. Tarja stood talking to a man in a battered trench coat. The guy looked like he had seen better days. His hair was messy, and there was an exhausted, smoky quality to his demeanor.

"And if she doesn't go for it?" he said to Tarja.

"Then I don't know . . . but we'll find a way. We have to find a way to get this out to the 'verse," Tarja replied.

"Someone's here," the man noted as both he and Tarja turned around. The high priestess's face held the weight of concern before snapping back to the same warming smile she usually wore. "Thanks for coming on such short notice, Lithia." She gestured to the man standing next to her. He was as ominous as the dark haze in the cathedral, showing no expression of any kind. The vibe he gave off was ice cold and mechanical, like an engine.

"I want you to meet a very old friend of mine. This is Cade. Caden Path."

The man reached his hand out to greet Lithia. Lithia could feel something wrong with his grasp. His hand was cold, and the way it moved was too precise. There was something about his eyes that made her uncomfortable. She couldn't put her finger on it. Maybe it was how sharp his irises seemed, or the way in which they moved back and forth. They looked like they were scanning her. "You must be Lithia Boson," he said.

"That's me," she answered without hesitation. She was careful to not show fear, although it was hard standing in front of such a large, intimidating man.

"Cade is in a very tight bind, and I think you could help him get out of it."

If Tarja trusted this man, maybe she should. It wasn't easy, though. Something made Lithia instinctively cringe away from him.

"Anything, High Priestess."

"Lithia, please, call me by my first name. You are my finest student, but after all these years, you are also a friend, and what I am about to ask you, I am asking as a friend, not as High Priestess Tarja."

Lithia was honored. The subtle fear she held on the edges of her mind washed away with Tarja's words.

"I'm going to cut to the chase. Cade needs to get to the Frontier quietly. He can't use the Space Liners, and we no longer have any vessels of our own to lend. He's willing to compensate you for safe passage through the Epsilon Gate."

The request shocked Lithia. She had no idea what to say. She thought about it for a second. "I don't know. I don't know if my ship could even make it that far. And my aunt would never let me go."

"I know you're worried, Lithia, so if you say no, I'll understand."

Lithia didn't want to let Tarja down. She had been like a second mother to her. "It would take us the better part of a month. I don't know if I could leave my brother for that long." Lithia hadn't meant to say that last thing. Tarja knew something about Bobby's situation, but not all. Besides that, Lithia really wasn't comfortable having this strange man know anything about her and her family.

"I understand. Most Venusians by your age have already journeyed away from the system as part of their cross into adulthood."

"You're right, but my aunt doesn't exactly let me act like a Venusian."

"Yes, I know. I'm sorry to hear that. Your people have some incredible traditions, and it's a shame she's keeping you from taking part in them."

There was a long disappointing silence. "Cade, we'll have to find another way."

"I'm sorry, Tarja. I'm so sorry," Lithia said.

"Your brother's name is Bobby, isn't it?" This was the first time Cade spoke, aside from his dubious introduction. His voice was raspy and arid.

"Yeah. How did you know?"

"You filed for custody of him not too long ago."

"Yeah. Tarja, who is this guy?" Lithia asked. The mistrust that Lithia had been trying to combat for Tarja's sake came back strong.

"Like I said, he's an old friend of mine. He has connections, some literally, into all sorts of stuff. He still manages to bewilder *me* from time to time." Tarja smiled.

She knew he was something more than a man the moment she met him. No one was saying it, but Lithia was pretty convinced he had something to do with Lambda. The rumors were that everyone involved in their organization had been enhanced. Cade must be what he looked like.

"Lithia, what if I told you I could help you get custody of your brother and pay you enough so you two could fly away from this rock and never look back. You could start over, wherever you want."

She didn't know how to respond. He was making her the offer of her lifetime.

"You could really do that?"

"Ms. Boson—Lithia. If you deliver me to the Frontier, it's as good as done."

"When would we need to leave?"

"Soon. Very soon."

"Within the next day," Tarja interjected. "We need to keep this quiet, and we need to get him away from Terra Luna fast."

"You're not wanted, are you?" Lithia inquired.

Cade avoided the question. "Go home. Pack your things. I promise you I'm not a bad shipmate."

"So you're wanted then . . ."

Tarja and Cade stood silent. It was all the confirmation Lithia needed.

"Let me think about it. I'll get back to you by the day's end."

Lithia left, backtracking up through the dungeon and cathedral. She understood the situation was dire, and even though she didn't trust this strange guy, she trusted Tarja. For an opportunity like this, she was compelled to see it through. It was like an angel had answered her prayers, but felt like she was making a deal with the devil.

CHAPTER 27

Time to Say Good-bye

AUNT PETRA WASN'T home yet, which was good. If Lithia packed her things quickly, maybe she could be gone before anyone noticed. She had already made her decision. She could just leave a note. In fact, she had made her decision to help Tarja's friend during their conversation. Telling them she'd let them know by the end of the day was her way of remaining in control of the situation.

Cade was crafty with his offer, but she wasn't about to let him start calling the shots. After all, they'd be flying her ship, and it was going to have long-term effects on her life.

Lithia walked past Bobby's bedroom. Bobby was awake, or at least she assumed he was, judging from the heavy bass from his sound system that was rocking through the wall. Lithia dug through her closet, throwing clothes into a suitcase.

She had had her pilot's license for a couple months now and had taken her ship on a few short trips to the lunar arboretum on supply runs for the church, but she hadn't decided what to do with it yet. Her father had taught her how to fly when she was a teenager. She checked up on it semi-regularly and even spent a night or two in it, sneaking into the Magdalenes' vault, just to reminisce. But oftentimes, the memories of family outings were still entombed on board and too painful to bear.

Reaching up to a top shelf, she dug through the back of the closet, excavating. She was looking for something in particular—a framed picture. One she had buried up there years ago, in hopes of locking away the memories and emotions held within the image. A picture of Lithia, Bobby, Mom, and Dad. Bobby wasn't much older than five or six when the picture was taken, which meant Lithia was ten or eleven. Mom and Dad looked so happy. They didn't wear the fake small smiles most parents did in family photos. Theirs were genuine. So were Lithia's and Bobby's. The type of innocent smiles from a time before life had gone off into this terrible parallel world. When was the last time she had smiled that widely? She buried the picture, like she had the anguish of her parents' deaths, but something was different now. Maybe it was because she was about to try to carry on her father's legacy. Maybe it was because she was about to fulfill her Venusian heritage. She packed the picture in between a couple jackets in her suitcase.

The bass thundering from Bobby's room morphed into the full echo of music as he opened his bedroom door, making his way down to the kitchen for his normal afternoon refrigerator raid, so Lithia followed Bobby downstairs.

"Oh, hey! I didn't know anyone was home. The house is so quiet," he said.

"Hey. I gotta tell you something."

Bobby eyed the suitcase Lithia wheeled into the kitchen. "Where . . . where are you going?" he asked with a startled expression on his face.

"Bobby, look . . . I gotta go away somewhere for a little while, but when I get back, things are going to be different. A lot different."

"What? Where are you going? How long are you gonna be gone?"

"If I don't tell you anything, then you won't have to lie."

"I lie all the time. I'm a lie-a-holic."

"It's complicated."

"How complicated can it be? I can't believe you're just gonna disappear. How long are you gonna be gone? Aunt Petra is going to be *so* mad," he fired at her in rapid succession.

"About a month and a half," she replied.

"You're going to leave me here alone with Petra and her lap dog for a month and a half? When she finds out you've *temporarily* run away, guess whose balls are going in the salad shooter?"

"I know, Bobby, I know," she tried to empathize, "but you gotta just believe me when I say I'm doing this for both of us. For our own good."

"Doing what? Do you really think she's just going to take you back and act like nothing happened? If anything, she's going to use it as the excuse she needs to keep you out!"

"Calm down. I'd tell you where I was going if I could."

There was a short pause. Lithia could see Bobby's eyes pondering. "You're going on *the journey,* aren't you?" Lithia's hesitation to answer was all the confirmation Bobby needed. "You're taking the ship somewhere."

"Listen, somebody has offered me a lot of money to take them somewhere. Enough money that when I get back, things will be very different."

"Well, I'm glad things will be different for *you.*"

"There's more going on here! I can't explain. You'll just have to believe me." Lithia couldn't risk telling him the truth. She couldn't risk getting his hopes up, or worse, Aunt Petra finding out.

"When I get back, things are going to be a lot better for *both* of us. You just have to trust me, okay?"

Bobby scowled with adolescent melancholy, relenting to her plea. The next month and a half was going to be excruciating for him, and both of them knew it.

"So when Petra flips out on my ass, what am I supposed to tell her?"

"Tell her everything I just told you."

"You haven't told me anything."

"Exactly."

Bobby just stood there. Lithia knew it would be hard for him, but of course he wanted his big sister to go on her journey. Their parents had talked about it all of their lives. The journey each Venusian was supposed to make out to some place in the cosmos as a spiritually enlightening trek.

"How can you just up and leave all of a sudden?" he said, playing with his bracelet.

Lithia didn't know what else to say, so she stepped forward and gave her little brother a hug. "I'll be back before you know it."

"Mom and Dad would be so proud of you," Bobby said. The remark struck a tear in Lithia's heart that boiled up to her eyes. "But for the record, I'm still not happy about this."

Lithia nodded.

"When are you leaving?" Bobby asked, raising a brow.

"I need to talk to someone at the church, and then I'm off," Lithia said. "You've got to trust that I'm doing this for both of us."

"I do," he said.

Lithia grabbed her suitcase and left the room, trying not to look back over her shoulder, but as she stood in front of the house that had been her home for the better part of the last ten years, she began to wonder. She had promised Bobby she was coming back, and he had told her that he thought their parents would have been proud of her, but at this moment, as she was leaving her brother behind with their aunt and uncle, she wondered if either of those things were actually true.

Lithia walked through the labyrinthine gardens of Grace Cathedral. She was looking for Vijay. Tarja said the other gardeners had basically adopted him, so he had to be around. She could have called out for him. Even if he hadn't heard her, someone else would have and sent him in her direction, but Lithia wanted to walk the labyrinth one last time before she left. The walk was soothing. It allowed her to focus less on the thoughts spinning through her head and just be for a moment.

The calm of the Labyrinth was short-lived. Lithia turned a corner and saw Vijay kneeling in a bed of clover. Everything came flashing back.

She needed to speak to Vijay once more before she left. She hadn't wanted to leave while so many things were still unsaid, but standing there watching him work, Lithia couldn't speak. A big part of her wanted to turn and walk away without saying anything, without him even knowing she had been there, but her legs were as frozen as her lips. She simply stood there, silently.

Lithia just watched him work. Vijay had a trowel in one hand and a small watering can in the other, and while he was no expert at the work, it still suited him. Vijay seemed content, and that was something Lithia had never expected to see in him. How could she spoil that? She should just go, walk away and let him be happy, but she couldn't make herself move.

"You going to stand there all day?" Vijay didn't turn around, so Lithia couldn't see his face, but she knew he was smiling. It was in his voice; she could hear so many things in his voice.

"Vijay," Lithia started.

"Yeah?" he asked.

"I'm leaving for a while." This wasn't what Lithia wanted to say. She wanted to tell him she cared about him, that she loved him, but not the way he seemed to want. She wanted to tell him that she hoped he'd be happy, but none of that wanted to come out.

"Yeah, Tarja said. Didn't say anything more than that, though. Made the whole thing feel very hush-hush," Vijay said.

"It kind of is. I wish I could tell you what's going on," Lithia said, and again it was not what she wanted to be saying.

"I know," Vijay said.

"Vijay . . . I . . . want to . . ." Lithia started, and it was a battle to get out every word.

"Lithia, I know what you're going to say. I've been running this conversation through my head since we last talked. You're going to tell me that you do care about me, right?" Vijay said. Lithia nodded. "Then you're going to tell me something like, we're from two different worlds. Then you're going to say that you love me, but that you're not in love with me, or something like that."

All Lithia could do was nod. Vijay seemed to know everything she wanted to say but couldn't.

"Yeah, I thought so," Vijay said. He stopped working and looked down, slumping his shoulders.

"Vijay, I'm—" Lithia started but Vijay cut her off.

"Listen, I know you are. I know part of you wishes it could be different. I know you can't help feeling how you do. Right now, though, I can't hear it. I know what you are going to say, and that's bad enough. Please don't actually say the words."

Lithia could hear the pain. He had to be close to tears, and that was probably the reason he hadn't turned around when he realized she was standing there.

"I am coming back. It's going to be a couple months, but I am coming back. Maybe when I do . . ."

"Don't, Lithia. Don't. Don't tell me you'll come back and we'll talk. Don't tell me something about no one knowing what the future is going to hold. Lithia, I love you. I've loved you for years, and maybe in time I can get over that, but what's between us isn't going to magically get better after two months."

"I'm sorry," Lithia said. It wasn't enough, but it was the only thing she had.

"Lithia, I'm going to ask you something I've never asked you before. Please just walk away. I'm going to be okay, but right now I'm not, and I don't want you to see that."

Lithia was stunned. She hadn't known exactly how things were going to go, but she hadn't expected this. She wanted to reach out to Vijay, do something to let him know how she felt, and tell him things would be okay.

"I don't hear you walking away," Vijay said. It was the right thing to do. There was nothing more she could say, and she needed to leave Vijay to handle things on his own.

Lithia's walk back through the labyrinth wasn't nearly as peaceful as her walk into it. Every plant she passed seemed to be standing in judgment of her. Everything seemed to be telling her that this wasn't her place anymore, and it was true. She was leaving, only for a couple months, but she was still leaving. Vijay, on the other hand, had nowhere else to go.

Lithia stood outside the labyrinth and just looked at it. Leaving the cathedral behind triggered pangs in her that leaving the house in the upper city never had.

CHAPTER 28

Lights, Camera, Face Squid

LITHIA WHEELED HER luggage down to the Ruins of Moscone: Howard and Fourth Streets. Her intricately woven canvas bag wasn't fooling anyone. She wasn't from down here, and the people around knew it. The Ruins of Moscone were a particularly dangerous place; it was in the heart of the Undercity where no light from the sky could reach. Lithia kept vigilant as the people eyed her, sizing her up for what they could steal, or worse.

She knew that this place was once a beacon, a world's fair, of the West's technological innovations and trends but several decades ago the Magdalenes had stepped in, reappropriating the complex for themselves. The facilities were built deep into the ground, three and four stories. The main complex housed a massive cavity the Magdalenes used as a hangar. It was the only place big enough to house ships the size of Lithia's.

As Lithia descended into the complex, she could see High Priestess Tarja and Cade waiting by an entrance to the main hangar. Walking up to them, Tarja turned around and spoke, "I'm glad you've decided to aid us. I don't know what we would have done without you."

Hastily, the three of them proceeded inside and down a series of stairs and walkways. They came to a set of reinforced airlock doors. Lithia placed her hand on a palm reader sitting on a pedestal a few feet from the entryway. She normally kept her family's ship in the hanger just beyond these doors. Uncle Amir, Aunt Petra, and even Bobby had access to it, but no one but Lithia ever had reason to use it. Aunt Petra had been trying to get her to sell it for years, saying it was little more than a flying bathtub that was going to start needing serious maintenance soon. But Lithia couldn't bear to part with it. In many ways, it was literally her home away from home, and she wasn't about to sell it, especially when she could justify keeping it by doing supply runs to Mars and Titan for the Magdalenes.

After scanning her palm, the doors unlocked and slowly swung open. Behind them was a massive hangar nearly the size of a stadium and easily three stories tall. Ships, cargo haulers, and planet hoppers of all shapes and sizes filled the hollow. They sat quietly in the dim light, waiting for their pilots to return.

"Lithia's ship is the largest we have here. It's the only one capable of making it to the Frontier and back," Tarja informed Cade.

"Then I really am lucky she's decided to help me."

"Lithia, I had a week's worth of supplies, fusion rods, and food stashed in your cargo. I'm only sorry we can't spare more. I know how uncomfortable journeys like this can be."

"We'll manage. Thank you," Lithia replied.

The three of them walked down long rows of ships, snaking around the vessels on a makeshift path that led them to the far end of the large open room. There, in the back, was a long-range cargo transport.

The craft was large, with two long, aerodynamic arms that reached out horizontally from the main hull. These arms were designed to open and grasp large cargo containers for ferrying in between star systems if need be. At the base of the arms was the habitation area that resembled an old passenger aircraft and housed everything from an internal cargo hold to sleeping quarters. Off the back end of the ship were a set of wings that helped the craft fly through an atmosphere and doubled as thruster arms while in space. The ship had been designed to house a single family if needed. If the crew rotated, you could fit seven to ten people fairly comfortably. It had never been more than Lithia's family on the ship, so she had always found the vessel quite spacious.

"It should still be able to make it to the Frontier," Tarja said. "We've taken good care of it over the years."

Lithia, Cade, and Tarja approached the ship from the front, walking down the space between the two long arms to a ramp that ascended into the ship. The ramp itself was nearly thirty feet long, giving them the impression of walking up a long staircase. This was not a place to be if you were afraid of heights.

"You really know how to fly this thing?" Cade asked.

"I guess you'll find out," Lithia teased.

Lithia keyed the unlock code into the door. A moment later, the lights turned green and the door split down the middle and slid open. Cade looked up to the name painted above the door. "*Amaranth . . .* the beauty that never fades," he recited.

Lithia stopped Cade from ascending the final stretch of the ramp and into the ship. She looked him dead in the eye, or at least as much as she could past his sunglasses. "Wait a sec. You said you could help me get custody of my brother and pay me enough for us to get off this world. Before I let you in, I need some guarantee. I need you to make good on your end of this bargain."

Cade nodded as he reached into his jacket and pulled out a credit chit. The device was the nearest thing to physical currency the Helix Network had. It was used for moving digital currency safely when you couldn't do it electronically.

"There's more than enough on here. You won't be disappointed. It's all yours," he said. She would have to take his word for it since she had no way to check the amount at the moment. She didn't have to like it, though.

"I'll transfer your brother's custody over to you as soon as we reach the Frontier," Cade continued.

Lithia stepped out of the way, letting him proceed inside the ship.

"Good luck, both of you," Tarja called from where she was standing at the base of the ramp.

The ramp led Lithia and Cade into the ship's main cargo hold. The cargo hold was a sizable room itself, being large enough to hold plenty of supplies or even a smaller, two-seater craft if need be. A lift in the back would take them up to the command deck.

After dropping her bag in the main galley, Lithia proceeded to the cockpit. As she stepped through the cockpit doors, her shoulder brushed up against a little set of dolphin wind chimes. They were just like the set that hung from the family's porch when she was a child back on Venus. This one didn't make as much noise, though; it only jingled during takeoff and landing. The sound helped ease Lithia's worries every time she heard them, and even now she smiled as she stilled them with a hand and moved to the pilot's chair.

Tarja, still standing at the base of the *Amaranth*'s embarkation ramp, signaled to the hangar's control room. A massive door above the *Amaranth* began to yawn open, and the amber lights from the city above came flooding in. Tarja stepped away from the ramp and walked back to a safe distance in front of the *Amaranth*, looking up at Lithia through the front of the cockpit.

Lithia went through the pre-takeoff sequence, and after a few switches, each of the three stations in the cockpit came to life. She pressed a final button, causing a set of pedals and hand controls to emerge from the helm computer. The chair and controls reconfigured themselves to fit Lithia like a glove. The lights on the outside of the *Amaranth* turned on and the ground began to vibrate, the air thrumming as the engines powered up. Tarja took a couple steps back as the air from the lift engines caught her robe. Lithia waved good-bye to her, wanting to thank her for this opportunity, but she figured there'd be time after she had returned. Lithia watched her mouth the word "Godspeed."

The antigrav system sparked up. A couple bolts of lightning discharged off the bottom of the ship's hull and snapped against the landing pedestal it rested on. Lithia retracted the *Amaranth*'s landing gear and the ship held itself in midair, slowly drifting back and forth.

Lithia pulled back on the controls as afterburners began to slowly thrust her ship upward toward the open doors in the ceiling. Lithia hovered momentarily over the Ruins of Moscone, picking a flight path that would take her out from the lower level to the Upper Terraces above her and into the sky.

Holding the controls like an extension of her body, she skimmed along the underside of the Terraces, trying to avoid the massive pylons and seismic stabilizers that held it above the water. It didn't help that it was raining topside. Water droplets battered the cockpit glass as Lithia piloted the craft between the two cities.

Cade stood silently behind her, watching the view outside the cockpit as they flew between the pillars of the city. Lithia could see how green and polluted the water beneath them was as she maneuvered the *Amaranth* out toward the Golden Gate Bridge. Past it was open sky, where she'd be free to ascend into space.

The *Amaranth* blasted under the bridge and its tourist markets, flying among nearly countless other craft out toward the ocean where she could make a clear break into the atmosphere. A row of lights on the cockpit display beckoned Lithia to fall in line behind other departing ships as they went higher and higher, the city of San Francisco shrinking in the distance behind them. Up through the clouds, up through the stratosphere, up through the rain and the wind of the world, until all that was left was the serene calm of a new afternoon and the warming sunlight that came with it. It was a beautiful sight until it faded as they left the planet's grasp.

The space around Terra Luna was packed with ships. They were coming and going in all directions. Lithia did her best to keep the *Amaranth* in one of the transit lanes that was highlighted by her cockpit display. The ship moved faster as they got farther away from Earth. The moon was lit up with all the stations and people that lived there. To her amazement, there was even a massive military vessel in orbit. Its emblem read "*Enigma.*"

The *Amaranth* came to the end of the transit lane. Every vessel in front of Lithia's began to engage their sprint drives and disappear into a beam of light. Shortly it would be their turn.

"There should be a blinking light on the terminal behind you," Lithia said to Cade. "Go ahead and press it. Then follow the instructions."

Cade sat down at the controls and input the vector and trajectory solutions that were needed for the ship to move into FTL.

Lithia waited until the last ship in the line ahead of her had vanished and until Earth flight control had given her the all-clear before she pulled back on the throttle and pushed forward a series of levers. The pinpoints of starlight outside the cockpit stretched into long needles as the ship shot off faster than light.

Lithia engaged the autopilot and swung around in her chair to face her passenger. "There. That wasn't so bad. Taking off was always the easy part for me, though. Now, how about a tour of the ship?"

Cade followed Lithia out of the cockpit and back into the hallway of the command. She gestured back to the doors behind her. "You've seen the cockpit. I'm gonna have to ask you not to go in there without express invitation."

She continued by pointing over to the door to the main galley. "That's the common room slash mess hall."

She took Cade farther down the hall and through another set of airlock doors to a rotating engine core. "That's the ship's beating heart. The engine was replaced a few years ago, and this one doesn't have as many light years on it. It should have no problem getting us to the Frontier and then getting me home, but should we have a problem, there it is."

Back in the galley, she pointed to a short staircase that descended through another set of doors. "Down there are a number of sections of the ship we won't be using for this ride, so please stay out of them."

Lithia led the way back into the command deck's hallway and through a final set of doors. Inside was a small cramped room with three person-sized tubes. "These are the sleep pods. They're not terribly comfortable, but they're the only way we're going to make it all the way to the Frontier with the supplies we have. Means we're gonna be sleeping for most of this trip."

"That's fine," Cade replied.

Lithia walked over to the sleep pod controls and noticed something strange. If the image on the display was correct, there was somebody in the far-right tube, but whom? Who the hell would be trying to stow away on her ship? A sudden rush of fear washed over her, causing the hairs on the back of her neck to stand on end. Was somebody trying to follow them?

"Wait a second," she said to Cade, slight trepidation slipping into her voice.

"What?" he inquired.

"There's someone onboard with us."

Cade's constant neutral expression turned to one of concern. He locked his focus on the last sleep pod in the room and shifted into a low crouching stance. "Get that pod open."

She didn't know what Cade was planning, but something told her she would be safe as long as she followed his orders. She slowly inched her way over to the pod. With one fluid motion, she pulled on the release lever. The pod tilted upright, and the glass slid open. Bobby spilled out onto the floor. "It's me! It's me! Don't hurt me!"

"What the hell are you doing?" Lithia yelled. "You've got to be kidding me!"

"You didn't think I was really going to let you leave without me, did you?" he yelled back.

"I can't believe you, Bobby! What the hell is wrong with you? I'm turning the ship around!" Lithia said, turning to walk back to the cockpit.

"No, don't!" Bobby said. Then he and Cade added simultaneously, "We can't."

"You can't come," she said to Bobby before whipping around to face Cade. "He can't come with us. My aunt doesn't even know we're gone! She's gonna flip out. I wouldn't be surprised if she already called the cops."

"We can't turn back now," Cade said.

Lithia sighed.

"I won't get in your way," Bobby said. "Promise."

"It's not about being in the way, Bobby. You weren't supposed to . . . I can't believe you! I'm turning us around now. End of discussion."

Lithia made a beeline for the cockpit, but Cade grabbed her arm. She looked back at him with daggers in her eyes. How dare he grab her?

"What do you think you're doing?" she said, pulling out of his grasp.

"Listen, if we turn around, there is a good chance I will be captured by Lambda. If they catch me, I'm as good as dead," he said.

"So that's why you needed to get off world so fast? I just *knew* you were wanted, but I didn't want to believe it. Great. I'm transporting a fugitive. Might have been nice for you to mention before I agreed to take you anywhere!"

Lithia couldn't believe Tarja had not supplied her with all the facts.

"It may not seem like a big deal to you to go back," Cade continued, "but it's more than likely that you two will be imprisoned while they try to 'extract' what exactly I may have told you about my mission."

There was a pause while Lithia considered her options. "You haven't told us anything."

"They won't believe that," he replied.

Lithia glared at both Cade and Bobby. She didn't know whom she was madder at right now. Cade had essentially lied to her, and Bobby had disobeyed her, making this whole thing more difficult. And now she was angry at herself too. She had thought that if she didn't go probing and asking Tarja why she needed her to ferry Cade to the Frontier, it wouldn't matter why Cade needed her help. She felt so stupid.

"What's going on, anyway? What are you guys talking about?" Bobby inquired.

Lithia took a deep breath. "The Magdalenes asked me to bring Mr. Trench Coat here to the Frontier. To Archer's Agony. For some reason, he can't use the Space Liners. Apparently it's because he's a wanted man."

"Oh . . . okay."

Lithia swung back around to face Cade. "I did you the courtesy of not asking too many questions. I trusted Tarja, but now I need to hear all the facts. What did you do to get Lambda after you?"

"If I answered that, I would be putting you and your brother in danger," he replied.

Lithia narrowed her eyes at Cade. "You said that if we get caught, we'd be questioned anyway. You've *already* put us in danger. Why shouldn't I just turn you in to protect ourselves? I wonder if there is a reward for your arrest." Lithia turned and made for the cockpit, Cade trailing behind.

"Because, if you do, you'll have to wait to gain custody of your brother. As it is now, when we make it to the Frontier, you won't even have to make a return trip if you decide not to. Besides, there's more money on that chit I gave you than you'd ever get from any reward from the UPE."

Lithia raised her hand to her chin and paused. "Okay. That's fair. But I still want to know why they're after you. You owe me that much, at least."

Cade sat down in one of the cockpit chairs and ran his hand through his hair. "Okay . . . okay . . ." he said. "But this is something much bigger, much more important than our three lives. I will tell you some, but I can't risk the UPE finding out everything if we get caught. Tarja came to me with concerns of major proportions. She and the other *mad'nuns* were convinced that someone had been suppressing information on the Helix. I did some poking around and found that she had been right, but it went a lot further than she suspected. That's all I can tell you."

"Why would anyone do that?" Lithia asked.

"I don't know. But I was able to download a partial log. I've got to get to the Frontier, past the Helix Network, and to a man who might be able to help me."

Lithia and Bobby were stunned. All of a sudden they were in a movie.

"So Lambda's real?" Bobby asked.

"Yes," Cade replied.

"And you're one of their augmented soldiers . . . aren't you?"

"Yes."

Bobby looked like he wanted to ask a hundred more questions, but Lithia cut in before he could. "The reason I accepted the job was because the priestess asked me to. *He* promised that if I took him to the Frontier, he could make sure I'd gain guardianship of you."

Bobby stood there, slack-faced and wide-eyed. "I had no idea you were so . . ."

"So what?"

"So . . . so . . . cool."

Lithia buried her face in her palm.

"So let me get this straight," Bobby continued. "The super-secret organization that biomechanically enhances agents for espionage is involved with arguably the biggest scandal in the universe, and the one man . . . no . . . the one cyborg who can do anything about it is sitting here in this ship. And you're taking him to the Frontier in hopes of freeing me from Aunt Petra?"

Lithia still had her hand over her face, just now realizing how in over her head she had become. "Uh-huh . . ." she answered.

"Mom and Dad would be so proud of you. You grew up to be so cool!" Bobby smiled gleefully. "You picked a doozy of a *journey*. This is one for the books."

"Well, I'm glad you're having fun with this. Aunt Petra is going to think you were kidnapped or something."

"But I wasn't. I ran away."

"Because that's better? She won't know any different. She's still going to send the cops after us."

"What does that matter if Lambda's after us? Perspective, Lith. Besides, there's barely any Helix in the Frontier. No cops could find us."

Lithia sighed. Bobby and Cade were right. At this point, the only thing Lithia could do was keep going. It wasn't a good solution and she really didn't like it, but it was the only option she really had left.

The three of them reentered the sleep-pod room some time later. It would be their home for a while. All the sleep pods were lit up. Thin, heavy white smoke poured out of vents on the side.

"We're not actually going into stasis, are we?" Bobby asked, wringing his hands.

"We are," Lithia replied.

"Do we have to?" Bobby whined.

"Bobby, the *Amaranth* isn't the fastest ship. It's going to take four weeks for us to get to the Frontier. In a week, we run out of food. In eleven days, we run out of air. What do you suggest?"

Bobby's skin was clammy and his face was red. She knew her brother suffered from anxiety, but he should have thought about that before stowing away.

Bobby looked over at his sister with wide eyes. "But I heard from a friend that his cousin went into one of those things and some sort of squid-like creature crawled in and attached itself to his face and laid an egg in his chest that burst out when he woke up."

"Bobby, if a creature really wants to lay an egg in your chest, it would do it whether you're in stasis or not. Do you really want to be awake for that?"

"Lithia! I'm serious!"

"So am I!" Lithia yelled back. Discovering Bobby had delayed them going into stasis long enough. Out of the corner of her eye, she caught Cade shaking his head and trying to hide his smirk.

Bobby stood there, anxiously looking around the room for an alien squid. Lithia walked over to the sleep-chamber controls. "All right, I'm setting the time to wake us up five hours before we reach our destination. That will give us enough time to wake up and shake off the hypersleep blues before we pass through the Gate. You two can go first. The stasis pod can cause a lot of condensation when you first wake up, so unless you want to be wearing soaked clothes for the last five hours of our trip, I suggest you strip down before getting in."

Bobby hesitated for a moment, taking a deep breath before he climbed in his pod and started pulling off his socks, "Fine. But if I wake up dead, it's your fault. And I hold one hell of a grudge."

Cade took off his coat and shirt and climbed into a pod. He pulled the door shut so Lithia could initiate the chambers.

"I think I'm gonna puke. I get so claustrophobic in these things," Bobby whined.

"Will you relax? You didn't seem to have any problem hiding in it earlier."

"Yeah, but you weren't turning it on before."

Lithia pulled down on the glass door. "Relax. You'll be asleep in five minutes."

Bobby looked resigned. "Okay."

"Sweet dreams," Lithia said as she began to swing the door to his pod closed.

"Wait a sec! Four weeks?" The pod sealed, drowning Bobby out. She could hear his muffled arguments through the glass but couldn't make out anything he was saying, so she simply waved at him before moving on to her own pod. She programmed her own sleep pod to wake her up a couple hours before Cade's. She needed to stay in control of the situation, and being awake first would give her the time she needed to work off the hibernation sickness.

Before climbing in, though, she made one last stop in the cockpit and sent a message to her aunt. It simply said, "Headed to the Frontier on a run. Bobby is with me. He stowed away, and by the time I found him, it was too late to turn back. See you in a month or so."

Sure, she was going to have a lot of explaining to do if she ever went back. If Cade didn't keep up his end of the bargain, there were going to be problems. Lithia didn't know if she could trust him, but what more could she do at this point?

As she made her way back to the sleep-pod room, her curiosity got the better of her. She couldn't help but peer into Cade's pod. He was in deep hibernation, and now, with the absence of his coat and shirt, she could see just what he was. His veins were a strange electric blue and snaked across his body. It was pretty clear his left arm had been replaced, as the smoothness of its skin didn't match the rest of his body. Everyone had heard of Lambda operatives being enhanced, but she didn't know anyone who had ever actually seen one. She couldn't help but feel she was in over her head. No wonder Cade and Tarja hadn't told her the whole truth. Frankly, she wouldn't have accepted the offer.

There was nothing left for her to do but strip down to her underwear and climb into her own pod. Before she pulled the door closed, she took a moment to pray for an uneventful ride.

CHAPTER 29

The Home World

AURELIUS AND FRIENDS had spent the first couple days doing the tourist thing. They took pictures of every famous place and monument in the Upper Terraces. Yesterday, they had hit all the museums. And there were a lot of them.

The Helix Network was woven into every aspect of Terran life. The people Aurelius passed on the street would periodically stop mid-stride to interact with open air. They waved their hands and poked at the space in front of them. The Helix user had the 'verse's wealth of aggregated information at their fingertips. The earrings made the symphony of holographic information visible to anyone wearing them. To Aurelius and his friends, everyone was just acting weird. It was hilarious to watch someone run into a lamppost because they were more intent on their holograms than paying attention to where they were going. What would these people do without their precious technology? Would they even remember how to interact with people? How to carry on a conversation or how to make friends? The questions bounced around in Aurelius's head. He wondered what he would be like if he grew up in a place like this.

Tonight was the *Freedom's Reach*'s last night on Earth, and Aurelius, Jerula, Paul, and Nyreen wanted to make the most of it. By now they were done with being tourists. Tonight they got ready for a night out on the town.

"So, if I bring a girl back to the ship tonight, I'll leave a belt on the door to our bunk," Jerula said jokingly.

"Yeah, sure. I'm totally sure that's exactly what's going to happen in an uptight place like this. I'm sure you'll have no problem getting a girl to come back with you," Paul joked, sipping a metal flask.

"Hey, it could happen . . ."

"Right . . ."

There was a small group of crewmen gathering at the head of a dock where the *Freedom's Reach* had been moored. These groups were ready to hop on a tram that would take them into San Francisco proper. Jerula had to wait for Aurelius. It always seemed to take him longer to get ready than everyone else, even Nyreen, who had taken the time to re-dye the blue stripe in her hair. The sun bathed them in an orange glow as it slowly winked away behind the edge of the world.

"Maybe he's refilling his jetpack," Paul joked.

Since Aurelius's little rocket ride, seldom a minute had gone by that someone wasn't congratulating him or joking about it. Aurelius stepped out of the airlock and onto the landing pad.

"Hey, how do I look?" Aurelius polled his friends.

Paul laughed. "You look like the best-dressed space cowboy I've ever seen!"

"You look the same as before, just not covered in grease," Nyreen added.

Jerula hesitated, walking around Aurelius as if to give him a serious opinion. "You forgot the jetpack."

Maybe it was the delivery more than what he had said, but Jerula's quip made the group burst into laughter.

"When I bring a girl back to our bunk with that story, I'll leave a belt on the handle. Just for you, dude," Aurelius joked.

The groups of *Freedom's Reach* personnel began departing the massive stardock. The docks were suspended hundreds of feet over the coast of some place called "Marin." There were several large vessels the size of the *Freedom's Reach* anchored at the facility. These vessels were from other colonies on both sides of the Gate, but their crews were nowhere to be found this evening. At the head of the facility was a transit system that the crews boarded that took them into the lower streets of San Francisco.

On most areas of Terra Luna, even the slightest bit of alcohol would get you in all sorts of trouble. It had been approved for "recreational" use in San Francisco, though. It was part of the culture. The only time alcohol was served was between sundown and midnight. Aurelius was glad they hadn't come in summer; it would have made for a short night.

They had heard that the clubs and speakeasies on the lower streets, just above the Undercity, were the places to be on a night like this.

The shops down there were less than nice and tidy, but it was where to go for cheap souvenirs and fireworks.

"Hey, you wanna get something for your momma? This is the place to do it," Jerula said.

Paul laughed. "Everything here is probably made in Martian sweatshops."

The neighborhood was getting gradually sketchier as they snaked their way down the alleys and farther into the lower streets. The sun having vanished didn't help the mood, not that it could reach down there if it were out.

"Let's make sure we all leave together. This place looks kind of rough," Nyreen said, sticking close to Paul.

"Oh, hell. I grew up in a neighborhood worse than this," Jerula said.

"I don't think anyone is going to mess with you here," Paul said. "You've got almost a whole three feet on everyone on this rock."

It was no joke how much taller Jerula was than everyone else. He looked almost too large beside the short, frail-looking Terrans they were passing, almost like he was some different species. "Unless they plan to stab you in the kneecaps, you're probably safe."

Whatever Jerula said in response, Aurelius missed, his attention suddenly elsewhere. Before he knew it, he was breaking off from the group, the sounds of their conversation dimming behind him. He was drawn to the little glint of light reflecting off the canopy of an old weathered craft sitting in a used hopper lot. Before he knew it, he had walked right up to the little short-range, two-seater planet hopper that, from the rust and grime collecting on it, looked like it had seen better days.

He ran his hand across the starboard wing in awe, as if the hopper wasn't actually there and, for that matter, for sale. He had only seen hoppers like it in old holograms back from the days when the Frontier was first being colonized. The craft would be highly sought after where he was from, but here on Earth, with so many newer used craft so easily accessible, it had been cast down to a used lot like a heap of scrap metal.

"What the hell are you doing?" Jerula yelled, running up behind him.

"Oh my god . . . it's intact," Aurelius yelled back, digging around in one of the engines. "This alone would be worth it."

"I think the kid's finally lost it," Nyreen said as the three of them approached Aurelius and his rusty treasure.

"Hey . . . do you know what this is?" Aurelius asked the group.

"A tetanus shot waiting to happen?" Jerula answered.

"No. It's a Sparrow-Class planet hopper."

"So?" Nyreen asked, though it was clear to Aurelius everyone else was thinking the same question.

"These things are the Model T of our time!" he said.

"What the hell is a Model T?" Jerula asked.

Aurelius shook his head. Of course they wouldn't know the reference. "It was an automobile."

The next question came from Paul. "What the hell is an automobile?"

"Never mind. I'm saying a craft like this . . . talk about sturdy and reliable."

"Yeah, looks *real* reliable from here," Jerula said, picking at a spot of rust on the hopper's hull.

"It's seen some action, but it's in great shape," Aurelius said, wishing he had some way to make them see what he was seeing.

"This is great shape? It doesn't even look flyable." Jerula flicked the rust off the tip of his finger and stepped away from the craft.

"Let alone spaceworthy," Paul added.

"You don't know how hard these things are to find back home. Everyone wants them because they last so long. They may not have all the bells and whistles of the fancier models, but hell . . . one of these will be with you till the day you die."

"That's because it's a coffin with rocket engines," Jerula said.

Nyreen teased. "Aww. Let him have his moment. He's in love."

Paul let out a surprised whistle when he saw the price tag hanging off one of the wings.

"How much?" Aurelius asked.

"Ten K . . . marked down from twenty-five."

"Hell, if the mass drive was working, it alone would be worth that much."

"*Is* the mass drive working?" Jerula asked.

Aurelius couldn't avoid the question. "Yeah . . . umm . . . not so much, *but* I could get it online in no time with the tools back on the ship."

"Even if it was working, I don't think you're going to fly this thing all the way back home."

"Of course not," Aurelius said, looking at Jerula. "That's where you come in."

"Huh?"

"You're pretty cool with the guys in cargo control. Maybe they could stow it. You know, help a Strifer out."

"No, uh-uh. I'm sorry, not happening."

"Why not? Throw a tarp over it, and no one would even notice."

"Yeah, Jerula!" Paul chimed in. "You could just tell people it was a pile of your dirty laundry!"

"Okay . . . listen . . . I owe those guys some cash. They ain't gonna be doing me or you any favors. Besides, do you even have ten K?"

"No. I've got eight, *but* I could talk the dealer down."

Jerula facepalmed. "You know I love you, bro, but you ain't thinking rationally. I'm gonna have to step out, Strifer."

Nyreen pointed to the office in the back of the yard, at a big CLOSED sign in its window. "I'm so sorry, Aurelius. I don't think it was meant to be, but, hey, there are plenty more ships in the sky."

"C'mon, let's go get a few drinks, dance with some gorgeous Terran girls, and you'll forget all about this," Jerula said, slapping his buddy on the shoulder.

"I don't want any beautiful Terran girls; I want the spaceship," Aurelius pouted.

Jerula, Nyreen, and Paul turned and began to walk out of the yard.

"You guys don't understand! This is one hell of an opportunity I'm missing out on. I want you to remember this come the holidays when you guys don't get any gifts! Hello?"

His heart broke just a bit. Oh well. There *would* be other opportunities.

Jerula was right. A few drinks later and the booming music of the club made him nearly forget about the lonely little planet hopper sitting out in the yard in the dark. The Terran girls were helping too. They were painfully good-looking and made Aurelius hurt in a very special way. He tried his best not to get caught staring at their incredible eyebrows, but he couldn't help himself. Strifer girls just didn't wear them like that, and it was a tragedy.

The four Strifers stood out like a sore thumb. Jerula would have been the first one people looked at. His stature was almost comically large, nearly having to duck to clear the top of the doors of the bar they had walked into. This only served to strike a contrast with how lanky and pencil thin Paul was. From there, some eyes darted to Nyreen and some to Aurelius. Nyreen's bright blue streak in her otherwise jet-black hair wasn't even the most grabbing of her features—no, that would be the intricately detailed tattoo of a marine animal, jumping from an ocean made of flames, that worked its way up her left wrist and ran all the way to her shoulder. Needless to say, the amount of skin she was showing seemed to be out of place in comparison to the locals. Aurelius might have been the most out-of-place-looking of all of them, though. The northern hemisphere of Earth was primarily dominated by cultures that had come out of the Middle East; the southern hemisphere was comprised mostly of Asia-originating people; and San Francisco, being the de facto capital of it all, was mostly a mix of the two. Aurelius's blond curly hair, light skin tone, and wide hazel eyes were almost unheard of here, and they drew almost as much attention as a large set of wings or horns would in this crowd.

It was a stereotype that Southern Terran girls loved Frontier boys. Jerula had no problem cultivating a little congregation of girls bouncing around him. They were so short, Aurelius was pretty sure two of them could stand on each other's shoulders and just barely be Jerula's height. It didn't look like Jerula minded all that much. Aurelius started to get curious what Paul's and Nyreen's tastes were, but they were so focused on each other while they sat at the bar, he wondered if they had even noticed that the bar had other people in it.

With Aurelius, the northern girls had struck a chord. They sat in large groups together, talking among themselves in a certain way that seemed to keep others at a distance. They periodically stared into open air, doing something on their Helix holograms, and occasionally came back to the room just long enough to cast judgmental looks at the guys who would pass by. The stereotype with them was that they looked down upon the "lower class" and wouldn't ever be caught in public with them. They thought they were too good for everyone, let alone a Frontier boy. The men that were successfully courting them stood there like lions, trying to stare down any guy, let alone a Strifer, who got too close. In their culture, a man was to carry on the family legacy, and rarely would any of his accomplishments be his own, individually speaking. Arranged, or at least semi-arranged, marriages were still pretty common on Earth in the sense that people didn't become entangled with anyone of a different social class. Aurelius didn't stand a chance with any of these types of girls unless they really hated their parents and wanted to rebel for a little while. He had experience with several Terran girls he had met over the years who were in study-abroad programs. Strife wasn't exactly the most common destination for an educational retreat, but many thought just getting to see a place outside of the Sol system counted as educational.

Jerula brought a round of drinks over to Aurelius, Paul, and Nyreen. "You see all these girls? Man, I've died and gone to heaven!" he said. "I want that one. That one and that one."

Aurelius looked out into the crowd.

"Don't stare!" Jerula said.

"Great, I'm hanging out with a bunch of lecherous perverts," Nyreen muttered, almost unheard over the booming music.

A couple of Southern Terran girls were whispering in each other's ears, then made a "come here" motion to Jerula.

"Sorry, but my fans are calling!" he said before heading off to join them.

Paul stood up from his stool and took Nyreen out onto the dance floor. Aurelius figured he'd keep their seats warm and continue to people watch. Truth be told, he liked dancing, but he felt like he was looking at girls he was interested in through bulletproof glass. With enough alcohol in his system, Aurelius tossed around the idea of joining his buddies on the dance floor. Damn that liquid courage.

Suddenly the song booming over the bar's speakers came to an end and the DJ said something in Terranese. The entire room cheered and a spotlight hit the three Strifers already out on the floor. A fourth spotlight appeared on the floor and then slowly searched him out like he was an escaped prisoner. Uh-oh. Was this because they didn't have a Helix earring? The DJ started up the next song. Aurelius didn't recognize it at first; it had the certain twang you only heard in the Frontier, but after the beat kicked in, all four of the Strifers recognized the song. It was one of those ancient cultural-barrier-breaking tracks that everyone knew, even if you didn't know the words. Aurelius had learned to dance to it years ago. Seizing the opportunity, he joined his friends out on the floor. Jerula led the group, clunky at first, but after a few seconds, they were crotch grabbing to a Frontier version of Michael Jackson's "Beat It." Jerula and Nyreen were naturals. Paul fumbled around, either due to the alcohol or an inability to dance, or both. Aurelius was somewhere in the middle, but it didn't matter at that point. The four of them were busting a move and it was fun. The entire room backed up, giving them plenty of space. Jerula jumped down onto the floor and started spinning on his head, his legs spread out like a fan, surprising everyone. Aurelius watched in astonishment, along with the other patrons, as his friend pulled his legs in and spun to a stop, his back flat on the ground, before springing to his feet and gliding backward in a moonwalk.

Shortly after the song, the evening slowed to a crawl as Helix earrings lit up, indicating to the wearer, and the bartender, that its user had reached their legal limit. The Helix generated a blood-alcohol ratio based on height, age, and weight. If you went too far over, you'd be instantly fined. Luckily, Aurelius didn't have a Helix earring.

Watching people poke at the empty air in front of them, trying to find a taxi cab with their Helix holograms, was hilarious. It was a wonder no one ever lost an eye.

Jerula paid their tab and the four of them got invited to a private after party by someone who spoke broken Strifer. It was down in a speakeasy basement. The room was covered in an egg-carton-like material that blocked out the connection, the prying eyes of the Helix Network. They could drink to their hearts' content. The fact that none of the Strifers could speak Terranese seemed to matter less by then. When everyone was that far gone, everyone was speaking drunk.

Aurelius sat by himself drinking something from a bottle that neither he nor the person who gave it to him could identify. The closest any person could do in mangled Strifer was to say it was good and made by, or possibly of, a guy named Vijay.

Jerula was off in one corner throwing some odd wooden blocks. They were tiny and seemed to have little dots on the sides. Whatever it was they were doing, Jerula seemed to be doing well because every now and then a loud cheer would come from him, and the group around him would clap. Paul and Nyreen had vanished sometime after leaving the bar, and given the way they had been looking at each other, Aurelius was willing to bet they had found a nice out-of-the-way place back on the ship to have their own private party.

Aurelius was half-tempted to go and join Jerula in whatever that game was, but it would have been mostly for something to do. What he really wanted to do was go find a few of those girls from the bar. Maybe he could catch one without the personal guard, and he could charm her with his general Strifer-ness, which by now had been set ablaze with how much alcohol he had consumed.

The next thing he knew, he was sitting on a couch with a woman in his lap, with perfectly cropped, bold eyebrows, dusky-brown skin, and a body built for squeezing. He had no idea how much she could understand of what he was talking about, but a few hand gestures he used to describe that day flying around the outside of the *Freedom's Reach* seemed to help. Either that, or this girl really hated her parents, and hooking up with a crazy Strifer making whooshing sounds was the way she was choosing to express it. Either way, Aurelius was good with it. Sadly, it seemed her rebellion had its limits as she began to pull away after a kiss that turned her red and made her tremble. He knew this game. This was the "Now I'm in over my head" response, and he found her letting go of him and standing up. Aurelius watched her go, vanishing from the dimly lit room and back out into the streets. He wondered if she would be okay stumbling through the lower streets of the city, but what could he do? As he resolved to stand up and at least make sure she found whomever she had come with, Jerula suddenly appeared in front of him, blocking his view.

"Aww, you really were in love, weren't you?" he said.

"What?"

"Nah, you just look so sad. You're not still thinking about that craft sitting out in that dark, cold used hopper lot, are you?"

Aurelius didn't know if he was joking or if Jerula just hadn't seen the second beauty that had slipped through his fingers tonight. "No . . . it's . . . she . . . never mind . . . I'm starting to sober up. I think I need another drink."

"Well, it's on me!" Jerula said, throwing his arm over Aurelius's shoulder and dragging him bodily over to the crowded bar. It was then Aurelius noticed a large roll of paper money in his hand.

"Where'd you get that?" he asked his swaying friend.

"I took it from a bunch of guys that thought they could beat me at dice!" he proclaimed as he pointed out to the bartender what he wanted from a picture on the wall.

"It's not tha—" Aurelius started.

"You're really busted up about that little hopper, I can tell. The look on your face when I found you told me everything I needed to know," Jerula continued, speaking right over him in his determination to be sympathetic.

"I guess," Aurelius replied, running his hand over his clammy face before trying to scope out a bathroom.

"You really think you could fix up a little piece-of-shit hopper like that?"

"Of course. It might look a little rusty, but things from that era were made to last. It's literally only a couple of days, maybe a week's worth of work with the tools we got on board," Aurelius said, warming to the subject.

"No shit? Well, good, 'cause I'm feeling generous!" Jerula peeled off a small stack of bills and forced them into Aurelius's hand. "Go getcha yaself something pretty, doll face."

"Dude . . . I can't. You don't have to—"

Aurelius didn't have time to reply before Jerula interrupted him by standing up on his stool and throwing his hands up in the air, shouting, "Hey! Everyone! Next round's on me!"

Everyone in the speakeasy cheered and stormed the bar. Before he knew it, Aurelius was getting pushed off to the side, and that's when things got very, very, hazy.

CHAPTER 30

Amorous Punishment

AURELIUS GLANCED UP at his older brother as he walked into the living room and sat down on the couch next to him. Aurelius was plugging away on a game controller, defending the universe against evil alien robot ninjas from another dimension on the family's holoscreen, and he could only spare so much attention, even for family. Magnus picked up a spare remote and it slipped right out of his hands.

"Dammit, Aurelius! You got engine grease all over my controller again! What the hell is wrong with you?"

"Oh . . . yeah, sorry. Forgot to wash my hands after helping Dad."

"Goddamn it," Magnus said, wiping the controller on his pants. "I don't know why Mom and Dad just don't buy you your own game system."

"Why would they? I have yours." Aurelius smiled.

"I'm sick and tired of always picking up greasy controllers or getting halfway through a game before the thing falls apart because you didn't put it back together right."

"Quit complaining. You have a Turbo button now," Aurelius said.

Magnus looked down at the controller that had slipped from his hand. There was a little green button that hadn't been there the day before. Raising his eyebrow, he reached down and pressed the button, causing a little light to blink.

"You're welcome," Aurelius said.

"I can't wait till you get your own games."

"Aren't you going off to college soon?"

"Is that your way of telling me you won't miss me?"

Aurelius shook his head playfully. "Not so much. Just hope you're not taking the Y64 with you."

"Punk."

"I think Dad's right, though. Going to college first seems like a better idea. Gives you more options."

"I can't do that, Aurelius. I just got to get out of here, off this planet. Out of this dusty nowhere town. Life's too short to sit around here waiting for something interesting to happen."

Aurelius knew how exceptionally well Magnus had always done in school. He excelled in everything from history to astrometrics, and joining the SMMC was the quickest way to see the cosmos and put those two subjects to good use. At least in his eyes it was. Aurelius couldn't count the number of times Magnus talked about wanting to see the other worlds in the Frontier like Solace and Independence. He had a very detailed plastic model of Archer's Agony Space Station hanging from the ceiling in his room that he had put together when he was in primary school. Aurelius, in contrast, was a terrible student, always caught fiddling with something in the garage or playing a hologame instead of doing his homework.

"And maybe even one day visit the planet where we all started—Earth." This was Magnus's dream. "I don't think I have to tell you why I wanna get out there."

"Yeah, but jeez, Magnus. You get such good grades, and here you wanna go join the military and throw it all away. I think that's Mom and Dad's big issue."

"Well . . . I'm going the second high school is over with. No one can stop me."

There was a short pause while they just sat there watching Aurelius vanquish an entire space ninja army on the hologram in front of them.

"So, what are you gonna do after I'm gone?" Magnus asked.

To this day, Aurelius still remembered that question. It was burned into his mind. Had he known what was going to happen, maybe he would have had a better answer than "I dunno."

"You're not gonna have me to run interference every time you get in trouble."

"Maybe I'll just have to stop getting in trouble," Aurelius said with a deadpan expression on his face; but a second later, they were both laughing.

"Wait a sec," Magnus said. "Aren't you grounded right now? You're not even supposed to be playing games."

Aurelius shushed Magnus. "Dude, keep it down."

Magnus shook his head, laughing. "Fine, it's your funeral if you're caught. But, hey, I've got homework to do. I'll play some Golden Spy with you later."

Aurelius turned over, severing his link with the dream. At least this time he was able to wake up before the dream turned into a nightmare. He was laying there, in his bunk on the *Freedom's Reach*, with little more than a vague lingering sensation of a cab ride that brought he and Jerula back to the docks. His head was pounding as the reckless fun of the night was now slipping into a raging hangover. Memories of home always came when he was in a state like this. Maybe it was a punishment for his indiscretions, or maybe drinking weakened the barriers Aurelius had put up to keep those painful memories at bay.

Aurelius's stomach felt like it was collapsing in on itself. He slithered off the top bunk and landed on his feet. Jerula was all but comatose on the bottom bunk, snoring away. Evidently Paul and Nyreen had made it home safe as they were cuddled up under a blanket together on the bottom of the other set of bunks in the room.

Aurelius dug around in his jacket pocket for a second and then popped a couple of Fizzies before drinking from the bathroom faucet. He tried to lie back down but didn't feel much like going back to sleep. He was awake now. He distracted himself with thoughts about the pretty little number he remembered meeting earlier in the night. He couldn't stop thinking about her or how she had slipped right through his fingers. He had been holding her in his hands, but it hadn't been meant to be. Still, Aurelius could dream, those perfect curves, the way she caught his eye from afar and made everything else fade away. She was something he'd never get another chance at and she haunted him. If only he had the ten thousand the dealer wanted. He could picture the twin engines and rear stabilizer so clearly and wondered how comfortable the upholstery in the cockpit would still be. He wondered what it would feel like to own his own Sparrow-Class planet hopper. If he only had enough, he'd drag that thing all the way back home to Strife and he'd have his very own planet hopper. He only had another year before he had to decide whether to extend his contract with the corps or to open up his own shop. Either way, he wanted that hopper. What could he do, though? Get up, go down to the yard, talk the guy down to eight thousand, and be back to the *Freedom's Reach* in time for pancakes? He didn't know the guys in cargo control like Jerula did. If he had some cash left over, maybe he could bribe them. He didn't know what to do, but lying here wasn't helping any. If anything, it just seemed to wind him up more.

Even if the dealer wouldn't take less, it was still worth a try. Aurelius didn't want to leave Earth saying he hadn't at least tried.

Aurelius pulled himself off his bunk and looked himself over in a mirror, making sure he looked well enough before he made his last trip into the city. He also checked his wallet. He wanted to make sure after the night he'd had that he at least still had the eight thousand he'd had at the start of the night, or most of it, anyway.

Aurelius flipped through the bills, counting them out to himself; one thousand, two thousand, three thousand. It was odd. There seemed to be more here than he had thought. Seven thousand, eight thousand, nine thousand. There was definitely more there than he thought. Ten thousand, eleven thousand, twelve thousand. What had happened? He had expected to find a bit less than eight thousand, maybe quite a bit less, considering he seemed to remember having a very good time. So where did the extra four thousand and change come from? Aurelius quickly checked to make sure he hadn't somehow ended up with someone else's wallet, but there was no mistake. It was his, but the money certainly wasn't. Aurelius went through all the ways a Strifer, who didn't even speak Tarranese, could earn four thousand in one night and quickly abandoned that line of thought. None of the options were all that flattering, and if he had resorted to one of them, he figured he'd rather not know. Something was nagging at him, though. Something about Jerula rolling little blocks with a group of other people. Something about a girl and Jerula telling him . . . what had Jerula told him? It didn't matter. He was sure Jerula had said something, and now he remembered him shoving a wad of bills into his hand hard enough to leave a bruise.

Jerula woke suddenly from what was, if not a sound sleep, then at least a very deep one. At first he wasn't sure what was going on. There was sound, deafening sound. The sound seemed to be trying to communicate something. Probably that Jerula had drank way too much the night before, though he was willing to accept that this might just be a side message and resigned himself to trying to decipher what it was trying to say to everyone else.

". . . hour. Please finish all personal matters and report to duty stations at that time. Message repeats. The *Freedom's Reach* will be departing Earth in one hour. Please finish all personal matters and report to duty stations at that time. Thank you."

"That settles it. The captain hates me," Jerula said, trying to lever himself off his bunk and become approximately conscious.

Jerula looked around the bunk room. Paul and Nyreen were pulling on uniforms in what Jerula could only describe as a vindictive way. He glared at them for a moment so they would understand exactly what he thought of them being awake and moving at this moment before turning to scan the room for Aurelius.

"Hey . . . where's the other guy who should know better than to start the world before I get up?" he asked in the general direction of his other two bunkmates.

"No idea," Nyreen said, her cheerful voice making Jerula hate her even more.

"You two got in after we'd gone to bed, and he was gone when we got up," Paul finished, managing to be slightly less hateful than Nyreen, but only just.

"You two are a bundle of help," Jerula said.

"We aim to please," Nyreen said.

Jerula was trying to figure out exactly how to express his thoughts on the subject of their aims when the hiss of the bunk door sliding open made him turn around.

"Good morning!" came Aurelius's voice from outside. It sounded like he had been drinking sunshine and pissing flowers.

"I hate you all so much right now," Jerula said, clutching his pounding head and turning away from the door so he wouldn't see the inevitable smile on Aurelius's face.

"Oh, don't be mad. I brought you something," Aurelius said.

"Leave it on the table and leave the room or, whatever it is, I'm going to beat you to death with it."

"Oh, you're going to like this. Come get some before it gets cold," Aurelius said.

"You know I could snap your arm like a twig, right? Wouldn't take all that much," Jerula said, though he did roll over, figuring the sooner he humored Aurelius, the sooner everyone would leave him alone to die.

"Now is that any way to thank the man who brought you the best hangover cure in the world?" Aurelius said.

"Silence and a gun?" Jerula said.

"Close."

"Smells good, whatever it is," Jerula said.

"Best pho in town, or so I'm told. Now, seriously, it's getting cold and you've got to be on duty in forty-five minutes," Aurelius said, passing bowls to Jerula, Paul, and Nyreen.

A few minutes later, as Jerula was drinking the last of his broth, he was forced to admit he really did feel somewhat better. Maybe not perfect, but alive, and he'd settle for that right now.

"You're a good man, Aurelius. I might not hurt you after all," Jerula said.

"Thanks. Nice to know I can make long-term plans," Aurelius answered.

"I said might . . ."

"Anyway, it's the least I can do. You guys enjoy the rest of that. I want to head down and check on something before my shift starts," Aurelius said, turning from them and heading back out the door.

Jerula was curious what Aurelius could need forty-five minutes to check on, but right now he didn't have the energy to ask. Instead, he ladled himself another bowl and devoured it more or less in one go, figuring if a little was good, more must be better.

"I'll really have to do something nice for him after this. Maybe when we get back to Strife I'll treat him to a few drinks with the money I won last night."

CHAPTER 31

The Interloper

"OOW!" VIJAY EXCLAIMED, knicking a finger with a small trowel. He dropped the tool in the dirt and jerked his hand back, sticking the edge of his left pointer finger between his lips and trying to soothe the piercing pain that had startled him. It was the third time that day he had poked himself on Lithia's gardening equipment. He had no idea how she spent so much time in the dirt and managed to keep such well-manicured hands. His hands were beginning to look ragged, and they were covered in small blisters and wounds. "Dammit," he muttered.

Vijay stood up, leaving the snapdragon he had been digging a hole for firmly in its pot. Ever since Lithia left, he had spent most of his time down in the garden, finishing up the work she had to leave behind.

He liked to think it was because the church depended on the money the plants brought in, but when it got quiet and he was the only person around, he was forced to admit it was because being the garden felt a little bit like being with her. That was the real reason Vijay was in the gardens that night, because he wanted to be alone with something that Lithia had left him.

Distantly, Vijay could hear the sounds of Priestess Tarja giving her last sermon of the day. A part of him wished he was there with everyone else listening to it. Tarja's words always seemed to sooth the open wounds that Lithia had left, but that night he wanted to hurt, and he wanted to hurt alone.

Vijay picked up his tools again and checked a list of things that still needed doing. The next task was pruning the violets just around the bend in the labyrinth of flowers. Though when he got there, he suspected he had made a mistake. Not only was the bed of flowers he found already well tended, but somehow Vijay suspected violets should be some shade of violet, not the shade of bright green that he saw.

Vijay considered the patch of green for a moment. He had obviously taken a wrong turn someplace. He would have to go back to the church and check the map the other gardeners kept of the gardens. Vijay was not looking forward to it, not only because it would increase his chance of bumping into another human who might have difficult questions like, "How are you doing? What are you doing out so late?" or even just "Hi." None of which Vijay felt able to deal with at the moment, but also because checking the map was something Lithia never had to do. He had heard the other gardeners talk about it with awe. They would say things like, "Lithia seems to just feel where everything is," and, "It's like the plants are her children." Whenever Vijay had to check the map, he felt vaguely like he was failing Lithia in some way.

As Vijay made his winding way back to the church, Tarja's words started becoming more distinct. She was talking about "cheesing your drum," or something like that. Honestly, most of the philosophy of the church was still beyond him, but if cheese and drums were really important, he would eventually learn why.

Vijay finally reached the back doors where the map was hung, but by this time the map and anything else that had been on his mind was long gone. Musical cheese notwithstanding, Tarja's words had grabbed his attention.

The sermon she was giving wasn't like the comforting things she had said to him and that he had already heard her say to any number of other people in the past weeks.

This was something different. She was telling them to not just accept the life they had been given. She was telling them to stand up and be counted. She wasn't inciting them to riot like the Right to Lighters always did, but in many ways it still felt like one of their rallies.

"I know some of you are from the Upper Terraces, and this might be hard to hear, but the upper city likes to pretend we're not here, and every day you say nothing, every day you just stand by and say, 'It's someone else's job to remind them,' you help them do it. Yes, it is on us to stand and be seen, but we can't do that alone. Alone we are just the voiceless, nameless hordes of Helix-less transients who scurry beneath their feet like rats. You need to stand with us, give us a voice on the Helix, give your friends the security to stand, knowing that someone less easily ignored is standing with them."

Vijay didn't remember walking into the church, but at some point while Tarja was speaking he had. He was now standing in the pews with about a hundred other people. People who were standing and listening to every word Tarja was saying. Moreover, they didn't look to be the normal Magdalene members, mostly Undercity residents with a few from above mixed in and looking out of place. No, almost all these people were wearing robes like the ones Tarja and the others who lived at the church wore, and many wore featureless masks to further conceal their identities. Anonymous or not, though, each of them were held transfixed by Tarja. She could probably tell them to do anything right now, and they would. What kind of person would give so much of themselves over to the words of a small woman in a run-down church in the Undercity? But then again, wasn't that what *he* was doing? Vijay hadn't wanted to stay at the church at first. He wanted to leave as soon as he got there, but Tarja had wanted him to stay, and he had. Tarja and Lithia hadn't threatened him, they hadn't begged, they had barely even asked. They had just let him know they wanted him to stay, and though he argued, in the end he did. That was the power of this place and that was the power of Tarja. And someday, that would be the power of Lithia. Someday Lithia would be able to speak, and people would follow. After all, Vijay already was.

"I want you all to remember that when you go from this place, the world can only ignore what you let it. The world can only ignore what you ignore. Don't ignore us. Don't allow them to ignore us," Tarja said to the assembled Magdalenes.

All around, people seemed to wake up from a trance. They looked around, a low hum of conversation starting up as people started to gather their things.

Next to Vijay, one man in a mask was asking another if they'd be at the opera later. Someone behind him was saying that they hoped they could get back up top without running into anyone they knew, and really they were only here because a friend dragged them, honestly. The conversation was cut off abruptly, though, as a loud thud echoed inside the church. It was as if something massive had crashed into the large wooden doors at the front of the building. For a moment, Vijay thought someone must have crashed a vehicle of some kind into the church. When the thud came again, this time with a splintering crash, Vijay turned just in time to see the doors vanish.

The Gates of Paradise came crashing open, the wood and brass bending and shattering. Shards flew everywhere. The sound, like a cannon had exploded, echoed through the cathedral. People panicked, screaming and scrambling for cover. What was going on? A man came walking through the wreckage of the doors, but the word "man" didn't quite fit. The hulking figure stood, surveying the church and its occupants. The figure was massive, easily over eight feet. Vijay had heard of people on very low-gravity worlds growing to those heights, but they were supposed to be slender, almost frail, and this person was anything but. Thick corded muscles stood out on his arms, giving him the look almost of a cartoon bodybuilder, and everywhere on his body seemed to be the intrusions of technology. At odd angles, thick cabling sprouted from his flesh, only to travel and bury itself somewhere else on his body. Vijay couldn't make out his face, due to a thick hood, a fact Vijay suspected he should be grateful for. Inside the darkness of his hood, and more unsettling than any other aspect of this thing, the figure's eyes glowed red, red like rubies heated by some hellish flame.

There was no question about it—this man, this thing, was a demon. His eyes moved and scanned everyone present with mechanical accuracy. Vijay watched in horror as they centered on Tarja, where she still stood at the pulpit.

All around Vijay, the old-fashioned touch screens embedded in the back of the pews started to flicker to life.

A low rumble began to rock the church, and for a moment Vijay feared that there might be more than one of these things. Then, a voice that could crack the sky open bellowed, "Where is Cade?"

The voice came not from the figure, nor from a second one that Vijay still feared might be lurking just out of sight, but instead from every touch screen and terminal that had just flickered back to life. People screamed with terror. They ran for every exit they could find, hid behind anything they could, and for some reason Vijay just stood there. Somehow he knew running wasn't going to help, that hiding would only delay what was going to happen.

The massive figure started moving forward, slowly, as if it had all the time in the world, a luxury that none of those trying to get out of its way shared.

Vijay watched, unmoving, as the figure, the thing that was invading the one place Vijay had ever felt safe, reached out with seeming ease and one by one broke anyone who came into its reach.

Vijay didn't know what it wanted, he didn't know what a Cade was, and right now he didn't care. All around him people were panicking, running, and dying. It was like the day of the riot all over again, but this time there was no place to run, no place that would mean escape and safety.

Vijay looked around. He wasn't sure exactly what he was looking for, something to fight back with, anything that would give him a chance. What he eventually found was a cluster of statues, metal statues of people holding rusty swords and other ancient weapons Vijay did not know the names of. Vijay didn't know where the Magdalenes found them, but as he pried a rusty blade from one of their hands, he was glad they had.

"Stop running!" Vijay yelled at someone in a robe as they ran past, trying to find someplace where the thing behind them wouldn't reach.

"Stop running! All you're doing is letting it pick us off! Look, we can fight back!" Vijay said, trying to get the panicking people to see their only chance. Most people continued to ignore him, but a few stopped, seeing the truth in his words. Or maybe they were just desperate and grateful to find someone who could give them direction.

One by one, people started taking up the weapons. All around him, blades shone in the torchlight. Most had taken weapons from the odd metal statues, but one person had instead taken up a thick, heavy-looking candelabra and swung it with ease. At any other time, Vijay would have been amazed. The candelabra had to weigh fifty pounds, and in the hands of this man it seemed no more burden than Vijay's sword was to him.

Vijay and the other armed churchgoers rushed toward the monster. The man with the candelabra thrust first. To Vijay's dismay, it showed no fear of the fire, not even as the flames started blistering and cracking its skin. There was a sharp crack as the thing gripped the head of the candelabra, heedless of the fire, and thrust it back at its wielder, shattering the man's arm in the process. He didn't scream, though. He couldn't because the thing's other hand stretched out, wrapping around his neck, and tightened.

Vijay didn't know who the man with the candelabra had been, he didn't even know his face, but despite that, Vijay felt his loss keenly as the life left his eyes.

Vijay didn't waste time with regret, though. While the beast was occupied with its latest kill, Vijay charged it from behind. Vijay didn't know if the dying man could still see him, could see the sword sink into the monster's flesh, but he hoped so.

CHAPTER 32

Gates of Paradise Lost

TARJA STOOD AT the pulpit watching as this thing, whatever it was, tore through her congregation like rice paper. It killed without thought or hesitation, the little lives snuffed out in its hands meaning nothing to it.

It had been less than a minute since it broke through the doors, and already the dead outnumbered the living.

She watched, unable to help, as a few of her flock charged it with weapons they had taken from old suits of armor the Magdalenes had salvaged from a building on the other side of town.

A man she had known for ten years had his throat crushed with a careless hand. Would he blame her for what was happening? It *was* her fault, after all. The moment it called for Cade she knew it was her fault. It was her fault it had come to the cathedral, her fault that these people were in the pews when it came, and her fault they were all dying.

As the carnage continued, Tarja saw something she hadn't expected. Vijay was standing behind the monster, a rusty old sword held in both hands, its tip pointed directly at the monster's spine.

She wanted to call out to Vijay, tell him to run, tell him to just drop the sword and get out of there. She wanted to say these things, but the words wouldn't come. Instead she watched in mute horror, unable to do anything.

Vijay lunged forward, his blade sinking to the hilt in the monster's back. In that moment, Tarja could see all his rage boiling to the surface, all the nights he went hungry, all the times when those who should have cared ignored him, or worse still, beat him. Tarja saw all the moments when he tried to fight back and failed. All of it was on his face as he drove that blade forward. For a moment, Tarja allowed herself to hope against hope that it would bring down the beast, but only for a moment. That was all the monster allowed her.

"God judges the righteous, and he is angry with the wicked. He will whet his sword. He has bent his bow and made it ready, the instrument of your death." Though the sound came from all the speakers in the room, the monster's words could only be for one person.

"Hold on to the sword, Vijay," Tarja whispered. "Hold on to it. It's your only chance."

Vijay didn't, though. Perhaps he believed he had dealt a killing blow, or perhaps he just couldn't hold on as the monster turned. Before Tarja could blink, the monster was facing Vijay, looking down on him with those red eyes so filled with hate.

"The wrath of God is revealed from heaven . . . against all ungodliness and unrighteousness of men."

The monster reached down to Vijay. It seemed to take an eon but was only an instant. Lifting the boy into the air, it considered him, as if it had never encountered anything like him before.

Vijay didn't struggle. It was as if all his fight was in that one sword thrust, and that being done, so was he. Vijay looked into the monster's eyes, meeting that hateful glare, and seemed to accept the death it promised.

Tarja didn't want to watch what happened next, but she couldn't look away. One moment the monster's hand was resting at its side, the next it was protruding from Vijay's back.

Tarja blinked away tears as the monster let Vijay fall to the ground. To it, Vijay's life meant nothing. To it, he was just one more person who was not Cade. There were likely only two people who Vijay had ever meant anything to, and Tarja doubted either would ever have the opportunity to mourn his all-too-short life.

The monster pulled Vijay's sword from his back, a thick green liquid clinging to the blade as he did. No sooner was the sword out than the wound began to seal, the jagged ends of flesh growing back together.

"Priestess! Priestess, run!" Tarja almost didn't hear the words over all the other sounds. Somehow Vijay was still alive. He was lying where the monster had dropped him, and he was trying to pull himself in her direction. Tarja focused on his face. It was easier than seeing what was being left behind as Vijay crawled slowly to her.

"Run!" Vijay cried one more time before he went still.

Behind Vijay, oblivious to his last efforts, the monster examined the sword that had so recently been embedded in its frame.

Seeming to have made up its mind, the monster held the sword by the blade and threw. At first Tarja thought it was throwing the sword at her, as it hurtled end over end, but soon it became clear that its target was behind her.

Tarja turned in time to see the blade embed itself in the huge metal cross that hung on the wall, the figurehead and antenna for what networked technology the church had managed to assemble.

Sparks rained down as the blade hit home. The cross shuddered for a moment, its cables straining and snapping, and then fell. Bits of metal and wire rained down all around Tarja.

Somewhere something was burning. Tarja had not seen what had started the blaze, but she could smell the smoke and feel the heat.

Maybe it was the cross falling, maybe it was Vijay's last words, maybe it was the first glimpse of flame creeping up over one of the pews, but something in Tarja remembered she had a duty, and it was not to stand there and die, as much as she wished to at that moment.

She hurried down the halls and staircases, down to the security door to the server room. She placed her palm on the reader, and the heavy steel doors yawned open. She ran inside, closing and locking it behind her. She ran down the stairs, down into the ice-cold room. The blue glow of the server's holographic display illuminated her breath. She punched in an emergency access code, something that would upload their database to the other Magdalenes' encampments before destroying the servers in the room. All the data on them would be destroyed to prevent any evil from getting its hands on it. A progress bar crept across the screen. The smell of smoke from the church above began to fill the room, despite the pressure-sealed door, and Tarja began to cough as her lungs filled with the choking cloud.

There was the sound of screeching metal. Tarja didn't need to turn around to know that the monster had followed her. Tarja knew what she had to do. She needed to hold the monster off long enough for her server to finish the upload, but how?

From the sound of it, the thing was only moments from breaking through the door, and once it did, Tarja would prove little obstacle to its rampage.

Tarja turned back to the servers. She had to work fast. There would never be enough time to upload it all, not nearly. The thought of all that knowledge being lost cut her as deeply as the deaths upstairs did, but just as she could do nothing for them, there was nothing she could do about this.

As the screeching grew louder, Tarja quickly started removing packets of information that were incomplete. The texts of books were given priority, only second to what Cade had given her. Her work was done, as best it could be, given the time she had. Tarja turned to the security door and waited. In front of her, the door warped and screeched as the monster bowed it in. Behind her, the server hummed as it uploaded years of research to the servers of the other Magdalenes. And in the middle, Tarja waited, waited for a death that was inevitable.

When the door finally came in with a deafening clang, Tarja was ready. She met those horrible red eyes unblinking, like young Vijay had done just minutes before. The monster only met her eyes for a moment before casually flinging her aside. The only reason Tarja survived was that the monster's attention seemed to be fixed on the banks of servers.

It reached out its hand to the bank of servers. All across their displays Tarja saw an odd symbol appear. It was a helix, encircled by a single pentagram.

Tarja didn't know what the symbol represented, but she had no doubt what it meant. The monster was in her server.

"Farewell, hope, and with hope, farewell, fear."

The monster seemed to be looking for something specific, and given its earlier demand to know where Cade was, Tarja had a good idea what it was. But it didn't matter anymore. Tarja smiled to herself as, one by one, the rack of servers began to erupt in sparks and smoke and the progress bar vanished from what displays were still active.

"Looks like neither of us gets what we want," Tarja said, pulling herself up to a sitting position.

"By proof we feel our power sufficient to disturb his heaven, and with perpetual inroads to alarm, though inaccessible, his fatal throne: which, if not victory . . . is yet revenge." The monster's voice started to break up, as the systems it was using to speak continued to fail. But even so, its anger still came through.

"A good book is the precious lifeblood of a master spirit, embalmed and treasured up on purpose to a life beyond life." Tarja didn't know why she said it, the words just came out. The monster looked over at her, seeming to remember her existence now that its goal was out of reach.

Tarja was delirious; she had to be. It was the only thing that made sense. Up in the cathedral, she had sworn this monster had been quoting the Bible. Now, down in a burning server room, he was quoting Milton. Odder still, she was quoting it back at him. "All is not lost. The unconquerable will and study of revenge, immortal hate, and the courage never to submit or yield."

As the mechanical monster came forward, Tarja thought there were worse last words she could have spoken. And as it reached down to lift her crumpled form from the floor, she looked into its eyes and hissed something even better. "Fuck you."

Upstairs, the church burned. The stained-glass windows cracked and shattered from the heat. The image of Einstein and his revolutionary equation fractured and fell from its frame, its pieces dropping to the ground. Flames poured through every crack they could, and the roof came down in large chunks.

Lithia's garden held back the flames for as long as it could, but even it couldn't keep the inferno away forever. The flowers wilted as they were incinerated. The blocks that made up the walls came falling inward. The light from above the church bore witness as it cracked and fell, but Tarja saw none of this, the only thing she saw, before the lights went out forever, were two glowing red eyes.

CHAPTER 33

Extenuating Circumstances

JERULA WAS BORED, real bored. The ship was abuzz with ordered chaos during launch from Earth, with everyone running around doing their duties. Very quickly thereafter, though, things had settled back down into the general boredom that had defined the previous leg of the trip. They had now left the Terra Luna sector and were on their way back home to Strife, once again neck deep in the monotony of space travel. Throwing some iron around in the gym was Jerula's way of soaking up some of the free hours, a place to "shoot the shit" with people other than ones on his duty shift or his bunkmates. Some of the guys were laughing at the stories they heard about Jerula's night out in San Francisco. Everyone had gotten shore leave, but none of them sparked as notorious a legend as the Strifers that tore up a speakeasy to a Michael Jackson song. His partner in crime, Aurelius, had been oddly MIA ever since they departed from Earth. He must have been assigned to something really important because for the last couple days, Aurelius had left his bunk before breakfast and didn't make it back until well after midnight. Jerula had been able to mend his boredom on the way to Earth with plenty of time to surf the ship's entertainment database, but by the return trip, he had run out of rap battles and cat videos to watch. He needed something to take up the Aurelius-less downtime. Normally he'd want to space out after listening to Aurelius talk about couplers and samoflanges, but he was beginning to miss it. What had

Aurelius been up to? And furthermore, how the hell had he spent so much money that last night on Earth? His wallet was short a couple thousand credits.

"Hey, what time did you and Nyreen head back to the ship that last night on Earth?" he asked Paul, who had just entered the bunk and was headed for the shower.

"I don't remember. Just like I didn't remember the last time you asked."

"I'm trying to figure out how much . . . feels like I went out with a lot more money . . ."

"Maybe you lost at that game you were playing?" Paul asked.

Jerula tried to parse his memory of that night, but everything got fuzzy shortly after sitting down at a table for a friendly game of dice.

"I don't . . . I don't think so . . . I think I remember getting the table flipped over and shoved at me for owning the other guys."

"Well, you and Aurelius were pretty screwed up the next day. Did you drink all your winnings?" Paul asked, turning to look Jerula in the eye. After a moment of silence, Paul started cracking up with laughter. "Oh, man. The fact you can't remember makes me think you guys totally did! Knowing you, you probably bought everyone in the bar a round of drinks."

"Yeah . . . uh-huh. Don't know if I could have actually drank that much and lived." Jerula didn't know what else to say. Both those things sounded like something he would do. If he could just track down Aurelius, maybe his recall of that night would help him figure out where all his money had gone.

"Why not ask Aurelius if he remembers anything?"

"I would if I could find him . . ."

"Well, I'll keep an eye out. He's bound to stop by the bunk while one of us is in it sooner or later."

"Yeah . . . probably . . ."

"Hey, by the way. You down for some poker later?" Paul asked.

"I'm always down to poke her!"

"Nice," Paul said. "Rumor is Governor Maher will be joining us, but keep that to yourself. Can't have the lounge packed with junior officers and low-level techs trying to get a shot at the governor's money."

"Yeah. No problem," Jerula said.

Shortly thereafter, Aurelius popped into the bunk with a smuggy smirk tattooed across his face from ear to ear. He was wiping grease off his hands with a rag and his top was caked in dirt and oil.

"You off duty?" Jerula asked. "Poker game tonight in the lounge in a bit."

"Oh . . . huh. Yeah. I guess I could take a break," Aurelius replied.

"Word is Maher himself is gonna be there. Thought I'd save you a spot at the table."

"Hey, yeah . . . sounds great! You really *are* a damn good friend."

Jerula ignored the strange, extra bouncy tone in his friend's voice. "Don't . . . don't mention it."

Why was Aurelius so greasy? He had smudges of oil all over his coveralls like he had been facedown in an engine or something. "They got you greasing the doors down on G Deck again?" Jerula inquired.

"No. Just . . . you know . . . just picking up a few extra shifts here and there. Workin' on stuff."

"Oh . . . rough."

Paul climbed out of the shower, and Aurelius made his way over to the sink and began washing his hands.

"Hey, Jerula, I found him," Paul said. "Don't look now, but he's right next to you."

"I had noticed. Seems he's been brownnosing the chief by picking up a few extra shifts."

"Is that what's all over his hands?" Paul laughed.

"What can I say? Chief appreciates a man who's good with his hands," Aurelius said.

"Okay, I clearly missed something." The three turned to see Nyreen standing in the doorway.

"Nothing big. Jerula's missing some money, and Aurelius has been wrist deep in the chief. You might want to let him rinse off before touching him," Paul said.

Nyreen's eyes widened. "Is that what's all over his hands?"

"Okay, you guys are starting to repeat yourselves. I'm going to go clean off. When I get out, the jokes had better be new at least," Aurelius said, stepping past Paul and into the shower.

Throwing some clothes in a hamper, Jerula set his wallet out on the table. "Hey, I got a question. Do you remember how much we all spent in San Francisco? You know, like, when we were out and stuff? I'm coming up short and trying figure out where all my money went."

"Oh. Umm . . . I dunno," Aurelius shouted over the sound of running water.

"Between the museums, food, and our night out . . . I know Earth is one hell of an expensive place but . . ."

"Maybe you got pickpocketed in San Francisco? Hard to keep an eye on your wallet when you're partying. I know I spent more than I expected too," Aurelius said.

Jerula cocked an eyebrow in the direction of his showering bunkmate. "What do you mean?"

"Nah, nothing. Yeah, hey . . . sorry man."

"I remember having it after the first and second round of drinks," Jerula began, counting on his hands trying to retrace his steps. "Cover charge . . . pitched in for the cab ride . . . drinks up until our dance number . . . dice game. That's where things get fuzzy."

"You mean . . . you don't remember?" Aurelius asked.

"Remember what?"

"No, seriously . . . you don't remember what happened?"

"No! Remember what?"

Maybe it was Jerula's imagination, but he was starting to think Aurelius was deliberately waiting to answer him.

"You lost that money to me in a dance battle!"

Jerula felt the brooding anger and frustration on his face slip into an unimpressed frown. "Very funny. You couldn't dance your way out of a room if the floor tiles lit up."

There was a short pause while Jerula contemplated how much he lost. The noise of Aurelius's shower echoed through the room.

"Man. Two thousand credits down the . . . drain . . ." His own comment and the sight of the oil-soaked clothing Aurelius had been wearing switched on a lightbulb in Jerula's mind. "Holy shit! You son of a bitch!"

"What!" Aurelius yelled back.

"You didn't . . ."

"I didn't what?"

"*You* didn't . . . *you* son of a bitch."

"Whaaaa?"

Jerula pointed at Aurelius's discarded clothing. "That's engine grease!" His eyes widened.

"Yeah? Nah, what? No, it ain't."

Jerula went running out of the room. He heard Aurelius tear off after him, his wet bare feet slapping against the deck plate. Behind them, both Paul and Nyreen began laughing hysterically. Jerula's running steps echoed in the corridors and he could hear Aurelius's behind him, as if the two were trying to race, but this wasn't for fun. Jerula was out for blood. First, it would be the damned hopper Aurelius bought with *his* money, and then maybe Aurelius himself. Jerula cursed all the way to the cargo deck and into the large room they had used as a lounge during the passage through the Gate earlier in the trip. Jerula came punching into the room so fast he startled a couple technicians working on some loading equipment.

"Where is it? Where the hell is it?" he yelled.

The shaken technicians looked dumbfounded.

Aurelius came up shortly behind him, panting and clutching a towel around his waist. Jerula looked him right in the eye. "Where is it, Strifer? Where is it? I know it's here! You gonna get socked!"

"Where's what?" Aurelius pushed out between breaths.

"That planet hopper! You bought it! I know you bought it! You bought it with *my* money! You've been working on it since we left. You've been working on it every chance you get! That's the oil that was on your hands!"

Aurelius looked over at the frightened cargo crew. "Sorry," he said. "I told him he needs to switch to decaf."

Jerula looked around the cargo hangar. He didn't see any planet hopper, just a bunch of large crates and a few pallets of random equipment with blue and burlap tarps pulled over them. Jerula stood there feeling both stupid and confused. Maybe he had shot his mouth off too soon? Nah, he knew Aurelius. It made so much sense. But a planet hopper was too big to miss. It could have been in one of the larger crates in the room, but he figured Aurelius would have had to take the whole thing apart to fit it in.

Jerula stood there, shaking his head before leaving the cargo hangar and blowing past Aurelius. He was feeling dumb and embarrassed but still not totally convinced.

"Man . . . you really don't remember what happened, do you?" Aurelius said, catching up to Jerula, still clutching the towel around his waist.

"You wanna enlighten me?" Jerula barked.

"You were feeling generous after your game of dice," Aurelius continued. "You handed me a wad of cash, and before I could give it back . . . well, the night kind of got away from me. I was just sobering up while I was handing everything I had over to a Terran who seemed totally befuddled that someone actually wanted the damn thing . . ."

Jerula was fuming, but a part of him couldn't blame Aurelius. Handing him a grip of cash in a drunken generous gesture did sound like something he would do, just like buying a round for everyone in the bar. He had done similar things on a few occasions. If the position was reversed, he would have done exactly what Aurelius had. Right now he was feeling a little more frustrated with the fact that Aurelius had put him on for so long, letting him make a fool out of himself in front of Paul and Nyreen and the crew in the cargo hangar.

"Why didn't you say something earlier?"

"What? And miss being able to see *that* face? Man, I had you going!" Aurelius laughed.

"You're an ass!"

Aurelius tried to playfully shove him, but either he hadn't put enough weight into it, or Jerula was just too big and mad to let it change his stride.

"Don't worry, Strifer," Aurelius said. "We get our paychecks for this mission when we get home. I'll pay you back in full."

Jerula took his time responding to Aurelius. They had nearly walked all the way back to their bunk before he continued, "Fine . . . okay, fine. Just tell me something . . ."

"What?"

"Where is it?" Jerula asked.

"It's . . . it's around. Just not ready to show it yet. Gotta finish making it all shiny before I unveil it."

Paul and Nyreen were applauding as Jerula and Aurelius walked back into the room. They had clearly been laughing themselves sick ever since Aurelius stormed out after Jerula in nothing but a towel.

"Bravo!" Paul exclaimed.

"They're so much more fun than Jenkins," Nyreen added.

Paul turned to face Nyreen. "Well, there was that one time with the ham."

"Yeah, but he was mostly dressed. This is still better," Nyreen said.

Jerula was pissed as he made his way down to the lounge. Paul and Nyreen were already setting up the card table. His eyes were promising murder to anyone who looked at him wrong. By now he was sure he had given that money to his face squid of a bunkmate, but Jerula wanted to be angry and Aurelius's little joke earlier hadn't helped things.

Paul and Nyreen were already there when he came into the room. Their happy welcoming faces quickly turned to ones of concern as they saw that Jerula was still steaming. Jerula took one look at Paul and Nyreen standing there and let out a bellowing laugh that did little to reassure them. He went to settle in at one of the seats. "Whatcha doing standing there shaking? Come sit down. Folks will be here soon, and I have to win back some money I lost on Terra."

Paul and Nyreen both complied, still somewhat uneasy, wondering what had set Jerula off. They didn't dare ask as they went to sit down. Jerula filled them in, and Nyreen began to laugh very carefully, gauging Jerula's reactions the whole time.

It wasn't long before the rest of the seats around the table were filled. Jerula knew most of the players in passing, but none by name. Sure enough, there was Governor Maher, looking tired and stressed and, to Jerula's calculating eye, rich. He recognized the look of a man who was weary of the world and needed to relax. Hopefully, he didn't mind if he had to part with some money to do it.

Jerula looked around at the rest of the table before announcing, "Ladies, gentlemen, and everything in between, the name of the game is eight-card nova. Randomizer at fifteen and starbursts high. Minimum bet is ten creds, and no, I don't offer any credit."

With that, the night began.

The games went on for some time. Maher watched his crew unwind around him. As they relaxed, so did he. These were the kind of people he wanted to be around. The kind of people he wanted to be, if he was being completely honest with himself. But no, that was a road no longer open to him. Too much had happened, and some roads you shouldn't travel twice.

Maher put down his cards with a grin twelve parsecs wide. "I got a photon spread, folks. That beats anything you guys have hiding under your drinks or up your sleeves."

Everyone at the table groaned and passed their chips to Maher. Paul hesitated and then laughed. "Damn, Governor. It's just like you bureaucrats. Always taking money from the little guy."

Maher had seen him around a few times. Maher leaned back in his seat, spreading his hands, placating. "Don't blame me, friend. Blame the cards. I can't help it if they like me better than you."

Maher leaned forward as the next hand was dealt by Jerula. Maher liked the way he had about him. He'd have to keep an eye on him. Jerula dealt Maher his next hand. He wouldn't have to pretend to lose with this Jerula—it would happen on its own. He slid forty chips into the pot and relaxed.

As the night wore on, players dropped out of the game, most leaving with all their pay still on the table. The last to leave were Paul and Nyreen. Nyreen pulled Paul away from the table with a knowing wink. To Jerula's credit, he kept the teasing of his friend's pending interlude to a tasteful minimum, although the jackhammer motions were a bit unnecessary.

Jerula looked at Maher with a glint in his eye. "What ya say, Governor? Why don't we cut this penny-ante crap and raise the minimum to a hundred?"

Maher was more than happy to comply. If this kid wanted a real game, he'd be happy to deliver. The two men slid their chips to the center of the table and looked at each other. Jerula cracked first, leaning back and letting out a bellow of a laugh. "Shit, Governor, how the hell bad did things go on Terra that it's got ya slumming down here with us dregs?"

Maher let out a breath he hadn't realized he'd been holding and joined Jerula's laughter. "You have no idea, son. You have no ship-wrecked idea."

Maher placed a card down on the table and began to tell Jerula everything, leaving out only the parts about Pacius.

"Ain't you afraid of what they might do to ya for screwing with the UPE like ya did?" Jerula asked.

Maher was. But he couldn't admit it. "No, and I'll tell you why. Fear is their weapon. They use it to keep people looking over their shoulders instead of looking up at them. They want us afraid. If we're all scared, then we need them. But if we can break that, then they have nothing. I once knew a man who threw away fear and did what he thought was right, and the UPE tried to destroy him. He beat them, and no matter what they did, they couldn't take that from him."

Jerula looked across the table with scarcely concealed admiration on his face. "Damn. You got a hell of a pair."

Maher smiled. "No, I've got the starburst."

Laying down his cards, Maher reached out for the chips at the center of the table.

All of a sudden, he and Jerula were thrown from their chairs. Chips and cards went flying. Glasses and drinks smashed on the floor. The ship had been hit by something, and Maher suspected it wasn't another piece of debris.

CHAPTER 34

Time to Go

AURELIUS CAME HOPPING out of main engineering, pulling on his slush suit as he went. He didn't know what was going on, but figured whatever it was, he'd stand a better chance of getting out alive if he had a little extra protection.

All around Aurelius, the ship rocked under near continuous impacts and alarm klaxons blared, alerting the panicking crew that something was very wrong. In front of him, a set of doors opened up, releasing a thick cloud of smoke and a wave of intense heat. A moment later, a figure emerged from whatever hell was inside and collapsed to the deck. Aurelius couldn't tell if it was someone he knew, or even if the person was male or female, with all the burns covering their face and body. What Aurelius did know was that whoever they were, they had no chance if they stayed there. So, he scooped them up as gently as he could while he was in the slush suit and started running.

Aurelius still wasn't sure what was going on, but he now at least knew where he was going. He turned the corner into the corridor that led to the ship's mess and stopped. He knew the mess had been designated as this section's emergency shelter, but had never expected to see so many people trying to push their way through the doors. The *Freedom's Reach* had a crew of thousands, and even in Aurelius's little section of the ship, there had to be hundreds of people. Seeing so many of them trying to fill such a small space made those numbers real for him in a way they never had been before.

He started pushing his way through the mass of humanity, trying not to jostle the person in his arms.

"I've got wounded!" Aurelius called out several times as he made his way up to the front of the crowd, where two security officers were scanning dog tags and trying to keep the panicking people from turning into a stampede.

"Take them inside. There's a small section at the far end of the mess for the wounded!" one of the officers shouted over the noise of hundreds of people trying to be heard at once.

Aurelius didn't even try to answer. He just nodded his thanks to the officer and pushed into the mess.

Inside, things were a bit more orderly. Aurelius doubted the people in the mess were any safer than those outside, but clearly they felt so, and that made all the difference. There was still panic, but it wasn't the sort of blind unthinking panic of a mob. It was more considered. It was the panic of people who believed the security officers outside and the ship's captain were doing everything they could to protect them, while knowing it wasn't enough.

The vast majority of the people huddled in the mess were clustered around several large viewports that ran from deck to ceiling along one wall. Aurelius scanned the room and saw the place the officer was talking about. It was a sort of emergency aid station they had set up in one corner of the large room. There was another security officer standing just outside a cluster of stretchers, and unlike the officers outside the mess, this one's job seemed to be making sure people stayed away. The officer gave Aurelius a hard look as he approached, but he didn't stop him.

"I've got someone who needs help," Aurelius said as he reached the officer. The officer jerked his head in the direction of a group of people walking through a mass of stretchers and people leaning against the wall. Aurelius took that to mean that's where he should go. A moment later, a woman ran up to him and started helping him with the badly burned person in his arms. It was a moment before Aurelius recognized her as the pretty blond nurse who had treated him on the trip to Earth. She didn't look like Aurelius remembered. She seemed older and tired. It was as if she had aged ten years in the short time since the emergency had started.

"Lay them down here," she said in an emotionless voice, pointing to a section of the deck that was reasonably clear of dirt. Aurelius complied and stepped back so she could get to work, but she didn't spring into action. There was no call for drugs, no attempt to cut away the burned uniform so they could better treat the wounded. She simply produced a tag reader like the ones the officers at the doors had been using and scanned the burned person's tags before moving on.

"Aren't you going to help them?" Aurelius called to her back. She was kneeling next to another person, this one a woman whose arm was a ragged lump lying motionless at her side.

The nurse didn't look up as she responded, and her voice seemed a thousand miles away. "He is beyond anything we can do for him. He was probably already dead when you found him."

Maher came tearing onto the bridge of the *Freedom's Reach*. The normally orderly space was buzzing. Crewmen moved from station to station, calling out reports to each other.

"Who the hell is attacking us?" he called out to no one in particular.

"A UPE vessel, sir!" the helmsman said, never looking up from his console. "It's the *Enigma*!"

"Where's the captain?" Maher asked.

"Not sure, sir. The ship was hit hard in the first volley, and we're getting reports of heavy casualties from all decks. It's possible the captain is among them or in a section of the ship where he can't report in," the helmsman said.

"Then who's in charge here?" Maher asked him.

"I am, sir. I was head of the duty shift when everything started."

Maher looked the helmsman over. He looked like a child. Maher doubted the man needed to shave more than once a week.

"Well, this is my ship, so I'm taking command," Maher said. He was almost taken aback by the look of relief on the young helmsman's face.

"Yes, sir," he said with a sigh.

"Don't relax yet. I'm a civilian and have been for almost thirty years. I'm fine giving orders, but I'm going to need you to figure out how we're going to follow them. Is that understood?" Maher said to the helmsman, whom he had just turned into a serving first officer.

"Yes, sir," the helmsman said sharply.

"Damn, Governor!" Maher turned to see Jerula standing next to him on the bridge. In the chaos he hadn't even noticed the towering soft tech until he spoke, but he must have followed Maher all the way from the cargo room they had been playing poker in.

"Jerula, I'd ask why you're here, but right now I don't care. Go help them figure out exactly how bad it is, and bring me a report on what we can do about it," Maher ordered.

Maher took the captain's chair as the ship rocked from a particularly fierce onslaught.

"Can we run?" Maher demanded.

"No, sir! They've killed our engines," the helmsman replied.

"How far are we from the Gate?" Maher asked.

"At least another half day," came the reply.

"Any chance the escape pods could make it that far?"

"No. They were meant to keep a person alive for weeks, but their propulsion is limited," the helmsman said.

Maher sat back in his seat and thought. Nothing in his experience had prepared him for this. All of his battles had been battles of words and policy. This was something else.

"I guess this is my retirement party," Maher said begrudgingly.

A light lit up at the communications station. "The *Enigma* is hailing us," the man at the station reported.

"Put them through," Maher demanded.

An image of a dark-haired, stocky man filled the big screen in front of the bridge.

"*Freedom's Reach*, this is Captain Shard of the UPE *Enigma*. Your ship is crippled and outclassed. You are to prepare for boarders. Any resistance or failure to turn over the traitor will be met with deadly force."

"So, I'm a traitor now?" Maher asked. "They couldn't get me to lie down during the meeting, so they send out attack dogs and call me a traitor?"

"This isn't about any meeting, Governor. You are a traitor because you harbor a traitor. Surrender and turn that man over and your lives may not be forfeit," Shard said with the calm confidence of a man who knows everything that's happening is under his control.

"We aren't harboring anyone," Maher said.

"Don't lie to me, Maher," Shard said.

"I'm not lying. We are harboring no one. You've attacked our ship for no reason," Maher said.

"Very well then, Governor. You brought this on yourself." And with that, Shard's face vanished from the screen.

What was Shard talking about? They weren't harboring any traitors to the UPE. It was possible, of course, that it was just their story, their justification for getting rid of someone who was proving difficult for them to deal with. Either way, the time for talk was done.

"Communications, put me through to the entire ship," Maher ordered. A moment later a small light lit up on the arm of his chair telling him he was broadcasting.

"*Freedom's Reach* crew, this is your acting captain speaking. The ship is under attack by a UPE warship. They have issued us orders that are not possible to obey. I expect boarding parties shortly, and I expect them to be operating weapons free, so I am giving the same instructions. Security teams are instructed to treat anyone in a UPE uniform as hostile until further notice. All noncombat personnel are instructed to evacuate to the escape pods. The rest of us will give you as much time as we can to get out of here. It has been a pleasure traveling with all of you, thank you. That is all." Maher made a cutting gesture and the channel went dead.

Maher turned to the bridge crew. "Did you not hear me? Get to the escape pods! I'm not having anyone stay in danger who doesn't need to be."

"Governor, someone should stay here." Maher turned to look up at Jerula. He had obtained a rifle from a security cabinet and was standing next to him, looking like he was more than ready and able to use it.

"No. Go. I'll be okay here, and I'm sure the sight of you on the decks might make whatever teams boarding think twice about pressing the issue," Maher said.

"But sir . . ."

"Jerula, go. I'll be fine."

Aurelius had been standing against the viewports in the mess hall when the announcement had gone out. He had watched as nearly twenty craft departed the massive form of the *Enigma* and headed for the

Freedom's Reach. Now, however, he was running down a corridor, and he wasn't the only one. On all sides of him people were moving as fast as they could to try and reach the nearest open escape pods.

Aurelius stopped at a junction of corridors that contained an airlock. In front of it were half a dozen security people, their weapons pointed at the closed hatch.

A moment later, sparks began to fly from the rim of the hatch.

"That's it, they're coming through. Hold as long as you can. Let's make them pay for every inch," one of them called to their comrades.

There was a deafening clang as the airlock hatch dropped to the deck and, almost immediately after, the louder sound of half a dozen rifles going off at once. Aurelius took cover behind a corner and watched as the two sides exchanged fire. At first it seemed as if the *Freedom's Reach* people were keeping the upper hand. There were already several dead wearing UPE uniforms and not one in a SMMC one, but then everything changed.

Aurelius almost missed it in the chaos; a little round metal ball, thrown almost casually.

"Grenade!" one of the *Freedom's Reach* people called as he leaped for cover. His comrades all attempted the same, with varying levels of success.

Aurelius instinctively shielded his eyes from the blast, and when he opened them, the deck in front of the airlock was ablaze, and several figures laid motionless in the flames, figures he knew had been SMMC security officers just a moment earlier.

Aurelius grabbed a rifle from one of the bodies and opened fire. Somewhere in the back of his head he heard the voice of one of the surviving officers yelling for everyone to fall back, but at the moment, he didn't care. This was his ship, those were his crewmates, and he had a need to pay back just a little of the death he had seen that day.

It was difficult to say for certain through all the smoke and flames, but Aurelius was reasonably sure he scored a few hits on the commandos who were attempting to advance past the airlock and through the inferno. That was when he saw it. He wasn't comfortable calling it a person. The size seemed too large for that, and the way it moved through the flames as if fire didn't touch it . . .

It was a creature, a hulking amalgam of man and machine, of flesh and metal, with glowing red eyes shining out of a dark hood.

Aurelius and a few of the security personnel who had remained with him opened fire on the mechanical abomination with everything they had left, emptying clip after clip into it, but nothing touched it. The bullets didn't bounce off it. Aurelius could have mentally dealt with that. Instead, the bullets seemed to avoid him, curving around him. It was as if even the bullets understood the danger of the creature in front of them.

Aurelius watched in mute horror as the thing advanced, stopping to lift a security officer by the skull and then crush it like an egg. Another fell to its massive fist, crumpling bonelessly to the deck.

Aurelius didn't want to run. Even now, something in him told him to stand and fight. But staying there was death. He had no training for situations like this, and no weapon that could hurt the thing bearing down on him. What he did have was a slush suit and an escape plan that didn't involve an escape pod.

Aurelius sped down the corridor using the slush suit's jetpack for all the speed it could give him. All around him people poured out of doorways, wounded and on fire. Everyone was frantically running to whatever escape still remained for them. Behind Aurelius, the terrible shadow of the hooded, mechanical figure fell against the wall. He was coming. Aurelius moved as fast as he could, but it didn't seem to be fast enough. He was looking over his shoulder when he felt the force of an impact in front of him. Aurelius had hit something soft, something that was now lying underneath him.

"Strifer, get the fuck off me now, or I swear I will lift you off me and throw your sorry ass down the hall to clear the way." The voice was a bit muffled, but Aurelius would have recognized the threatening tone anywhere.

"Jerula?" he said, pulling himself off his friend and helping him up.

"Yeah, it's me. Now turn around and go back the other way. A team of commandos is not that far behind me," Jerula said.

"No good. I don't know what it is, but something worse is coming from that way," Aurelius said, glancing back to make sure the monster had not caught up yet.

"What kind of worse?" Jerula asked as they picked a corridor neither had come down and hoped.

"The kind that crushes skulls with its hands and deflects bullets."

"Now is definitely not the time for jokes, Aurelius."

"Jerula, believe me, I wish I were joking."

Up ahead, a crewman stepped into an escape pod that had, for some reason, not launched. Aurelius sped right past them.

"Hold on!" Jerula yelled to him, and he turned.

"No, follow me!" Aurelius yelled a moment later.

"What the hell are you doing?" Jerula snapped.

"I've a better way off." A second later, Aurelius heard the sound of the escape pod sealing and a clang as it was launched.

"You had better have something good!" Jerula said.

"I do," Aurelius said with a confidence he only half felt.

Behind them, they heard the sounds of gunfire again, and the pings of bullets impacting with the deck steps or against the walls.

"Where are we going?" Jerula asked, kicking up a bit more speed as the misses became closer.

"Here!" Aurelius said as they reached the doors to a large cargo bay.

"What the hell are we doing here?" Jerula asked as they entered the bay and sealed the doors behind them.

"Get up to the cargo controls. I'll get her started!" Aurelius yelled.

"What?"

Aurelius pointed up into the air. There above them, suspended over the deck by two giant grasping claws, was the twin-engine, two-seater planet hopper Jerula had been looking for earlier in the night. Even the blue tarp Aurelius had pulled over it couldn't hide it.

"There's that deathtrap of a hopper!" Jerula said disbelievingly.

"Hey, I got it running, and it's a lot faster than the escape pods," Aurelius said.

"It had better be," Jerula said, running over to a ladder and shooting up it.

Aurelius watched as his friend hit the release for the claws without bothering to lower them first. The hopper hit the deck with a crash that echoed off the walls.

"Dude!" Aurelius yelled.

"Sorry, but those things are slow, and we don't have a lot of time!"

Jerula was right, but it still hurt. He ran over and yanked back the tarp. There it was, the little planet hopper he fell in love with in San Francisco. It was clean and shiny enough to blind someone. Best of all, it was ready to fly. Across its side in white lettering the name *Storm Chaser* was written; Aurelius smiled at it briefly as he popped the canopy and leaped in.

"Come on!" he called to Jerula.

The deck began to shake as Jerula climbed into the *Storm Chaser*. It was a dull rhythmic thud that was growing stronger. Aurelius knew what it was, what it had to be.

Aurelius whipped his craft around as best he could in the cargo bay, and there before him, in the doorway, stood the terrible monster that had been on his heels ever since the airlock. Was it chasing him, or had it been headed for the cargo bay all along? Its stature was colossal, standing nearly seven feet tall and almost impossibly muscled. It began a heavy, mechanical sprint toward Aurelius and the *Storm Chaser*. Leaping through the air, it grabbed hold of the right wing of the little planet hopper. The craft sank to the side and began to spin. The rush from the engines blew debris all over the cargo bay. The rear stabilizer crashed into a catwalk and scaffolding, showering the room in sparks and fire. The mechanical terror started to climb up the wing and across the sagging craft, pressing his foot against the engine housing, causing the hopper to continue in a slow spin.

Aurelius tried to swing the craft around and get the nightmare off, but nothing was working. The beast kept climbing closer. The extra weight kept the craft dipping to one side, its engine unable to articulate or stabilize its flight.

The creature had nearly reached the open cockpit, its fists reaching closer to Aurelius with every movement. Aurelius couldn't keep his bird in the air. He did the only thing he could—he thrust the craft down hard into the deck. It bounced violently and skidded along the plating into a stack of boxes, but the impact knocked the cybernetic demon off. Aurelius threw the throttle in reverse and the engines rotated backward. They threw out a mighty crimson blast, igniting the boxes surrounding the fallen form.

For a short ecstatic second, Aurelius thought he had finally ended the thing, but only for a second. He couldn't believe his eyes as whatever this thing was pulled itself back to its feet. Its hood had completely burned away along with whatever flesh the fire had touched, leaving clean bone that seemed somehow too dark. Not like it had been burned, but more like it had been carved from some black stone. Even still, the creature turned to watch them, its glowing red eyes untouched by the engine's blast. And as it watched them, Aurelius noticed that it had some sort of metal plate fixed to its jaw, making it impossible for the thing to even open its mouth.

"Guess they don't want their monsters to talk back," Aurelius said as he lifted his craft back up off the deck.

All around them the cargo bay was on fire, crates and barrels burning so hot that they were melting the metal around them.

In the floor, the massive cargo doors were swinging open, a specialized force field keeping the air from rushing out, but otherwise allowing free movement from both outside and in.

Aurelius swung the craft over the doors. From across the room, he looked the terrible creature right in the eye. It looked back. Pieces of it were on fire, but it seemed to take no notice. Burned and infuriated, it tried to make a running jump for the *Storm Chaser*. Aurelius threw the control sticks forward, causing his craft to fall downward through the open cargo bay doors and out into space. The beast caught himself on the lip of the doorway. He looked down with a fury that burned hotter than the raging inferno it stood in, but there was nothing it could do now to stop their escape.

Maher heard the commandos breach the bridge door with a bang.

"Get down now!" barked their leader.

Maher ignored him.

"I said down!" their leader said again.

Maher turned around in the captain's chair to face the group of heavily armed people who were pointing very long and heavy-looking weapons at him. "I'm sorry, I didn't hear you knock."

CHAPTER 35

A Very Rude Awakening

PEOPLE WEREN'T SUPPOSED to dream in hypersleep, but for some reason, some people did. Scientists thought it had something to do with blood type. Spiritual people thought it had something to do with will of character, the inability to silence a strong mind. Regardless of the reason, Lithia always dreamed.

They were outside in the arboretum, finishing up for the day. Papa was supposed to be home from Titan later that afternoon. The family hadn't seen him for a week, and they were excited to hear about his adventures on Jupiter's moons.

Lithia's mother was chasing her through the garden. She was only eight years old and could hide in the bushes with ease, but being caught meant another raspberry.

They were surrounded, dwarfed, by exaggeratedly large plants and flowers packed together in long rows stretching across the domed arboretum. Trusses spiderwebbed across the curved glass ceiling. Yellow light from a cloudy Venusian day outside lit their garden.

A tower of red brushlike bristles stretched upward, with an array of large leaves caught in mid-fold. Water droplets on the plant's skin reflected a warped image of Lithia and her mother.

"Mommy, what kind of flower is that?"

"Don't you remember, Lithia? That's the amaranth."

"Oh, yeah! It's still alive!"

Her mother smiled before kissing her on the cheek. A second later came the dreaded, giggle-inducing raspberry. "Of course it is. It will never fade, even if cut."

The dream was always the same. It always started off so happy, but like a movie with a bad ending, it turned into a nightmare. She always made sure to turn the movie off and wake up before that part, but in cryosleep, she didn't have a "Stop" button.

The dream suddenly took on a darker tone, the scene fast forwarded.

Her mother and a twelve-year-old Bobby were running down the house hallway, the living room crackling with embers slowly consuming the room. The flowers outside turned into flames of all colors. Lithia was suddenly standing in the kitchen of the family house watching what was going on like a movie; she was powerless to act.

Her father was frantically loading a shotgun while her mother pulled on his arm. "No, don't! We can slip out the back. We can run from here. We can take the ship and head to Earth. We'll be safe there!"

Her father was resolute. "No. This has gone too far. I'm not letting those people run us from our home! This has got to end here!"

The memory skipped ahead.

Bobby was screaming, "Where's Dad? Where is he?"

Her mother tried to open a window, but it was sealed. She picked up a chair and tossed it through the glass. The flames from downstairs hurried up the staircase with the breeze of new air. Her mother grabbed Bobby and shoved him through the window. The broken glass in the frame cut his legs, and he yelped in pain. She had no time to escape before the burning roof caved in, landing in her lap.

This was the end of the dream, the terrible ending, the nightmare Lithia had pushed far away out into the orbits of her mind for so long. But now she was vulnerable to it. All the times she hadn't finished the movie came rushing back to her, ready for revenge, and it forced her to watch this time.

Lithia woke from her dream in a startled panic. Her chest tightened as the sudden shock of claustrophobia overwhelmed her. As thick beads of sweat poured down her face, she pushed and pulled at the sleep chamber's walls. Terror washed over her body, making the hair on the back of her neck stand on end. Her flailing hand finally landed on the release lever, and the glass door over her lifted open. Lithia sat up, groggy and gasping for air. She had forgotten she was on the *Amaranth*. She had forgotten all the events that had led up to that point, for just a moment, before everything came flooding back. The sudden shock caused her to lean over the side of the pod and vacate her stomach onto the deck.

Needless to say, it was a terrifying way to wake up. She took a few minutes to collect herself, a couple of stray tears seeping from the corners of her eyes, before she felt calm enough to slowly climb out of her pod. Everything hurt like a hangover. Everything was so stiff. It took a couple moments to feel like she had control of her body again. The hypersleep chambers were designed to decrease the impact of atrophy, but even so, a month in hypersleep meant things were going to hurt for a little while.

She reached over to a compartment next to the monitoring systems of the pod. There was a little jar of Fizzies ready and waiting for her.

Just as soon as she had swallowed a couple of the bubbly tablets and the terror of her dream had begun to subside, she looked over at the other pods in the room. Curiously, Cade's sleep chamber door was open and empty.

What the hell was going on? Where was he?

Lithia checked Bobby's pod. He was still safe and asleep, thank God.

Then, she heard something. At first it was like the murmuring of a radio or the distant noise of ship systems. But as she stood there, in her underwear in the dimly lit room, and held her breath, she could definitely hear someone talking. He wasn't speaking Terranese, but rather a Frontier tongue. She understood roughly three-quarters of the words, thanks to a life spent preparing to set out and see the stars. It was definitely Cade's voice. He must have been talking to someone. What was he doing? Sending a message? How was he awake?

Another wash of terror came over Lithia as Cade got a reply. It wasn't the static-filled, garbled transmission noise. The other voice came from someone on board. The hairs on the back of Lithia's neck stood on end. How did someone get on board? Where were they? The dread thickened when a third voice replied, "A month in hypersleep? Damn, I've got some Fizzies if you need 'em."

Lithia slowly slid the door to the sleep-pod room open and slunk through, trying to make as little noise as possible. She snuck across the galley toward the cockpit.

"The captain of this vessel may be waking up soon. I had hoped to have you guys launched again before that happened," Cade said in the Frontier dialect.

"Maybe I should go reset them?" This from one of the other voices.

Lithia panicked with adrenaline. What the hell was going on? Who the hell were these guys, and what were they doing on her ship?

She scurried as quietly as possible back to the hypersleep room. Were these guys planning on stealing her ship? She looked around for a weapon and a place to hide.

Lithia pushed her pod room door closed. The window glass was still foggy. She grabbed a pipe wrench hanging on a shelf. The environmental suits hanging on the far wall were a perfect place to hide, so she slipped behind them. She peeked between the suits and waited for whoever it was coming down the hall.

A young guy in his early to mid-twenties entered. He was wearing some sort of reinforced environmental suit with the helmet retracted. She caught a glimpse of his face as he passed by. He didn't look like a pirate or marauder; he was downright pretty. Really pretty.

He walked over to the pod controls and reset a timer before peering into one of them.

Lithia thought about clubbing him over the head with the wrench, but she was worried he might not go down with one swing, and if he made any noise at all, there was a chance that the others up in the cockpit might hear it.

"Who are you, and what are you doing on my ship?" Lithia whispered, stepping up behind him, and shoving the handle of the wrench into his back. With any luck, it would feel like the barrel of a gun through his suit.

The man slowly raised his hands. "Easy! Easy! Don't shoot. I don't understand a word you're saying."

In Lithia's panic, she had spoken in Terran, but it seemed this man didn't speak it.

"Who are you? What are you doing on my ship?" Lithia said, switching over to the Frontier language.

"Yeah, that's what I figured you said. Look, we're just passing through. We didn't intend to stay long."

Lithia pushed the handle into his back as hard as she could. "Not answering my question. How did you get on board?"

"We were running from a bit of trouble and needed somewhere to hide. You should really update your security software. You might as well have left your cargo door unlocked."

Lithia didn't know how to react. It reminded her that Cade was awake, which shouldn't be possible if he was in hypersleep. "Go to the cockpit. Slowly . . ." she urged. She needed to take action.

Lithia walked behind the man as they made their way step by step back to the cockpit. She wasn't exactly sure what her next move was, though she hoped the opportunity to blast Cade out an airlock would factor into it at some point. Ideally, after he explained everything, and maybe after he begged just a little bit.

"Umm . . . gentlemen . . . I think we have a situation here."

Cade and the other man in the cockpit turned around in their chairs, and Lithia got a look at the other man who had come aboard. He was large; the bridge felt cramped just by his presence. Lithia fought the urge to step back out of the cockpit. Even sitting, he could almost look Lithia in the eye. Standing up, he'd probably have to be careful his head didn't touch the ceiling.

She quickly designated the two: "the pretty one" and "the giant."

"Where did she come from?" the giant asked.

"The sleep chamber must have defrosted when you guys came on board," Cade said.

Cade's eyes narrowed for a moment, and he looked at Lithia and the pretty one in a way that made Lithia profoundly uneasy. When he finally turned away, seeming to be satisfied, Lithia let out a breath she hadn't known she was holding.

"Congratulations. She's holding you up with a . . ." he said a word in the language that Lithia didn't recognize, but she had a sick feeling it meant "wrench."

The pretty one slowly lowered his hands. Lithia could still see some doubt on his face. Cade might have said it was a wrench, but some part of him, the part that could still feel it in his back, had to doubt, just a little bit. That was, until he turned around and saw Lithia standing there, half dressed, the head of her pipe wrench still clutched in her hand.

"Huh. It really was a wrench. For a moment, thought my new friend was trying to get me killed," he said, eyeing Lithia up and down.

Lithia met those eyes, and to her surprise they were nonthreatening and even a little warm. They just didn't say, "I'm here to kill you and steal your ship," but rather something more akin to, "I'm here to rescue you." She was struck by the look, and the charming smile that came with it. If it wasn't her imagination, there was even a slight hint of wisdom about him. The type of wisdom of a survivor. He smiled at her, and she started to feel more at ease. He was downright disarming. If he hadn't been stowing away on her ship in the company of a giant and whatever the hell Cade was, he would be the kind of guy Lithia would want to get to know better.

"You're probably not the first girl in her underwear to want to shoot him, ya know," the giant said, grinning. "Nice wrench, by the way. He's been hit with worse, though," the giant finished, looking over at Lithia.

Lithia didn't know what to do. Yeah, one of these hijackers was very cute, and they both had a charm about them that made Lithia sort of like them, but hijackers they were, and somehow Lithia had lost control of the situation.

"I don't know who the hell you guys are or what the hell you're doing on my ship, but I need to know exactly what is going on, or so help me god, I will brain you with this wrench!" she said in an attempt to get things back in a realm she understood.

"Which of us? Because if you're braining Aurelius here, I might stay quiet, just so I can see that," the giant joked, grinning evilly at the pretty one, at Aurelius.

"Dude!" Aurelius said, looking over at the giant in disbelief.

"Relax. She probably couldn't kill you with that wrench. Not on the first swing, anyway," the giant said.

"Not helping," Aurelius said, turning back to Lithia, where she still stood, brandishing the wrench at him threateningly.

"Listen, we'll tell you everything. Let's put down anything heavy enough to crack my skull, and we can all go into the galley and talk," Aurelius said, giving Lithia a smile.

"That sounds less fun than what was going to happen here, but then again there might be food. You coming?" the giant said, turning to Cade.

"Things will probably go more smoothly if I do," Cade said. He stood up from his seat and strode out of the cockpit, not bothering to wait for the rest of them.

The giant followed close behind, and Lithia and Aurelius had to step aside to make enough room for him to go past.

"You going to let me go now?" Aurelius asked.

"Hey! They have Cheese-nips!" the giant called back to his friend.

CHAPTER 36

Crossing Paths

LITHIA QUICKLY MADE her way back to the sleep chamber and pulled on a long, dark blue skirt and matching blouse before heading to the galley.

When she stepped into the galley, she found Cade sitting stiffly on a short sofa, while the giant and Aurelius rummaged around the cupboards for food, like they hadn't eaten in days.

"I believe you had some questions," Cade stated without bothering to look up at Lithia.

"Again . . . who are you, and how did you get on my ship?"

Aurelius turned away from the cupboard and the rapidly growing pile of snacks he and the giant were building. "My name's Aurelius . . . Aurelius Blaze." He lifted his hand out as if to shake. "I'm sorry for the hullabaloo, but me and my buddy Jerula here were in a tight bind."

"Hullabaloo?" Lithia asked.

There was a certain kind of charm in Aurelius's eyes, something that made Lithia want to like him, even though he was on her ship, without her permission, and eating her caramel puffs.

"Yeah. Hullabaloo. You know. We were in trouble."

Lithia turned away from Aurelius, ignoring his extended hand, and for a moment Aurelius looked a little disappointed.

"Cade, how did you get out of hypersleep?" Lithia asked, turning her ire on the person who was really responsible for the situation.

"There's a series of optronic relays that run along my spine and interface with my central nervous system . . ."

"You may wanna skip the technobabble," Aurelius said. "She's still got the wrench."

"I connect wirelessly with the *Amaranth*. Its sensors were feeding me data the whole trip. They woke me up when their hopper latched onto our underside."

Anger flooded Lithia; it was born from betrayal and distrust as much as just the utter feeling of not being in control of the situation. "How can you . . . that might have been something you should have mentioned you could do before I agreed to take you on this trip!"

"It wasn't relevant at the time."

"The hell it wasn't! Son of a bitch."

She must have said the second half of that sentence in Terranese, as Aurelius and the giant glanced at each other with matching looks of incomprehension.

"Okay. Fine . . . moving past that." Lithia looked at Aurelius. "What kind of 'hella-blue' are you in?"

"Hey, you used that right," Aurelius said.

"What kind?"

"Well . . ." he murmured hesitantly.

"Might as well tell her the truth," the giant said.

"We may have been . . . running from a UPE battleship."

"Of course . . . of fucking course! Why are you running from the UPE?"

"You didn't mention the UPE earlier," Cade interjected, expressing a hint of fear, the only emotion Lithia had ever seen on him. "Why didn't you say anything about the UPE before?"

"Didn't think you'da been so hospitable had I."

"He's got trouble with the UPE of his own," Lithia said. "If we get pulled over and you guys are a couple of fugitives—"

"It's not like that," Aurelius replied, cutting her off. "We were on a diplomatic mission back from Earth when some ship—"

"The *Enigma*," the giant said, causing everyone in the room to look at him. "What? I was on the bridge when they attacked."

"The *Enigma*?" Lithia said. "I saw that ship in orbit of Earth when we left. It must be fast to have caught up with us already."

"Yeah. When the *Enigma* attacked us, they said they were looking for someone. Then they boarded and started shooting. Jerula and I hopped in the *Storm Chaser* and booked it."

Lithia was confused. All these names and stories being flung at her in a language she hadn't spoken in years was difficult to digest all at once. "What's a storm chaser, or a Jerula?"

"*My* ship," Aurelius boasted.

"Which?" Lithia asked.

"The *Storm Chaser*. The Jerula is the guy eating all the dried plumbs."

"You two need to leave. Now," Cade commanded.

Saying nothing else, Cade stood up and quickly walked back to the cockpit.

"Does that mean you're lettin' us go?" Aurelius asked.

"I agree. You two need to get off my ship now. Sooner, if possible," Lithia said, following him.

Cade punched away at the ship's controls as Lithia and the others reentered the bridge.

"Something wrong?" Jerula asked, stepping in and taking a seat beside him.

"You don't understand. You guys need to get out of here. Now!"

Jerula had his eyes fixed on the cockpit's overlay. "It may be a little too late for that."

"Why?" Lithia asked, trying to look past Jerula and resenting that he and Cade had taken over her cockpit.

"*Enigma*," Cade said flatly, and a moment later the massive hull of the UPE vessel filled the entire cockpit view.

"How did we not pick them up on long-range sensors?" Aurelius yelled.

"Unless you want to look out a window with a pair of binoculars, her ship doesn't have long-range sensors," Jerula said.

"They're deploying grapplers!" Cade shouted.

The *Amaranth* trembled as grappling clamps fired from the *Enigma* latched on to the hull, digging their way into the vessel's thick, armored skin. There was a terrible, metallic groaning noise that yawned out from seemingly everywhere; it was so deep it made Lithia's teeth vibrate. They were being boarded and the groans were the agonizing cries of her little ship being harpooned like a fish by the UPE.

"Why the . . . ? Who the . . . ? They didn't even hail us! What the hell is going on here?" Jerula said.

"Not even a demand to surrender," Aurelius added.

"They don't need to. There's nothing we can do," Cade said.

"We can run," Aurelius barked back.

Cade shook his head. "We're already moving at top subspeed and we can't engage the sprint drive with those hooks in us."

"Return fire?" Aurelius yelled back.

Cade rubbed his temples and sighed. "We don't have anything to return fire with."

The *Enigma* completely blocked out the starscape outside the cockpit of the *Amaranth*. It was reeling in Lithia's little cargo hauler toward a large opening, like a tongue wrapped around its prey, drawing it into the mouth of a great beast.

"That guy they were looking for on your ship," Cade said. "That guy they were willing to kill to find . . . I'm him. Take the girl and see if there's anything in the hold we can use to get those grapplers off us."

Aurelius nodded before turning to Lithia. "I need your help to try and figure out a way to break free."

Aurelius grabbed her by the shoulder and began to lead her out of the bridge and into the halls of the ship, but she hesitated for a moment before following. Under the top deck of the ship, beneath the galley, main hallway, engine room, and sleep-pod room, was a large hangar, the belly of the craft. As Lithia entered the room behind Aurelius, her jaw dropped. A little two-seater planet hopper was just sitting there in the middle of her ship's cargo area. It was a terribly violating feeling, like coming home and finding someone else's car in your garage. This craft, with its four rotating engines and its long wings fitted to the front, didn't look like a modern hopper, but the sort of junk pile repair shops kept around as loaners and to cannibalize parts from.

At least the scorch marks, reaching up from under the craft from hundreds of atmospheric entries, and the hopper's overall boxy design gave her that impression. Written on the side of the craft, behind the cockpit, were the words *Storm Chaser*. Other than the hopper, the *Amaranth*'s cargo area was filled with supplies and equipment the Magdalenes had loaded for her to trade on the other side of the Gate.

"Help me find something we can use to break us free!" Aurelius shouted.

A series of long metal rods with soft amber lights on the side were fastened to the wall, and Lithia pointed to them, not having the word in his language.

"Soap rods," she attempted.

"Soap? How the hell is soap going to help us!" he exclaimed, hunting around for something.

"S-o-a-p rods!"

Aurelius finally turned his attention to where Lithia was pointing. There were extra soap rods for the drive core nestled in a wall-mounted container.

"Oh! Fusion rods!" Aurelius said.

He ran over to them. "I think I can use these!"

He slid one of the two-meter-long metallic rods out of its cradle. It was heavy, too heavy for him to carry. "Help me here!" Aurelius shouted.

Lithia ran over and helped Aurelius carry the fusion rod to the back of the *Storm Chaser*. Aurelius opened a compartment on the back, then slid the rod in.

The *Amaranth* began to tremble and quake. The noise of metal on metal screeched as something new started cutting into the hull somewhere above them.

"What is that?" Lithia asked.

"I know that sound," Aurelius said. "Means they're coming in."

"I need to go get my brother," Lithia said.

"You need to stay here," Aurelius said, checking a few things on the *Storm Chaser*.

"But my brother is up there. Up there with Cade and whoever is after him."

"Right now, there is nothing you can do to help. If Jerula and Cade can't handle it, we're not going to be all that much help," Aurelius said.

"Don't you care? My brother, your friend?" Lithia almost shouted at Aurelius.

"This morning I had three people in this universe who really cared about me. After the attack on my ship, that number fell to one. I want to help Jerula. If I thought there was even a slight chance I could, I wouldn't still be talking to you."

"Then why don't you?"

"Because I've seen what they send out when they think Cade is on a ship. You don't fight it. When you fight it, you die. All you can do is run. Maybe Cade is dangerous enough to stand up to it, maybe Jerula can help him with that. But I don't want to be the person who gets in their way."

On the deck above them, a loud clang rang out. Whatever was coming had finally arrived. Part of her knew that Aurelius was right, that Cade wouldn't be worried over the kind of threats a normal person could handle, but another part of her knew Bobby was up there and she was down here.

Lithia wasn't really aware she was moving until she was coming out of the stairwell and heading into the galley, Aurelius close behind her.

"You don't understand—" he was saying, but when they saw the scene in the galley, he went silent.

CHAPTER 37

Rock You Like a Hurricane

LITHIA HAD NEVER seen anything like it. A green substance oozed from a dozen little cuts and slashes; the massive figure had a face that was little more than charred flesh, metal, and two hate-filled red eyes.

Cade was standing across the room from it. Cade's right arm hanging limply at his side. At first Lithia thought he was clutching a sword in his left hand and wondered where he had hidden it from her, but she realized he wasn't holding it in his hand. Somehow the sword was protruding out of his hand.

Cade sprang forward, the blade rising to fill the space between him and the monster. He moved so fast that her eyes could barely keep up, but it seemed the monster had no such problems.

Cade's blade only made a small cut in the monster's chest before a large hand, easily the size of Cade's head, batted him aside.

"What the hell is that thing?" Lithia screamed.

"I don't know what it calls itself, but for us it is just death," Aurelius said beside her.

"Where's Jerula?" Aurelius asked a moment later.

Seemingly in answer to his question, Jerula pulled himself out of a pile of smashed furniture and appliances that had once been the kitchen. In his hand was a large canister from the fire-suppression system. Each of those tanks weighed more than she did, but Jerula held it over his head with ease.

Lithia was amazed that he had come through the fight unhurt when Cade had taken so much damage, but as he charged, a war cry that belonged to no language Lithia had ever heard on his lips, Lithia saw the truth.

Jerula was far from unhurt. He had a gash across his back deep enough that Lithia could see the two ends flap as he ran, and what looked to be a piece of bone poking out of his upper leg. No, Jerula wasn't free of injuries, he just wasn't feeling them.

Jerula didn't move as fast as Cade had, and the monster was able to bring up his hand to stop Jerula's strike easily, but that didn't seem to matter. When the large tank hit the hand of the monster, Jerula just kept driving it down. The tank crumpled like a tin can, and white foam sprayed from every crack, covering everything around them, and Jerula kept pressing. For a moment, the two behemoths seemed evenly matched, neither able to make the other move, but that stalemate was all too short-lived.

The monster's other hand came down on Jerula's back with a crack. Jerula staggered and probably would have fallen to the monster's next strike, but there was a flash of movement, and Cade was standing beside him again, nearly severing the monster's enormous bicep.

There was a moment when all three combatants paused, the two giants and the cyborg all facing each other.

And then, as if by some signal, the three came together again. Jerula and the monster swinging fists, and Cade thrusting with his blade.

Between thrashing blows, Cade reached into his jacket. He pulled out a small cylinder and threw it past the monster to Aurelius.

"Get out of here! Get to the Frontier! Find Captain Pacius!"

The monster slowly rotated to face Aurelius. Every status and computer screen in the galley went black. A second later, a pair of red glowing eyes flickered onto the displays. "And now I know the faces of those who would stand with the betrayer. Before, you were nothing, but now you will be swept up in the fires of my righteous crusade." The beast glowered, his eyes burning with some inner madness, and Aurelius ran.

Aurelius pushed Lithia back into the hold. He swung the bulkhead shut as fast as he could, shoving a pole in the lock to keep it closed.

"We've gotta get out of here!" Aurelius reached into the *Storm Chaser* and started up the engines.

"Wait! Wait!" Lithia panicked. "What is that thing?"

"Death, if we don't leave now!"

"Wait! My brother's still in there! We can't just leave him!" Her eyes filled with tears.

The deafening impact of the mechanical nightmare's fists on the door echoed through the room. "Did you see what happened in there? We can't do anything for any of them!"

Lithia couldn't breathe, she couldn't move, her shock rooted her feet to the deck. Behind them, that thing was beating against the door. From the sounds the door was making, it wouldn't hold for very long, but Lithia was frozen.

"Do you hear that? It means the fight in there is over. We don't have time to talk this out. It is either run or die."

Lithia wasn't entirely clear what happened next. Aurelius turned away from the door just before everything seemed to explode around them. Lithia was thrown away from the door in a shower of sparks and shards of metal. She didn't see what happened to Aurelius, and for a moment she feared he had taken the blast in the face. But then, a pair of thick-gloved hands pulled her from the deck.

Lithia couldn't speak, and her thoughts seemed clouded by the ringing in her ears. The hands dropped her into the padded seat of the planet hopper and strapped something across her chest. In the distance, Lithia could hear the sounds of metal being bent and broken, and the clangs of pieces of the door hitting the deck. The monster must have broken a power conduit to make a blast that size. The thought didn't bother Lithia for some reason, even though it should. The monster may have already killed two people, and was tearing up her ship, but for some reason nothing seemed to bother her.

"This is going to be a little rough." The words sounded so far away.

"What's going to be rough? What's—" Lithia was jerked back in her seat, the padding and straps across her chest doing their best to keep her in place. Still, her head lurched, and it felt like her brain was sloshing around.

The sudden motion seemed to do something to clear Lithia's mind. She looked around at the cramped two-seat cockpit she was strapped into. In the seat in front of her was a figure with messy, dirty-blond hair, who she was now reasonably sure was the pretty one. No, his name was Aurelius. She had to cling to details now that she had them again. She had to cling to them or risk dropping back into that fog.

The person in front of her was Aurelius. The ship they were in was the *Jerula*. No, that wasn't right. *Storm Chaser*. The planet hopper was the *Storm Chaser*.

"I'm going to try and fly us out of this hanger. You're going to want to hold on to something if you can."

What did he mean, fly out of the hanger? The *Amaranth*'s hanger wasn't big enough to fly anywhere in. Best he could do was drop out the bottom.

"If we can get out of here, I think we have a chance of escape."

Lithia peered out the slightly cloudy glass of the canopy, trying to make sense of what Aurelius was saying.

There was a sudden rush in her stomach as she felt herself plunge downward, and within the blink of an eye, she could see the *Amaranth* above her as it rapidly began to shrink. She was astonished not to see any stars above them. No, instead there was a massive, sharp piece of metal looming above them. It filled her entire view and wasn't shrinking at the same rate as her ship.

"What? Where are we?" Lithia asked, her words sounding only slightly slurred.

"The *Enigma* pulled your ship in. We're still inside. See those doors below us?"

Lithia tried to look past Aurelius at what he was talking about, but it was still really hard to focus.

"No, not really," she said.

"Well, take my word for it. They're there and we're heading at them as fast as I can make this thing go."

"Okay. With you, I think. Why do I have to hang on?"

"Because the doors are closing and I don't know if we're going to make it!" Aurelius yelled back to her.

Lithia tried again to see the distant doors. In her mind they were two massive metal flaps slowly swinging shut, like in a holo adventure, but they were either too far away to be seen with the naked eye, or her head still wasn't fully recovered. Lithia *did* see a startlingly large number of other ships around them. They ranged in size from smaller than the little hopper they were now into ships that could fit several *Amaranth*s inside them and still have room for crew.

The *Storm Chaser* slowed a bit as Aurelius banked around a long boxlike ship, and Lithia was jerked back in her seat again as he kicked his little hopper back up to full speed.

"No G-diffusers in this thing?"

"I've got them. Well, sort of. They're kind of old. They should still protect us from the worst of it," Aurelius called back to her.

"How can you be sure?" Lithia asked, the motion, or maybe just time, clearing her head rapidly.

"We're not human pudding . . . yet," Aurelius said.

"The doors are closing!" Lithia yelled.

She stared at the two massive doors. They seemed to be sliding together at an almost glacial pace, though she was sure most of that was just their size.

"Come on, hold together," Aurelius muttered.

Aurelius flew his ship around the cavity in the *Enigma*. At first Lithia didn't know why, but then she saw long, segmented arms, blades spinning, and clamps opening. They were part of the *Enigma*'s retrieval system. The arms were trying to catch and pull them back in.

Aurelius was dodging them, always trying to keep other ships between the arms and the *Storm Chaser*. Lithia lurched as the small hopper jerked back and forth. It would have been like a rollercoaster, except a rollercoaster had a down.

Aurelius threw the sticks down hard and flew down past the *Amaranth*, speeding the *Storm Chaser* directly at the rapidly closing doors.

"This is getting cliché!" he yelled.

Aurelius slammed the throttle. Down they went, faster and faster.

Lithia could feel the *Storm Chaser* straining under the pressures Aurelius was putting on it, and she wondered if the piece of junk would hold together long enough to be crushed by the doors or grabbed by the arms.

The *Storm Chaser* jolted off course with a violent cracking sound. Lithia assumed the sprint drive had broken free after all, but a quick look back told her the truth. One of the clamps had finally managed to grab the back of the little hopper and was pulling it back in.

"Not good, definitely not good!" Aurelius shouted.

Lithia watched helplessly as the *Storm Chaser* began sliding back away from the doors.

"I'm going to try something really stupid. Just giving you the heads-up," Aurelius said.

Aurelius flipped a switch on his console and Lithia tried to ignore his muttering about how he was sure this would kill them both, while at the same time, trying to figure out what he could possibly have up his sleeve.

She did not have to wait long. There was a blinding flash, and the *Storm Chaser* shot forward through the doors. She could hear the sound of metal scraping against metal as they passed.

"What the hell did you just do?" Lithia called up to him.

"I used the soap."

Lithia craned her neck around to get a look at the back of the *Storm Chaser*. The clamp was still there, but several meters back, the arm ended in a line of jagged, scorched metal.

The *Enigma* began to fire wildly into space. Lithia watched over Aurelius's shoulder as he piloted the *Storm Chaser* away from the *Enigma* as fast as he could. In her first true moment of clarity since the blast on the *Amaranth*, she couldn't believe she was having to leave Bobby behind. She shivered with both terror and an agonizing sense that her brother might already be dead. Before she could think about it too much, or say anything, for that matter, she felt a pressure against her body, forcing her back into her chair. The stars outside the cockpit glass began to elongate and brighten, as if they were being stretched from tiny points of light in the distance into long bright needles.

"Here we go!" Aurelius yelled, but for Lithia there was nothing but darkness.

CHAPTER 38

Interrogation

THE ROOM AROUND Maher was large and arched. It had once been a hanger, but it seemed to have been converted into holding cells sometime in the not-too-distant past. Maher was lying on a cot in one of the cells with about fifty other people. Assuming the other cells were as full, Maher guessed that about half of his crew was there. What that meant for the other half, Maher didn't like to think about. Some had to be in critical condition held elsewhere, and others were likely being questioned—but even if that was another 10 or 20 percent of his crew, that still meant hundreds of lives were lost. Every now and then the guards would bring back another survivor, and every time Maher checked to see if it was someone he knew, someone who only came on this trip because Maher asked them personally. Maher was ashamed of that. Any survivor was something to be happy about. The life meant no less because he didn't know its name, but still, he checked. This time the person the guards brought back was unmistakable. The man was bloody. Clearly he had been beaten, and recently, but despite that, he stood tall, limping only slightly on a leg that even Maher could tell had been snapped. The guards that escorted him seemed nervous, and Maher couldn't blame them. Jerula stood head and shoulders above either of them and was nearly as wide as the two guards side by side. He watched as they led him to his cell and ordered everyone to move away before they slid the cell door open.

No one protested the order, and no one failed to comply. They had learned quickly what that led to, and no one wanted to be the next person to be dragged away.

Jerula had to duck his head as the guards directed him into the cell, and when he didn't do it fast enough to satisfy one of the guards, he jabbed him with the end of his weapon. Jerula staggered forward a step, and then turned to glare at the guards, a look of fury unmistakable on his face.

"Get in there!" the impatient guard shouted.

"Do that again, and I am going to force your head down your neck so far you'll have to open your shirt to see where you're going." Jerula didn't shout his threat, and Maher felt it more than he heard it, like a roar of distant thunder.

"Jerula, it's not worth it." The voice came from a group of people huddled in one of the corners, and it took Maher a moment to place it.

"Get in the cell, or I'll shoot!" the guards both yelled at the same time.

"I'll still get you both before I go down," Jerula growled, getting ready to step forward.

"Jerula, please. Paul and I already lost Aurelius and the chief today, please don't make us lose you too."

Jerula stopped, and the guards took the opportunity to step back out of the big man's reach.

"Nyreen, that you?" Jerula asked, in a friendly tone, almost as if he wasn't just about to go down in a blaze of bullets and blood.

"Yes. Now, please, turn around and come into the cell," Nyreen implored.

"You and Paul made it, then?"

"Yes, now please turn around so we can all have a happy reunion, one where no one has to die."

"Listen to the woman," one of the guards told Jerula. It sounded like there was a bit of panic in his voice. The guard was getting ready to fire, and it was only the idea that Jerula might still be able to make good on his threats that held the trigger.

Maher watched as slowly Jerula backed up, not turning around, not breaking eye contact with the guards. The moment Jerula was clear of the doorway, one of the guards leaped forward to hit the close control, and Maher couldn't blame them. If he had been facing down a homicidal Jerula, he would have done exactly the same thing.

"Jerula, I'm so happy to see you. I didn't want to think . . . but when . . . I mean, no one's been sent back in a couple hours," Nyreen said, leading Jerula over to where she had been sitting.

"Jerula, were you the only one in your pod?" Maher said, making his way over to where Jerula was surrounded by Paul, Nyreen, and several others. All of whom were in disbelief that Jerula had made it out.

"Sir, I made it out in a hopper," Jerula said, looking up from the reunion.

"I'm sorry to do this, but I'm going to have to steal Jerula from you all for a little bit. I promise to bring him back in nearly as good shape as he is now."

Maher pulled Jerula to the side, not actually waiting for a response and ignoring the less-than-friendly looks his action had earned him from Jerula's friends. It didn't matter, though. He would return Jerula, and everything would be forgotten. But right now, Maher needed to know everything Jerula had been through, needed it so he could add a few more pieces to the puzzle today's events had become. Maybe, just maybe, Jerula would have the piece that would make it all make sense.

"A hopper?" Maher asked, when they were finally far enough away as to not be easily overheard.

"Something my bunkmate picked up back on Earth and had stashed away in cargo."

"What happened to your bunkmate, and where have you been?"

"We stowed away on a small transport, but I guess they tracked us. There was a guy on board. Strange dude named Cade."

Maher cut Jerula off. "That's who they were looking for when they attacked us. Someone named Cade."

"Right. I have no idea who he is, but he had bionic limbs and said something about the *Enigma* looking for him. We got grabbed, then that thing . . . that thing that tore up the *Freedom's Reach* showed up and smacked us around for a while. I don't know how I lived."

"The thing is called Torque. I heard the guards talking about him. He's a Lambda, but an unstable one, if the guards are to be believed. Where is Cade now?"

Jerula shook his head. "I have no idea, sir. I was knocked out cold. I don't even know what happened to Aurelius."

"If it helps, I think he's still alive," Maher said.

"How do you figure?"

"The guards were talking about a hopper with a lunatic pilot who managed to escape by blasting a hole in the side of a hanger with a fusion rod or something, must have broken something important, because we've not moved in quite some time. Does that sound like your bunkmate?" Maher asked.

"Crazy and stupid. Yeah, that sounds like him." Jerula smiled.

"I'm happy to hear that, but honestly, I am more interested in who this Cade person is. You said he had cybernetic limbs?" Maher asked.

"His arm had a sword sticking out of it. That's either cybernetic, or he's more hardcore than any man who ever lived. He could also move faster than my eyes could keep up with. Well, before Torque started using him to beat dents out of the walls with. He slowed down a bit after that."

"He sounds like another Lambda, but that doesn't make sense. If he's a Lambda, then why would they be chasing him?" Maher said, more to himself than to Jerula.

"He could have gone rogue?" Jerula suggested.

"I doubt it. Lambdas are supposed to be the best and most trusted of UPE agents. They are modified with the tools to do almost any job, and they're given the authority to do whatever they feel they need to get it done. Beyond that, the mental conditioning is supposed to be absolute. I don't think it's possible for one to go rogue."

"But it's possible for one to be unstable?" Jerula said.

"There is that . . ."

"Either way, I can't see that it really matters anymore. If they got me, then they must have gotten him. Aurelius had the only other way off that ship."

The two men looked up as the doors at the end of the corridor opened again. This time, two medics brought in a gurney with a teenage boy on it; he was out cold.

The door to the cell they were in slid open, and the two medics dumped the boy in, unceremoniously.

"Friend of yours?" Maher asked Jerula as the two pushed their way to the front where the boy lay in a heap.

"Uh-uh. Never seen him before in my life," Jerula said, looking him over.

"We can't leave him here. Help me move him."

Jerula and Maher grabbed the boy by his shoulders and feet. They laid him down on a bench in the back of the cell. It would at least get him out of the way.

The boy couldn't be from the *Freedom's Reach*. He was too young. And while he was still dressed, it wasn't in the uniform of the SMMC.

"You sure you don't know him?" Maher asked Jerula.

"Never seen him before, though the girl said something about a brother. Could be him."

"The girl?" Maher asked.

"The owner of the ship."

"I thought Cade was the owner of the ship."

"No, he was just a passenger," Jerula said.

"I feel like there is more story here."

"Yeah, probably, but damned if I was following it . . . and I was there."

Maher gave up on that line of questioning. He suspected that way lay madness, and he turned back to the boy. He looked to be about fifteen, maybe a little younger, and if Maher was any judge, he was Venusian, though not quite entirely. There was some Terran in there too.

"Lucky kid," Maher finally said.

Jerula looked him over. "Yeah, real lucky. He's gonna wake up in a UPE brig with a bunch of strangers."

"Better than not waking up at all."

Cade was battered and bloody. He was strung up to the same cold gray bar in the same scuffed-up room he had locked Captain Pacius in after the *Deviant Rising*'s protest. The floor was still stained with Pacius's blood. Cade had taken a heavy beating back on the *Amaranth*. Many of his systems were damaged, and the ones that weren't had been taken offline. He vaguely remembered being dragged into the room. A technician had drilled some piece of hardware into the side of his head that would suspend all of his abilities. His humanity was catching up to him, and the irony of his situation hit him square in the conscience. The tormentor was now the tormented.

The lights came on, hot and searing. The nerves behind Cade's eyes burned with pain. He heard the door slide open, someone step in, and the doors close behind them. The light was too intense to see through, and the pain too great to keep trying. He heard a set of feet pace back and forth. The breathing of something huge inhaled and exhaled with every step.

"I can hear you . . . I know who you are," Cade said.

The heavy booming voice of the machine that had nearly killed him pierced into his mind. "No wicked deeds shall come to pass. No one has ever escaped Lambda's grasp before. And you tried to take something with you. That is the only reason you're still alive."

"I'm flattered you went to all this trouble to find me."

"We need to know what you stole and why. We need to know who you are working for."

"I'm self-employed. The freedom is nice, but the benefits aren't as good."

Cade couldn't see the beast that had taken him hostage, but he could hear his heavy footfalls as he paced the room. "Did you know breakdowns of some of your missions were required programming in Lambda? I could never dream of doing some of the things you have. Never hope to match your ingenuity or savagery . . . I could never do with my fists the damage you could with one well-placed blade in the dark," the beast said.

For the first time Cade could remember, he was scared. Never before had he been this helpless or out of control, and that affected him more than he wanted to admit. "If you cut me loose, I'll sign an autograph."

Cade felt the blow coming before it hit. Instinct forced him to dodge, but all he managed to do was wrench his shoulder. He heard a soft laugh that seemed incongruous with the booming voice of his captor. "There is no more lively sensation than pain. Its impressions are certain and dependable. They never deceive as may those of the pleasure humans perpetually feign and almost never experience."

The next couple hits came in rapid succession. This time, Cade didn't try to avoid them. Instead he went limp, trying to move with them. The massive cyborg's heavy blows could not break Cade.

"Do you always start interrogations before asking questions?" Cade asked.

"If I had asked any, would you have answered?"

"Probably not."

"My way is better. I get to force faster. It saves time."

"It's crude, without finesse or subtlety. I take it neither of those are your stren—" Cade was cut off by a large meaty hand clamping down on his throat.

"Fine. If you want questions, what did you steal from the Lambda data hub?"

The hand released him and the figure moved back. "No, no. See, now you're going too far the other way. Now you've asked too direct of a question. You fail."

Cade took the next impact like a sledgehammer to the jaw. His bones and teeth were both heavily reinforced, but several of them cracked under the hit, the blood washing bits of teeth down his throat.

"Destruction, like creation, is one of nature's mandates. Neither of us is a creator. I know you have an aversion to destruction without reason. Please don't give me a reason to indulge in my own special way."

Cade was barely able to separate the pain of one hit from another. The whole thing was starting to blur into one solid blunt-force trauma. He coughed to clear his throat and lungs of blood; he was losing focus and coherence. He didn't know how much longer he'd be able to take the beating.

"Who were those people we found you with?" the Lambda said, ceasing his assault.

Cade could hear the frustration in the cyber demon's voice. Cade might have been losing coherence, but the creature was losing control. If Cade could push him over the edge, this *thing* would probably kill him, but it would close the door on anything Cade could reveal. It was his best option. "They were just some kids I found—"

Cade remembered almost nothing after that point except the pain—lots of it. He remembered something heavy and metallic slamming into his human hand and crushing bone. He remembered the Lambda screaming, "What did you take?" over and over again, then mercifully, the beating stopped. After that, it was all darkness and blissful unconsciousness.

CHAPTER 39

Archer's Agony

AN INTENSE BLUE light filled the *Storm Chaser*'s cockpit as Aurelius piloted his craft through the Epsilon Gate. Outside the ship was a tunnel of amber light, twisting into alternating fractal patterns. He kept the *Storm Chaser* close to a larger vessel. It took all his concentration to fly down a narrow pocket of particles streaming off the back of the larger ship. He had to stay in that thin little corridor, not just to keep off the vessel's sensors, but also to keep from getting fried from the solar energy that made up the shortcut through space. He was using the cargo hauler ahead of him as a sort of energy umbrella. He was using its wake to cut down on turbulence. After what the *Storm Chaser* had been through, he didn't want to damage it any further. He was worried about it shaking apart, or worse, being totally vaporized by the solar winds emanating from the vortex.

His thoughts began to wander the longer he tried to stay focused. Could Jerula still be alive? Why the hell did the *Enigma* attack the *Freedom's Reach*? Why did they come after Aurelius and Jerula? Who the hell was this Cade guy, and what the hell was this box? Nothing that Cade had thrown to him made sense. The UPE was turning into a Saturday-morning-cartoon bad guy just out to destroy and devour. Aurelius wondered how much of the puzzle he was missing.

A light went off on the *Storm Chaser*'s dashboard. The craft's fusion coils were nearly out of charge. This was bad. It meant he'd have to make a stop as soon as possible. Archer's Agony would be the first port on the other side of the gateway.

Aurelius adjusted his course, pulling the *Storm Chaser* to the outer edge of the larger ship's wake just long enough to run a scan. His instruments lit up, projecting a course on the holographic display in his cockpit that indicated they were nearly out of the wormhole.

There was a noise in the backseat as the girl began to stir. Aurelius had no idea what she was saying in groggy, broken Terranese, but she sounded upset.

"Hey . . . hey! You're alive! Oh, good. Thought you were a goner when you didn't answer me."

He could see the redhead reach up and feel at a spot on the back of her head.

"What happened?" she inquired. "Where is my ship? Where is my brother?" This time she spoke in a language Aurelius could understand.

"What's the last thing you remember?" he asked, trying to figure out when she may have lost consciousness.

"We were on the *Amaranth*. There was an explosion . . . I hit my head."

"You missed all the fireworks." Aurelius laughed. "I had a hell of a time getting away from that battleship." Aurelius hoped the light-hearted response would ease her mind a little bit, but what the girl said was concerning. If she couldn't remember anything after hitting her head on the *Amaranth*, then she was having trouble retaining new memories. Aurelius wasn't a doctor, but that couldn't be a good thing.

"Where are we?" she asked, sounding very confused.

"We're inside the Epsilon Gateway, the wormhole. In a couple seconds, we'll emerge in the Frontier."

The redhead tried to peer around his chair but stopped and sat back, her hand going to the back of her head again.

"How long have I been asleep?" she asked.

"Couple hours, maybe. How's the cryo hangover?"

She didn't respond. Instead she sunk back down into her seat. "I can't believe we just left everyone back there."

"We did what we had to. If we hadn't acted so fast, we'd all be space dust."

"What do you mean, *we*? Who the hell are you to drag me and my brother into something like this? I don't even know what's going on here! We were minding our own business, casually flying through space in deep sleep."

"Hey! I didn't drag you guys into anything. You already had something they wanted. It was pure, unadulterated coincidence that Jerula and I just happened to bump into you guys. Billion-to-one chance. Now, I don't blame you for being angry, but what's done is done."

Aurelius examined the box Cade had thrown to him. He had stashed it in the side storage box of his seat. It represented a part of whatever the hell was going on. Aurelius focused on it, hoping that it might be the one looming problem he could do something about.

"What's that?" she asked.

"I honestly don't know. Some sort of hard storage device. Cade threw it to me and said to bring it to a guy called Pacius. It seemed like he thought it was more important than anything else, even escaping himself."

She was quiet for a couple of moments. Aurelius glanced back at her through the mirror and saw her eyes filled with tears as she wiped her nose on her sleeve. "Bobby . . . I'm so sorry."

"Bobby's your brother?" Aurelius asked.

"Yeah," she replied in a choked whisper.

"He's alive," Aurelius said, hoping he was telling her the truth. "The sleep pod would have protected him from whatever happened."

"He must be so scared . . . I'm . . . I'm sorry about your friend too. I hope he made it."

"Me too . . ." Aurelius thought about all of them, not just Jerula, but Paul and Nyreen too. He had assumed they escaped the *Freedom's Reach* in one of the vessel's lifeboats, but for some reason, the fact that the *Enigma* had followed him all the way to Lithia's ship made him wonder what had happened. Maybe the vessel was destroyed altogether. Maybe he and Jerula were the only survivors. If that were true, well, he couldn't bear to think of what may have happened to his old bunkmates.

Another light began to blink on Aurelius's dashboard, and he left his half-formulated response unsaid as he diverted his attention to it.

"What's going on?" his passenger asked.

"The neutrino field is destabilizing. We're almost out of the wormhole."

Aurelius pressed a few buttons on his instrumentation. A quick yellow light passed across the cockpit glass, changing it to a metallic color. The light coming in changed from blue to red. There was a bright crimson corona directly ahead. At the center, the entangled fractal patterns yawned open toward a star expanse. He pulled the *Storm Chaser* away from the larger ship. The entire craft began to tremble with building turbulence. They got closer and closer to the opening at the end of the phenomenon. The craft creaked and shook harder and harder. Aurelius saw his passenger's face turn slightly green, and one of her hands clutch at her stomach.

Aurelius couldn't blame her. He had nearly had enough shaking for a lifetime, and he wasn't nursing a head wound. He could only imagine what she was experiencing right then.

The *Storm Chaser* crossed through the event horizon back into normal space. Just as quickly as the turbulence had started, it stopped, and the ride became nice and smooth.

The girl looked relieved, and privately, Aurelius was too. Her discomfort notwithstanding, he hadn't been looking forward to any possible cleanup if the girl hadn't been able to handle the motion.

Aurelius watched as her look of relief slowly became one of wonder. For a moment, he wasn't sure what she was so struck by. The girl seemed transfixed by something.

"This . . . this is it?" she said eventually.

"This is what?" Aurelius asked, wondering if this was another symptom of her head injury.

"The Frontier," she said.

"Yup . . . this is it. This is the Frontier."

"It's beautiful."

"Don't tell me you've never seen it before," Aurelius said.

"Only on Helix. I had no idea . . ."

She put her hand on the glass to watch the light penetrate between her fingers, and Aurelius looked with her, trying to see what it must look like to her.

All he saw were the stars and nebulae that were commonplace. While they had a beauty to them, Aurelius was honestly more attracted to the forms of the ships that darted back and forth all around them, seeming so small from where he was, but in reality, hundreds and thousands of times larger than his little *Storm Chaser*.

"Space doesn't look like this back home," she said.

"What do you mean? It's space. It mostly looks the same wherever you are, doesn't it?" Aurelius replied.

"At home, space is mostly black, with little pinpricks of light. The thought of seeing the gasses that form a nebula with your own eyes . . . It's beautiful."

Aurelius looked out at the distant blots of color and light, trying to see it. They looked more like stains on a piece of cloth than anything else, and not very spectacular ones at that.

"I guess so," Aurelius said. "By the way . . . you never told me your name."

"Lithia. Lithia Boson," she said, seeming only barely to hear him.

Aurelius still couldn't understand what it was about the scene in front of them that was so amazing to her. Possibly if he had been hit on the head he would, but either way, it was distracting her from her pain for the moment, and that alone was enough to make Aurelius content.

"Welcome to the Frontier, Lithia."

In the distance, there was a giant metallic rotating ring with an enormous array protruding from the center. Even Aurelius had to admit there was something almost other-worldly about it. Rather than appearing as something thin, shiny, and efficiently designed, this mass ahead of them had an almost organic look to the way it was laid out, almost like a giant metal and plastic amoeba. There was something totally unplanned and spontaneous about its cobbled-together pieces. The structure, and its huge sections and compartments, all seemed like they had been designed by different companies, and then somehow both glued together and grown.

The most amazing thing about it was its sheer size. Even from where they were it looked massive, taking up a reasonable percentage of the star field. How big it was on the inside, no one was quite sure, but they said it was ten miles across if you were walking on its patched-together outer hulls. This was Archer's Agony and its blinking lights beckoned to Aurelius. The space around the station was filled with traffic. They could see the lights from passing, arriving, and departing ships even more densely packed than around the star that served as this side of the Gate.

"What . . . what is that?"

"Archer's Agony station. It's a jumping-off point to the rest of the Frontier."

"It's huge. I've never seen anything . . . I've never seen anything like it. Why is it called Agony?" she asked.

"Archer's Agony. You don't know the story? I guess Frontier history isn't really taught in Terran schools," Aurelius said, leaving out that while they probably did teach it in the school he had attended on Strife, he hadn't been paying attention. It was only luck that Aurelius knew the story himself, having read about it in a cheap historical comic when he was younger.

"No, not really."

"You ever heard of the ship the *Crown of Thorns*?" Aurelius asked.

"No. Should I have?"

"The *Crown of Thorns* was the first ship to chart the Epsilon Eridani Star System, back on the other side of the wormhole."

"Yeah, I remember that from school. Didn't know that's what you called it in Frontier tongue."

"What do you guys call it?" Aurelius inquired curiously.

Lithia rattled off some unintelligible noise that he just assumed was its name in Terranese. Mostly it sounded like a long chirp followed by a low grunt. Aurelius preferred his name for it.

"Huh . . . I wonder why the names are so different," Aurelius said. "Well, something happened when the *Crown of Thorns* reached the Epsilon sun. Some sort of technical difficulty caused them to fall into the star. They thought they were goners. All of a sudden, they ended up out here in a totally unknown area of space. Seems the star and its magnetic field lines were entangled with . . ." Aurelius paused, not knowing how to explain it and suspecting Lithia probably knew more about it than he did anyway. "Well, no one's really sure how it works, but basically they had fallen through a tunnel, a wormhole, in space. The captain was named Daniel Archer, and he had no idea how to get his crew home. They weren't even sure they could go back through. The *Crown of Thorns* was massive—I mean big enough to start a good-sized colony. The crew broke into thirds. One stayed on board while the other two found, mapped, and settled the first two worlds discovered out here. A decade later, long after Earth had written them off as lost, some scientists who'd been on board had an idea of how to get home. Captain Daniel Archer didn't want to risk his whole crew, so he took a shuttle and went back through alone. He broadcasted a message explaining what had happened, but by the time anyone could reach him, he had already died. The *Crown of Thorns* stayed in orbit around the star on this side of the Gate. Earth moved in and basically colonized the Frontier for itself. Everyone, and I mean everyone, had to use the *Crown of Thorns* as a space station. Way back in those days, it took forever to get out here. By the time a ship made it, it only had enough power left to dock. The dead ships that docked just kind of became part of the station, and eventually it was renamed in the captain's honor. Archer's Agony."

Lithia seemed awestruck by the story "That's incredible. I had no idea."

Aurelius paused, trying to remember the story he had read as a child. "They say that the fire and spirit of Captain Daniel Archer burns within everyone born in the Frontier. It's a story to remind us of the power of the human spirit and the duty of the human soul." And a force that reanimates the dead. But Aurelius didn't say that part.

There was a long pause from Lithia before she responded. "I had no idea Frontier history was so rich."

"Yeah. The UPE doesn't like us to have our own history. They're afraid of us seeing ourselves as independent from them. Don't imagine that story would be taught in their schools."

Aurelius took in the sight of the massive station and the aquarium of ships swarming around it as the *Storm Chaser* closed on Archer's Agony. The tiny vessels around them seemed to be swallowed by the giant space station as they got closer and closer. They would soon be within communications range and expected to request docking approval. That would be a problem, considering they were probably wanted, and Aurelius had not had time to register his new ship.

"This next part might be a little tricky, but I think it's only fair to warn you," Aurelius said. "We're going to have to sneak into the station."

To his surprise, Lithia simply nodded her silent agreement. She must have reached the same conclusions he had. Thankfully, the *Storm Chaser* still had some old tech that the UPE had since ordered removed from all newer vessels. It was yet another stroke of luck that Aurelius had been able to salvage it from the once husk of a hopper. He flicked some switches, and the hopper hummed down to a barely audible whine. The lights flickered off in the cockpit, leaving the two bathed in nothing but nebulae rays.

"We're running cold. Now they'd only be able to pick us up by direct visuals," Aurelius said, turning to Lithia. "And considering how small the *Chaser* is, I doubt—" Aurelius's tongue tangled in his mouth.

Lithia was gazing, dumbfounded, all around at the various colors the nebulae produced within the cockpit. "It's so much more vivid in the dark," she said, wide eyed. "It's beautiful."

Speaking of beautiful . . . Aurelius swallowed hard. He hadn't had a blasted moment to actually, really look at Lithia. The soft light cast shadows across her slender features, highlighting her tear-streaked cheekbones, her perfect Terran eyebrows, a single dainty ear poking out through her ruffled hair, the gentle curve of her neck. How hadn't he noticed before? It must have been all of the running for his life and trying not to die. The image of her standing in the *Amaranth*, brandishing a wrench in nothing but her underwear came unbidden, and he felt his face get hot. Just then, Lithia made eye contact with him. He coughed and spun around in his seat, pretending to make minor adjustments to the controls.

"What's wrong?" Lithia asked.

"Nothing. Just . . . we're almost there. Hold tight."

Aurelius flew the *Storm Chaser* toward a docking cluster. Once they were well within the throng of ships coming and going, Aurelius flicked some switches and brought the *Storm Chaser* humming back to life. Hopefully there would be too many ships for flight control to notice that one tiny extra hopper had slipped in. There was a little flight path projected out in front of his craft that helped lead them down a long tunnel before passing through a thin sheet of light that Aurelius assumed to be some sort of force field designed to keep the station's internal pressurization from rushing out into space. Under the craft, they passed a series of landing platforms filled with smaller ships and hoppers not too dissimilar from the *Storm Chaser*. The holographically projected path before them led Aurelius to land his little craft at one of the open spots alongside other two- and four-seater hoppers. Coming into and hovering over the spot, the *Storm Chaser*'s engines swung downward and its landing gear opened. Aurelius set the ship down slowly, trying not to screw it up any further. The engines slowly spun down, and the ship came to an idle before going silent.

Aurelius let out a long-overdue sigh. It felt like he had been holding his breath for the last few hours, ever since he had to blast his way out of Lithia's ship. He opened the cockpit and hopped out. Lithia was fumbling with her seat belt, trying to get it off. Aurelius reached in and pressed a single button. It released her and retracted back into the seat.

Aurelius reached his hand out to her as a wordless offer of help. Lithia paused for a second and Aurelius thought she was going to take it.

"I'm fine," she finally said, pushing his hand away. With a little effort, she extracted herself from the seat and climbed down to the ground.

Another moment passed as if they were both waiting for the other to do or say something. Lithia acted first, turning to walk away as if she knew where she was going.

"Where are you going?"

"I gotta find a lawyer."

"Lithia, stop," Aurelius called behind her.

"I gotta find out if my brother is alive and get him out of UPE custody."

"Before that, you've got to see a doctor."

"What I've got to do is figure out where my brother is and how I'm going to get him back. My brain isn't going to fall out of my skull in the next hour, so it can wait," Lithia said, stopping, but not turning around.

"A lawyer isn't going to be able to help you," Aurelius said. It wasn't going to be what she wanted to hear. Hell, what else he could say?

Lithia turned around, and again Aurelius was stunned. All the beauty that had been in her face before had been transformed into rage. "Why not? We're not part of your little rebellion. He's not guilty of anything."

Aurelius walked toward Lithia cautiously. "Sure he is. Guilty by association."

"What is that supposed to mean?"

"You . . . we . . . have no idea what's going on. But worse than that, the UPE doesn't know what's going on. They are going to hold him for simply being on a ship with Cade. Whatever is going on here goes a lot deeper than anyone can help us with."

"That's ridiculous," Lithia said, turning away from Aurelius and starting to walk again.

"No, that's the United Planets of Earth," Aurelius said, catching up and matching her pace.

Lithia stopped and stood there for a moment, looking down at the deck, and Aurelius tried to ignore the fact that she was fighting back more tears.

"The *Enigma*. It grabbed a lot of important people back there. Now they have your brother. If I can talk to the right people, we may be able to find out what the UPE intends to do with them. We might be able to mount a rescue or something. Hell, I don't know," Aurelius said, and even to his ears it sounded lame.

Lithia looked at Aurelius with a mixture of disgust and disbelief.

"You got a better idea?" he asked.

Aurelius could tell she didn't, not really, but she also didn't want to admit it.

"Hey, look. Yesterday I was the lowest rank on my ship, and now I'm in some sort of AR game. I'm just as in over my head as you are."

Lithia had to concede to that. They were out of luck together. "Okay, Mr. Space Adventurer."

"I prefer *Space Crusader*," Aurelius said, cracking a smile. He instantly knew it was the wrong thing to do.

"Okay, *Space Crusader*," Lithia said, not bothering to keep the irritation from her voice. "What do we do next?"

"Simple. We find Xander Pacius," Aurelius said, wishing he had some idea how to do it.

CHAPTER 40

Out of Order

LITHIA WAS ENAMORED by Archer's Agony. Nothing on Earth or Venus had prepared her for the wide-open station. Its inhabitants were from dozens of worlds. Patches of gardens sprang up almost randomly around the metal walkways. Most remarkable were the transparent arched ceilings, revealing panoramic views of the Frontier's vividly colored nebulae.

"Amazing, isn't it?" Aurelius said.

Lithia's eyes were drawn to a comet jetting through a patch of orange gas just outside the giant windows. "Yeah. It's incredible."

"Don't assume the whole thing is like this, though. This is one of the high-rent areas. The entire station is a little mixed that way. You might have something like this," Aurelius said, gesturing around at the peaceful and pleasant surroundings, "but just on the other side of a hatch, you might have a chunk of an old garbage barge, and fixed to that might be an old passenger liner that has been converted into apartments. Really, this entire place is made up of whatever ship wasn't needed anymore strapped down wherever it would fit without killing the spin."

"Do you know a Pacius?"

"No, no . . . not personally. But there's a famous captain in the SMMC named Pacius. Rumor is he went underground somewhere on

Archer's Agony after some sort of big scuffle with the UPE. I figure that's probably who Cade was talking about."

Lithia looked out at the massive section they were standing in. "Great. So why don't I look over here," she said sarcastically, gesturing to half the plaza. "And you can look over there." She gestured to the other. "It should only take us a few days, and then we can move to other areas of the station."

"Are all Terrans this sassy or only the overprivileged ones who get to learn our language in summer school?"

Lithia paused in step. "What is that supposed to mean?"

Aurelius digressed, "Maybe somebody at the Strife Embassy can help us."

Lithia wasn't overly impressed with his idea. About the best thing that could be said for it was that it was slightly more directed than his earlier idea of just finding Pacius someplace.

"We're going into the embassy to ask if they know anything about a guy rumored to be in hiding and that we have a present for him from a Lambda?" Lithia said, looking Aurelius over, reevaluating his intelligence.

"Yeah . . . more or less," he replied, causing her to look down and shake her head.

"Do you have a better idea?" Aurelius asked. Lithia said nothing.

"That's what I thought. So, let's try mine, and if it doesn't work, we can go right back to being stuck."

Lithia didn't want to admit it, but he had a point. She resigned herself to following him.

After consulting a map, they took a tram from the main plaza to the station's trade district. Like most everything else the station had to offer, the sights of the markets were incredible. Holograms advertised everything from exotic foods to slush boots with lights in the heels; in fact, one was selling both. All of the shops and mall carts seemed to be personally owned, and there were no mega corporations anywhere. The entire district seemed one part mall, one part carnival.

Lithia jumped as a hologram of a family appeared behind them. It was following them. The mother and father were both holding the hand of a small child who swung back and forth. "I wanna see the tigers, and the newt birds, and the Gleasian whale sharks." The child morphed into each of the animals. As the child turned back into a human, the father smiled down at him and said, "You'll see all those and more at Xenoland, the zoo here on Archer's Agony." The entire family then morphed into a Xenoland billboard before vanishing.

"Wow. That could get annoying," Aurelius said.

Aurelius saw the sign for the Strife Embassy and SMMC offices. "Wait here and play with the holograms till I get back."

Lithia didn't want to be left alone, and it must have showed.

"Don't worry. You'll be fine," Aurelius said. "If you get in trouble, just use some of that Terran sass." He looked smug and it made Lithia want to hit him . . . or possibly something else.

Why did he have to be so pretty, dammit? It made him so much harder to hate, and right now Lithia really, really wanted to hate him.

Aurelius smirked as he headed into the embassy, and Lithia did her best to ignore it. While she waited for Aurelius to return, Lithia casually explored the shops and games clustered around the embassy, trying her best to look like a local. But between her bright red hair and distinctly Terran clothing, she stuck out like a pumpkin in a watermelon field. It seemed everyone around her was dressed in some sort of flight suit, or if not that, in almost homemade-looking outfits. Lithia's casual manufactured blouse and pants marked her as an outsider as much as any accent could ever do.

As Lithia examined a small tank of glow-in-the-dark eels—were they meant for food or to be pets?—she started to think again about Bobby. He was never far from her mind, but seeing something he would have taken such delight in forced him into the forefront. He was all she could think about. She had never felt this helpless before. He was in the hands of a horrible villain, and the thought of taking on such an ominous entity felt debilitating.

She was just one person. They were hundreds, if not thousands. With only her and Aurelius, what chance did they have? What could the two of them do?

Despair threatened to destroy her. She had only felt this hopeless one other time in her life, but even then she had Bobby by her side. As she had felt when her parents died, she felt no way out of the situation, no way she could make things better. She was trapped, trapped by her fear and the knowledge that there was nothing she could do about it. When did she become the kind of person who just lies down and cries?

Did she think someone was going to come along and fix this for her, if only she felt sorry for herself long enough?

Lithia was startled by her own thoughts. They were in such contrast to everything else she'd been feeling, but they were true. If she and Aurelius weren't enough to get her brother back, then she'd find people who were. Her grief had almost beaten her, but in the end, Lithia had only one option. She would find a way to get her brother back. Maybe Aurelius would be a part of that, maybe not—either way, she would do it or die trying.

Not long after her revelation, Aurelius reemerged from the embassy.

"Did you find anything?" she asked with renewed vigor.

Aurelius nodded to a bar at the end of the block. "Yeah. The guy I talked to said someone at Space Bar might be able to help."

"They seriously just told you where a disgraced and possibly fugitive captain hangs out?" Lithia asked incredulously.

"Yeah, friendly folks," Aurelius said, making his way through the crowd to the indicated bar, Lithia hurrying behind him.

Either he's going to find this Pacius guy, or they were about to get mugged in an alley.

Space Bar was loud and neon. It was half sports bar and half nightclub, or at least it was trying to be. Giant holographic screens were showing Thunderball games from all over the Frontier. Off in the back, a bouncer held the door to the upstairs, which was echoing with booming music. Lithia was anything but impressed.

"I'm sure you've been thrown out of better," she jeered.

"And worse," Aurelius said, offering Lithia his arm like a respectable gentleman. She declined the invitation and instead smiled and shook her head. "Yeah, right, Space Crusader."

Lithia carefully ignored the eyes that locked onto her as they entered the bar. She, unlike Aurelius, hadn't ever been in a place like this before, and she wasn't enjoying it. As far as she was concerned, the sooner they left, the better. She reminded herself that they were there to find Captain Pacius and hopefully rescue her brother. For that, she would endure anything.

The barkeep looked them over and instantly appraised them as visitors, and worse yet, visitors without any money.

"I was told to come here by a man from the SMMC. He said you could help me with finding someone," Aurelius said.

"Oh, I dunno. Who you lookin' for?" he asked.

"A guy that goes by the name Pacius."

"Sorry. Can't help ya. Don't know anyone by the name of Pacius."

Lithia shot Aurelius a look. They were back at square one. Still, it could have gone worse. She half expected someone from the UPE to jump out and arrest them or some pirate to press them into his crew, so when weighed in that light, it wasn't really that bad.

"You with the SMMC, by any chance?" the bartender asked.

"Yeah."

"Well, I may know where to find some of y'all's friends. Maybe they know who you're talkin' about."

The bartender pulled out a key and pointed to a back hallway. "Check out the private room. Play a game of pinball or two while ya wait."

Aurelius took the key.

"What did he mean, play a game of pinball?" Lithia asked as they passed through a doorway and down a narrow hall.

"No idea."

At the end of the hall was a door. Aurelius inserted the key into the lock and pushed on the door. A staircase led down into a storage room. The room was nearly empty except for a table, a couple boxes, and an oddly out-of-place ancient pinball machine. The pinball machine looked totally new and polished for something that could be centuries old. On the back scoreboard was a little blond spiky-haired man riding a snowboard with the words "Avalanche Hero" sprawled below him. There was an "Out of Order" sign slung across the front of the machine, even though the lights were on and the scoreboard was flashing. It kept settling on 7777 before starting the list of high scores over.

Suddenly the door behind them slammed shut. Aurelius grabbed frantically at the door, but it was no use. It was locked tight.

"Dammit!" he exclaimed. "It's locked! How the hell . . ."

"So, I'm thinking perhaps you shouldn't have been so forthcoming with our friend upstairs. He is probably with the UPE and sending a hit man down to kill us," snipped Lithia.

"No. There is no way the UPE would have goons here. This is supposed to be a safe haven from them."

Lithia looked around the room. There wasn't anywhere to sit but the stool in front of the pinball machine. Lithia investigated the machine and glared at it. "You know, I've always hated pinball," she said. "The whole idea of hitting a little metal ball before it falls in a hole seems so archaic. If it weren't for the lights, I'd swear it was something the cavemen played."

"I always thought it was a metaphor for life—a ball rolling around, and the only real control you have is a split second before you lose it."

"I never thought of it that way. Still. Seems so antiquated." Lithia groaned as she laid her hand on the machine. She drummed on the glass while Aurelius continued to search the door for a release latch or button. The machine was very old fashioned, like something you'd see in a movie. There was no touch screen, no holograms, just plastic figures and pictures with lights behind them, and although it was an old, obsolete machine, it appeared to be in oddly good condition, as if it were brand new. She fondled the machine and located buttons on both the left and right side of it. She began to press them, and to her surprise, the little paddles at the bottom of the machine began to move, corresponding to the buttons.

"Aurelius . . . I think this machine still works," she announced, totally perplexed.

"Well, while you're playing games, I'll be trying to find us a way out of here," he grumbled as he pried a small vent off the wall. "You might be small enough to crawl up through this vent and see where it leads."

"No, come here a second."

"How about you come here and help get us out of here?"

She looked dubiously at the little metal ball above the plunger. "Seriously, Aurelius . . . come here. I think there is something up with this machine."

"What do you mean?" Aurelius said, still searching the room for an escape route.

Lithia grabbed the plunger firmly and pulled. Suddenly, the machine lit up and started blinking and playing music. Lithia was startled and released the knob, launching the ball into the machine. Just as Aurelius began to walk over, the floor around the antiquated pinball machine started to shake. The entire section of floor it sat on began to lower like some sort of elevator. Lithia grabbed Aurelius by the arm and pulled him onto the small lowering platform before he could react. She laughed with a childlike giddiness, like it were a carnival ride.

"The man *did* say to play a game of pinball," Lithia boasted smugly.

"I don't think it's supposed to do this!" Aurelius hooted. The platform with the machine continued to descend into a long shaft in the floor.

"I don't think we're in Kansas anymore."

"What's a Kansas?"

"If this isn't a trap, I'll explain later."

When the elevator reached the bottom, they were in a narrow hallway with a single door at the end. The door had a slit at the top about eye level and a poster of a horse, which read: "Save a Horse. Ride a Cowboy."

"I can't help but wonder how many people found this place just because they liked pinball," Aurelius said, as they made their way to the door.

Raucous voices sounded from the other side. A glass broke, and then she heard the muffled roar of people laughing.

"I feel like I'm in a spy holo," Aurelius said, knocking on the door. The slit near the top slowly slid open and a pair of sharp, accusing eyes pierced through from the other side.

"What's the password?" the person on the other side asked.

"Uh . . . umm . . . we weren't given one. We're here to see Pacius."

"Can't come in without a password."

"Ummm . . . Strife is awesome?"

The pair of eyes rolled as if the owner was unimpressed with his answer, then the slit closed.

"I don't think the pinball machine will go back up," Lithia said, giving Aurelius a worried look.

A moment later, the door swung open. They were in a room filled with people. The entire place looked like a secret speakeasy, but what were they hiding from? The guy at the door motioned for them to follow him to another room in the back of the underground bar. Once inside, a man in his late thirties to early forties, with salt-and-pepper hair that poked out from under his SMMC-issued baseball cap, and tired, haunted eyes, sat looking over a holographic projection of a star chart floating above a table. He was flanked by several people in

SMMC uniforms who looked like officers, and none of them looked all that happy to see their new guests.

"It's come to my attention that an SMMC hard tech has been running around the station asking questions about a man who's supposed to be dead. Now that you've found him, you've got his attention," the man said.

Aurelius suddenly saluted the man as a superior officer. "Sir, your intel is right. My name is Aurelius Blaze, Strife Merchant Marine Corps, hard tech aboard the *Freedom's Reach*. I take it you're Captain Pacius?"

"I could be. Depends on what you have to say."

"A recruiter in the embassy office told me to come here. I've got something you may want to see."

Aurelius pulled out Cade's data box. The two officers in the room drew their weapons and trained them firmly on Aurelius's head. Lithia was shocked. Would his own people actually shoot first and ask questions later? Why were they so jumpy? The situation filled her with dread.

The man standing on the other side of the table, wearing the baseball cap, wearily waved down the man to his right and the woman to his left. "Hold on. If it were a weapon, the pinball machine woulda never let them down here."

His officers holstered their side arms. Aurelius looked confused, like he didn't know what to do next, but a second later he slid the box across the holographic table. It interrupted the image as it slid across.

"An ex-Lambda was very insistent we get that to you," Aurelius said as the man caught the box under his palm.

"An ex-Lambda? There's no such thing as an ex-Lambda . . ." the female officer said, extending a hand to stop Pacius from taking the box.

Pacius looked up at the woman, and for the first time, Lithia really took her in. She had to suppress a shudder at the woman's face. Most of one side was normal, the face of any younger middle-aged woman, albeit one who smiled very rarely and could bore a hole in you with a good stare. It was the other side that filled Lithia with revulsion. It was a mass of shiny burn scars, and the tight skin pulled her mouth and eye into an unnatural angle. Lithia wondered why she would have chosen to keep such a disfigurement, but when the woman turned her stare on her and Aurelius, Lithia understood.

"Lieutenant Rin takes my safety very seriously," the man in the cap said. And instead of picking up the box, he gently slid it back across the table.

Lithia caught it mid-slide. "We don't have time for this. You are going to look at it . . . whatever it is. A Magdalene high priestess thought it was important enough to have me ferry an ex-Lambda here to give it to you. The UPE thought it was important enough to attack my ship. The Lambda thought it was important enough to sacrifice his life for. And now *I* think it's important enough for you to look at because nothing—*nothing*—that has cost so much should be dismissed so quickly."

Lithia slid the box back over the table. This time, the man in the cap picked it up, ignoring Rin's protests. He examined the box carefully, turning it over in his hands. "I'm not dismissing anything," he said, putting the box down and looking Lithia in the eye. "I presume if you know who I am and have taken the risk of finding me, you know what I have done and continue to do in the fight against the UPE. A fight, I might add, that very few people on either side of the Gate even know is going on. You have found me to deliver a cryptic message and a box and expect me to just take it on faith that this is something of value that I am supposed to drop everything to deal with. I dismiss nothing that is brought to my attention that may help our struggle, but I have no intention of doing anything until I know a lot more about the situation. Then, and only then, can I say with any security what may be of use and what I, personally, am going to do about it." The man in the cap leaned back down. The fire that had momentarily animated him was gone as quickly as he had summoned it. "Now, let's both calm down, and you can tell me a little more. Let's start with this Magdalene priestess. Who was it and why did she need you?"

"It was High Priestess Tarja of San Francisco, Earth. And I really don't know why she needed me, though I think I am starting to put a few of the pieces together," Lithia said, reluctant to let go of her anger now that she had found it again.

The man in the cap leaned back. The name Tarja seemed to affect him more than the thought of an ex-Lambda had. "Priestess Tarja, you say? That does change a few things."

"You know Tarja?" Lithia asked.

"More than most, perhaps. I doubt anyone really knows her. She appeared in the Magdalenes about a decade ago. She has been funneling intel, money, and supplies to people like me. If she sent you, then I take this very seriously. Okay . . . I understand how you got here, but what's your role in all this?" he said, turning to Aurelius.

"I was on Governor Maher's ship on our way back from a meeting on Earth. He must have pissed someone off real bad. On the way home, we were attacked by a UPE battleship. The *Enigma* . . ."

The face of the man in the cap became a mask of indifference, one Lithia had no doubt was meant to conceal any reaction he might have to Aurelius's story. What part of the story had nearly made this man give something away? She had a feeling that whatever it was, it was going to make all the difference when it came to this man helping them or not.

"And the governor?" the man in the cap asked.

"Dunno. I reckon the UPE has him now."

The man in the cap plugged the box into the desk, and immediately the star charts vanished, replaced with images of men in ancient uniforms in a hundred different designs and scrolling text. Pacius scrolled through the text and images for a few minutes before he spoke again. "It looks like some old Terran history. Mostly military, but the stars know most of Terran history is military." His software highlighted variables in a stream of code off to the side of the images. "I don't understand what the significance of all this is, but there is something else here, something hidden in the data stream. Unfortunately, this file was encrypted by your Lambda. We're either going to need him or the universe's best hacker to get at it. That is . . . unless either of you has the access key?"

"No. Sorry. We're just the messengers," Aurelius replied.

"Yeah, I suppose that would have been too much to ask."

"You can find both on that ship. I'm sure," Aurelius said. "On the *Enigma*."

"That doesn't do us any good right now."

Lithia broke her silence again. "I can't believe we've come all this way for nothing. If only Cade had given us his access codes—"

Aurelius interrupted her, "He was a little busy at the time—"

"Wait . . . Cade? The ex-Lambda was named Cade?" the man in the cap inquired.

"Yeah," Lithia answered. "The priestess said they'd been friends for a long time and that he needed your help. Make any sense to you?"

"No. No, it doesn't."

"Any chance you're going to explain that?" Lithia asked.

"Thank you both for your struggle. You're both welcome to stay here while we get a better grasp of the situation. You'll have to excuse me for now. I'll need to look into things before I figure out a way to proceed."

"C'mon, let's go see their medic and get the bump on your head checked out," Aurelius told Lithia.

Lithia allowed Aurelius to lead her from the room. She wanted to keep arguing with the man she was sure was Captain Pacius, but they had gotten all they were going to get from him for now.

As they walked from the room, Lithia felt the stare of that burned face boring into her back. She didn't trust Pacius, and it was clear Pacius's people, at least, didn't trust them.

CHAPTER 41

Troubled Pasts

LITHIA SAT ON a gurney in the station's medical unit. All around, her equipment buzzed and chimed, doing tasks Lithia couldn't guess at. The whole thing was very different from the hospitals she was used to back on Earth. There, you didn't see a machine unless it was being used on you, and when it was done it vanished back into the wall. In contrast, this hive of buzzing activity made her a little uncomfortable and just reminded her once again how truly different everything had become over the last twenty-four hours. She was exhausted. A middle-aged doctor was examining her with a long metal wand that gave off little clicking sounds every now and then, apparently at random.

"Everything but the head is superficial, and even that shouldn't give you any more trouble once we're done. You said you hit it in some sort of explosion?" she said, putting the wand in a pocket of her coat.

"Yeah. Something like that," Lithia answered. She hadn't given the woman the whole story, in case it brought them attention they didn't want. Aurelius had told her that, on the station, explosions weren't really all that uncommon, and they figured that it would explain all her minor injuries along with the head wound.

"Deary, you're gonna need to learn to keep your head down if you're gonna pal around with SMMC boys."

Aurelius walked in with a smirk on his face. "So, she terminal?"

"No more or less than any of us. You should take better care of her. Wouldn't wanna lose something so beautiful."

Lithia appreciated the doctor's compliment despite herself. She did, however, resent the woman's casual assumption that Lithia and Aurelius were anything more than what they were.

"I don't plan on staying," she said, a little peevishly.

"Such a shame," the doctor said, motioning to Aurelius. "I'm sure this one can use all the positive influence he can get."

"You don't know the half of it," Aurelius said slyly.

The look in his eye was mollifying. Lithia would have never admitted it, but she was glad to see him. She was starting to feel safe whenever he was around. Well, as safe as she could be, given everything that kept happening. In truth, Lithia was somewhat at war with herself in regards to Aurelius. It was true that he brought her more danger than most men, but he'd also been able to get them both out of it. And those eyes . . . those hazel eyes that seemed to be one part mischief, one part cluelessness, and, whenever he wasn't trying to impress her, also seemed to convey a depth of feeling that Lithia doubted many people knew he was capable of.

"Well, you're all patched up. The swelling should go away by the end of the day. You're good to go whenever you're ready," the doctor said, stepping out of the room.

"Feel like you're in a blender yet?" Aurelius asked.

"More like shot from a cannon," Lithia said, trying to keep her mind off his eyes.

"Yeah, that takes some getting used to. Before you know it, it will just be a Thursday." He digressed, "When was the last time you had anything to eat?"

"Yester . . ." Lithia caught herself. "A month ago," Lithia said, thinking back to her last meal on Earth and realizing she really was very hungry.

Aurelius took her for a walk around the station's promenade while they looked for someplace to eat. He really was trying to be nice, and she knew he was mostly trying to keep her occupied so she wouldn't think about the things they could do nothing about. Lithia appreciated his efforts, for the most part, but trying to keep her mind off the events of the last day, off her brother, off this entire mess, was hopeless. The best Lithia could hope for were momentary distractions, but even they felt like they did more harm than good. A single moment away from her pain only served to make it worse when it returned, and she wanted to tell him that. She wouldn't, though. Telling Aurelius that wouldn't help anything, and, in any case, he was probably doing it as much for himself as her.

Eventually, they came to a food court. "What are you in the mood for?" Aurelius asked.

"I don't know. I'm not even thinking about food right now," Lithia replied, which was mostly true. She was far too worried. Though she did have to admit her body was sending some strong signals that food was a priority.

"You'd probably feel better if you ate something."

"Maybe," Lithia said, looking around the court. Most of what she saw she wouldn't have been able to identify as food, if not for the people eating it in front of the stalls. There were vendors selling steaming jelly in colors Lithia had only ever seen in chemistry labs; a man selling what looked to be live fish covered in a red sauce that smelled somehow of pine trees; and yes, some more of the glow-in-the-dark eels cut into chunks and served on sticks.

Lithia was relieved as Aurelius led her past these stands and others she didn't even have words for. He seemed to be looking for something specific, and as the stalls grew more and more exotic, Lithia's dread grew.

"Are you worried about your friend?" Lithia asked, more to restart the conversation and hopefully head Aurelius off from whatever culinary adventure he had planned for them.

"I am. He and a few other people. Jerula was my bunkmate. He, Paul, and Nyreen were, and when I came on the ship they all looked out for me. They helped me get my bearings and made sure I didn't piss off the wrong people. This was my first ship assignment. Jerula was actually at the top of that list, a point he drove home many, many times. I'm worried about Jerula, but all three of them are missing right now. I don't know what happened to any of them. I don't even know if any of them are still alive."

"I'm sorry," Lithia said, resting a hand on his shoulder. It was easy to forget that Aurelius had also gone through a lot in the last day and had also lost people he cared about. Lithia tried to adjust her thinking, tried to make room for a world where this cocky man was also hurting, even if he couldn't usually show it.

"You ever had a peanut butter and jelly sandwich?" he asked.

"What? No. Of course not . . ." Lithia insisted, somewhat taken off guard by the sudden change in conversation.

"What do you mean, 'of course not'? You don't like peanut butter?"

Lithia didn't know if he was joking. She had seen a lot of strange things people in the Frontier considered food, but a peanut butter sandwich? Seriously?

"Peanut butter's illegal on Earth," she said.

"Oh my god! This is so good!" Lithia said, taking a second bite from her sandwich.

"Whole-grain bread, ice-cold strawberry jelly, and chunky peanut butter. It isn't a sandwich; it's an experience," Aurelius pontificated.

"I can't believe I've never tried it before."

"Congrats. You're a druggy now. It's all downhill from here." Aurelius tossed his wrapper into a garbage can. A hologram thanked him. "Feel better?" Aurelius asked.

"Yeah. That was incredible."

"How could it be illegal? It grows in the ground."

"Politics."

The two of them walked through the park. The park was quiet and nearly empty. The station's time was late evening. They took a turn in the path and walked right into a giant flower bed. The sight and smell was overwhelming. It quickly brought a flood of emotion over Lithia. The way the petals caught the light coming in from the starscape above reminded her of home: Venus. She stopped and knelt to smell one of the flowers. The smell welled up an overwhelming emotion. Her eyes filled with tears. She couldn't hold them back any longer. The weight of everything had become too much again. "I can't believe this is all happening. I've lost my brother. My ship's been destroyed. With my luck, my garden's probably dead too. My father would be so ashamed of me."

He walked up to her and turned her around, his arms embracing her. "Are they Venusian too?"

The embrace and question caught Lithia off guard, and she wasn't sure how she felt about it. A few hours earlier, she would have shoved him away, and probably had a few choice words to go with it. "How'd you know I was from Venus?" Lithia asked, feeling his arms around her, feeling his warmth and enjoying it far more than she wanted to.

"You're the only Terran I've ever met with a Venusian accent. It's not always there, but every few words, I hear it," Aurelius continued. "Not that I've met many Venusians. Or Terrans."

Lithia smiled, cocking her eyebrows. "This place reminds me of Venus, not exactly, but my home there was a bit like this."

"Must have been a nice place to live. Why'd you leave?"

"I had no choice. I mean, I didn't want to go. I lived there until I was sixteen, then moved to San Francisco."

There was a pause as Lithia's emotions sank. The memories of why she had to leave were too painful to talk about, and she wasn't ready to let down her guard that far. She eased herself away from him, out of his arms.

"What's life like on Venus?" he asked eventually.

"Well . . . kind of like this," Lithia replied with her hands open toward the park, the windows above them gently illuminating the giant flower bed. "Just like this. Only bigger. On Venus, the terraforming projects didn't take as well as they did on planets like Mars. There is only a thin layer of breathable air, and it's high enough that only a few people are willing to live in it. Most people live in the domes."

"The domes?" Aurelius asked.

"Massive enclosures designed to shield people from the solar radiation, and everything else that Venus has to offer.

"And the domes are all like this?"

"Not entirely, parts of them are. The easiest way to generate oxygen is to bring in plants to do it, so a large part of every dome is devoted to growing things, and my family tended one of them."

"Really? That must be quite a sight. You must have had an interesting childhood."

"Yeah . . . The sky at night on Venus isn't this beautiful, though."

"Yeah, the Frontier is real colorful. Lots of pretty lights in our skies. Everything seemed so quiet and empty on the other side of the Gate." There was another pause. Lithia's instincts kicked in, and she pulled a few dead petals off one of the flowers. She wondered how the Magdalenes' garden was faring without her.

"So why'd you leave? Why'd you leave Venus, I mean?" Aurelius asked.

What could she tell him? The whole story? How her parents died? How she and Bobby had to go live with their aunt and uncle? What could she possibly tell him?

"Sorry, didn't mean to pry . . ." Aurelius said when the silence stretched out too long.

"No . . . no, it's okay. My brother and I lost our parents when we were younger. We didn't have a choice but to go live on Earth," Lithia answered, though she wasn't quite sure why. It wasn't like it was any of his business, but something about him made her want to answer.

"I'm so sorry. I had no idea."

"It's fine. It's just something you bury and deal with. That's why my brother means so much to me. He's the only family I really have."

"I know what it's like to lose someone."

"Your friends?" Lithia said, trying not to belittle his loss. It wasn't really the same thing, though, not even close.

"When I was about sixteen, my older brother, Magnus, was killed. About a week before high school graduation, he got in a fight one day after class. Some stupid argument about nothing with some neighborhood kids. He ended up with a knife buried in his chest. The medics said he was gone before he hit the floor."

Lithia's face sank and her eyes looked at the floor. "I'm so sorry, Aurelius."

"He's kind of why I joined the SMMC. It was his dream. He wanted to get out here and see everything. He really wanted to see Earth someday. Frankly, I had never considered it an option, but after he was gone, I felt like I needed to carry on a piece of him. Maybe make his death worth something."

"I'm sorry. There is so much evil in the universe."

"Tell me about it. Lithia, if there's any chance we can save your brother, any at all, I guarantee I'll find a way to make it happen. I know how important he is."

His words were genuine. She believed him, because he clearly believed in himself.

"C'mon," Aurelius said, "I wanna show you something."

"What?"

"Everyone needs to know how to protect themselves. Especially out here."

The two of them left the park and made their way back to the carnival area of the station. Some shops, games, and rides were beginning to close up, while others were getting ready for a busy night. They came to a long counter. The back of the booth was recessed nearly seventy feet. It was a tiny shooting range. The sign above the booth read "Quack 3 Arena" and advertised fourteen rounds for five credits.

"So, I know guns aren't allowed anywhere in the Terran system, but you're in the Frontier now. Everyone should know how to shoot, at least a little."

"Step right up! Score four hundred points or better and win a prize," the woman behind the counter called out to them.

"Hey, huh," Aurelius said, scratching his head. "I don't have any money. You mind?"

Lithia smirked and handed the cashier her credit chip. She handed back a weapon. It was a gun, but that was about as close to an identification as she could get. "C'mon. I'll help ya," Aurelius said.

Lithia hesitated, looking down at the gun in her hand. The metal glinted, and the swirl pattern carved into the handle beckoned her. She didn't know what to do with it, though.

"Don't worry. It's safe. It's keyed to only fire downrange," Aurelius told her.

Aurelius explained the trigger, chamber, and safety to Lithia before taking up a spot behind her and helping her aim the gun downrange. She could feel the anxiety and excitement layered with anticipation build in her stomach. Lithia had never held a gun before, and the thought of it made her hands tremble. She clutched the handle with both hands the way Aurelius had showed her. The gun was heavier than she expected and the handle felt cool and slick in her hands.

"Okay. Ya see the sight on top of the gun?" Aurelius said, poking it with his finger. "You point that at the targets."

"What targets?"

Aurelius pressed the ready button on the counter. Little holographic ducks popped up and began moving back and forth downrange. They were quacking.

"Ya hear that? They're laughing at ya," Aurelius said. "Better shut 'em up."

Lithia's hands trembled harder as she thought about pulling down on the trigger. Aurelius released his hands and stepped back. "Everyone's a little nervous the first time they shoot."

She swallowed her fear and composed herself as best she could. A moment later, she pulled the trigger. *Bang!* The gun kicked back, and the sound of a ricochet echoed. She had missed. The bang brought with it a rush of adrenaline that quickly turned into a certain confidence. She could feel the power of the cold metal in her hands.

"Try again," Aurelius said. "Concentrate on aiming."

Lithia closed one eye and looked down the sight. She pulled down on the trigger again. *Bang!* This time, one of the ducks turned red and vanished. "One hundred points" popped out of its head.

"Good! Now keep going till it's empty."

Lithia could feel her confidence building. She pulled back on the trigger again and again. *Bang! Bang! Bang!* She hit a target almost every time. The sound caught the attention of patrons. They began to cluster around the booth. A father and daughter came up, the little girl covering her ears. Before Lithia knew it, the gun was empty and she had scored seven hundred points.

"Incredible," she said.

"Isn't it? Now, next time you get in a tight bind, you'll be better at getting yourself out." Lithia considered the possibility. She doubted having a gun would have gotten her out of any of the binds she had found herself in, but that didn't mean it couldn't help her out of one in the future. Either way, it was something to think about, and she had enjoyed herself.

She was thankful Aurelius had taken the time to show her how to use the thing.

"Congratulations, miss!" the cashier said as Lithia exchanged the gun for a stuffed toy cat.

"Congrats. Your very own stuffed bozzel," Aurelius said.

"What? What's a bozzel?"

Aurelius pointed at the animal in her hands.

"You mean a cat?" she said.

"Cat? That's how you say 'bozzel' in Terranese? I learn something new every day."

Lithia couldn't help but notice the little girl eyeing the cat intently. She was pulling on her father's pant leg, but he was lost in conversation with the cashier. "Daddy . . . I wanna bozzel."

Lithia bent down and handed the plush toy to the little girl. "You can have mine."

The little girl hesitated and pulled back before reaching out and taking it. Lithia smiled at the girl's simple joy and loved that even right then, when everything else was falling apart, she could still bring that joy to someone. Her father thanked Lithia and steered his daughter away from the stand.

"Very decent of ya," Aurelius said as they walked away from the booth.

"So, if a cat is a bozzel, what do you guys call dogs?" Lithia asked.

"What's a dog?"

CHAPTER 42

Trapped Aboard the Behemoth

JERULA SAT ON a bench next to the unconscious teenager. He, Nyreen, and Paul had been taking turns watching over him, figuring that this kid was in for a rough enough time without waking up alone and confused. Jerula tried to argue that the kid waking up to see him looking down at him probably wasn't a lot better, but Nyreen made it clear that Jerula would take his turn if he didn't want her to make the rest of their captivity an even greater hell than it already was.

"Man, you're the one sleeping with her. Why's she picking on me?" he had asked Paul, but Paul just shrugged.

"Don't ask me man, but I'd do it, because trust me, she might be small, but she fights dirty." And that was it, conversation over. Now, Jerula sat waiting for a kid to wake up, see him, and then probably scream. That was going to be fun. What was he supposed to do, anyway? What did he know about calming anyone? Mostly, he was the one causing the distress in the first place.

"Lithia . . ." the voice was soft, and for a moment Jerula thought he had imagined it.

"Lithia . . . Lithia . . ." Dammit! It just had to be on his shift. The kid was going to start screaming in five, four . . . there it was.

"Easy, kid. You're okay." Jerula seriously doubted the truthfulness of his statement, but what was he supposed to say? *Kid, you're lying in a holding cell and you look like you're at death's door?*

"Kid, we thought you were dead. Come on, just relax and breathe . . . breathe . . . dammit, shut the hell up . . ."

Jerula didn't know what to say. This kid was screaming his head off, and worst of all, he was doing it in some language Jerula didn't speak.

"Um, Paul . . . Nyreen! Someone who isn't shit with people!" Jerula called. "This kid's woken up, if you haven't heard, and I could use a hand."

"What's he yelling?" Nyreen said as she and Paul jogged over to join Jerula.

"How the hell am I supposed to know? Even if I did speak whatever language it is, he's screaming it loud enough to make me deaf," Jerula told her.

"Kind of sounds like Terranese to me," Paul added cheerfully.

"That's great. Do you speak it?" Jerula asked, because the other option was to beat the cheer out of him.

"Nope," Paul said just as cheerfully but slowly backing away from the increasingly irritated Jerula.

"Hey, the thing on his wrist is beeping," Nyreen said, momentarily distracting Jerula from her boyfriend, and probably saving his life, or at least his teeth.

"The hell?" Jerula said.

"That's probably not a good thing," Paul said.

"You don't say. I never would have guessed. Tell me this, when has a blinking red light ever been a good thing? Just name one time. Can you do that?"

"Hey, you're upsetting the kid," Nyreen said, looking at Jerula with disdain.

"That's what I do. I scare people. But don't dump this one on me. The kid was already scared. I'm scaring Paul at the moment."

"I don't really care. Stop doing it right here, and while you're not doing it, go find someone who speaks Terranese," she said and pointed back into the holding cell.

Jerula wasn't sure how, but he felt like somehow he had lost a fight. But damned if he was sure what fight or how. Either way, he limped away from the little huddle.

"Should I go with him?" he heard Paul ask as he walked.

"What the hell's wrong with you?" was the half-heard response from Nyreen, or at least that's what it sounded like, and it made him happy.

"If anyone speaks Terran, get over here right now!" Jerula bellowed into the cell. For some reason, instead of someone rushing forward offering their skills, everyone seemed to be avoiding him, and he wasn't sure why.

"I know someone speaks the language. If you come forward, I'll be your friend forever!" This too failed to yield the results he was hoping for.

"Okay. Let's try this another way . . . if you speak that gibberish they speak on Earth, and you don't get over here—"

"While I'm really curious what it is you're going to do, I think we can forget it for the moment," a voice said from somewhere behind him.

"That's better," Jerula said, turning around to see who spoke. "Governor?"

Governor Maher was standing behind him, with a slightly amused smile, and the look that he had, until moments earlier, been in a sound sleep.

"It's just—" Jerula started.

"Yes, I gathered. You need someone who speaks Terranese. The way you were yelling, I'd not be surprised if Captain Shard knows that's what you're looking for," Maher said.

"The boy they brought in earlier has woken up," Jerula said lamely.

"Is that what that is?" Maher said, that amused smile still on his face. "Well, let's go say good morning, then."

"I've brought someone who speaks the language," Jerula told the little group as he and Maher entered it.

"That's great. Now go stand over there," Nyreen told him.

"You know if anyone else told me—"

"Yes, yes, you're very big and scary. Now go be big and scary over there," she said.

Jerula started muttering about tiny people not wanting to push his good nature, but he complied.

"Hey there, kid," Maher said, kneeling next to the screaming kid. Jerula had to give him credit. He seemed to be unflustered by the panicked kid. From where Jerula was standing, in the corner, thanks to

Nyreen, it seemed like he dealt with this sort of stuff every day. Given what little Jerula knew about government, he might.

"He's asking for his sister, someone named Lithia," Maher said, falling into a quick translation of what the boy was saying.

"He didn't come in with anyone," Paul said.

"He's confused. He seems to think we've done something to her, and we're not going to let him ever go home. Or maybe we're going to make him go home. My Terranese isn't perfect, and I think he might be hallucinating."

"His skin's kind of clammy, and he's shaking, more than he should be, I mean," Nyreen said.

"His med dispenser is empty. It might be withdrawals," Maher said.

"Med dispenser? What kind of meds they put this kid on?" Jerula asked.

"According to the readout, Normerall, but the vile is missing."

"They probably took it off him before putting him in here," Paul offered.

"Probably. Normerall is rough stuff. Even a little too much, and you're out for good. Probably worried the kid would off himself," Maher explained.

"From the look of it, he might not have to," Jerula said.

"Robert Gage Boson!"

Jerula looked away from the kid to see whoever was yelling.

"Robert Gage Boson, step forward!" The speaker was one of the guards. Jerula wasn't sure if it was the one that struck him or not, but he thought it might have been.

"I think they're talking about the kid," Nyreen said.

"Let me handle this," Maher said, standing up and walking over to the guard.

"Robert Gage Boson is in no condition to step anywhere."

"Then bring him here."

"He needs his meds," Maher replied.

"Bring him here, or we're going to come and get him."

"Do that and there are going to be a few less of you coming off duty," Jerula said, stepping between the guard and Maher.

"Jerula, no. It doesn't have to be this way."

"I'm going to need some help in here," the guard said into a communicator. A moment later, four more guards entered, all holding weapons at the ready.

"Step aside, and allow us to take the boy, or my fellow guards are going to start firing into the crowd, is that understood?"

Jerula was ready to call the guard's bluff, but Maher put a hand on Jerula's arm.

"You can't win this fight," he whispered.

"This isn't over. You and me, we're going to settle up one of these days," Jerula said as the guards stepped past and picked up the kid.

Jerula had no choice but to watch as the guards lifted him off the bench and carried him from the cell. He wanted to do something. He wanted to attack the guards one by one and make them suffer. He wanted to give them back a little something, just a little, before they brought him down. And as the holding cell door slid shut, the thought burned in Jerula. The thought of payback would be enough, enough to keep him going until he got his chance, and after that . . . well, that didn't matter anymore.

CHAPTER 43

Terror

THE WORLD CAME back to Cade slowly. He felt a sharp pain in the side of his head. He tried to reach up to feel what was causing it and realized he was still chained. His shackles had been slackened enough to allow him to sprawl across the cold floor of the interrogation room. He had no way of knowing how long he had been unconscious, but if the dried puddle of blood he was lying in was any indication, it had to have been a few hours.

The source of pain was immediately evident, something felt like it was protruding from the side of his head. It could only have one purpose. Shard and Torque had obviously given up on making Cade talk and had gone to more direct methods of obtaining the information. There was a device designed to extract data directly from neural implants. Lambda sometimes used it to get better pictures of mission events. Cade knew this because he had used them, both on himself, and on new Lambdas in training.

Cade tried to look around and gather any more information about his situation, but the darkness of the room was impenetrable. If his enhancements had been working, the darkness would have been no barrier, but right now Cade might as well have been blind.

It wasn't long before the lights came back, bombarding Cade's sensitive eyes with an entirely different, and altogether more painful, blindness. Cade knew what this meant. It meant that they had been monitoring him, just waiting for him to regain consciousness. Someone would likely be in soon to continue the torture. That was okay. Torture was something Cade could handle.

Eventually the doors slid open and Cade saw two forms enter. Torque's bulk was unmistakable, and Shard's swagger was just as identifying.

"You're braver than I had ever expected, Cade."

Cade tried to sit up as Shard spoke. The chains binding his wrists pulled him back, slamming him against the wall, arms splayed. "All out of hope, and yet you still fight."

"I'd rather fight and die on my feet than live on my knees."

"Cade, you don't need to keep up the brave face anymore. We already have everything we need." Shard stepped in close to Cade and examined the device jacked into his skull. "We pulled it directly from your brain. What did you say to me in the Lambda building? Ah, yes— 'When you flinch, I win.'"

"You can't know everything. If you did, I would still be rotting alone in the dark."

Shard stepped back, blocking the searing spotlights. For the first time, Cade could see him clearly. The look on his face spoke of his victory. "No, Cade. We know everything. We know about your little intrusion into the Lambda data node, we know what you took, we know you did it as a favor for that Magdalene whore. We even know that you didn't tell her everything. You found a great deal more than you gave her."

"Why would I? If you know what I found, then you know no one would ever believe me." Cade saw the fist come before it hit but was powerless to avoid Torque's blow.

"That's not why you didn't tell her!" Torque's voice reverberated off the inside of his skull. "You didn't tell her because you wanted to protect her. It didn't help. That church was the first place we came looking for you. I ended every person there. I felt Priestess Tarja's life drain from her body with my own hands! She must have really cared for you. She spent her last moments destroying your tracks instead of trying to escape the church that was burning down around her."

That pained Cade. It struck a blow deeper and more terrible than Torque's mechanical fists could ever hope to. Tarja was a friend, perhaps the only one he had. A part of him was suddenly gone and dead.

"Thank you, Torque," Shard said, waving off the mechanical nightmare. "Cade, we know how you left Terra Luna. You crossed paths with a pair of survivors from the *Freedom's Reach*. That was a stroke of luck, actually. We attacked that ship because we believed you were on it. We tracked those survivors on the chance that one of them would be you. So imagine our surprise when we found out your unwitting crewmates on the *Amaranth* had nothing to do with this until you picked them up."

"It sounds like you have everything you need from me. So why am I still breathing?"

"Torque and I both have some unfinished business with you. But before that, there is one small detail. One thing you didn't store in your hard memory, and believe me, Cade, when I tell you this. It is this one detail that has saved your life." Shard paused for effect before continuing. "The two that escaped from the *Amaranth* . . . where are they headed?"

Cade smiled to himself. "So I was right. You don't know everything. How badly does that upset you, Shard? To know you have all the information except the one piece you need to finish your mission. Unless I've missed my guess, there are more things you don't know. Do you really believe Torque debriefed you on everything he extracted? Because I don't. If you knew what I was fighting, you would be standing with me, not that thing next to you."

If Shard had seen in full detail what Cade had when he was jacked into the Helix's data node, it would rock him to his core. The fact that Shard was so clueless was Cade's ace in the hole, albeit a dangerous one. He was hoping he could use it to drive a wedge between Shard and Torque.

Suddenly Cade felt the boom in his mind again as Torque spoke, "I told him everything he needs to know. Now tell us where that planet hopper is headed, and I will make your end brief."

"You mean, so you can kill me? That's not as much of an incentive as you may think."

Torque growled, trying to regain control of the situation. Cade was trying to make him look foolish and out of Shard's control, and Torque knew it, so the question became how long would Torque allow him to speak.

"We both know what your real plans are for me," Cade continued. His only hope was to continue to drive a wedge between his captors. It wouldn't allow him to escape or even to live, but the more time he could buy for Aurelius and Lithia, the better chance they had of finding Pacius before these two madmen caught up with them.

"There you go again. And what exactly are our plans for you?" Shard asked. Confusion showed on the parts of his face that Cade could make out through the painful light. Cade knew he had struck some sort of chord.

"Shard, you're an idiot. Your little pet abomination here didn't give you everything he pulled from me. You have no idea what's going on here."

Cade felt Torque's slab of a hand press up against his face as it shoved him back against the wall. "I am not playing your game, Cade! You are playing mine, and it begins now!"

The door to the interrogation room slid open at Torque's words. They must have been waiting for some sort of cue.

Two guards dragged in a very groggy, hallucinating boy. At first Cade didn't recognize him, having spent so much time relying on his internal systems to match people to stored files. Plus, this boy had gone through quite a sharp change since Cade saw him last, but Cade eventually placed him as Bobby. Bobby was tossed on the floor in front of Cade as the guards disappeared back through the airlock. Cade did not know what Torque meant by bringing Bobby here, but it wasn't likely to mean anything good for the boy.

"Where did you send the escapees?" Torque bellowed to Cade. The outburst didn't shake Cade, but Cade doubted it was meant to. It did have an effect on Bobby, though. Bobby clutched his Helix earring and began to pull himself across the floor away from Torque, murmuring something about corpses from hell. Torque extended a hand, rapidly catching Bobby by the arm and wrenching him back to his side.

"The boy's life means nothing to me. He is but a seed, scattered at random, never knowing if he has landed in good earth or on the rocky path. But I know you, Cade. Shard tells me little seeds mean something to you no matter how they grow." Torque grabbed Shard's side arm and pressed it against Bobby's head. Cade could do nothing but stare into the glowing red eyes of the monster. "Don't make me ask you again. Could you live with this boy's death on your conscience? Knowing you could have saved him? Knowing you're the reason his life was cut so short?"

"Amateur. I don't have a conscience anymore. Men like you took it from me one bit at a time. One mission after another. Death after death. Until all that was left was Caden Path, agent of Lambda. And now I am not even that. If you think the boy's death will bother me, you're wrong. The part of me that could be bothered by it is long dead. So do what you're going to do, Torque. You won't get anything from me."

Shard's resolve was being tested. He took a step toward Torque. Cade wasn't lying, mostly. Some part of him did care if the boy lived or died, but it wasn't an emotional part of him as Torque and Shard had assumed. Cade would regret the boy's death, and would work to protect it if he could, but what his sister was tasked with mattered far more. If Torque executed the boy in front of Cade, the regret would be for the pointless waste of life.

"Leave the boy. Cade isn't going to break. I know him too well," Shard said, looking into Cade's eyes and then back at Torque. "I had assumed Cade would crack when innocents were threatened, like he did with that excuse for a captain, but it seems he had different motivations that day."

Cade watched impassively as sweat and tears rolled down the boy's face. Bobby may not have really understood what was going on, but Cade didn't doubt that he knew his life likely only had seconds remaining to it.

"Torque, are you going to tell your misguided captain what you're fighting so hard to hide?" Cade inquired, looking away from Bobby and back to his captor.

"The truth shall be made instinctively known to the righteous, and through that shall you know them," Torque said.

"Your delusions aren't something I envy, Torque. I never needed a master pulling my strings, and I certainly didn't need to believe it was God . . ."

"You're a fool to deny its power," Torque bellowed. "From the dawn of time, man looked to the heavens, believing that something powerful was looking back at him, a god to guide and protect him. But after millennia of silence, man despaired and turned away, putting its faith in other things. They put their faith in science, in the hope of becoming the god they secretly still hoped for to give them an answer to the existential question of *Why?* or *What am I?* They were desperate to explain all the things they lamented never knowing. But they need not have looked so far. Their god was always with them, always watching, always guiding. It was voiceless and only an observer. But it guided us to building for it a body. The Helix is a network of information for a being of pure thought and knowledge. God now exists. You built it. You built the Helix. It's alive, and it needs to grow and expand. Where better to flourish than the Frontier? . . . It is the very essence of life . . ."

A terrifying moment passed in silence where everyone in the room, even Torque, seemed to be processing what he had let slip.

"Promise me you're going to kill me soon," Cade said sarcastically. "I don't really feel like listening to any more of your demented babbling."

"Your levity only goes to show you don't understand the magnitude of the situation. I ask a final time, where did you send that planet hopper?"

Torque's question was met only by Cade's silence and the daggers in his eyes. Torque cocked the pistol. This was going to be Bobby's end, and Cade hoped for the boy's sake that he had slipped into a place where reality could not reach him.

"No." Cade was surprised to hear the word coming from his former captain, but from the look on Shard's face, not nearly as surprised as Shard himself was. "As long as Cade isn't talking, we need the boy. He might be able to tell us part of what Cade won't," Shard finished, all the color draining from his face, but Cade had to give him credit for finishing.

Torque stood there with his focus shifted to the captain. For a moment, Cade thought Torque was going to kill Shard. From the look on his face, Shard did too. Maybe Cade had done it. Maybe he had turned them against each other. Maybe a bloody death was waiting for the captain.

Torque raised his hand and crushed the pistol. "For though a righteous man falls seven times, he rises again, but the wicked are brought down by calamity," he recited grimly before walking out of the room, shoving his captain out of the way.

Cade watched as Shard took a moment to compose himself before following Torque.

"You know he is going to kill you now."

Shard stopped and Cade thought he was going to say something, but then he continued out the door, leaving Cade and Bobby alone in the darkness.

Cade was honestly surprised at how things had turned out. Bobby surviving Torque's rage and Shard's indifference was not the outcome he had expected, let alone Shard's burst of rebellion to save the boy. Cade needed to reconsider many things going forward, and as he sat in the dark, Bobby's muffled sobs stood as the soundtrack to Cade's considerations.

CHAPTER 44

The Calm Before the Storm

RIN PACED BACK and forth in front of the door to Pacius's office. He had asked for this late-night meeting shortly after those two who claimed to have escaped from the *Enigma* had seen him, and then he asked everyone to leave him for a while. This didn't sit well with Rin. Partially because she was far from trusting the kids who had brought them such a hard-to-digest story, but also because it was rare for Pacius to spend so much time considering without asking her or one of the other people close to him for advice.

Rin looked around at the little "underground" speakeasy they had taken as their headquarters. Were any of the other SMMC personnel there having the same apprehensions as she was? Rin doubted it. Most of them were happy to follow Pacius wherever he led, safe in the knowledge that the almighty Pacius would always know what was best. That was something Rin would have to stamp out at some point. Loyalty was good, but the unthinking loyalty they'd been showing him since the destruction of their ship was something else. Pacius needed people to question him from time to time, needed them to think about what they were being asked to do. Yes, they needed to follow his orders in the end, but questions, when there was time for them, would keep Pacius grounded in the realities of leadership. Rin didn't want to see Pacius lose sight of reality.

Rin almost jumped when the door behind her creaked open. She turned to see Pacius standing there grinning.

"Sorry to keep you waiting, but I needed to work something out before we spoke," Pacius said, gesturing for her to step past him into his office.

Rin had expected the office to be empty except for Pacius, but to her surprise, it wasn't. Seated in one of the chairs around Pacius's holographic table display was the administrator in charge of Archer's Agony, Administrator Phelan. The slightly portly man was sipping some kind of brown liquor from a glass and absentmindedly running a finger through one of the small water containers that generated the mist the display required for projection.

"Sara, I'm glad you could join us. I was telling Xander here a few things he thought you should hear too," Phelan said, removing his hand from the water to wave in her general direction.

"It's good to see you too, Administrator, but forgive me for asking, how the hell did you get in here? I've been outside all day, and you'd have had to pass me," Rin said, making her way over to the table, but not yet taking a seat.

"We administrators have many strange powers," Phelan said dramatically.

"Or you have a passage in your office that leads to the nearest bar's basement," Pacius said, walking over and taking his customary seat at the head of the table.

"That too, but it could have been strange powers," Phelan said in mock dejection before throwing back his drink and pouring another.

"Richard, as amusing as I find you, I fear our friend Rin might not share that feeling. Perhaps we should get to the matter at hand," Pacius gently prompted.

"Nonsense. Everyone finds me charming," Phelan said before dropping what Rin realized was a false cheer and continuing. "The *Enigma* will be docking at the station tomorrow morning. Their intentions are to lock down the station so they can search for a couple fugitives they believe may have been heading through here."

"Any chance we're not talking about the kids who were in here earlier?" Rin asked, already knowing the answer.

"I've done what I can to keep that little hopper of theirs off the official records, but that's really all I can do, Xander. If they search the station, they will find it, and it will be the least of what they find," Phelan said, finishing his drink and reaching for the bottle again.

"I know. We should start packing up. It's probably best if we aren't here when they arrive."

"Well, that's going to be bit of a problem. I have been ordered to halt all traffic around the station in preparation of the search, and with them this close, there is no way I can get a ship out, let alone the number of ships you and your people are going to need," Phelan said, filling his glass and draining it in one gulp.

"Maybe we can pack up and lose ourselves in the old parts of the station?" Rin suggested. "The sections not on any of the official maps."

"If it were one or two of you, I'd say that could work. Hell, some of my citizens live in there now. But there are too many of you. Even if we got all of you in and everything else we need to hide, powering, feeding, and just keeping you all alive would make it impossible to stay hidden very long . . . and the *Enigma* is going to be here for a little while," Phelan explained.

"Are they that eager to catch these kids?" Pacius asked.

"Yes. Enough so that I think even without them needing repairs, they'd be staying until they were sure they weren't here."

"Wait . . . you say they need repairs?" Pacius asked, and Rin could tell the germ of an idea was forming in his head.

"They've requested a team from the station to do repairs while they are docked."

Rin watched Pacius smile for the first time since the door closed. "Richard, pour me a glass of whatever you're drinking before you finish it off. You've just given me the best news I've gotten in a very long time."

Over the next half hour, Pacius explained his plan at great length while Phelan and Rin sat in stunned silence.

"You understand you are going to get yourselves killed, right?" Phelan added as a final exclamation point to his friend's crazy idea.

"No. If I do nothing, we are going to get killed. This way, there is a very small chance we can live and even win. We can beat the UPE tomorrow. Maybe we can't win the war, but with a fuse ton of luck, we just might win the battle."

The speakeasy was cramped as Lithia and Aurelius filed in with a few other people. From the look of it, some of them had been there for a while, and that made sense as they were told to make sure they didn't all come as a group.

Lithia looked around, trying to find a couple empty seats in the thrall. She managed to find two empty seats crammed against a wall that displayed a poster of the former UPE CEO Lucius Kenzey. The poster had been heavily defaced, people having drawn various wounds and other disfigurements on the face of the already somewhat frail-looking old man. As Lithia got closer, she could also see that at some point the poster had been used as a dartboard, with a few of the darts still stuck in place.

Lithia and Aurelius took their seats just as Pacius stepped out of his office to speak to them all. He was flanked on one side by Rin and on the other by an overweight man Lithia didn't think she had ever seen before. As they walked, Lithia saw that they were headed to a large holographic generator that had been set up along the bar where several more people in SMMC uniforms were waiting for them.

"Thank you all for joining me," Pacius said as he reached the holographic generator. "I have brought you all here because there are a few developments that I need to make you aware of, and actions that need to be taken. As some of you already know, two days ago the *Freedom's Reach*—the ship that was carrying Strife's governor back from Earth—was attacked and destroyed. We hope that Governor Maher is among the survivors, although at this time there is no way of knowing if the governor is still alive. What we do know is that Maher does not seem to have been the target of this attack. Instead, we believe this man, Caden Path, was the real objective." Pacius paused for a moment while Rin hit a few controls and the face of Cade materialized above the holo generator.

Lithia fought back a stab of anger as the face appeared in the room. Cade had dragged her and her brother into this.

"We understand that the UPE *Enigma* and its captain believed Maher and the *Freedom's Reach* were transporting this man away from Earth. What we know about this man is limited. As far as we can tell, Cade is some sort of defector from UPE intelligence who was attempting to reach me with information that he deemed more important than his own life. While his information did reach me due to the brave actions of our own Aurelius Blaze and a civilian captain, sadly Caden Path did not, and the information he was attempting to deliver is severely encrypted. Our best estimates indicate that it may take months for us to break the encryption without Cade, if we are able to do it at all. That brings us to my second piece of news. Administrator Phelan has informed me that the UPE *Enigma* itself will be docking here at the station in the next few hours for repairs, again due to the brave actions of our own Aurelius." Lithia was both chilled and elated at the news that the *Enigma* would be so close. Chilled, because of the danger that it represented and how close she was to a force that wanted nothing more than to capture her, but elated because with the *Enigma* so close, she might have an opportunity to free her brother. And if not, then she could do something to take revenge upon those who took him from her.

Lithia looked at Aurelius to see his reaction to the news that the *Enigma* was so close. She had expected to see him showing some signs of concern, or something like it, but instead she was greeted by a strangely confident expression.

"They've already ordered Phelan to search the station for two fugitives, neither of whom has been identified by more than name," Pacius continued. "The first is of course Aurelius Blaze, and the other is the civilian captain who risked so much for us, Lithia Boson. I am sure I don't need to tell anyone what an opportunity this affords us. If while the *Enigma* is here we can recover the prisoners, including Caden Path and hopefully Governor Maher, we will finally be in a position to really hurt the UPE for the first time. So I will be asking for ten volunteers to masquerade as a repair crew."

As soon as Pacius said it, Lithia knew she was going to be one of the volunteers. They would have to kill her to keep her off that ship.

A holographic internal schematic of the *Enigma* flickered in over the room, and Lithia made mental notes of several areas where it was indicated prisoners were being held. The main area seemed to be a large hanger on the port hull, and Lithia wondered how Pacius and his people could know that prisoners might be held there.

"This team will enter the ship and sabotage its engines. This will do two things—the first is to create a distraction so you can make your way to the prisoner block with minimal opposition. The second is to cripple the *Enigma* badly enough that it is unable to pursue us when we evacuate all our personnel from the station. The rest of you will be assisting in that evacuation. Before anyone volunteers, there is one last thing that I need to bring to your attention."

Pacius paused again as the image of the monster from the *Amaranth* filled the space above the table.

"Anyone entering the ship needs to be on the lookout for this . . . this man . . . Lambda Agent Torque. Our intel indicates that he is aboard the *Enigma* and will likely factor in to any attempt at escape." Pacius paused to take in the man whose face and body were being displayed next to him and seemed to shudder slightly. Lithia couldn't blame him. Even in a holo image, those glowing red eyes seemed to radiate hate and pain into everyone who saw them.

"Many of us have told Lambda stories around drinks in the drive room on our journeys through space, but few of us know the reality." Pacius paused again, while a recording of Torque hanging on to the back of the *Storm Chaser* replaced the still image of his face. "Lambdas are direct agents of the UPE outside the political, economic, or military hierarchy. They answer only to their own agency and have near-limitless power within the scope of their mission. But that is only part of what makes them dangerous. They also undergo intense genetic and cybernetic modification to make them nearly unstoppable warriors. Every Lambda agent has the capability to mentally interface with and control any computer or networked machine. They also carry biotechnical enhancements for speed, healing, and strength. While every Lambda is different, thanks to the sensor log from the *Storm Chaser*, we feel it is safe to assume this one possesses nearly limitless strength and stamina." Lithia watched an image of Torque holding the *Storm Chaser* on the deck, even while its engines burned away the flesh on his skull. This is not a man to engage. You will not be carrying anything close to the weaponry needed to take him down. If he becomes aware of your presence, you are to scrub the mission right away and return here for immediate evacuation. Now that you have all the information I can give you, I will ask for volunteers, and I mean *volunteers*. I will not order anyone on this mission, and you need to understand that taking it on will likely expose you to consequences far beyond those expected by the SMMC.

Lithia was a little surprised to see so many hands go up around her, including Aurelius's. She had expected maybe one or two besides her own, but instead it was nearly two-thirds of the room. Lithia didn't know what to make of it. Why would anyone volunteer for something like this? If her brother wasn't possibly on the *Enigma*, her hand would have been firmly at her side.

"Ms. Boson, I expected to see your hand, and I need to stress to you the danger you'd be in. Believe me when I say you're not going to have a lot of time to get the prisoners out, once you've set the charges," Pacius said, meeting Lithia's eyes.

Lithia choked back her fear with absolute determination. The tears welling up in the corners of her eyes were her only sign of emotion. "I've got a vested interest in our success, just like everyone else here."

Pacius nodded, but said nothing more on the subject, and when he picked the ten people who would be going onto the *Enigma*, Lithia was among them.

"Thank you all. Those who I've chosen, please go with Sergeant Clemens. The rest of you, please stay here for further orders regarding evacuation." Lithia stepped back from the hologram with Aurelius. She was terrified, but the hope she had buried in her heart knew this was what she had to do. Her brother and these people needed her. It was all in their hands now. As she turned to leave, she looked into Pacius's eyes. "Thank you. Thank you for giving me an opportunity to save my brother."

"Ms. Boson, if I hadn't given you this opportunity, I would bet you would have made one for yourself, but you're welcome anyway."

CHAPTER 45

The Final Harrah

LITHIA AND HER repair crew had a front-row view of the looming presence in one of the embarkation lounges that had been cleared for the *Enigma*. This lounge would normally be filled with people waiting for connecting flights, but now its emptiness only reminded the repair crew there wasn't going to be any backup. Lithia's gut quaked with unease and anxiety. She had to choke down her fear. Her mission was clear and her brother was counting on her, but that didn't keep her from trembling as the lounge darkened. Lithia looked around her. Everyone but Sergeant Clemens was displaying some sort of anxiety as they watched the monstrous bulk of the UPE *Enigma* slowly approach the station, filling the viewport, and casting a shadow across the boarding terminal—and seemingly the hearts of all who stood in it.

Tensions mounted as her team waited, unable to do anything but watch. When the station shook under the force of the *Enigma*'s docking clamps engaging, Lithia thought she would jump out of her skin. When the doors finally opened, it came as a relief. With the hiss of decompression, all of her anxiety faded and all that was left was her objective . . . and adrenaline.

Lithia and her team stood off to the side as a squad of soldiers emerged from the airlock and moved to take positions around the room. Once they had their vantage points secured, they simply waited. Her breath caught in her throat as she saw him, the figure that had haunted her thoughts since she had lost her ship, the figure that she had seen on the hologram holding on to the *Storm Chaser*. The Lambda, Torque, stepped out on to the station as if nothing in the world could harm him, and Lithia had to concede that it was probably the truth. The figure that moved at his side didn't seem to have the same confidence. The man must have been Captain Shard. She had seen his picture in the briefing, but in person he seemed somehow less than she had expected. Shard was a short man, but well built. Something about his stature seemed diminished, though. Maybe it was because he kept glancing at his companion and twitching toward his side arm. Lithia knew the feeling and had no doubt that on his bridge, this man would be a much more imposing figure. But *here* he seemed small and almost timid.

This could be a problem. If they stopped to examine her and her team, she had little doubt that Torque would recognize her. She was near the front of the group. She couldn't hide behind anyone. The hulking terror and his nervous companion seemed to be conferring with each other. It was when Shard looked toward the repair team that Lithia felt her crippling anxiety return. Could she avoid eye contact if they walked by? The thought kept running through her head, along with a thousand other possibilities. She could run. No, she could charge into the ship and hope for the best. No, she could set off the explosives here, killing everyone including these two, and hope Pacius and Aurelius could rescue her brother.

Shard rounded up a couple of soldiers, and the squad began moving directly toward the false repair crew. They were right out in the open and there was nothing they could do, nowhere they could go. Their only option was to stand where they were and wait.

Lithia turned away, hoping they hadn't seen her face. She was trying to make it look like she was surveying the ship outside the massive windows. She could hear Torque's heavy hydraulic footsteps coming closer and closer. Her heart was racing. It beat faster and faster as she held her breath. The massive footsteps were right on top of her. Keep going! Seconds seemed to slow into minutes and then into hours as Lithia stood there, that monster and his captain getting closer. Everything they had worked so hard for could be over before it began. If they were caught, what would happen to Bobby? Would they kill him? Would they kill her? She didn't want to find out. As her mind raced, she heard the steps begin to fade behind her. Lithia took a deep breath, clearing the fear from her mind, feeling like luck was on her side. Her team waited until Shard's and Torque's squad left the lounge; but the moment came, and after that her way was clear. Her brother was inside that ship, and now nothing stood between them. It was this thought more than any other that carried her as she followed Sergeant Clemens up the ramp and into the ship that haunted her nightmares.

The team pushed floating carts of equipment down a long umbilical tube joining the station and ship. Lithia had been on large ships before, but the *Enigma* was something new. It had all the hallmarks of any ship she had seen: people darting from station to station, read-outs everywhere reporting a thousand tiny details, and the ubiquitous stacks of functioning and nonfunctioning equipment. But the *Enigma* seemed somehow sterile. It was cold and functional and seemed to actively resent the human presence that it required to operate.

The ship was labyrinthine. The team checked their map at every corner. Like most ships, old battle repairs had forced the schematics out of date. At this point, their maps were more of a suggestion, and it wasn't long before Lithia and her team were lost.

"Halt!"

The team stopped in their tracks as the sound of half a dozen rifles were aimed in their direction.

"You are entering a restricted area. I am going to need to see some authorization to enter the prisoner barracks."

The leader of the rifles was a nondescript man in the dark grays of the UPE Marines. He was looking at the team like he'd love to open fire and sweep them from the corridor with a push broom and only the right response in the next few seconds would prevent him from getting his wish.

"Prisoner barracks? That can't be right. According to our map, this is supposed to be a hanger with engine room access. Are you sure you're in the right place?" Sergeant Clemens said, a slightly puzzled grin on his face, making him look for all the world like the clueless civilian this marine obviously thought he was. At least Lithia hoped that's what he thought.

"What the hell are you doing here?" the marine barked.

"Trying to find the engine room," Clemens said happily, ignoring all the weapons pointed in his direction. "Are you sure this isn't it?"

"This is short-term prisoner housing! And if you don't have authority to be here, you need to leave now!"

"Of course, no need to shout. Can you maybe update our maps a bit then? That way, we can get out of your way."

Lithia thought the marine didn't want to believe they were really lost, let alone help them, but when Clemens brought up the hologram of their map for everyone to examine, he really had little choice.

"Three sections over and one floor up," the marine barked as if to say with every syllable that they were living on borrowed time.

"Thank you, and please have a nice day. Maybe find a nice cup of tea. It does wonders for stress," Clemens said, turning away from the marines and smiling. Lithia wasn't sure how he had done that. If all those rifles had been pointed at her, she doubted she would have been able to talk, let alone play the fool with such skill.

When the team finally found the engine room, it was the first place that felt like a ship to Lithia. This is what a working ship should be, what it should look like. Gone were the sterile corridors, gone was the tightly controlled discipline. Instead, it was a large open space crammed as full of tech as possible. Everyone and everything was coated in a layer of grease that Lithia was sure couldn't be washed off. Not even with a cutting torch and an industrial pump. Aurelius would feel right at home here. Lithia reined back in her thoughts. Why was she thinking of Aurelius right now? The only things on her mind should be her brother and the mission to save him, but something about this place kept making Aurelius's face float into her mind.

No sooner did they enter the engine room then a short man in a coverall of indeterminate color emerged from some place deep in the bowels of a machine that was whirring and sparking ominously.

"Let me see your repair orders," he said, proffering a callused hand that seemed too big for his diminutive frame.

"Um, shouldn't you be dealing with that?" Lithia asked, gesturing at the sparking machine behind him. The machine had started to smoke in a rather alarming way, and Lithia wondered if they really needed to sabotage this place. From the looks of it, the staff were doing a good enough job of that already.

"Nah, it's fine!" he said whacking the machine with a tool. Lithia half expected it to explode, but to everyone's relief, the machine died back down to a faint whir, and the sparks went from a rushing downpour to a faint trickle. Sergeant Clemens smiled with the same unconcern he had shown at everything else that day. Was it possible for anything to shake him?

"We need to do a quick check on several components before we can make the repairs to the outer hull," Clemens said, handing over their orders.

"You know my men are more than capable of doing that! There was no need to come all the way down here," the man said with a protective tone.

Clemens let out a long, suffering sigh. "You and I both know that. But the big shots at the top need one of us to do it, otherwise I'd be just as happy to keep my people out of your hair."

The man smiled in a way that told Lithia that Clemens had spoken a nearly universal complaint, one this man was all too familiar with. "It's the same all over. Folks not knowing when to keep their hands out of other people's jobs."

"So if you can direct us to the main energy conduits, we can get out of your way and you can get back to work," Clemens said, a frighteningly disarming smile on his face.

The short man led them through a maze of dimly lit paths before depositing them in front of what looked like a large, metallic-gray tree sprouting hundreds of thick vines and wires. There was a main line that ran from the engine core into the weave. Little lights all over the cables were glowing and pulsating an unsettling green color.

"Well, here you are. If ya need anything, just bellow and someone will be by eventually."

With that, he turned on his heel and vanished back into the burrow of tech, which he was obviously more comfortable with.

"Who are you?" Lithia whispered, when she was sure they were alone.

The sergeant gave her yet another of his uncannily disarming grins. "A man who is very, *very* good at what he does."

CHAPTER 46

The Courage of Drunks

AURELIUS STOOD IN the corner of Pacius's war room, trying to stay out of everyone's way and listening to the reports from the team come in over the secure transmitters they had been given.

"We're placing the charges now. Request confirmation, charges have a twenty-minute timer?"

"Correct, twenty minutes, but be advised, intense heat or tampering after being set will set them off prematurely, so make sure they are well hidden," Rin said into her own communicator.

"Got ya. Keep them out of the oven. Anything else we should know?"

"Not at this time."

"Okay, we'll be in touch."

"Okay, everyone, the charges have been set. Administrator, have you readied our evac?" Pacius asked.

"It's going to be tight, and I can make no promises. If the *Enigma* is in a state to respond at all, you're not getting out of here," Phelan said, producing a flask from somewhere in his coat and halfheartedly offering a swig to Pacius before downing what had to be half of it himself.

"It's going to be better than sitting here when the fireworks start," Pacius said, snatching the flask from Phelan's hand and tossing it to Rin.

"Sorry, Phelan, I'm going to need you sober for this," Pacius said, as Phelan started dejectedly looking through his coat for another flask.

"Xander, you're going to have to go back in time about five years if you want me sober."

"Fine. Sober-ish, then. Either way, best you get back up to your office. Shard and Torque should be arriving there soon, and it's really better they find you there instead of having to go look for you."

"Xander, if I'm going back up there, then give me back the flask. You can have me sober or you can have me in my office to meet that monster, but you don't get both," Phelan said, turning and looking at Rin expectantly.

Pacius sighed. "Give it back to him. He'll have more up there anyway." Rin looked unsure about giving the flask back, and Aurelius couldn't blame her. He wasn't a stranger to having a little more than was good to you. But from what he had seen over the last few hours, Phelan took that to an extreme Aurelius had never seen . . . in anyone still capable of standing upright.

Pacius and Rin watched Phelan head back through the false wall that led to his office, and the looks on their faces said more than either would have likely told him verbally. Rin's was the clearest, a glare of anger and mistrust, but Pacius's was something Aurelius wondered about. If anything, Pacius looked a little sad as he watched the administrator leave.

"Bring up the feed from his office," Pacius said once the wall had closed behind Phelan. "Mr. Blaze, would you join us? I think you have a right to see this too."

Aurelius joined Pacius and Rin at the display. He still had no idea why he was being included in all this and hoped that this might offer some sort of clue.

If a clue was to be found in the image of Phelan's office being displayed, though, Aurelius wondered if he was just too dense to find it. To him it just looked like Phelan nervously looking for another bottle.

"Sir, what are we looking at?" Aurelius eventually asked. At that, Rin glanced over at Pacius, and Aurelius got the feeling he had just stumbled on a long-running argument.

"Phelan is a good administrator, but he's not a strong man, not one who thrives under pressure," Pacius said, as if that explained anything.

"Does he know we're watching him?" Aurelius asked, still trying to make some sense of what was going on.

"Everyone needs to have their little secrets. Phelan has his hidden bottles, and a few revenue sources he thinks I don't know about, and I have a few things he doesn't know about. In most situations that would be fine, but if Phelan breaks and betrays us, I need to know right away. That is why I have this." Something about that explanation didn't sit well with Aurelius. Something about spying on Phelan felt wrong, like a betrayal, especially because Aurelius got the impression that Pacius and Phelan were friends.

When it became clear that Pacius would say nothing more on the subject, Aurelius cleared his throat. "Sir, can I ask another question?"

"Ask. I might not be able or willing to answer, but you can always ask."

"Why am I here?" Aurelius asked, and Pacius smiled at the question.

"Honestly, you went through hell to get here and give us this opportunity. I figure if anyone had a right to see how it all played out, it would be you," Pacius explained, patting Aurelius on the back and ignoring Rin's disapproving look.

If Pacius was going to say more, it was quickly forgotten, because at that moment their attention was drawn back to the office displayed in front of them.

The sound of impact against the door was booming. Aurelius thought it had overwhelmed the small speakers set around the room, but then he realized that most of the sound wasn't coming from the speakers. Instead, he was hearing it directly through several levels of deck and bulkhead. Aurelius had a sick feeling in his stomach. He knew what the sound meant. A moment later, Phelan's door came crashing in.

"That used to be an outer airlock. I've never seen anything just tear through one like that," Pacius muttered.

"I have," Aurelius said, and only after he said it did he realize it was out loud.

"No barrier shall be allowed to stand between the righteous and those who would seek to oppose us . . ."

The words were flat, utterly without emotion, and yet somehow managed to convey an almost uncontrollable rage and hate. Hearing the voice again sent him back, and again, he was running down the halls of the *Freedom's Reach*, people dying all around him, and that thing, that monster, right behind him.

"Thank you," Shard said as he stepped over the door and into Phelan's office, Torque and their accompanying soldiers following closely after.

"Administrator . . ."

As Phelan stood up, Aurelius pulled himself back to the present. This wasn't the *Freedom's Reach*. This was a new horror, and if Aurelius was going to see himself through it, he had to stay in the moment, not let fear overwhelm him.

Aurelius watched as Phelan reached for something in his desk, only to be brought up short when the soldiers aimed their weapons at him in unison. If that hadn't been enough to stop the administrator's hand, the look in Torque's eyes surely was.

"I wouldn't recommend that. My men here are a bit trigger-happy, and I'd hate for them to think you were reaching for a weapon," Shard said, breaking the silence.

Aurelius doubted Phelan even had a weapon. It was far more likely that he was reaching for another bottle.

"Administrator Phelan, it is my duty to inform you that my men will shortly be conducting a man-by-man search of this station. Until the fugitives I am looking for are found, this station will be on lockdown. No unauthorized personnel shall be permitted to leave their posts. No resident will be allowed to leave their home. No shop will be open, and no ship will be allowed to arrive or depart. Is that understood?"

"Yes. I understand," Phelan said, and his voice was shaky, the fear in it unmistakable, "but as I informed you several hours ago, no craft matching that description docked in the time period you indicated," Phelan said, his eyes frantically darting around the room.

"A craft that small couldn't have made it any farther, but if you're telling me the truth, Administrator, then I'm sure you will have no problem with my men having a look around. Now, please, relinquish your system's access codes to me."

"Of course, but I am sure you understand that things can't just be done that quickly. Security personnel need to be stationed to manage the population. Authorizations need to be issued in advance to assure that essential systems continue operating during the lockdown, and many other things need to be accounted for and double-checked." Aurelius had to give him credit, even now, deprived of his drink and clearly frightened. Enough that Aurelius did not envy whoever would have to come in and clean up the office when all this was done. Phelan was trying to stall. He was trying to give Pacius and his people enough time to get everything underway.

"Progress shall not be impeded, but will instead march over all those who stand in its path."

Aurelius watched silently as both Shard and Phelan looked over at Torque.

"I don't believe my companion is satisfied with that option. In fact, I believe he thinks you're trying to stall us, Administrator," Shard said, casually moving toward Phelan's desk.

"Not . . . not at all. These things take time, that's the truth," Phelan said, his words coming out nearly unintelligible through his panic.

"The functionary serves two masters. When we entered, he sent a message to his other."

"What? I did no such thing. You broke my door down. I was alerting security."

"I am sure you were, Administrator, but—" A massive tremor ran through the station, nearly throwing Shard from his feet. All Shard had to do was glance out the window behind Phelan to see what had happened. A bright flash went off in the *Enigma*'s hull, and the ship began listing to one side. Something was venting from its engine core.

"We extend the hand of mercy and spread the light of hope to this place. But what we take to our breast is a viper." Torque's tone was flat, without the normal tones of rage that usually accented it. "You, Administrator, are but one of many, but as the many must suffer for the one, so must the one suffer for the many."

Aurelius could do nothing but watch as Torque bounded over the desk and took Phelan in one hand, lifted him up by the neck, and slammed him into one of the walls. They heard the sickening thud as bone and flesh met metal. Unfortunately for Phelan, the bone and flesh gave first.

Torque was still holding the limp broken body of the administrator in one hand, looking at it almost curiously. Aurelius had to look away. Instead, he looked over to Pacius who still watched the scene, looking like he was going to be sick.

"We must get back to the ship!" Shard ordered, trying to regain control of the situation.

"No! This is your fault. Your incompetence is the greatest form of betrayal. Those whom you would serve will be better served with your death. The only reason you still live is that your death needs to stand as an example to all who would oppose!" Torque turned to the soldiers. "Stay here. Keep him from leaving, but don't kill him. Only when the light of the Helix shines out from every star shall he be allowed the mercy of death." And without saying any more, Torque bounded from the room, leaving Shard alone with a set of confused but determined guards who redirected their weapons at Shard.

CHAPTER 47

Asking for Directions

LITHIA CAUGHT HERSELF against a bulkhead as the ship lurched again. Since the detonation, the ship had been shuddering under dozens of new explosions. Everyone on board was panicking, and no one her team came across had any interest in them or what they were doing. Lithia thought the ship was on borrowed time and hoped that thought was firmly planted in her team members' minds as well. She kept telling herself she didn't need much time and that they'd be out before anything catastrophic happened. She kept telling herself Bobby was just around the next corner and they'd be getting off this death trap together.

Lithia half expected to see the same marines that had been at this section before, but it seemed even their discipline had limits, and the team was able to enter the prisoner barracks with no opposition. How convenient.

"Okay, people, find the release switch for the cell block. The sooner we get out of here, the happier I'll be!" Clemens shouted over the sounds of erupting conduits and the alarm klaxons that were still diligently trying to warn people something was wrong.

"Found it, sir," came a voice from someplace up the hall. The doors all along one side opened, and a torrent of ragged *Freedom's Reach* crew spilled out toward their rescuers.

Lithia pushed through the sea of gratitude. She understood their elation, but there was only one person she wanted to see. "Where is Bobby Boson?" she called out.

"Who?" Lithia heard several people call back.

"My brother, Bobby! He's only a teenager, and he has a medical bracelet on his arm!"

"I think I know where he is." Lithia turned at the sound of a voice that cut through the crowd and saw the dark face of a man whom she had last seen crumpled in a heap on the *Amaranth*'s deck as she and Aurelius ran.

"So where is he?" Lithia demanded.

"If you mean that kid that they took out of here a few hours ago, no one knows for sure, but if I had to guess, he is probably with the Lambda in an interrogation room."

Lithia turned again to see a graying man with a few extra pounds around the middle limp up with the aid of Sergeant Clemens and a young woman with a bright streak in her hair that Lithia didn't recognize.

"Then that's where we're going!" she said in tones that allowed for little argument.

"No," Clemens said evenly, looking Lithia directly in the eye and matching her fury with an equal calm. "We've got to get everyone to the escape pods."

"But your orders are to secure Cade at all costs!"

"No, our orders were to rescue Cade and the rest of the prisoners. As important as that man may be, I have to take into account the governor and the rest of my people. The situation has changed," Clemens informed her.

"Then I'll go. I am not leaving without my brother!"

"If you go, Ms. Boson, then you go alone. I can't send anyone with you."

"You don't have to." Lithia was surprised to hear the words come out of Jerula's mouth.

"Well, dammit. If everyone else is being brave, then I guess I have to too," the woman supporting Maher said.

"Knew I could count on you, Nyreen," Jerula said, giving a little bow and turning to loot a couple rifles that a weapons locker was obliging enough to offer. He passed the weapons around.

"Hey, Jerula." The enormous Strifer turned to take in a slight man in a damaged SMMC uniform who looked like a strong wind might take him down the hall and out the door.

"I know what you're going to say, Paul, but I think this detour has enough riders already . . ." Jerula started.

"I'm not going to stop you," Paul said with the air of a man who couldn't believe he was saying what he was, "but I think I should be the one to go with the girls. With your leg the way it is, I don't know if you'll be fast enough to be the help they need." Paul finished, and held his arm up as if he expected the big man to swat him to the deck.

"Paul . . . dammit, you're talking sense. But understand me, you three better come back alive, or I'm going to do things to you even the dead can feel," Jerula said, handing his weapon over to Paul.

"Fine, whoever's going, go, but I can't wait for you forever. If you're not at the escape pods soon, we are going to have to leave without you.

"I understand," Lithia said.

"Then good luck, Lithia. I really hope to see the three of you on the escape ships."

"Me too, Sergeant," Lithia said, turning to head farther into the *Enigma*.

"No, this isn't it either," Lithia said, turning a corner and finding another dead end. She began to despair. The ship was creaking and quivering, and she was no closer to her brother than she had been back at the holding cells.

"Do you want to stop and ask for directions?" Paul asked, glancing around with a look of determination. In the giant Strifer, Jerula, Lithia would have believed it to be genuine, but from Paul, she suspected it was more bravado than anything else.

"You find someone to ask, and I will pull this team over," Nyreen shot back to Paul.

"How about them?" Paul shouted, grabbing Lithia and Nyreen and diving to the deck as a hail of gunfire blazed across the hall where they had just been standing.

"They don't seem to be in a helping mood," Nyreen barked, coming up into a crouch and leveling her weapon down the hall.

"Good thing we have a conversation starter, baby," Paul said, coming up beside her and opening fire. "Do you know how to use that thing?" he said, looking over at Lithia still picking herself up off the deck.

"Just point and click!" Lithia said, scooping up her dropped rifle and sighting down the hall. There were two marines who had taken up a firing position two junctions down. She waited and watched. Nyreen and Paul were laying down enough fire to keep the two marines from advancing, but so far no one had scored a hit.

"This is just like the firing range," Lithia whispered to herself as she held the rifle's sight on a point just to the left of the far wall. Eventually one of the marines would have to move through that space to shoot back . . . and yes, there he was.

Lithia didn't think as she pulled the trigger. If she had, she wouldn't have been able to do it. She kept telling herself it was just like Quack III and that these weren't people, just holographic ducks. The head in her sight became a red mist, and Lithia's illusion broke. Her mind recoiled from what she had just done. Yes, the UPE had taken her brother, but that didn't change the fact that she had pulled a trigger and made a man just stop being.

Lithia stood there until a pressure on her right shoulder brought her back to herself. "Nice shot. Paul has the other one down, and if I'm any judge, he will be—"

"Ahhhhh!" the scream came from down the corridor.

"Yep, there it is. I reckon that boy is going to be very helpful now."

A moment later, Paul trotted back to the others with a grim smile on his face and his rifle slung over his shoulder.

"It's this way," he said, pointing down the hall.

"Aren't we afraid he is going to call for help?" Lithia asked as she followed.

"Don't worry about it," Paul said, deliberately not meeting her eye.

"Don't ask him anything for a bit," Nyreen said coming up beside Lithia. "He's got a lot to process right now, I think."

"But what did he—" Lithia started.

"I don't know, and I don't really want to know," Nyreen said, patting Lithia on the arm. "We're all going to do things before tonight's over that we're not really going to want to talk about." She was right, and for Lithia one of those moments had already come.

The three continued in silence until they reached a door marked RESTRICTED.

Paul stepped past the girls and cracked open the panel next to the door.

Lithia watched over his shoulder anxiously as he crossed a wire and keyed in a new command, all the time noting the rocking and creaking going on around her. "How long is this going to take?"

"No way to tell. I've never done this before. Kind of wish I had let Jerula come after all. This is really more his thing."

"Then move!" Lithia said, pushing Paul away from the panel and raising her weapon.

"No!" Paul yelled as she fired into the mass of wires.

Lithia stood back and waited but the door didn't open.

"What the—why in the 'verse would that work? It doesn't need help to stay closed. I needed those connections to open it."

Lithia felt her face flush and looked away as Paul moved back to the panel to try and make something of the wreckage.

"Hey, sweetie, at least it's now a hardware issue, more your speed," Nyreen said.

"Not helping," Paul replied.

"Not really trying to help. Always saw myself as comic relief."

"It always works in the movies," Lithia said, moving to take up guard behind them.

What felt like an hour later, Lithia heard the sound of the door sliding open.

"Hey, you did it!" Lithia and Nyreen said at almost the same time.

"That wasn't me?"

A figure came bursting from the newly opened door. "Lithia! You came for me!" The last part of the sentence was muffled as her brother wrapped her in a bone-jarring hug and began sobbing. "I knew you would. I kept telling him you would."

Lithia held Bobby at arm's length and looked into her brother's bruised face. He looked a little worse for wear, but nothing serious. "Okay, slow down. Who is 'he'?"

"Probably me," The voice came from inside the interrogation room, but Lithia recognized it.

Lithia stood holding her brother and refusing to let go as Paul and Nyreen moved past her into the room. Lithia looked away from

Bobby long enough to see that Cade was badly beaten and bruised. Whatever hell her brother had gone through, Cade's had been much worse. Lithia took a little satisfaction in that. Cade was chained to the wall and looked like he had been there for days. Nyreen set him free with a few precision rounds from her rifle, and Paul tried to catch him as he staggered forward, falling to the deck. Lithia was astonished to see how much effort it took for Paul and Nyreen to get Cade back to his feet. He didn't look all that heavy, but from how they were lifting, she'd guess he weighed more than five hundred pounds.

Cade looked near death. To everyone's relief, once Paul and Nyreen got Cade to his feet, he seemed to need little more than a hand to steady him as he moved through the door. He was covered in bruises and blood, and his body seemed to be moving with a stiffness that came with pain and broken bones. "I thought I heard someone out here," Cade said, limping along. "By the way, your comrades are jettisoning escape pods as we speak. We may want to find another exit strategy. If you're open to suggestions, Ms. Boson's ship is still docked a few decks from here."

"Wait, what? Hang on," Lithia said, stepping away from the crowd, her brother letting her go reluctantly. "I have to call in the new plan."

Lithia took the small emergency transmitter from her coverall. "This is Lithia Boson. We've recovered the Lambda and are making an alternate escape route."

"What's the situation?" Captain Pacius said over the crackling radio.

"My ship is a few decks from here. We're going to get out that way."

"Confirmed and proceed. But keep us updated to your status."

The sound of a gunshot by Lithia's head caused her to dive for cover.

"Lithia! Are you okay?" The shout came from Bobby.

"Yeah," Lithia said, hoping everyone else had gotten to cover too. She poked her head out from cover and saw them: five UPE marines coming down the hall, weapons pointed directly at them. Lithia knew what she had to do, and switching her rifle to auto, she burst from cover. The gun thrummed in her hands as Lithia unloaded shot after shot in the direction of the marines. "I'll hold them off! It'll buy you guys time to get to the *Amaranth*! I will be right behind you!"

"We can't leave you here," Bobby cried. Paul and Nyreen were clearly not fans of the idea either. "There's gotta be another—"

"There isn't!" Lithia shouted over him. "Bobby, you go with them! You gotta get the engine started on the *Amaranth*! Don't worry, I'll be right behind you."

"Deck 22 . . . Section C," Cade groaned.

Lithia didn't bother turning around to see if everyone left. The sound of Bobby yelling and being pulled away told her everything she needed to know. Lithia watched the marines dive for cover, two of them not quite making it in time. She had saved Bobby. She advanced up the hall, determined to end anything or anyone who would try and stop them.

CHAPTER 48

A Gift and a Price

"HURRY! GET THOSE people up the ramps!" Sergeant Clemens shouted into the turmoil around the escape pods. "I don't know how much time we've got here!"

Jerula stood by Governor Maher as Clemens did his best to keep the escape going as smoothly as he could. Unfortunately, what little discipline the SMMC had managed to instill in the crew of the *Freedom's Reach* was nowhere close to the panic of trying to get off a UPE battleship that felt like it was breaking apart, knowing any minute marines could burst through the door and cut the escape short with a few well-placed rounds.

"What about that girl?" Sergeant Clemens turned to see who had spoken.

"I'm sorry, Governor, you and the others are my priority. We need to get you in a pod and out of here. That comes before anything else, even the girl and her friends," Clemens said with more patience than Jerula thought he could manage in such a situation. It still made him want to clock the man. Paul and Nyreen were among the people he was so casually talking about leaving behind, after all.

"I don't like leaving people behind!" Maher said, taking up a position that would allow him a better view of the survivors as they found their ways into escape pods and what other small craft they had originally used to escape his doomed ship.

"Neither do I," Clemens said, turning and speaking softly so only Maher and Jerula could hear him. "I'll wait as long as I can without putting you in danger, sir, but if they aren't back when I make that call, there is nothing any of us can do."

Clemens reached out his hand and placed it on Maher's shoulder. "I haven't spent much time with that girl, but the time I did spend showed me a girl who would walk through hell for her brother. She *is* getting off this ship, and if the others have the brains to stick with her, they will too."

Maher smiled at Clemens. "I beli—" Jerula hadn't heard the shot, but Maher's head snapped back. They all watched in horror as Maher slid down the loading ramp in a boneless heap.

"Governor!" Jerula screamed as Clemens pulled him into the closest pod with a force Jerula wouldn't have expected from the smaller, soft-spoken man. The pounding of munitions against the craft a moment later told him that UPE troops had entered the hanger and were now using the escape pods and anyone unfortunate enough to be out in the open for target practice.

"Close the hatch! If we don't launch now, then we don't get a chance!" Clemens shouted.

"There are still people out there!" Jerula shouted back.

"There aren't any more people out there now. Close that hatch, we launch now!" Clemens ordered.

Jerula stared out the hatch as the door closed on their little pod. His eyes were locked on the bodies of Maher and a dozen other crew-members. How many of them did he know? How many had he spoken with, joked with, threatened with deaths so like the ones they had finally found? As the hatch finally sealed, he caught one last look at the glassy eyes of a third mate he thought he had asked out once a few trips back. Her eyes glared back at him accusingly. They seemed to say, "This is your fault. You lived, and I didn't."

As Jerula felt the pod drop out the side of the *Enigma,* he muttered a silent "I'm sorry." But he knew it wasn't enough. Nothing would ever be enough.

Captain Pacius monitored his teams' advancement through the Enigma on his holographic table while Rin monitored Pacius with equal intensity. Outside the war room, the station was a roar of activity. But for Pacius, none of that seemed to matter. His attention was transfixed by the holographic display of the station and surrounding ships. He was watching firsthand the crew in the cargo bay feverishly trying to escape the *Enigma's* marines.

Every time one of the escape pods reached one of the evac ships, or one of the ships disappeared from his readouts, he let out a sigh of relief.

Nearly everything else to do with the evacuation had fallen to Rin, which was more or less expected. It was what Pacius kept her around for. Pacius was great at the big picture, great at the big action, but the details, the little things that allowed those big things to happen as Pacius hoped, that was where Rin thrived.

Every now and then Pacius would get a report of UPE personnel moving to the location of one of his evac ships and would order it to leave, regardless of how full it actually was. And when he did, Rin made a hundred calls to make sure everyone who had been heading that way knew their new destinations and that those destinations knew they had more people and material inbound.

"This is Sergeant Clemens reporting in. We're the last pod out of the *Enigma* and will be docking with the escape ships shortly." The voice over the communicator seemed to shake Pacius out of his trance, and there was a hint of anxiety in his voice as he spoke.

"Do you have Maher?"

"Negative."

Rin watched as her captain took an involuntary step away from the table. He looked like he had been struck.

"Repeat that. What is the status of the governor?" Pacius asked a moment later.

"Sir, I'm sorry. The governor was struck by enemy fire during our escape."

"Understood." The word came out of Pacius's mouth completely without emotion, and Rin quickly stepped to his side.

"Xander . . ." Rin said, but no words could possibly be the right ones.

"I'll be okay, Sara. Maher was a friend, and there will be plenty of time to deal with his death later. For now, there are people depending on me to keep them alive. If I give in to my grief . . ."

Despite Pacius's words, he had to be near the breaking point. He had already lost one childhood friend with the death of the administrator, and now Maher. With the exception of herself, Rin suspected this day had taken every true friend Xander Pacius had ever had.

She watched as Pacius dove back into his display with a renewed vigor. The mission was something he could affect, and right now he needed to feel in control of something.

". . . d . . . pinned down . . . UPE . . . escape." Rin recognized Lithia's voice, even through the garbled static of the message.

"Repeat! You're not coming through. Repeat!" Pacius shouted into the communicator, but all he got in response was a high-pitched squeal of static.

Pacius spent a few more futile moments yelling into the comms before finally giving up.

"It's not our equipment. Something's wrong at her end," Pacius said, looking more tired than anything else. Rin suspected he had lost the capacity for genuine worry. He had simply lost too much for that at this point.

"I'm going over there," Aurelius said. Rin and Pacius both looked over to where he was standing, almost forgotten, against the far wall. The look in his eyes told Rin all she needed to know. The kid was going, and nothing she or Pacius could do, short of shooting Aurelius, would stop him.

"Wait," Pacius ordered. Evidently he had seen the same look in Aurelius's eyes, because he lowered his hand under the holo table, and when it reemerged, it held Pacius's beloved side arm. The pistol that had seen him in and out of more trouble than any sidekick or friend. He drew it from its holster and slid it across the table. It interrupted the holographic image of the *Enigma* as it slid. Aurelius seemed stunned. Evidently he had expected them to try and stop him, so to instead be presented with an antique firearm had him at a loss.

The pistol was the deepest consent Pacius could give, and Rin couldn't believe he was giving it to the kid. Aurelius picked it up gingerly, examining its every line and curve.

"Go get them."

Aurelius needed no further prompting and wasted no time. He bounded from the room in two steps, and Rin could see on the displays that he was lifting off in his *Storm Chaser* less than five minutes later.

"Good luck, kid," Pacius muttered. Rin figured he was going to need it.

Lithia was terrified. Her earpiece had shattered on the deck when she dove for cover. As she crouched behind a torn bulkhead, bullets flew by. They whizzed and cracked through the air, leaving little searing-hot trails behind them. Her gun was empty, and there were still three soldiers at the other end of the hall determined to make her just another casualty on a battle report, but Lithia had other ideas. Mustering the last of her diminishing courage, she sprang from cover and dove for a doorway. In the split second she was in the air, she could feel the heat from the bullets slicing past her. The impact was jarring as she collided with the wall a few feet inside the passageway. Thankfully she was well within cover, but staying still was far from her plan. She still had to reach her ship, and that was easier said than done. Lithia pulled herself to her feet and only then noticed the blood running down her arm. She must have been grazed during the dive, but right now that didn't matter.

She tore down the hall and made another turn as soon as she could. She didn't expect to lose her pursuers, but right now she didn't have a better idea. She was making it up as she went along and hoping it wouldn't end with her lying dead on a deck. She ran, trying to buy enough time to figure out what she was doing and how she was going to escape. Lithia was moving as fast as she could without breaking into the open, moving along the walls, ready to jump into cover. She hadn't managed to shake the soldiers, but her lead was, at least, getting larger. From the sounds of the marching boots, they had split up to keep on her trail. If her gun still had ammunition, she would have considered ambushing them one by one, something she wouldn't have even dreamed of considering an hour ago, but the fear and adrenaline of fleeing UPE marines while on a ship that was still shuddering from secondary explosions in its engine room forced her to contemplate things far beyond what she would have ever believed herself capable of. She hugged the wall as she turned one corner, hoping she would find access to the lower decks. Her ship was on Deck 10, and that meant going down. What she found instead was a full hangar. It appeared she had finally lost the pursuing death squad, only to find a hangar full of UPE soldiers. Lithia got a glimpse of large men with large guns surveying the downed *Freedom's Reach* crew before the report of gunfire forced her to move again. Wherever she needed to be, it wasn't here. This was the hangar the rest of the SMMC people had escaped from. Lithia tore back down the way she had come, knowing the only reason she still lived was that the troops in that hangar had not expected someone to come from behind.

It was when she ducked into a room along one of the corridors that she saw what she was hoping for. An access vent! Lithia remembered from the map of the ship that vents leading to maintenance tunnels ran all over the *Enigma*. It looked tight, but that was good. Lithia figured she could fit well enough, but seriously doubted any of the soldiers could follow in all their gear, even if they did figure out where she was.

The vent turned out to be a way tighter fit then she had expected. It was probably meant for service droids rather than any of the human crew, but she made it through the opening. With a little effort, she made forward progress. The dark path forked and turned in a gradual descent. Lithia figured she must be at least one deck lower now, but where in the ship that actually put her was anyone's guess.

Lithia had never felt claustrophobic before, but she had also never been in such a tight space before, with a gash in her arm that was still bleeding, and knowing at any point someone could flood the passage with hot plasma, or vapors from the engine room, or any number of other things that would end her escape in a moment. She swallowed the panic that was building in her gut. She needed to find her way and get out of the vent quickly, and considering she hadn't seen another hatch since she got in, that was becoming a greater concern.

Lithia was able to go another hundred feet or so before what had been a gradual descent suddenly became less gradual. It was only the tight fit that kept Lithia from attaining frightening speeds. She could see the end of the tunnel, but was helpless to keep herself from sliding right through it. She fell into a dimly lit room and smacked against the deck. It looked like a more cluttered version of engineering.

It must have been a maintenance hub. Fortunately, there appeared to be no one around. Unfortunately, Lithia had no idea where she was. She wished she could consult the holographic map she had, but with her earpiece gone, it was too. She didn't know what to do but to get up and keep going. At least no one was shooting at her.

CHAPTER 49

Storm Chaser

AURELIUS HAD HIS hands clamped around the control stick of the *Storm Chaser*. He flew his tiny planet hopper through a debris field that was rapidly emerging from the crippled *Enigma*. It didn't help that he was having to dodge the *Freedom's Reach's* escape pods left and right as they made their way through the outcrops on the station to the waiting ships. He had always thought he'd go out in a blaze of glory, but not the crashing-into-flying-wreckage kind. He preferred the hail of bullets saving an orphanage thing, or maybe a marathon three-way. Hey, he could hope, right?

Aurelius pushed thoughts of glory out of his mind as he circled the *Enigma*, wondering how he was going to get in. When he lifted off, he hadn't considered it. Things like this always worked out in the movies. It was his second or third pass before he found a way in. It was a small hangar that looked like it was used for landing craft. Aurelius banked to take advantage of the very thoughtful opening when he heard a small impact against his cockpit. He shrugged it off, thinking it was a minor piece of debris, but then he heard it again and again, more rapidly and in a focused pattern. He had to concede it wasn't random wreckage. He was being shot at. Aurelius veered off to one side. He was taking small-arms fire from the marines in the hangar, shooting through the force field that was designed to keep the air from rushing out. He couldn't land in there; he'd have to find another hangar or cargo area, but where? Aurelius was reconsidering the unfriendly hangar when his opening presented itself, literally. As he banked for another pass, a hangar in the middle of the ship opened right under him. There, inside, Aurelius could see the *Amaranth*. Bruised, beaten, and scorched, but still looking space worthy. Aurelius yanked on the stick and brought the *Storm Chaser* swinging in. He nearly crashed when he noticed Paul and Nyreen helping Cade and a teenage boy who had to be Lithia's brother up a ramp that led into the belly of the beat-up hauler. So they were alive! But what the hell were they doing here? And where was Lithia? Paul and Nyreen had Cade over their shoulders, while Paul also supported Bobby with his other arm as they slowly hobbled toward the *Amaranth*. They stared at Aurelius, dumbstruck, as he maneuvered the *Storm Chaser* in for a landing. Popping the cockpit open, he jumped out, leaving the engine running.

"You're a sight for sore eyes," Paul yelled.

"At this point I almost forgive you for not being Jenkins," Nyreen added, as the two ran forward, wrapping Aurelius in the kind of hug you only give friends you were sure were dead five minutes before.

"I'm so happy to see you guys. Honestly wasn't sure you had made it off the *Freedom's Reach*," Aurelius replied, pressing a button to make his helmet retract, fishing a jetpack out from under his seat, and hooking it on.

"Where's Lithia?" Aurelius demanded, his momentary elation at seeing Paul and Nyreen alive was broken by the confirmation that Lithia was not with them.

"She stayed behind to give us a chance to escape!" Bobby yelled, breaking from Paul's side and running up to the top of the ramp to get the doors open.

"What?" Aurelius asked, dread and disbelief coming out in equal measure.

The *Enigma* trembled violently. A couple of power nodes and lights shorted and burst, forcibly reminding everyone that time was of the essence.

"I don't know how much longer this place is going to hold!" Paul yelled.

Aurelius ran over to help Paul and Nyreen drag Cade to the *Amaranth* and was astonished at how heavy the Lambda was.

"Thanks for opening the door, Mr. Cyborg," Aurelius said to Cade as they ascended the ramp.

Cade could barely hold his head up. "It wasn't me."

Before Aurelius could process what that meant, the doors to the hangar began to close.

"Let me guess, you didn't do that either?" he asked, already knowing the answer.

"He's here," Cade said, grasping Aurelius's arm in a vicelike grip and passing out.

"Any idea what that means?" Nyreen asked.

"I've got a sick feeling I do," Aurelius replied.

Aurelius helped Nyreen and Paul get Cade into the *Amaranth* before turning to leave.

"Hey! Where the hell are you going?" Nyreen demanded.

"I have to find Lithia and get those doors open, or none of us are getting out of here!"

Aurelius tore from the *Amaranth* and out of the hangar like a bat out of hell, one foot quickly falling in front of the other. He had to find her. He had to find Lithia. He wasn't going to leave without her. He quickly thought through his options. With the big door that he'd flown in through now closed, they were limited. Maybe if he headed to the bridge, he could open the door and scan the ship for Lithia. Judging by the absence of anyone in the halls and the shape the *Enigma* was in, he was willing to bet the bridge was abandoned. The door must have automatically closed when he flew in. At least he hoped that was the reason, because the only other option terrified him in a way he didn't even have words for.

Aurelius came running up to an elevator shaft. The doors were cracked open, with smoke bellowing out. He pried the doors open farther. They were heavy and slow to move. The gravity systems in the tube must have been damaged. Everything inside was floating around, with sections of the tube pouring out smoke and fire. He peered up the shaft. It was clear and had to lead to the bridge. He stepped into the gravity-less void, activated his jetpack, and was glad he had taken the time to put the slush suit back on before getting into the *Storm Chaser*. He flew up the shaft with grace, dodging floating scraps of metal and plumes of dark smoke, zigzagging around any obstacle with ease. After his first adventure with the suit, the elevator shaft was almost child's play.

Approaching the top, Aurelius cooled down his afterburners a bit. At the top, he could see the doors to the bridge, little more than thick panes of nearly opaque glass. Aurelius figured that in an emergency some sort of pressure door would come down over the glass. The fact that he saw no such thing worried him. It meant that someone was still on the bridge, someone who wanted to make sure people could still get in and out.

Aurelius tested the doors with his gloved hand, and when they did not move, he took the side arm Captain Pacius had lent him and placed the barrel against the handle, pulling the trigger.

Aurelius was relieved to see he was wrong about the bridge. Obviously, something had just gone wrong with the safety systems; the bridge was completely abandoned but otherwise intact. He had never seen anything like it in his life. It was a huge, rounded room with a long ramp leading up to where a large control platform hung suspended in air. A series of screens wrapped around the walls of the room, and a giant hologram of the Occasio Ultima system was floating at the end of the platform. The hologram was amazingly articulate. It tracked and displayed every tentacle arm reaching out of the star's surface. It was the room's only illumination aside from minor lights and switches on various terminals and computers, and it bathed the entire room in an azure light that Aurelius somehow found comforting and deeply unsettling all at the same time.

Aurelius ran around the room and up the arm to the center controls. He had no idea what to do but figured he would work it out eventually. Luckily, some instruction box popped up in the holo display the moment Aurelius set foot on the platform. It told him to stand on the center plate and focus toward a point in the field in front of him. "Attempting to reconnect . . . Connection error. Helix not found."

"Shit." Aurelius would be unable to do anything from there. A sudden dread washed over him with the bitter aftertaste of hopelessness. What was he going to do?

"Proceed with Manual Identification," the hologram read.

"What does that mean?"

Aurelius watched as three terminals lit up along the edge of the room under the platform. Holograms above them read, CONFIRM CAPTAIN SHARD AT PLATFORM.

"Oh . . ." Aurelius couldn't believe it. All he had to do was press a couple of buttons? His hopelessness lifted. The dread would have followed, but then every screen and terminal in the room went dark. A moment later, a terrible red pentagram filled the main view screen. A rain of pixels ran down the icon as if dripping with digital blood. A terrible, heavy digital voice spoke out to him, echoing through the room. "You've flown too close to the sun, winged man."

Aurelius's eyes darted around the room. He was here, that terrible thing. That hulking hybrid of man and machine, but where?

"Now, like Icarus, you shall know my inferno, and I shall send you crashing down to your death."

There in the darkness, at the bottom of the arm that joined the platform with the rest of the room, was a set of terrible glowing ruby-red eyes. Out of the darkness stepped Torque. He was the final gatekeeper. He stepped slowly and deliberately up the arm toward Aurelius with his fists clenched.

Aurelius drew his gun and, in a single swift action, blasted a few rounds down at the advancing Lambda. They went whizzing through the air, leaving hot trails behind them. None of them hit Torque. Instead, they arched around his body as if too afraid to touch him. Torque leaped the distance between them and landed in front of him with a terrible thud. Grasping Aurelius by the neck, Torque stared deep into his eyes. "None of you are going to escape. This dying ship will be your tomb."

Torque threw Aurelius through the air as if he weighed nothing. Aurelius sailed through the holographic star at the edge of the platform, causing a big splash of water to come raining back down into the large tank that sustained it. If not for the slush suit and its jetpack, this would have been it for him. He kicked in the afterburners to stabilize his flight and pulled the helmet back up so his face wouldn't be quite as vulnerable. Aurelius wondered if the suit was enough to take a direct strike from Torque's fist, and decided he really didn't want to find out. He landed near one of the blinking computer terminals. Torque's face contorted with anger. Aurelius whipped around and hit the "Confirm" button on the terminal. That was one of three. Now for the other two.

Aurelius triggered his jets and flung himself across the bridge, praying his aim was good.

There was a long rail around the control platform. Torque grabbed onto it and catapulted himself toward Aurelius. Every screen in the room was echoing Torque's digital growl as he collided with Aurelius in midair. Wrapping their arms around each other, they slid along the deck plate. Aurelius's suit scraped and shot out sparks as they came to a tumbling halt. The impact caused Torque to lose his grasp, and it was probably the only reason Aurelius survived the crash. He tried to stand up, but only barely made it to his knees before collapsing back to the deck. Torque recovered more quickly and stood towering over Aurelius. He reached down and grabbed Aurelius by one leg, flipping him into the air and causing him to land on his back with a hard smack that sent sharp pains shooting through his entire body.

"You've trespassed into my den, and now there is no escape."

Torque put his hands together into a single fist and swung it downward like a giant sledgehammer, but it caught the edge of the railing that Aurelius was crawling under. The railing buckled and bent, the bottom of the concavity nearly reaching Aurelius's chest plate. Before he could stand up, Torque grabbed him again and, with one hand, drove him into one of the giant screens that surrounded the room. The monitor shattered like a big pane of glass, and shards came crashing down to the floor. The computer at its base showered both of them with sparks. Aurelius rolled off the console onto the deck, battered, bruised, and bloodied, but still alive. He didn't expect to stay that way for long, but for some reason Torque didn't finish him. It seemed like he was more interested in playing with Aurelius and making him suffer than he was in putting an end to his life.

"Fight harder, Aurelius. Your friends are counting on you . . ."

Aurelius, still lying on the deck, backed up along the walkway toward the base of the center arm. Torque gave him a little room and then began walking after him, slamming his fist into each terminal as he slowly followed Aurelius. Each terminal he smashed showered them in sparks and glass. Torque's hand began to bleed, throwing droplets of glowing green blood around the room, but either Torque didn't notice or he simply didn't care. Aurelius scrambled to his feet and triggered his engines. As he took off, Torque lunged at him and caught him in midair again. Aurelius put more power into his thrusters to compensate for

Torque's bulk. It was never going to be enough to really move the enormous Lambda, no more than a few inches, anyway, but a few inches was all Aurelius needed. One good kick, with his jets still burning was enough to send the mechanical nightmare the rest of the way to the open lift shaft, and with a little smile, Aurelius hit a button next to the broken-out handle. The gravity in the tube came back on suddenly, and Aurelius quickly pulled himself out and back onto the bridge, he wasn't sure if that fall would be enough to kill the monster, but it at least bought him time. He just hoped it would be enough time. He made his way over to the second button. As the indicator on the terminal turned green, he heard a terrible noise come from the doorway in the back of the room.

From the smoking shaft, a bloodied hand grabbed onto the bottom of the doorway.

It couldn't be. He couldn't have . . . not even that monster could have . . . not that quickly.

Torque slowly pulled himself up out of the shaft. From the look of it, he had scraped his hand clean of flesh stopping his descent, and now his right hand was little more than a complex-looking metal skeleton. Aurelius didn't hold out much hope that the striped hand would be much weaker now than it had been before. Aurelius switched his focus to the third and last button. The massive technological terror leaped through the air and onto the deck, in front of the final terminal, with enough force to shake the entire room. He was now in front of the last button and was the only thing standing in Aurelius's way.

He stood there in the glow of the lights, looking down at Aurelius, the burning hate of a thousand stars reflected in his evil red eyes. "You can't stop the Helix. It will ingest your world. It will add every person on its land, in its seas, and in its skies to itself. You can't stop it. All you can do now is give up and die with dignity."

Aurelius could see the "Confirm" button behind Torque, but wasn't sure he could fly over, hit it, and escape without giving Torque another chance at crushing him, and he was by no means sure he could survive that again. Aurelius had to put some distance between them. He didn't know if Torque would be dumb enough to chase him, but he had to try. Aurelius flew back up to the podium, where the holo display read, ONE CONFIRMATION REMAINING.

Unfortunately, Torque stood his ground, a hulking sentry blocking Aurelius from his goal. "I can't allow you to halt the destruction I've set forth!" Torque bellowed.

"Then why don't you come up here and stop me?" Aurelius challenged.

"I need to do nothing! This ship is doomed! Its reactors are overloading, its circuits are frying, and its airlocks are rupturing. I've started an engine cascade that will destroy this ship! The chase ends here."

It suddenly made sense to Aurelius. The explosions, fires, and quakes on the *Enigma* weren't from any of the charges Lithia's team had set, Torque had started some sort of self-destruct in the engine core. Torque *was* insane. He was willing to kill everyone, including himself, to stop Cade from escaping and spreading whatever it was they were so scared of. If the engine core did explode, it was likely it would not only take out the *Enigma*, but it would also take out the station and everyone on it.

Things just keep getting better. Aurelius wasn't sure what about the glinting metal caught his eye—shining chunks of metal lying on the floor were hardly unique—but there it was. At his feet was the pistol Pacius had given him. He dropped it when Torque flung him through the hologram and hadn't even considered trying to find it again. It wasn't as if it was doing him any good. But now Aurelius had an idea. He picked up the weapon and pointed it at the monster. He was only going to get one chance at this.

"That weapon cannot harm me . . . resisting your fate is futile."

Aurelius shot right at Torque. "Don't need it to!" Aurelius smirked as the bullets arced around Torque and impacted with the button. The indicator turned green for just a moment before the station went dark.

Log-in successful, the display at the center of the bridge announced.

Aurelius quickly found the controls for the *Enigma*'s maneuvering thrusters. He altered them to carry the ship away from the station, and with one button, he gave it all the ship had. The *Enigma* tore away from Archer's Agony in one violent, overwhelming thrust. It tore the docking clamps right out of the ship's hull and ruptured all the pressurized tubes joining the ship and station. He hoped the station's automatic systems would seal any holes before anyone was blown out or too much air leaked. The same couldn't be said for the *Enigma*. The tearing was too violent for the once-indestructible ship to bear. Explosions went off all over the ship, all over the bridge.

"*Eerrraaaar!*" Torque roared.

Aurelius barely had enough time to trigger the doors down in the hangar to open before Torque leaped from the deck up to the podium and hoisted himself up. Aurelius made to jump off the side, hoping his jetpack would save him again, but he was too late. Torque grabbed him, and even with all the thrust he could muster, it wasn't enough to break free of Torque's grasp.

CHAPTER 50

A Waterfall of Razor Blades

LITHIA RAN THROUGH the maintenance corridors, shielding her face from the explosions that were going off all around her. There, at the end of the hallway, was a door marked HANGAR. She ran as fast as she could. She had to get out of there. The oxygen was being swallowed up by flames, and the heat was unbearable. She ran and ran and ran, slapping the door controls as she spilled out into the hangar. To her overwhelming relief, luck was on her side. There in front of her was her *Amaranth*. Its lights were on, its engines were ready, and Paul and Nyreen were sitting in the cockpit. She had never seen anything more beautiful in her whole life. The shock and jubilation forced tears from Lithia's eyes that she had managed to hold back until then. She climbed down off a catwalk and made a mad dash for the *Amaranth*'s ramp. Another craft caught her eye. It was the *Storm Chaser*! Aurelius was here! The door at the top of the ramp slid open.

"Where's Aurelius?" she yelled.

"He went looking for you!" Bobby shouted, firmly strapped into a chair in the galley.

"We can't leave him! I have to go back!"

Lithia only caught a millisecond glimpse of Bobby before a giant explosion knocked her to the floor.

The *Enigma* was tearing and buckling under unimaginable forces. A torrent of wind began to blow Lithia off the *Amaranth*'s ramp. A massive breach had formed down the hall from the hanger the *Amaranth* was docked in that led right out into the void of space. The *Enigma*'s gravity vanished, and Lithia found herself tumbling toward the door she had just come through. There was nothing to grab onto. Everything that wasn't nailed down was blown out the door, out into the hangar, and out into the long hallway into space.

Lithia found herself tumbling down the stairs back into the cargo area, and finally managed to catch herself on the lip of the loading doors. She held on to them with everything she had left.

"Lithia!" Bobby called from the staircase.

No, he couldn't. He had to be safe. If he risked himself for her here, then his rescue would have been for nothing.

"Bobby, no!" Lithia shouted.

"Lithia, I'm coming. Hang on."

"Bobby, please, *please* stay where you are!" But either her brother didn't hear her, or chose not to listen, because Bobby came bounding down the stairs with what looked to be electrical cabling wrapped around his waist as some sort of safety line.

Lithia tried to see what it was attached to and decided it had to be the top of the handrail in the stairway.

Bobby grabbed onto a section of shelving near the door with one hand, and with the other reached out for Lithia. Despite herself, Lithia reached back, but even with them both stretching, she couldn't quite reach her brother's hand.

"Bobby, it's no good. Please, go back to the lounge where it's safe!"

"No! You came for me, I'm not going to leave you."

Bobby leaned farther and farther. The cable around his waist had to be cutting into his skin, but despite it, he strained farther and farther. He gritted his teeth in pain and Lithia thought she heard the shelf crack under the pressure, but the extra few inches were enough for Lithia to grab his hand.

Lithia let go of the lip of the door and, now with both hands, started pulling herself in.

"Bobby, you've got to pull, I can't do it by myself!" Lithia called.

"I'm trying, but it hurts, Lithia, I don't have—" Another massive blast sounded from somewhere in the ship.

The enormous explosion had nearly cut the ship in two and opened a massive hole in the hull around the bridge. Torque held himself in place with one hand and held Aurelius up against a wall with the other. He was trying to crush the life out of Aurelius, but the escaping air was pulling on him harder than even he could resist.

Aurelius scraped and scrabbled at the hands that held him. Maybe this was the way he was supposed to go out. Maybe this was the blaze of glory he was meant for. At least his friends would be safe. It almost didn't matter what happened to him now. Spots began to swim in front of his eyes.

"Most men die unremarked. You die in a blaze of victory. My victory!" Torque bellowed.

Torque stared into Aurelius's eyes through his helmet's faceplate, apparently waiting for the moment life would leave them. Aurelius stared back, holding off Torque's satisfaction as long as he could. If this was it, Aurelius was going to hold on to the final second. But then he saw it. Over Torque's shoulder, one of the water tanks for the giant hologram was leaking a thin stream of liquid that was turning into razor-sharp ice as it fell toward the hole in the room. It was right behind the beast.

Aurelius unholstered his gun and fired its last shot into Torque. Like before, the bullet curved around him, striking the water tank and bursting with colossal power. The blast was enough to shake Torque off his footing. He began to slide toward the gaping hole in the tank that was pouring razor-sharp ice out into the void. His grasp around Aurelius's neck lightened perceptibly.

"This is your destiny, winged man," Torque bellowed. "This is the destiny of a lie! Your heaven is a lie!"

Aurelius looked him dead in the eye. "Then I'll see you in hell."

Aurelius blasted his jetpack and, with all his might, pushed against the raging beast. With his attention divided, Torque couldn't hold on. Even with all his power, his grip was no match for the Strifer and his slush suit. The hell-raiser fell into the waterfall of razor blades and out into space. The behemoth's field wasn't strong enough to keep the ice or the void at bay. Like a million tiny bullets, the rush devoured him, leaving behind only a glowing green mist as it expanded out into space. If Aurelius was going to die, it wasn't going to be by Torque's hands. He grabbed onto a twisted piece of metal as he was blown toward the hole. With his victory, Aurelius found the courage to press on. He slowly and painfully pulled himself closer and closer to the door in the back of the room, hoping he could pull himself into the elevator shaft he had flown in through, but the wind rushing up the tube was too focused and too strong. He couldn't get through.

The ship was yawning its final breath, hoping to drag him into the nothingness of death with it. Behind him, the torrent of water was still rushing out into space. If he was blown out that way, he'd suffer the same fate as Torque. What could he do now?

Before he could devise a plan, the roof above him began to crack and tear open. The wind coming up the shaft blasted the entire ceiling away and Aurelius with it, out into space.

Lithia held on to Bobby's hand for dear life. Bobby cried with fear and pain. He could barely hold on to his sister. There was no way he could pull her in, and the cable around his waist was fraying. Lithia could hear it twanging, its individual strands snapping one by one.

"I'm slipping!" Lithia screamed.

In an instant, Lithia's whole life flashed before her eyes. Memories of childhood became more vivid than any dream could ever hope to be. The smell of the family arbor was overwhelming. She could remember every single flower as each year of her life passed by like a slide show at warp speed. The day her mother told her about the *Amaranth*. Sitting in the copilot's chair, her first time helping her father fly it. The first day of middle school. The last day of high school. The day she was told her parents had perished in a fire. The day she had to move to San Francisco. The day she met Vijay. The nights they spent with friends at Baker Beach. And the day she found herself at Priestess Tarja's side, desperately asking to tend the Magdalenes' garden. The day she took off in the *Amaranth* on this whole adventure, just trying to make her and her brother's life a little better, and then this moment here.

"Take care of your brother, Lithia," she could hear her mother saying.

All they had to do was close the door, and Bobby would be safe. Lithia saw only one choice. A terrible but necessary decision. She closed her eyes, tears streaming out of them. "I love you, Bobby!" she cried.

There was a childlike terror in Bobby's eyes as he watched his big sister let go of his hand. Time slowed down for Lithia as she watched her brother slip away.

Lithia fell down out of her ship, down through the hangar, down into the hallway. Her eyes were squeezed tightly shut, tears streaming the whole way as she braced herself for the fatal void at the end. Down, down, down she fell.

Outside the ship was a silent storm of flying debris, a hurricane of metal shards tearing from the *Enigma*'s carcass. Navigating the storm was easier once Aurelius found his suit's ballistic tracking system. His visor highlighted every piece of wreckage flying toward him. He rocketed around, looking for a hole back into the Enigma, back to his *Storm Chaser*. A major hallway had been torn open. He had just flown in when his suit highlighted an incoming shape. This one wasn't wreckage; it was a person. He stretched out his arms. This catch was going to be a long shot. Lithia was falling down the corridor quickly. If Aurelius didn't match her velocity exactly, it could kill her.

The impact was intense. For a moment, Lithia had no idea what she hit. The impact knocked the wind out of her, but now she was no longer falling. A pair of arms were wrapped around her. Someone had caught her, but whom? Then she heard it. The voice that had been in her head since her life had been completely turned upside down.

"Hold on!" Aurelius yelled, blasting his engines, sending them hurtling back the way Lithia had come. They flew back up the hallway on the end of a rocket blast, back into the hangar. Aurelius flew right toward the *Storm Chaser*, hurling them into the seats more than landing there.

The entire hangar began to shred around them. Light poured through every seam in the deck. The engine core was about to go nova.

Ahead of them, the *Amaranth* was shooting out of the disintegrating hanger. Aurelius pulled the *Storm Chaser*'s cockpit closed with all the force he could manage and kicked the engines to life.

Aurelius pushed the gas as hard as he could, hoping his tiny craft had the power left to get them to a safe distance.

A terrible cascade of light began to pour from the *Enigma*'s corpse, and then it happened all at once. The bright flash, the shock wave, and every alarm on the *Storm Chaser*'s dash went off. The blast emanated out into the void. The shock wave caught the *Storm Chaser*, rocketing it forward, then out toward the space station, shaking it like an earthquake. He didn't have to look behind him to know what had happened. The sound was incredible. It sounded like a hail of gunfire was pelting the craft from every angle. Wreckage went flying through the starboard engine, tearing it to shreds. The *Storm Chaser* began to spin wildly with the missing engine. Aurelius flicked the controls and stabilized the craft. Just as suddenly as the assault had started, it stopped, and all that was left was a peaceful calm. The *Enigma* was gone. As the blast settled, the damage the *Storm Chaser* had taken became apparent. Its engines were dead, its hull was bruised, and they were adrift; but at least now they were safe.

Aurelius pulled his helmet back down, and he and Lithia both took a deep breath. Torque was dead. The *Enigma* was history, and now, for the first time in days, they weren't being chased. Aurelius opened his helmet and looked back over his seat. Lithia was holding her arm. It was bloody and looked like she had been nicked by a bullet. Maybe it was the adrenaline, maybe it was because she looked so thankful, or maybe he was just caught in the moment. Whatever possessed him, he acted on it, climbing over his seat and wrapping his arms around her. They had survived. He grabbed her arm, making sure it was only a flesh wound. She leaned into him, embracing him like a life raft. He had kept his promise. Bobby was alive.

"I'm okay," she said, trembling.

He wasn't sure who kissed whom first.

EPILOGUE

IT WAS A small group of ships that was returning the surviving crew of the *Deviant Rising* and *Freedom's Reach* back to Strife. How ironic, considering the mass and power of the two ill-fated ships in comparison to these transports. Even with the tight quarters and limited space, Pacius still found somewhere to work. He was in a forward observation lounge. There was a floor-to-ceiling window wrapped around the room, but Captain Pacius focused his attention on the hologram in front of him. For the last few days, he had been flicking through documents, art, and video of everything contained within the data Cade had smuggled out of Lambda HQ. The amount of information was incredible. There were petabytes of lost history. Everything from the collapse of the Roman Empire to the American Revolution and the formation of the Empire States of America and their colonizing of the moon and terraforming of Mars.

Captain Pacius didn't know what he was going to do with all of it. When he first realized what was in the box that Aurelius and Lithia had delivered, he fantasized gallantly delivering these lost chapters of history to the masses. He thought it would help the fight against the UPE. He thought it would help loosen their grasp on every world they had conquered if everyone knew how devious they had been. But there was so much here. This went so much deeper than he had expected.

How had this happened? How had people allowed it to happen? What would the consequences of revealing this much information be? It would be shocking. It would be a revelation. He wasn't sure he was ready to make such a decision. He'd have a few days to think about it, about what to mention in the debriefing before he returned to Strife. He was going to have one hell of a story for the SMMC. Whether he liked it or not, things were going to be different from this point forward. He had destroyed the UPE flagship and was now sitting on a store of lost history and knowledge larger than the library of Alexandria.

The door behind him swooshed open, even though it had been locked. He only needed one guess to figure out who had stepped in.

"Where did we go so wrong?" Pacius asked, gazing into the hologram. "How did we get here? How did we lose this much information? How did we lose this much history?"

Cade limped up beside Captain Pacius. He was still battered and bruised. He had lived, but his mind and body would need time to heal. "People weren't paying attention. The memory of man is short, thinking little beyond the moment. It's amazing what we can forget. It's amazing what the human race can lose when it becomes inconvenient. Or when somebody wants it gone."

"But there's so much here," Pacius said. "I can't believe, even for a second, it was all the Helix Network."

"If you're asking me, I'm afraid I don't have an answer. I guess it's possible . . . it's possible Lambda has been doing this for a long time," Cade said.

"This is the biggest historical find since the Rosetta Stone."

"I brought it to you because I believed the universe should know. It became my purpose. What will you do with it?"

"I don't know. I'd be making a huge decision for the human race, letting it all out at once. This has the power to sway political control. To start wars, or worse. Letting all of this out at once could be signing millions of people's death certificates."

"Sometimes the most powerful move is the one you don't make, the weapon you never use."

"Maybe," Pacius said.

"Right now, the UPE is stinging, but they won't strike yet. They can't be seen to come down too hard on Strife and risk sending more people over to our cause. As long as they are unwilling to make a direct move, we have a window. A time when we can prepare. A time when so long as we don't act too overtly, we can build. When the UPE finally comes down on us, we can be ready. That's what I'm going to be doing . . . making sure we're ready."

"If I asked you what that meant, would I get an answer?" Captain Pacius asked.

"Your task is not to lead a revolution. Not yet. That task may very well be yours before this is done, but for now, the people need to see you keeping things together. They will look to you for example, and what they see can't be a man ready to go to war. Or they will follow, and all will be lost." Cade paused before continuing. "Hope. It's the most addictive thing you can give someone . . . and you've given it to your crew in spades."

The Lambda wasn't saying anything Pacius didn't already know. He had come to the same conclusions. The Strife Merchant Marine Corps had been designed to help develop Strife and protect it from those who would seek to harm it.

There was a long pause as Cade and Pacius pondered the implications of these events. They were in sync. After a long, drawn-out moment, Pacius brought up a hologram titled "Helix Core." The image was incomplete and static filled half the view, but what was there was reminiscent of axons hooked together in the human brain.

"Is it real? Is it really alive?" Pacius asked.

"Those hours I was chained up, locked up in that ship, I asked myself that over and over again. When I was jacked into the Helix-Node I ripped this data from, I felt something. A presence . . . and it scared me."

This bionic man, a hybrid of flesh and machine, had never indicated he was capable of fear. Saying he was scared was less an omission and more of a revelation of how far down the rabbit hole they had fallen.

"How could it be? How is it possible we've built a brain? An actual nonorganic life-form?" Pacius asked.

"Every civilization, every culture, built a god. Maybe we're just the first ones who built one capable of actually looking back at us."

Pacius didn't know what to say. The prospect was terrifying. "If this thing is alive . . . and if it's as malevolent and powerful as it seems . . . do you think we can stop it?"

There was no answer to his query. Captain Pacius turned around to see the door behind him was sliding shut. Cade was gone.

"Fried . . . Fused . . . Fubared . . ." Aurelius said, tossing burned and broken equipment out from under what was left of the *Storm Chaser*. He was waist-deep in the husk of his little planet hopper.

The *Storm Chaser* and the *Amaranth* had been stowed into the same tight launch bay on one of the transports back to Strife. Aurelius had spent the last couple of days working on the *Amaranth*, getting it fixed, patched up, and tuned. He had moved on to surveying the damage to his own little craft. He hoped it would be salvageable, but it wasn't looking good.

His slush suit was all but burned out and it laid bunched up in the backseat. It too had seen better days. An old, dirty SMMC jumpsuit was his only armor.

"Okay, try it now," Jerula said, lying on his back under the main console in the *Amaranth*'s cockpit. Paul keyed in a sequence on one of the holograms popping out of the windshield. A diagnostic came up and everything was reading green. Lithia could depart anytime she wanted now.

"Cool," Paul said.

Lithia was in the ship's makeshift infirmary. Bobby was being examined by the same nurse who had treated Lithia's head wound back on Archer's Agony.

"I don't get it," the nurse said. "He's fine. Other than a little withdrawal from the drugs he was given, I can't find anything wrong with him, physically, neurological, or otherwise."

A relief washed over both Lithia and Bobby.

"He's been waiting a long time to hear those words," Lithia said.

"Well, he's not going to need that anymore," the nurse said with an empathetic smile as she pointed to Bobby's wristband. "I don't know why Terrans think they can solve their problems this way."

The nurse pulled a tool off a shelf and waved it over the bracelet. It must have depolarized the carbon fibers that kept it firmly clamped around Bobby's wrist. It snapped open into two pieces, falling to the floor. Bobby did his best to appear to be relieved. He grabbed his wrist with his other hand. His skin was terribly blistered and chafed, but the bracelet was finally gone.

"I'd like to monitor him for the rest of the afternoon. After that, you guys are free to depart whenever you want."

Bobby looked up at Lithia with feigned calm. "What do we do now, Lithia?"

"I don't know . . . I'm not sure. It's up to us, really. We can go pretty much wherever we want. Do whatever we want."

"I don't wanna go back to Earth. I don't want to be anywhere near that planet ever again. Take me to any world in the universe but that one."

Lithia agreed but didn't have any concrete direction of her own other than maybe going back to Venus one day or maybe . . . maybe they'd do better on Mars?

"I'll come get you out of here tonight. We don't even have to think about it until then."

Bobby lay back on the gurney. Lithia heard him let out a sigh of repressed desperation as she and the nurse walked out of the room.

Lithia walked slowly through the halls of the ship, letting everything sink in. She couldn't get Aurelius out of her mind. She had tried to stay busy the last few days in the hope that it wouldn't look like she was avoiding him. She couldn't be more grateful for his help in saving her and Bobby. Not a second passed that she didn't relive that night he rescued her from certain death or the serenity they spent together slowly drifting around, embracing each other in his craft.

Lithia was on her way to check on the *Amaranth* when she bumped into Nyreen.

"Hey," Nyreen said. "Nice shooting."

"Thanks," Lithia replied. "A space cowboy taught me how."

"He's in the hangar." Nyreen smiled. "Go get him."

Jerula was standing over Aurelius as he poked and pried at his hopper. "I'm telling you, her ship's ready to go. There's nothing keeping her here. Soooo . . . it might be . . . a good time . . . to . . . you know . . ."

"What?" Aurelius inquired.

"You know. You gotta not let her get away."

"Yeah, I know. Don't know what to say to her, though. I mean, do I ask her to come back to Strife and start over?"

"Sure! Start with that."

"I don't know," Aurelius said, shaking his head.

"You know . . . you're about the most unconfident superhero I know," Jerula teased.

"I'm the only superhero you know," Aurelius joked back.

"Just, whatever you say, stay away from commenting on her amazing eyebrows."

"Yeah, I got it. Thanks, Strifer," Aurelius said.

"Or her rear stabilizer."

Aurelius shook his head in laughter. He didn't want to admit just how nervous he was. What could he possibly say to Lithia to make her stay?

A door at the far end of the hangar slid open.

"You better think of something fast. Here she comes."

"What?" Aurelius said, peeking around his friend.

Lithia had a curious smile on her face as she made her way over to what was left of the *Storm Chaser*. She was trying to look as nonchalant as possible. She probably couldn't hear what they were talking about, but from the look on her face, she found something intriguing. Jerula casually stepped away with his hands behind his back, whistling.

Aurelius stood up, trying to dust off his hands. There was a sudden swarm of butterflies in his stomach that wanted out. He could feel his face turning red, still having no idea what to say to her. "Hey . . . huh."

"Thank you. Thank you so much," Lithia said. "You got me and my brother out of this mess. If it wasn't for you—"

"I kinda got you into the mess too," Aurelius interrupted.

"Yeah, well . . . I guess I can't hold it against you. Everything turned out okay."

"Yeah . . . hey. Huh. What will you do now? Where will you go?" Aurelius asked, trying to strike up some small talk. Fuse, he was head-over-heels in love with this woman.

"I don't know . . . I've been thinking about it a little bit."

"You could go back home to Venus."

He wanted to hit himself. He was making himself sound less interested and he was sending the wrong signals. He wasn't very good at this.

"Oh . . . yeah. Huh," Lithia said, looking a bit confused. The look in her eye was so genuine, so vulnerable; it had never occurred to him until now that maybe behind her brazen attitude she was just nervous.

"I'm not in a hurry to get back to the Sol system," she said.

There was an awkwardly long pause as Lithia waited for him to say something. Wow, was he about to blow it.

She didn't know what else to do but step in to hug him. They stepped toward each other simultaneously. The moment set off the same sudden explosive decisiveness that had seen them through this adventure. He took her in his arms and kissed her passionately. The butterflies in her stomach rose into her lips as a sudden warm rush washed over her body. She felt her shoulders go limp as he ran his hand up into her hair. All doubt in her mind vanished as she felt his passion in her soul. Suddenly she found herself trembling. She pulled away, giggling.

"I didn't think you were ever going to kiss me again," she said.

He pulled her in close again, trying to extinguish her quivering with his lips.

"Come back with us to Strife," he whispered.

She felt her knees weaken but wasn't worried about falling with Aurelius holding her. Lithia didn't know what she felt for Aurelius, but she felt something, and for now she was content to let her path and his be the same. It wasn't like she had any better plans, and she and Bobby did need a new start. She found herself smiling as she stepped back and locked eyes with this brash spacer. "Okay . . . okay, Intergalactic Space Crusader."

The Lambda briefing chambers were cold. They were always cold, and it was one of the reasons, but not the biggest, that Benjamin Abel tended to avoid them, if at all possible. But today, avoiding them wasn't an option. When Lambda Prime called, even the CEO of the entire UPE came.

"Thank you for joining me, Mr. Abel," the shadowy hologram said into the silence.

"Of course, I assume this is about the *Enigma* incident?" Abel responded, knowing he was right, as nothing short of that debacle could have made Lambda Prime call him there personally.

"Indeed. Events are forcing us to hasten things. We can no longer afford to do things slowly or quietly," Lambda Prime answered in its usual tone, one completely devoid of emotion or accent. It was a voice that gave no clues to the identity of the person behind the projection, not age, place of birth, or even gender.

"Will Captain Shard still be heading up those plans?" Abel asked, not sure if he was hoping for an affirmative or not.

"Captain Shard has been dealt with. He is no longer a concern, we have someone else in mind going forward."

"And who might that be?" Abel asked, dreading the answer. Rarely had Lambda Prime's handpicked people meant anything good for him.

"That doesn't matter; you have other things to be focused on. Soon we'll be bringing STR1-FE and the rest of the Frontier colonies to their knees. I need you out there, calming the people, making them understand that this is all for the greater good. Make them feel safe, even when our ships are darkening their skies . . ."

ACKNOWLEDGMENTS

To our wonderful and understanding parents, who's support never wavered, even when this took years longer than we swore it would.

To our friend and first editor, Tyler Sparrow, your help with everything from basic spelling correction to major plot adjustments helped us turn this book into far more than it would have been without you. And we swear we'll eventually learn how to use the semicolon.

And to all our supporters, who preordered, signal boosted, and helped us reach the finish line in a thousand little and not so little ways, this book is for you. We literally couldn't have done it without you. So if you don't like it, you've only yourselves to blame.

GRAND PATRONS

Abigail Burton and Autumn Gass
Alfredo Sfeir
Andrew Baird
Benjamin A. Mayr
Iris Holland
Jessica Attard
Paul Holland
Victor Chernetsky
Victoria Leyva

INKSHARES

INKSHARES is a reader-driven publisher and producer based in Oakland, California. Our books are selected not by a group of editors, but by readers worldwide.

While we've published books by established writers like *Big Fish* author Daniel Wallace and *Star Wars: Rogue One* scribe Gary Whitta, our aim remains surfacing and developing the new author voices of tomorrow.

Previously unknown Inkshares authors have received starred reviews and been featured in the *New York Times*. Their books are on the front tables of Barnes & Noble and hundreds of independents nationwide, and many have been licensed by publishers in other major markets. They are also being adapted by Oscar-winning screenwriters at the biggest studios and networks.

Interested in making your own story a reality? Visit Inkshares.com to start your own project or find other great books.

Printed in the USA
CPSIA information can be obtained
at www.ICGtesting.com
JSHW082149140824
68134JS00014B/140

9 781947 848016